When Angels Battle

MaryLu
Tyndall

When Angels Battle

Guardians of the Saints, Book 2

©2022 by MaryLu Tyndall

ISBN: 978-1-7344420-7-6
E-Version ISBN: 978-1-7344420-6-9

Library of Congress Cataloging-in-Publication Data is on file at the Library of Congress, Washington, D.C.

This book is a work of fiction. Names, characters, places, incidents, and dialogues are either products of the author's imagination or used fictitiously. Any similarity to actual people, organizations, and/or events is purely coincidental.

Cover Design by Ravven
Editor: Louise M. Gouge

RANSOM PRESS

Foreword

Dear readers, this book is a work of fiction, an adventurous, romantic story that I hope will not only entertain you but will strengthen your faith. Based on many years of personal research into the Scriptures and end-times prophecies, I have presented one possible scenario of what the first half of the Tribulation might look like. This is the seven year period prophesied in Scripture also called Jacob's Trouble or the Day of the Lord. Though there are many different interpretations of the book of Revelation, I did my best to portray the events as they might happen. Of course, none of us really know how these things will play out. This is not a theological study but rather a glimpse of a loving God who is forced to send judgment on a world who rejects Him. In doing so, He hopes to save as many of His children as He can. In addition, the story portrays the overwhelming deception that God's enemy will use to destroy mankind and how Tribulation saints who walk in the love and power of God will be willing to sacrifice their lives for Jesus. Having said all that, if you're ready for an intense spiritual ride, then turn the page and let's get started!

Check out my When Angels Battle Pinterest Board as you read.

Now I saw when the Lamb opened one of the seals; and I heard one of the four living creatures saying with a voice like thunder, "Come and see." And I looked, and behold, a white horse. He who sat on it had a bow; and a crown was given to him, and he went out conquering and to conquer.

When He opened the second seal, I heard the second living creature saying, "Come and see." Another horse, fiery red, went out. And it was granted to the one who sat on it to take peace from the earth, and that people should kill one another; and there was given to him a great sword.

When He opened the third seal, I heard the third living creature say, "Come and see." So I looked, and behold, a black horse, and he who sat on it had a pair of scales in his hand. And I heard a voice in the midst of the four living creatures saying, "A quart of wheat for a denarius, and three quarts of barley for a denarius; and do not harm the oil and the wine."

When He opened the fourth seal, I heard the voice of the fourth living creature saying, "Come and see." So I looked, and behold, a pale horse. And the name of him who sat on it was Death, and Hades followed with him. And power was given to them over a fourth of the earth, to kill with sword, with hunger, with death, and by the beasts of the earth.

Revelation 6:1-8

The fourth beast shall be a fourth kingdom on earth, which shall be different from all other kingdoms, and shall devour the whole earth, trample it and break it in pieces. Daniel 7:23

Chapter 1

Fort Lauderdale, Florida, eighteen months into the Tribulation

AR-15 tight in her grip, Nyla Cruz led her team through the darkness. At well past midnight *and* the ten o'clock curfew, no one stirred on the shadowy neighborhood street. A buzzing sound drew her gaze to a streetlight flickering on and off. Something moved beneath it. Nyla snapped her weapon in that direction. A cat darted down the sidewalk. One of her troops behind her chuckled. She faced forward again. They expected no trouble from the quiet, humble house they approached—the one with the shades drawn and the ever-so-slight hum of singing inside. But in this crazy world, you could never be too careful. The past year as a New World Union Peace Keeper had proven that fact to Nyla more than once.

Halting before the white picket fence, she signaled Marco, her second-in-command, to take two men around back in case the *Deviants* made a run for it. Next door, the curtains shifted slightly across a window, allowing a shaft of light to penetrate the darkness. The shadowy outline of a woman peered out. The *snitch.*

Nyla groaned. She hated snitches. Even ones who aided the New World Union, as this lady had done when she'd reported that her neighbors were holding illegal meetings. Even so, she'd ordered the woman to stay inside and not do anything that would give them away.

The curtain swung shut. Nyla moved toward the front door, the light footfalls of her troops following in her wake. Shouts emanated from inside the house, joyful shouts, happy shouts, accompanied by the sound of a guitar and singing. Odd. Joy and happiness had been in short supply these past months after war had ravaged much of the world, multiple plagues had struck, the world economy had collapsed, and a tsunami had dramatically altered the Eastern Seaboard of what once was the USA. Not to mention the abduction of millions by the Neflams. So many people dead or...just gone. Rare was the family who had not lost someone to one of those disasters.

"Blessed be the name of the Lord! Bless His holy name!"

Though muffled, she could now make out the words of the song coming from within the house. She would never understand these *Deviants*. Doctors called it a personality disorder. Politicians called them terrorists. Nyla just called them crazy.

Raising her night-vision goggles, she signaled for Bait and Roman to bring the bar-and-hammer forward. The other three men positioned themselves behind them, Glocks at the ready, their eyes on her, waiting for her command.

Her command. She still found it hard to believe she was the Team Leader of Florida PK Team 88. It had taken her a year, clawing her way through prejudice, bureaucracy, and more hard work and risk than she'd thought possible, to be able to lead a team of nine men and one woman. And since then, her team had done great things to aid the New World Union in bringing about peace and security, at least in Nyla's little part of the world.

"New World Union Search Warrant. Open up!" she shouted.

The singing halted.

"New World Union Search Warrant. Open up!"

Nothing.

She tried the door handle. Locked. Nodding toward Bait and Roman to bust in, she gestured for the others to be ready.

BAM!

The ram hit the door. Wood splintered. Screams blared. Bait and Roman leapt out of the way and Nyla charged inside, followed by the others. She leveled her AR-15 on a crowd of fifteen people huddled in a circle, holding hands. Instantly, they released each other, eyes wide, as they backed away from the intruders.

Her troops moved with practiced precision, circling the Deviants and leveling their weapons upon them.

"This is an illegal gathering!" Nyla shouted. "Everyone, hands in the air!" She signaled for Mason and Labre to search the rest of the house. "Is there anyone else here?" she asked.

An elderly man, hands raised, moved toward Nyla. "No one else."

"Give me that, nice and slow." She gestured with her gun toward the book the man had dropped. "And the rest of you, get out your VaxPasses."

The man held out the book, and after lowering her weapon, she thumbed through the pages. A Bible. A *real* Bible, not the NWU-permitted version but the archaic one filled with prejudice, racism, and hate. The one that had misled so many, caused so many wars, and held mankind back from evolving into the master race the Neflams had hoped for when they'd seeded Planet Earth.

The one that had stolen her parents.

Heaving a sigh, Nyla glanced over the Deviants—a few old people, a middle-aged man, a young couple, a college-age girl and boy, a few teens, and three men in their thirties. Though fear appeared in some of their eyes, none of them wept, no one cowered, not one of them ran. *And* none of them shouted angry words at her. One even smiled her way.

Nyla held up the Bible. "Just having this is a felony, not to mention reading it. This entire meeting is a felony." She nodded toward Bait and Crane. "Check their passes."

The two men closed in on the huddle of Deviants, demanding to see their mobiles, while Mason, Labre, and Marco returned from searching the house with a shout of "All clear."

"None of them have a VaxPass, Commander, only NWU IDs." Crane covered his mouth and backed away from them. Bait did the same.

Resisting the urge to join them, Nyla stood her ground. She had learned long ago never to show fear, even with the spread of a killer plague. One that these ignorant rejects from the past refused to eradicate by taking the mandated vaccines. She'd thought most of these fools had been rounded up already.

Placing her face mask around her nose and mouth, she instructed her troops who had not received the fifth booster to do the same, then leveled a hard stare at the old man, who must be their leader. "That's three strikes, old man. An illegal gathering, an illegal Bible, and no VaxPasses. Arrest them all at once!"

The man nodded toward the other Deviants as if to reassure them. But what possible reassurance could there be as her troops swarmed in, yanked their wrists behind them, and snapped them in steel restraints? They were going to be locked away in a FEMA Reformation camp, probably for the rest of their lives.

A stream of bright light split the air in front of her, followed by a strange sensation, not altogether unpleasant. She turned to Marco. "Did you see that?"

He shook his head. "What?"

"Never mind."

The old man faced Nyla, an odd smile on his face as Mack yanked his arms behind them and locked them together.

"Come on, old man." Mack jerked him toward the door.

Still, his smile remained as he passed her. "God bless you, young lady. May He open your eyes."

Grunting, she shook her head. Like she said, bunch of crazies.

Ranoss could hardly bear to watch the arrest and persecution of yet more holy saints, especially at the hand of Nyla. How many more of God's precious children would she send to their deaths before she removed the blinders from her eyes?

Xoran, who stood beside him, glanced at Marco as he entered from the back of the house. Though the top of Xoran's helmet only reached Ranoss' chest, the short warrior angel more than made up for his stature with his muscular body, which he'd often used as a weapon.

Ranoss had his own special weapon, a flaming crossbow whose arrows had the power to send demons straight to the bottomless pit if they hit their mark precisely. He'd been practicing much lately, for he knew the battle was about to get intense.

Xoran's eyes followed Marco until he stopped beside Nyla. "I must never question the Father's hope for these two, but there are days…"

"I quite agree, my friend," Ranoss shifted his mighty stance. "'Tis most hard to watch, this constant defiance of the true way—the *only* way. I have not the patience of the Almighty in these matters. I long to fight, to defend and protect, as is my training." He gripped the hilt of his long sword. "But how to battle the darkness when she embraces it?"

Several angels passed by them, nodding at Ranoss and Xoran, as they accompanied their wards being hauled off in handcuffs.

One of them, Turian, stopped before Ranoss. "Good to see you, my friend. 'Tis been a while."

"Indeed. At least a hundred earth years." Ranoss glanced at the retreating saints. "Which one is yours?"

"The old man who spoke up. John Bailey. I've been with him since his birth." Turian's sad glance followed John out the door. "The Father tells me he will die soon. For his faith."

"'Tis good news for him," Xoran added.

"Aye. I will be with him until the end, and thereafter, I am granted the privilege to escort him home."

"What joy there is to be found in such a task." Ranoss's gaze landed on Nyla, who now ordered her troops to search the house for more incriminating evidence. "'Tis something I long to do with my ward."

"I must leave. 'Twas good to see you again." Turian nodded at them both and followed John out the door, leaving only Ranoss, Xoran, and two other angels in the room.

With the departure of the holy saints and their angels, all light vacated the house.

Ranoss gripped his crossbow and plucked an arrow from his quiver. He knew what was coming.

The shadows appeared, filtering through walls, windows, and doors, vile specters in all shapes and sizes with malformed faces and bodies, some stiff and brittle, others undulating and fluid. A familiar stench followed them in. Malevolent eyes spotted the warriors and shrank back, snarling. But they didn't leave. They didn't *have* to leave, for they were invited here by the men and women who had invaded this holy abode.

"You wanted to see me, Captain?" Nyla poked her head in the door of Captain Martin Jennings' office and entered when he gestured her forward. She had barely removed her battle gear and put on her civilian clothes when Captain Jennings requested her presence in his office.

"Marco," she exclaimed, surprised to see her second officer—*and* her boyfriend—standing before the captain's desk. Pleasantly surprised, for the man was even handsomer in his street clothes than in his uniform—something she could not say of most men.

Marco smiled and gave her that wink of his that always stirred her blood. With his jet-black waves, just the right amount of stubble on his chin, and those bedroom eyes, she expected he stirred many a woman's blood.

"Shut the door, please." Captain Jennings glanced down at a document on his desk and then leaned back in his chair, lacing fingers that seemed too long for his hands across his rounded paunch. Gray streaked through what remained of his hair and bags fit for any overnight trip puffed beneath eyes that had the ability to inflict punishment with one sharp look. Thankfully, that was not the look she saw in them now.

"Miss Cruz, your record is exemplary." He shook his head as if he found the fact shocking. "Just in the past six months, you have raided twenty-five illegal assemblies and brought in more than five hundred Deviants. Astounding work."

Pride buzzed through her. "I couldn't have done it without my team, Captain. The best in the county."

"Maybe even the state." Jennings stared back down at Nyla's record. Was the man going to give her a raise, an award? But why was Marco here?

What did it matter? She *was* exemplary, wasn't she? She was successful, good at what she did, and on her way to even bigger things. Perhaps to become a Global Peace Keeper, travel the world, not be stuck in some Podunk county in Florida.

She took a breath, awaiting the good news. If only her parents could see her now. But of course that was not possible.

Jennings shifted on his chair, the creak echoing through the small office. "What do you know about Daniel Cain?"

Nyla's eyebrows rose. "He's the most famous Deviant pastor in all of Florida, and maybe even the entire North American Region. Word is, he's responsible for starting at least fifty underground assemblies and spreading his heresies and lies to thousands of weak-minded people."

Marco cast her a sideways glance.

"Yes." Jennings sighed. "And he's also spread his cult north into Georgia and the Carolinas, brainwashing people there into believing in a God that doesn't exist and that the Bible—that racist, homophobic trash—is the actual Word of this God. We've been hunting him for over a year." Jennings blew out a huff of disgust. "He is a danger to society and the advancement of mankind."

"We know all this." Marco shrugged. "We've had every available officer on the lookout for him."

Nyla agreed. The man's picture had been blasted across all their mobiles. A huge award and promotion awaited anyone who captured him. Everyone was on the hunt for Daniel Cain, but thus far, he had eluded all detection.

Jennings rose from his seat and pressed a hand on his back. "Yes, but now we have a lead. A man by the name of Calan Walker, an ex-Navy SEAL. We think Mr. Walker is Daniel's bodyguard."

"Bodyguard? How would we know that if we have not seen Daniel?" Nyla asked.

"Let's just say I have a reliable source."

Marco crossed arms over his chest. "Okay, so we arrest this Walker guy and *convince* him to tell us where Daniel is."

"That's one way." Jennings' lips grew tight. "A sloppy way. But it's highly possible the Navy SEAL doesn't talk, as he's been trained, and then Daniel goes even further underground." He rubbed his chin. "I don't want to risk it."

An uneasy feeling took root in Nyla's gut. "What does that have to do with us, Captain?"

"We're going to put someone on the inside."

That uneasy feeling grew into a bubbling brew. "We aren't trained to do undercover work."

"True, but you are the perfect person to attract Mr. Walker." Jennings' gaze locked upon Nyla.

"Attract?" She shared a glance with Marco, who looked even more uneasy than she felt. "You mean as in *physical*?"

"I do. Word is, he used to be quite the ladies' man."

"I don't—"

"He is a man of habit," Jennings continued, ignoring her. "He jogs on the same beach every morning. We merely put you in his path, and then you use your charm to meet him, become his friend, and slowly convince him you're seeking this God of his. That's it."

"Why can't you just put a tail on him?" Marco interjected.

"We've tried. Many times. But he always eludes us, crafty bugger."

Nyla blew an agitated sigh. "You can't be serious. Daniel and his followers will find out who I am, what I've done. If they don't already know about me."

Jennings shrugged. "We'll take care of that." Planting both hands on his desk, he leaned forward, the look she—and many fellow officers—feared finally blazing from his eyes. "You're fired."

Nyla swallowed, heart sinking like a stone in mire. "What?"

Marco groaned.

"Not really, of course," Jennings straightened with a smile. "But it will be on your record until your assignment is done. Fired for spreading conspiracy theories and expressing sympathy for the Deviants."

Nyla bit her lip. *This can't be happening!* "But, Sir—"

"It's the perfect cover, Cruz, and you know it. It will get you in their door. They are always looking for new converts."

Marco shifted his stance. "Why not choose some other pretty woman? There are plenty who work here."

"But none with Nyla's training, should she find herself in danger."

He was right, of course, and Nyla knew it. Still, fired? Not exactly the reward for hard work she was looking for.

"Once you get into the underground church," Jennings continued, "you just have to play along until you meet Daniel. When that happens, you can tell us where he is going to be, and we'll pull you out and go in and get him. Easy."

For someone else, maybe, but for her? Spending days, maybe weeks, with the very people she hated and hunted?

Marco's face had become steel. "I don't like this."

"That is not my concern." Jennings eyed him. "However, you will be Nyla's handler. She will meet with you on a regular basis to give you updates."

Marco's jaw seemed about to burst, but to his credit, he remained quiet.

Nyla didn't like it either, but at least she'd still get to see Marco. He was one of the few people she trusted in this world. "But what about the viruses? Most Deviants aren't vaccinated."

"Which is why I've scheduled you for your fifth shot today. With it, you'll not only be fully protected but the completed graphene nanotracker will let us know exactly where you are at all times."

Which was precisely why she'd been avoiding the fifth booster. Not that she didn't believe in universal vaccines to protect mankind, but she'd heard that the graphene they'd inserted in each booster would fully assemble in the fifth one to form a working tracker. Perhaps she had a bit of her mother in her, after all, because the idea of someone… *anyone* knowing where she was at all times seemed a bit Orwellian.

"I don't suppose I have a choice," she finally said.

"This word comes directly from PONAR. Putting Daniel Cain out of commission is at the top of his list."

The President of the North American Region? Yikes. Nyla swallowed.

"If you can bring us Daniel Cain, Miss Cruz, there's no limit to how high you can go in the New World Union."

Well, if he put it that way. She smiled. "When do I start?"

When He opened the third seal, I heard the third living creature say, "Come and see." So I looked, and behold, a black horse, and he who sat on it had a pair of scales in his hand. And I heard a voice in the midst of the four living creatures saying, "A quart of wheat for a denarius, and three quarts of barley for a denarius; and do not harm the oil and the wine." Revelation 6:5-6

Chapter 2

I can't, Marco. Not tonight." Nyla took a step back from the man, who even in his civies looked more like a Spanish god than human. Moonlight threaded silver through the light of the street-lamp in front of Marco's apartment building, creating a halo around him that confirmed her suspicions. Her gaze dropped to his well-formed physique. She knew too well what existed beneath his tee-shirt—rounded, firm muscles that rippled over his arms and torso, muscles she had caressed many a night. With thick, black, wavy hair, a slight scruff on his chin, and dark-lashed eyes that were far too attractive for a man, Marco Torres was the desire of every woman on the NWU Peace Teams.

But he was hers. Or he had been for the past six months. *All* hers.

"Come on, babe." He slid toward her and ran a finger down her cheek. "Who knows how long we will be apart if you snag this bodyguard."

"If?" Nyla gave him a sarcastic smile.

"Well, of course you will, a hot mama like you." He grinned seductively.

"You can flatter me all you want, but I'm really not staying. I promised—"

He drew her into an embrace, his unique spicy scent suffocating her senses. Lowering his head, he nibbled her neck. Her breath escaped, and she nearly gave in. *Nearly.* Ah, but the man caused her to feel sensations she'd never felt before.

Gathering all her self-control, she pushed from him. "I mean it, Marco. I've got to get home to my grandmother."

He stared at her for a moment, his eyes shifting between hers, a slight hint of anger within them. But that couldn't be. Marco had always been a gentleman. Finally, his expression sank into a boyish sulk. "I hate this, babe. I'm going to miss you."

"Me too." Wind tossed a strand of hair into her face, and she eased it behind her ear. "But I'll catch this Daniel guy quick and be back in your arms soon enough."

He nodded and gave her a half-grin. "Okay. I'll walk you home."

"No need. I can take care of myself. Besides, it's only a few blocks and way past curfew." And she never went anywhere without her Glock. Turning, she started down the sidewalk before she changed her mind, casting one last glance over her shoulder to wave goodbye. But Marco was already gone.

Nyla quietly slid her keys onto the wooden stand by the door. The last thing she wanted was to wake Tata. The poor woman suffered from so many ailments that if she was finally asleep, Nyla wanted to keep it that way.

Snoring rumbled from the couch. Kyle, Nyla's brother, was a different story. He hadn't taken the disappearance of their parents well. That, coupled with losing his baseball scholarship to Florida State when the war broke out, had crushed all his dreams. Sure, he'd only been eighteen at the time, but instead of manning up to help her take care of Tata, he'd sunk back into his two favorite addictions—video games and pot. Now, Nyla was the sole breadwinner in a world where both bread and wealth were in short supply.

She slid all four locks into place and turned on the alarm. As usual, Kyle had forgotten to set it. Glancing around, she made her way through the living room to the three small bedrooms in the back and wondered why anyone would bother breaking in. They had nothing of value except maybe some food in the fridge. Yet, now that she thought about it, lately she'd seen people hungry enough to kill for a bag of chips.

"Is that you, Pajarito?" The scratchy voice emerged from the first bedroom, halting Nyla. No matter how quietly she tiptoed, Tata always heard her come home.

"Yes, Tata." Nyla entered to find her grandmother sitting up in bed, Bible in her lap. Light from a small lamp on the nightstand glistened in the older woman's long gray hair tumbling down her nightdress. She smiled, that gentle smile so full of love, it was easy to ignore the missing teeth.

"How was your day, dear?"

"Tata. What have I told you about having that out in the open?" Nyla pointed toward the Bible. "Or anywhere in this apartment. I could lose my job."

"Some things are more important than jobs." Tata patted the bed for Nyla to sit.

She slid onto the soft mattress, shaking her head. How many citizens had she arrested for possession of the very book that sat right here in her own home? Many a night she had contemplated stealing and burning it while Tata slept. But the banned book of myths seemed to bring such comfort and joy to her grandmother, she couldn't bring herself to do it. Her only consolation? None of the teams would ever think to raid *her* apartment.

"I just don't get it, Tata. Mom and Dad are gone because they believed in this book. And here you are, caught in the same lies."

Tata caressed the leather-bound volume as if it were made of gold. "I just wish I'd read it before."

"Then you'd be gone too."

"Exactly, my dear." Her grandmother patted Nyla's hand.

Nyla huffed and slid hair behind her ear. "We don't know how bad these reformation camps are. You might not have survived."

Tata's smile was so sweet, so filled with confidence. "They aren't in reformation camps, dearest. They are in heaven."

Ridiculous nonsense. But Nyla refused to argue about it anymore. She took Tata's hands in hers, so bony and...cold? "You're freezing." Releasing her, she pulled the covers up onto Tata's lap. "Have you had anything to eat? Something warm?"

Tata shook her head. "Some crackers this morning, but Kyle ate all the soup."

Nyla forced down her anger. She'd deal with her brother later. "I'll go make you something." She started to rise, but Tata pulled her back with more strength than Nyla thought possible.

"No need. I'm not hungry." Tata's eyes grew moist as a look of concern tightened the wrinkles on her face. "There's so many going without these days. People dying of hunger everywhere. Food lines that go on forever. Even those who have jobs can barely afford to feed their families. I have no right to complain."

Nyla nodded. She saw firsthand the pain of the famine every day on the job. How many families living on the street had she escorted to FEMA camps, where at least they'd get meals and a roof over their heads? For others, she'd found them too late. "It's been a rough year and a half for the world, I agree. Though World War III was short, the nuclear exchange left irreversible devastation in many countries, especially the former USA. Then, with all these natural disasters caused by climate change, it's no wonder the farms aren't producing enough food. Plus the corona viruses and smallpox affecting farmers and transportation workers. But there is hope, Tata. Now that the New World Union, under the direction of the Neflams, has brought peace and unity to the world, things will get better, you'll see."

"This isn't climate change. This has all been prophesied in this book you hate so much." Tata lifted up the Bible.

Nyla bit her lip. Why did every conversation end up back to that blasted book? She hated that book, hated what it had done to her parents and so many others. And now what it was doing to her Tata.

"A quart of wheat for a denarius, and three quarts of barley for a denarius; and do not harm the oil and the wine," Tata said.

Nyla gave her a confused look.

"From Revelation. It means it will cost an entire day's wage to buy a loaf of bread, but those who are rich will keep getting richer."

"And *we* will be one of those rich, Tata." Nyla smiled, hoping to lighten her grandmother's mood with her good news. "I've been put on a special assignment that, if I succeed, could mean a huge promotion and a giant raise, and then I promise we'll have all the food we need."

"I'd rather be hungry than see you caught up in this evil global system."

"My *global* job is the only thing keeping you, me, and Kyle living as well as we do." She regretted her tone instantly. Sure, they had their NWU universal income, as did everyone else, but it was barely enough to buy a pittance of food, forget decent housing and transportation.

Tata seemed about to say something, but instead a look of sorrow sagged her features.

Nyla ground her teeth. She'd wanted to cheer her grandmother up, but she'd gone and done the opposite. As usual.

"I'm sorry, Tata." She squeezed her grandmother's hand. "I just want the best for you and Kyle."

"I know you do, dear. I don't know what I'd do without you. I love you so much."

Nyla pushed to her feet. "I love you, too. Now, put that thing away"—she gestured to the Bible—"and get some sleep."

Out in the kitchen, Nyla opened the fridge—a half-loaf of bread, two eggs, and a pint of orange juice. She slammed it shut and leaned her head on the door with a sigh. Hadn't she just bought lunch meat, milk, cheese, and fresh vegetables? How could they be gone so soon? Did Kyle have a clue that most people didn't have access to fresh food? No, of course not. It was all she could do to remind him to save some for Tata.

Back in her bedroom, Nyla quickly undressed, placed her Glock onto her nightstand, and tossed an old tee-shirt over her head. One glance at the clock revealed it was well past midnight. She needed to sleep. Tomorrow would be a big day. But her body was strung tight with all that had happened. Spots ran around in her cage, and Nyla opened it to retrieve the crazy hamster. "What have you been up to today?" She drew Spots to her cheek and smiled at the way the hamster's shifting whiskers tickled her skin. After caressing the top of her head—one of the hamster's favorite things—Nyla placed her back in the cage and gave her a treat. Silly to keep a pet during these trying times, but for some reason, Nyla couldn't part with her. Spots was all that remained of a normal life and having her nearby always brought a smile to her face.

Looping her unruly brown hair into a loose knot on top of her head, Nyla knelt before a wooden chest and opened it. A familiar scent drifted around her, soothing her, warming her, and she drew a deep breath. Though it had been over a year, her mother's unique sweet smell had not disappeared. Faded, yes, but it still lingered on the few items of her mother's Nyla had managed to salvage—an old dress, the throw blanket her mother always snuggled with, a few books, her favorite earrings, the round pillow she held at night, and a family photo album. Nyla knew the scent would soon fade away, and she feared that most of all. Would she even remember the smell when it was gone?

Reaching inside the chest, she pushed aside the clothing, lifted a loose piece of wood at the bottom of the chest, and pulled out the necklace.

Sitting down on the floor, she held it up. Moonlight filtering in from the window spun a web of silver light around the cross as it dangled in the air. Nyla closed her hand over the shimmering gold. Her mother had given the cross necklace to Nyla on her sixteenth birthday. Nyla had worn it for a while to appease her mother, but she felt like a hypocrite and finally stopped. She didn't believe the same way her parents did, and there was no sense in giving them false hope.

"Oh, Mom." Closing her eyes, Nyla lowered her head and pressed the necklace to her forehead. "Why did you and Dad have to be so foolish?"

She would never forget the day they disappeared. It replayed in her darkest nightmares night after night. The chaos that happened afterward gave her little time to grieve, little time to process what had occurred.

They'd lost everything during the weeks following the *disappearance*...when the bombs hit and the tsunami struck— house, cars, and most of their belongings all gone, except these few things of her mother's they later found in the rubble.

"Will I ever see you again, Mama?" Tears flooded her eyes, and she hung her head.

"Look how she clings to the cross, Ranoss. 'Tis a positive sign," Zhaviel said.

"She keeps it only to remember her mother," Ranoss returned with a grunt.

"'Tis something, at the least. With Kyle I have no such sign of light." Zhaviel sighed and glanced out the door where his ward still slept. "In truth, I find myself quite restless. There's not much to do when all he does is pollute his body with drugs and play mindless games."

Ranoss nodded. He did not envy Zhaviel's assignment, nor any of his assignments these past millennia. He was the angel of those who used pharmakeia to escape the sorrows of this world. Even his battle dress reflected the depression and bondage of these fallen sons of Adam, all dark leather from head to toe with his spiked club gripped tight in his hand.

Indira appeared before them, the usual smile on his face. His white hair fell to a fur-lined silver cloak that covered bright chain mail for protection. In his hands, he carried a book of blessings for the aged righteous. Ranoss had never seen him without it. Indira faced Zhaviel. "The Father would not have assigned you to him were there no hope. Be strong, young warrior."

Zhaviel frowned. "I would trade with you in a minute, Indira, to watch over such a one as Mary, or Tata, as Nyla calls her."

Indira's gaze drifted to the room next door. "She finally sleeps. But even so, I must be on the lookout for the enemy. Her light is bright and growing brighter. She becomes more of a threat each day."

Ranoss kept his gaze on Nyla, seeking a flicker of light in her spirit, longing for her to listen to her grandmother. "Nyla has a good heart. She cares for her grandmother and brother. But will it be enough?"

"Keep the faith, Ranoss," Indira drew his silver blade. "I must go. I sense danger." The aged angel disappeared into the wall.

Zhaviel nodded toward Nyla. "Her new assignment may prove challenging, Ranoss."

"Indeed. Already the spirits of deception, lies, betrayal, and prejudice assemble around her." Aye, he *saw* them. They, along with other dark spirits, had been watching him, keeping their distance, yet salivating at the chance to join the others already tormenting Nyla from within. The most powerful among them—hatred—stared at Ranoss with red, fiery eyes. Once Nyla infiltrated the Father's saints, she would open the door for the others. And her last state would become worse than the first.

Then what hope would there be for her?

And you will be hated by all for My name's sake. But he who endures to the end will be saved. Matthew 10:22

Chapter 3

Nyla had always loved the beach. There was something powerful and majestic about the sea, and yet oddly soothing. She'd grown up in Oklahoma, a place as flat as a pancake and as cold in winter as the Arctic. At least it felt that way, especially when the wind was blowing. Which was much of the time. Childhood memories of those days always brought a smile to her lips, though so much had changed since then, they seemed more like a dream to her now. Her parents moved them to Fort Lauderdale ten years ago, nearly eight before the arrival. She remembered the first time she saw the ocean, a glittery blue diamond dancing in the sunlight all the way to the horizon. And she fell in love. After that, she'd spent every minute she could on the beach.

Spreading out her towel, she dropped her bag and plunked down to sit on the sand. She adjusted her sunglasses against the glare of the rising sun and glanced down the shore. The entire landscape had changed so much after the tidal wave, it was hard to imagine this was the same place she'd spent many an afternoon during her college years. Where once palm trees waved majestically on shore, now nothing but flattened rotted trunks remained. The few high-rise hotels that had not been knocked down by the massive wave looked like sun-bleached skeletons peppered by dark, gaping holes where windows once had been. Much of the white pristine sand was gone too, dragged out to sea when the waters receded.

But things were recovering. Buildings were being rebuilt, trees replanted, and sand shipped in from other beaches.

"Lookin' good, babe." Marco's sexy voice rang in her ear.

"Where are you?" She scanned the shoreline and finally saw him waving at her from behind an outhouse several yards from her position.

Nyla laughed. "Great place to hide."

"Yeah, you should smell it. No one would dare come near."

Voices drew Nyla's gaze to her left, where a family was setting up umbrellas and spreading blankets. Absent were the children she used to see running toward the water with buckets and shovels. She still didn't understand why only the younger children were taken and not teenagers. The Neflams had said that all the children needed to be taught the truth, even the ones from non-Deviant families. But why couldn't the little ones remain with their parents while they attended reformation centers? It all seemed so cruel, but the Neflams knew best.

A gust of wind blasted over her, tossing the edge of her blanket and cooling the sweat on her skin. One thing about Florida hadn't changed. It was still stinking hot, even in April.

A couple in their thirties set up chairs down by the waves. Nyla sensed a dark cloud of sorrow around them. So far, none of the children and none of the adults had returned from the reformation camps. What could possibly be taking so long? Of course, the NWU had announced it could be up to seven years before they'd see their loved ones again. Afterward, there had been protests, even riots in the streets, but with all the mayhem that had been going on in the world at the time—the tsunami, war, the arrival of the Neflams, and the famine—most people focused merely on surviving. Besides, who could argue with a master race of aliens?

Nyla swatted a mosquito away. She didn't want to think about it. The past was the past, and it only reminded her of her parents. The future was the only important thing now, making the world a better place, a safer place, a place without wars and violence, without disasters caused by climate change, a place where social and economic equality ruled, a place where everyone could pursue their dreams in peace. And the higher up in rank Nyla went, the more influence she could have. Not to mention enough wealth to take care of Tata and Kyle.

"Tell me when you see him," she said into the wind.

"Should be any minute now," Marco replied, then after a pause. "I miss you already."

Nyla smiled. "I haven't got his attention *yet*." She pressed a finger on her ear. Hard to believe such clear sound could come through something the size of a pin head. And it was waterproof too. But at least this Walker guy wouldn't be able to see it.

"Has Jennings told everyone I'm fired yet?"

"Heard he was going to announce it this morning."

Shaking her head, Nyla grabbed a handful of sand. Nearly a year of hard work, and it would all disappear just like this sand slipping through her fingers.

"I know what you're thinking." Marco's voice chirped in her ear. "You got this, girl. You'll get this Daniel guy and be a hero, probably even get promoted big time."

Warmth sped through Nyla that had nothing to do with the rising sun. Marco knew her so well. "You mean *we*. We're in this together, Marco."

She could almost hear him smiling. "You got it, babe."

Nyla stood, untied the sarong around her waist and let it slip to the ground. She might as well get in the water and be ready.

A whistle rang in her ear. "If this Walker guy don't bite, I will!"

"Stop it. I need to focus," Nyla responded playfully as she made her way down to the surf and waded through the first incoming waves.

"He's coming. You got three minutes."

The beach was more deserted than usual at this time of morning, but Calan didn't mind. This was *his* time, a time to exercise both his body *and* his spirit. There was nothing like watching the sun rise over a magnificent sea to remind one of God's glorious creation. Not that Calan needed reminding. The Father was always with him. He could sense Him deep within his spirit, could hear His loving voice radiate through his thoughts, and feel the power of the one Name on his lips that was above all names.

With each thud of his bare feet into the wet sand, he whispered a praise to the only Father Calan had ever known, the One who had rescued him in every way possible. He stepped up his pace, his breath coming hard and fast. He had to keep himself fit if he was to complete his mission. His SEAL training had taught him that. Failure was not an option. He could make no more mistakes.

Rays from the sun warmed his right cheek while a breeze cooled him from the west. Light and dark, heat and cold. The world had always been gray to him, but no more. Lines had been drawn, right and wrong, lies and truths, good and evil. Calan had learned that the hard way. But then again, he seemed to learn everything the hard way.

He smiled, watching two gulls fly away as he approached. Life went on. At least some of it. Millions of animals and people had died in the past eighteen months, leaving a weighty fog of emptiness and sorrow draped over the world, as if creation itself had sunk into a deep depression. Calan still found it hard to believe he had survived this long. Now he was on the most important mission of his life. A little over five more years to go, *if* the Father so deemed it.

He stepped up his pace even more, pushing himself until every muscle burned. Sweat slid down his bare back.

A scream pierced the air. Splashing drew his gaze several yards offshore where arms flailed and a head disappeared beneath the waves.

Calan charged into the surf and dove in. The warm Atlantic rushed over his body as he plunged arm after arm into the water and kicked with all his might through the waves toward the place he'd last seen the person. Halting at the spot, he spun around, searching for any sign of him. Then inhaling a deep breath, he dove beneath the surface, sweeping his hands out in every direction. There. He touched something solid. A body, floating lifelessly through the sea. Grabbing the person around the waist, he sped for the surface and forced her head above water. Yes, the *him* was a *her*. And the her was not breathing. Thrusting one arm beneath her shoulders, he quickly swam to shore.

By the time he carried her out of the water, she was already coughing and spitting out water. Thank God.

He laid the woman gently on the sand and turned her on her side to vomit out more water. But she seemed to be breathing just fine. In fact, she opened her eyes, blinked a few times, and then stared up at him. He'd never seen such beautiful eyes, light brown, the color of creamed coffee. And those lashes. Long and thick and beaded with glittering water.

"Are you all right?" he asked.

Nodding, she attempted to sit, and Calan took her hand to help her.

"I'm fine. I'm sorry. I don't know what happened." Her breath came in heavy spurts as she stared out over the ocean.

Strands of wet dark hair hung down her shoulder over a bright yellow bikini that left little to the imagination. Oddly, Calan hadn't noticed up to that point. But now... He shifted his gaze away. "You shouldn't be out that far if you can't swim, miss."

She faced him, squinting in the sunlight. "I *can* swim." She bit her lip. "Or I thought I could. I got dizzy. Not sure why. It's not like me."

"Well, I'm glad I came along when I did." Calan glanced both ways down the shore. Empty except for a few small groups of people. No one would have seen her go under. God must have arranged for Calan to pass by right at that time. He silently thanked Him.

"You saved me. Thank you, Mr...."

"Calan. Just Calan. And you're welcome."

"Not many would have bothered in today's world."

She was probably right about that. "My pleasure, miss."

"Nyla. Nyla Cruz." She extended her hand. He shook it. Firm, confident, yet soft. A good handshake.

From a beautiful woman. A weakness of his. In a prior life. But obviously, from the way his body was reacting, still a temptation. He stood, seeking the Spirit within for strength. A heaviness, a darkness swirled about the woman. A normal sensation from most people he met these days.

He forced his gaze away yet again. "I better get going. Will you be okay?"

"How can I ever thank you? Can I buy you a coffee or something?"

"No need."

"Lunch? Please let me repay you." She struggled to rise, and Calan reached for her hand and helped her to her feet.

"Like I said. No need." Then shifting his eyes once again from her body that had curves in *all* the right places, he jogged away, yelling a "nice to meet you" over his shoulder.

Nyla stared at Calan as he raced away. Was it her imagination or was he running much faster than he had been before? From her? She huffed, unable to take her eyes off him. She had not expected Calan Walker to be so...so...*good-looking*? He wasn't drop-dead gorgeous like Marco, but he had a presence, a masculine ruggedness that surprised her. And a kindness, a genuine kindness shining through his eyes that she rarely saw in anyone.

"That guy must be gay," Marco chirped in her ear.

She smiled. No way. Not the way he was looking at her, or trying *not* to look at her. She'd never met a red-blooded male who didn't ogle every inch of a pretty woman in a tiny bikini. But this guy? He seemed intent on focusing elsewhere, as if it caused him pain to enjoy a sexy woman's body.

"Maybe he just didn't find me attractive." Not that she believed that, but she needed a compliment right now to lift her crushed ego.

"Impossible, babe."

And there it was.

Turning, she kicked her feet in the sand as she made her way back to her towel. "Guess I failed at the most important mission of my life."

Anisian marched up to Ranoss and Xoran. "Greetings, mighty warriors!"

Ranoss tore his gaze from Nyla and smiled. He hadn't seen Anisian in over two-hundred years. "Anisian." Attempting to stretch up to the giant angel's tall stature, he gripped his arm. "Who are you assigned to?"

"Calan Walker."

"What a blessed gift from the Father of Spirits," Xoran said.

"Indeed, though it hasn't always been so with this human." Anisian turned to watch his ward as he spoke with Nyla. "See how the spirits of lust and fornication spin about his shield of light, seeking entrance. Yet he makes every attempt to not look at her. The Father is pleased."

Ranoss grimaced. "She is wrong to tempt him so."

"But they must meet," Anisian said. "And so they have."

"It begins now," Xoran added.

"As it must." Ranoss shifted his boots in the sand, watching as Nyla exposed more of her body to the human male. Lust and fornication opened their salivating jaws toward Calan, and drawing his blade, Ranoss started toward the couple.

Anisian threw out his arm to hold him back. "Not yet, my friend. The Father tests Calan. He must pass on his own in order to grow stronger."

Ranoss growled. "Why does the Father not allow us to engage these foul spirits? We could do much good before they cause these sons of Adam to fall."

"Because he has given them free will," Anisian said. "They must choose the light. They must choose to fight the darkness. Then we can engage."

Xoran chuckled. "Your ward, Calan, must not give you much opportunity to fight. See how he resists her."

Anisian nodded, obviously pleased. "Yet he has his weaknesses, his insecurities."

Ranoss released a heavy sigh as Nyla made her way to her blanket, a host of demons accompanying her. "She did not entice him. How will they get together now?"

Anisian started after Calan. "I must leave. Trust the Father. His plans never fail."

And in his place shall arise a vile person, to whom they will not give the honor of royalty; but he shall come in peaceably, and seize the kingdom by intrigue. Daniel 11:21

Chapter 4

Calan, gun in his holster and flashlight in hand, slipped through the back door of the abandoned warehouse. Daniel had summoned him, and he was anxious to speak with his mentor—*had been* all day—but he had to go through the motions of his job, his *cover*. Being a security guard for NeirLoom Corporation at their biggest warehouse barely helped pay the bills, but the added benefits were out of this world, literally.

Weaving among the scattered crates of office furniture, Calan made sure the few cameras mounted on the inside walls captured his face before he moved toward the back where the offices once had been. He wanted his employers to see him doing his job. *If* they even bothered to look. After the economic collapse and the Great Reset, NeirLoom had been forced to sell off most of their merchandise. They'd taken a huge hit financially and had never recovered. Who needed office furniture when so many companies had gone belly up and most people were quarantined at home due to the virus? The tsunami, war, and famine had only made things worse, and now only a few pieces of furniture remained out of what once had been a warehouse stuffed with merchandise.

Why NeirLoom kept him on, he couldn't say, except the owners wanted to keep the place free from squatters, a common problem after the collapse. Drawing a deep breath of air that always smelled like the inside of a commercial airplane, Calan took the stairs down to the basement, stopped at the locked door, and gave the secret knock.

A muffled voice emerged through the wood. "He who endures to the end."

"Shall be saved," Calan responded.

Within seconds, the door flung open, and Max ushered him inside. After clicking the locks back in place, he gave Calan his usual bear hug, a specialty of the large man who had been such a comfort and encouragement to the saints.

"Good to see you, brother."

"And you, Max. Is he here?"

"Yes. He's expecting you." Calan followed Max into the large room that used to be a storage space for extra furniture and office supplies. Empty for years, it provided the perfect meeting place for the saints of Fort Lauderdale, Zion's Nest, as they called it. Comfortable couches and chairs, along with tables and lamps, circled the oblong room that was roughly the size of three living rooms. Various carpets softened the cement floor, while black posters boarded up the few slit-like windows lining the walls near the ceiling. Musical instruments crowded one corner, and from the other, the scent of fresh baked bread emerged from a small kitchenette.

Calan nodded to the few people sitting in a circle reading the Scriptures, all friends of his, and then stopped to compliment Max's wife, Carolyn, their resident cook, who stirred a pot of soup on the stove.

"Smells delicious." He glanced into the bubbling liquid as Max kissed his wife on the cheek.

"Have some," She giggled at her husband's attention, then gestured toward the soup.

"I will. But first I need to speak with Daniel." Tribby leapt on the counter and rubbed her head against Calan. "Hello, little one." He stroked the black cat's fur.

"Get that thing off my counter!" Carolyn waved a ladle at the cat, but then smiled when Calan picked it up. "You and that cat," she said.

"He's a stray just like me." Calan set Tribby down on the floor, and he bounced away. "I know you can't resist a stray."

"I can when they put fleas in my food." She returned to her cooking.

Max gestured toward the back of the room. "He's been in there praying for hours, but he told me to send you right in when you get here."

Daniel rarely interrupted his prayer time for anything. "Wonder what's up," Calan said.

"No idea. But you know Daniel."

Nodding, Calan walked toward the back, knocked on the closed door of what was once a small office, and quietly entered. Daniel sat on a cushioned chair, his elbows on his knees, his head in his hands. Upon hearing Calan enter, he lifted his gaze, smiled, and gestured to a chair. "Sit."

With light hair and a fit physique, Daniel was only seven years older than Calan, but he held himself with the authority of an elder. Calan still could not believe Daniel had chosen him to be his protégé. Him? A man who had failed at the most important things in his life? Yet this man—this man on whom the presence of God sat so strongly—saw something in Calan no one else did.

He slid onto the seat across from Daniel. The man's blue eyes shone with such brilliant clarity and peace, Calan shifted his gaze away, glancing over the warm room that served as a private place of prayer for anyone who needed it. A large wooden cross hung on one wall, while across from it, someone had painted a mural of Jesus high on a cliff, reaching for the one sheep who had wandered away from the flock. A desk stood in the corner, a stack of illegal Bibles and various papers scattered on top.

"Have you been practicing your gifting?"

Daniel's question brought Calan's gaze back to him. The man was never one for small talk. "Now and then." In truth, being able to sense evil before it arrived made him uneasy. They were surrounded by so much darkness, especially now during the Tribulation, that he hated the responsibility of warning the others in time. What if he sensed things wrong? What if he neglected to detect a threat until it was upon them?

"You have other gifts, too," Daniel said. "One will become more obvious soon."

Calan sighed, unsure whether that would be a good thing or not. More gifts meant more responsibility, and there were days he just didn't know if he'd be up to the task. His thoughts drifted to the girl on the beach, and the reason he'd been wanting to speak to Daniel. Plus, he needed to change the topic before Daniel anointed him with oil and told him he would walk on water. "I rescued a woman from the ocean this morning."

Daniel smiled, that knowing smile that always set Calan on edge, as if the man could read his thoughts.

"She was very beautiful," Calan continued, suddenly regretting that he mentioned that particular fact. "But there was darkness around her."

'You sensed the enemy?"

"Very strong. But there was something else." Calan leaned forward on his knees. "A spark. Maybe I'm crazy, but I thought I saw a spark of light deep inside her."

Daniel nodded. "There is hope for her, then."

Calan shrugged. "I won't see her again, anyway. Really strange, though. She seemed intent on seducing me."

"The Lord is pleased you resisted her."

Warmth flooded Calan. He knew that. But to hear it from Daniel meant the world to him. "Wasn't easy." Calan laughed. "She was *very* pretty."

Daniel grinned. "So you said." He leaned back in his chair. "Yes, I remember well those days when women threw themselves at me."

Calan studied his friend and smiled. "You *knew*. You already knew that I met this woman." Why did these things still surprise him.? It was one of Daniel's gifts—the gift of knowledge.

Daniel shrugged it off. "The Lord would not have told me if it weren't important."

Important? Calan couldn't see how.

"You are learning," Daniel said. "You have the gift of discernment, just as the Father said."

Calan glanced at the wooden cross. He'd made a vow to the Lord to never repeat the mistakes he'd made in the past. In fact, to make up for them. And he intended to keep that vow, along with his promise to protect Daniel at all costs. If discernment would help him do that, he was all for it.

Daniel scrubbed the stubble on his chin. "So, this girl, what is her name?"

"Nyla, something. Cruz. That was it."

Daniel's brows rose. "Interesting."

"Why?"

"You don't recognize her name?"

Calan shook his head.

"She's the team leader for one of the NWU Florida PK Teams, responsible for arresting and imprisoning several of our brothers and sisters."

Horrified, Calan leapt to his feet. "What?"

Daniel laughed. "God has such a profound sense of humor, doesn't He?"

Calan only stared at him, not finding anything funny about the situation at all. For one thing, she could have arrested him on the spot.

Daniel inched forward on his seat. "Word is, she was just terminated from her position."

"What for?"

"It was all over the news today. Apparently she expressed sympathy for us *Deviants*, as they call us, and she was also overheard questioning the narrative of the Neflams and the existence of God."

"Whoa. From a Peace Keeper?" Calan raked back his hair. "So, maybe I was supposed to say something. I didn't sense that." But of course Calan was no Daniel. He glanced at a clock on the desk. "I better get out there and do my rounds for the cameras." He rose. "So, is that what you wanted to speak to me about?"

Daniel nodded. "You'll meet her again. God has told me."

Nyla tossed and turned, her mind reeling with a horrible nightmare in which she'd lost her job, was disgraced in the eyes of all her friends and colleagues, and was slammed all over the news and media as an evil lunatic and a traitor to the NWU.

Squeak, squeak, squeak...Rubbing her eyes, she heaved a sigh. Crud. What was that hideous noise? *Squeak... squeak... squeak.* Willing herself to wake up from her terrifying dream, she rolled over in bed, opened one eye, and saw Spots spinning on her hamster wheel. She chuckled. Someone was up bright and early and ready to exercise. *Not* Nyla.

The nightmare she'd been having became more real the more her mind and memories sparked to life. Not a nightmare at all. But her new reality. Tossing off her covers, she swung her legs over the side of her bed and dropped her head into her hands, raking back her tangled hair. Her eyes landed on her laptop, still open to the news article that had caused her to cry herself to sleep. Yes, cry. Not exactly a good trait for the Team Leader of the best PK team in South Florida. But then again, she no longer held that position. According to the news, she was a traitor, a Deviant. An enemy.

She knew Jennings had to discredit her in order to make her cover solid, but this was too much. The story of her "betrayal" and "termination" blasted across every local news station. Everyone in the city, county, and most likely state and world knew. If she had known this would happen, she would have done all in her power to turn down the assignment. As it was, she'd failed to lure the apparently too-saintly-to-lust Calan Walker into her seductive web.

Yet another insult she'd been forced to endure.

Rising, she opened Spots' cage and retrieved the ball of warm fur. "You still love me, don't you?" She drew the hamster close and caressed the top of her head. "What a sweet girl."

Things could be worse. At least Nyla would still collect her salary, though off the books, Jennings had said. At least she could still take care of Tata, Kyle, and "you, sweet thing." She held up the hamster and kissed her furry cheek. Spots wiggled her nose, sending her whiskers twitching.

"I know, I need to shower." Nyla smiled. All was not lost. Marco had buzzed in her ear last night that Jennings was working on another meet. He buzzed other things too, sensual things, that made Nyla regret her decision not to spend the night at his place.

She carefully placed Spots back in her cage and gave her a yogurt treat. Then tossing on a robe, she headed to the kitchen to make coffee for Tata.

Kyle slouched on the couch, watching the news.

"So, you got fired?" He snorted. With disdain or ridicule, she couldn't tell.

Opening a cupboard, Nyla pulled out the can of coffee, deciding to ignore her brother.

The news blared on. "Chinese troops have been subdued in Taiwan and hostilities cease for the time being as NWU Prime Minister Aali has successfully initiated talks. Additional peace talks are still in progress between Pakistan and India as well as North Korea." The gorgeous blond who was giving the news turned to her male colleague beside her. "What an incredible leader and peace maker Minister Immu Aali is. The world is fortunate to have him."

"No wonder he won the Nobel Peace Prize last year for the treaty he forged between Israel and the nations, strengthening the Abrahamic Accords," the man chimed in. "No one else has been able to bring peace to the Middle East." They both smiled at each other and then back at the camera before going to a commercial.

There was only enough coffee to make a few cups. Nyla frowned. She'd have to make enough for Tata and then head out for her own.

Immu Aali appeared on the screen. The man was handsome, Nyla would give him that. Much like Marco, his looks were dark and exotic, but there was a presence about him—a hypnotic power—that penetrated the screen and filled the room.

"I am confident," he began in his charming accent, "that, with the Neflams' help, we shall see complete world peace soon. Though it has been a difficult hurdle to overcome the nationalists, the ten world regions we have formed are quite willing to give up their national sovereignty in order to create a New World Union of combined cooperation. A world where no nation or region will attempt to dominate another and all will work together to create peace, harmony, and a balance with nature that will blossom across our globe, end climate change, famine, and all wars, and stop the spread of infectious diseases that have so recently ravaged our population."

Nyla stopped to stare. The man was mesmerizing. His words brought comfort and hope to a world devastated by tragedy after tragedy. This was the reason she worked so hard. This was why she did what she did—her purpose. And this was why she must continue her current assignment, no matter the cost. World peace and the advancement of humankind was at stake.

"Yeah, yeah, yeah..." Kyle switched the station off and picked up his virtual reality headpiece.

Nyla returned to making coffee. "Come on, even *you* can see this guy is good for the world, a born leader. We've needed someone like this for a while now, and he came on the scene in the nick of time."

"I'll believe it when I see it. Besides, how are we going to live now that you got canned?" He fired up a game, hesitating before putting on the headset. "It isn't true, is it?"

"What?"

"You aren't one of those *Deviants*?"

"Of course not." She wanted to tell him the truth, but Kyle had never been able to keep his mouth shut. Jennings had made her promise to tell no one, not even her grandmother. "It's just a misunderstanding. I'll be back at work soon."

"What are we going to do in the meantime?"

She turned on the coffee pot and stomped into the living room. "I don't know. Maybe *you* could find a job." She raised a sarcastic brow.

"You know I'm sick." He scowled, his hand reaching for the bottle of CBD pills on the table.

Darting forward, she grabbed them.

"Hey!" Anger fired from his eyes—lifeless, sad eyes that pricked at Nyla's conscience.

"It's time you stopped doping yourself up and become a man. I need you, Kyle. Grow up!"

"Sorry if I never live up to your expectations! Or Mom and Dad's." Growling, Kyle sat back on the couch with a huff that reminded her of a spoiled teen being asked to do chores. But Kyle wasn't spoiled. He had never been spoiled. Her father had seen to that. Where other teens were given cars, expensive clothing, and all kinds of freedom, Kyle had to work to earn a car. He had a curfew and responsibilities around the house. Sure, their father had been tough on him, maybe too tough, but their parents had taught them both the value of hard work and respect.

Then why was he behaving this way? She sighed, staring at him. He had not taken the disappearance of their parents well. He'd been there, as had Nyla, at the very moment they vanished before their eyes. Mom had reached out for Kyle, a tearful pleading in her eyes, as if she knew what was about to occur. It was only a millisecond, but the love pouring from her face was overwhelming. Kyle had always been a vulnerable, emotional kid. He had always been the weak one. Mom had called him an empath, someone who feels things much deeper than most people.

Maybe Nyla was the one responsible for spoiling him now. She'd coddled him after that, taken care of him, tried her best to be a mother to him. But she'd only driven him deeper into depression and drugs.

She settled her voice. "I need your help."

"For what? What's the point? Even if this guy brings world peace, one-fourth of the population has already died from the plagues, war, the quakes, tsunamis, and famine." Kyle stared at his feet, where as far as she could tell, he wore the same hole-ridden socks he'd worn two days ago.

He was right, of course. The events of the past eighteen months were enough to make most people curl up in a ball and give up. Nyla didn't have that luxury.

"Yes, all that sucked. But things are getting better. There won't be any more wars now that the world is divided into ten regions. The ten presidents are good people chosen by the Neflams. The plague is dwindling, the vaccines are working, and if we take better care of the planet, there won't be any more famines and quakes. Things will settle down."

Kyle huffed. At twenty, with his curly dark hair and tall physique, he was growing into a handsome man. If not for the perpetual frown on his face. "Lot of good the vaccine did. Most people who took it ended up dying anyway."

"That's conspiracy, and you know it. It was the next virus, smallpox, and other plagues that killed those people. Besides, the new booster shots offer full protection. You heard what the Neflams said, how they are perfecting the human race, survival of the fittest and all. And they are teaching us how to incorporate technology with biology. Someday, we will live forever. It will be glorious."

"Those Neflams creep me out," Kyle spat out. "Besides, if this is how life will be, I don't want to live forever."

Nyla growled inwardly, growing weary of his complaining. "How about you stick around for a few years and get a job? I could use your help with money."

"I'm here with Tata all day. Who else is going to watch her?"

"She can take care of herself." Nyla bit her lip. Most of the time.

"She's eighty."

"I'm not dead yet." Tata's scratchy voice emanated from the hallway where she emerged, shuffling along with a walker she'd named Ralph.

"Tata." Nyla approached and helped her to one of the chairs in the living room. "I made coffee."

"Why do you think I came out?" Tata smiled. "The glorious scent of fresh-brewed coffee. Share a cup with me, Kyle. Cheer up. We are alive and have food. All blessings."

Kyle attempted a smile. "If you say so."

Nyla poured them both a cup. Her com piece buzzed, and she flipped it on as she headed into the bathroom.

"Morning, gorgeous." Marco's voice made her smile, despite the angst of the morning.

"Hey, handsome."

"Jennings has a lead. Feel like getting a coffee?"

"You have no idea."

For we do not wrestle against flesh and blood, but against principalities, against powers, against the rulers of the darkness of this age, against spiritual hosts of wickedness in the heavenly places. Ephesians 6:12

Chapter 5

Nyla jumped in line at Ernesto's Café stand on Ocean Drive and kept a wary eye on her surroundings. Apparently, Calan had been spotted at this coffee shop most mornings, no doubt as addicted to coffee as she was. They weren't the only ones, apparently, considering the size of the line. It amazed her that people had money to spend on treats like fancy espresso. The universal income given to every law-abiding NWU citizen barely paid for basic necessities, which left most people seeking employment in an economy still recovering from the crash. Hard times for sure, yet maybe to these people in line, a good cup of coffee was a necessity, something to look forward to in a world devoid of so many of its former pleasures.

A warm, humid breeze wafted in from the sea, drawing her gaze to the glassy blue water, always so calm in the morning. Only a few ripples caressed the shore, glittering like diamond ribbons in the morning sunlight. Seagulls pecked at the sand, looking for crabs or leftover food to eat, while several people set up their towels and umbrellas. After the tsunami, it had taken awhile for everyone to feel safe on the beach again, but slowly, more and more came out to enjoy a day in the surf and sun.

Voices raised at the front of the line, and Nyla jerked her attention to a patron showing her mobile to the clerk in the stand.

"What kind of crap is this?" the woman yelled.

"I'm sorry, ma'am, but your social score does not meet the NWU standards to order coffee," the young barista stated with all the emotion of a robot. "Next." He gestured toward the person behind the woman.

The woman wouldn't budge. "But why? I don't understand."

"Move out of the way, lady," the man behind her shouted as others in line groaned.

Every inch of Nyla's training itched to jump into gear and do what she'd been trained to do—assess the situation and act in the best interests of peace and civility. But she no longer carried a badge, no longer had an ounce of authority.

She ground her teeth.

Finally, just when it looked like the others in line intended to shove the poor woman aside, she skulked away, cursing under her breath. A shred of sympathy wove its way through Nyla's heart. It was only coffee, but still...*No.* She snapped her gaze away from the woman. Obviously, she'd done something wrong to lower her social score, and she deserved her punishment. It could be something as small as jaywalking or littering or posting a racist slur online. Or it could be much worse, such as speaking out against peace and harmony with Planet Earth.

"Hey, babe, get me a cappuccino too, will you?"

Nyla smiled. "I'd love nothing more than to share one with you face to face."

"So, you miss me already?"

It had only been a day, but yes, she missed Marco, his sensuous smile, the way he looked at her, his kiss...ugh. She blew out a sigh. She had to be strong.

"Mr. Wonderful is heading your way."

Nyla stiffened, but then quickly attempted a relaxed stance.

Someone fell in line behind her, shadowing her from the sun. Resisting the urge to turn around, she stepped up to order. "Iced cappuccino."

"Miss Cruz?"

She spun around, shielding her eyes from the sun, and glanced up. "Mr....Mr.—"

"Walker. Call me Calan."

"Ah, my rescuer." She gave him her widest smile. "So, maybe I *can* buy you that coffee after all?" Turning, she held up her mobile to be scanned.

The barista waved a wand over it and let out a groan of disgust. "This must be the day for social dissidents."

Calan shouldn't have been surprised to run into Miss Cruz again. Daniel's words from the Lord always proved true. He just hadn't expected them to happen so soon. But here Miss Cruz stood in the flesh, albeit a more covered up flesh than the last time. Which Calan was thankful for.

He'd had to restrain his laughter at the look on her face when the barista wouldn't sell her any coffee. You'd have thought the young man informed her she was going to jail. For such a pretty face, it sure could scrunch up into a red ball of rage rather quickly. She started to yell at the man, but then kept touching her ear as if she had an ache, and stopped. Finally, Calan showed his mobile to the man, paid for her drink, and ordered his own.

Now, as they sat on a bench facing the sea, he found himself wondering what to say. Unlike Daniel, Calan wasn't outgoing and charming. He was a warrior, a protector, and not particularly good at intimate conversation. Especially with beautiful women.

Salty wind blasted over them from the sea, sending her lustrous hair whirling behind her. "Thanks for the coffee," she said, pressing a finger over a small scar on her neck. "I'm so embarrassed."

"Don't be. These social credit scores are draconian. I'm sure you didn't do anything wrong." But of course he knew exactly what she'd done wrong, if Daniel had his information right. Nyla's firing from the Peace Keepers would lower her score significantly, not to mention any suspicion of sympathy toward Deviants.

She took a sip of her coffee. "It's okay. I better get used to it."

"Planning on committing a crime later?" Calan smiled.

A hint of mischief appeared in her light brown eyes. "You never know." She gazed back out to sea. "So, what do you do, Calan?"

Squinting from the rising sun, he rubbed sweat from the back of his neck. "Security. I'm a guard for NeirLoom Corporation."

"Nice." An odd expression twitched on her face, and she touched her ear. Facing him, she gave him a seductive smile that seemed suddenly out of place. "Thank you again for saving me the other day *and* for this coffee."

Was she flirting with him? "Sure." Calan glanced down the beach. He and Daniel and a few of the saints were supposed to meet here in a few minutes, and he didn't want to introduce Nyla to them. Maybe she was curious about God. Maybe she wasn't. Calan's job was to protect Daniel until he could be sure. In fact, he really had no idea how to steer the conversation to spiritual matters.

He finished his coffee and tossed the cup in a can beside the bench. "Want to take a walk?"

Nodding, she stood, and shuffled through the sand ahead of him. Tight shorts and a white tank top hugged her curves perfectly as her curly brown hair waved across her back. Calan swallowed and looked away, seeking the Spirit within as Daniel had taught him. Darkness. He sensed darkness around her. If she *was* seeking God, there was little indication.

Lord, a little help here? He caught up with her, and they reached the wet sand and started walking.

"So, what do *you* do, Miss Cruz?"

"Nyla. If you can believe it, I used to be a NWU PK. A team leader, in fact." She stared at him as if gauging his response.

Calan didn't flinch. "Used to be?"

"Yeah, just got fired."

"I'm sorry to hear that."

"It's okay. Maybe it wasn't the right job for me." Wind blew her hair across her face, and she eased the strands behind her ear. "Let's just say I didn't always agree with what we were doing."

"Ah, so that explains your social score."

She flashed him a smile. "Exactly."

"Well, just between you and me, I don't agree with everything they do either." He wouldn't say more, just leave her an opening if she wanted to share. But he suspected Nyla Cruz was no dummy. The NWU had listening ears everywhere, and it was never safe to state an opinion contrary to the mainstream views.

She fell into silence as they both fell into step, a comfortable silence, which was odd for him with anyone. A wave swept out before them, flattening the sand into a glistening bed. Their bare feet sank into the moist silt as a bird chased the water back out to the sea. Somewhere a bell rang, people chattered, birds squawked, waves tumbled on shore—all sounds becoming muffled as Calan sensed an approaching darkness. It slithered over him like an icy foam, draining all warmth from his soul.

He glanced around for the source. Up ahead, he spotted Daniel and two saints heading toward them on the beach.

Grabbing Nyla's hand, he spun them both around and started back.

"What are you—?"

"Sorry, I gotta get to work. I forgot."

The chill turned to ice, prickling his skin. Dread consumed him, threading through his body, tightening his nerves, squeezing the breath from his lungs.

"No weapon formed against me shall prosper," he whispered too low to be heard over the waves. "Be gone in Jesus' name!" The chill left. A wave of relief spread over him as he breathed in the sea air.

Nyla glanced at him as if he'd lost his mind.

But the sense of evil remained, floating around her. *She* was the source. He must do everything in his power to keep Nyla Cruz away from Daniel.

A familiar voice hailed him from behind.

Drawing his sword in one swift motion, Anisian marched toward the couple. He'd sensed the mounting enemy forces before he'd seen them. Now they surrounded Calan and Nyla as they walked down the beach—circling, spitting, and seething, gathering more troops, and finally drawing their weapons.

"To the battle!" he shouted to Ranoss, who was already running beside him, crossbow armed and pointed.

In the distance, Anisian spotted Nazare, Daniel Cain's guardian, and two other warriors dashing toward the fight. Good. It appeared from the large number of enemy troops something important was about to happen, something they were trying to stop, or perhaps encourage?

Nay, to stop. The voice of the Commander of Heaven's Armies spoke within him. The same voice that had given him the command to fight.

Spotting the warrior angels, the demon creatures spun about, weapons raised, red eyes flaming, putrid foam emerging from between their sharp fangs....

And the battle commenced.

The chime of blade on blade filled the air, along with the groans of pain from the dark ones when the warriors hit their mark.

Anisian hefted his blade and swung it down upon a particularly large demon. The vile creature met it with the force of its own sword, sending a tremble through Anisian. This one was strong. But not strong enough. Forcing him back, Anisian leapt to the side and cleaved his blade across the creature's chest. He groaned, a hideous, blood-curdling groan, fuming and foaming at Anisian before he disappeared in a puff of black smoke.

Spinning around, Anisian ensured his ward, Calan, was well, then searched for more enemies to battle. Ranoss fired a flaming arrow from his crossbow, striking one of the dark ones in the head. It exploded in globs of black slime all over the sand. Across the way, Nazare battled two of the loathsome dark ones. Anisian headed toward him to help, but Nazare dispatched them one by one with ease. The large warrior's reputation preceded him as one who, much like Samson of old, could fight off many of the enemy at once.

Sensing danger, Anisian swept his sword behind him, slicing a demon in two. An ear-piercing scream filled the air as an incoming wave swept the two dark halves out to sea.

"Anisian!" Nazare's shout turned him around to join his two friends in battling the remaining demons. Ranoss fired arrow after arrow, never missing his mark, while Nazare knocked aside dark fiend after dark fiend, left to right, as if he were clearing a path. Anisian took a position behind them and near their wards to dispatch any hellions that got through.

Finally, all the enemy's forces disappeared, some in black smoke, others in black sludge, all leaving behind their putrid stench and an icy chill.

Breath heaving, Anisian sheathed his sword. "Well done, mighty warriors. May God be praised."

Nazare nodded his way with a smile. "I fear this is only the beginning, my friend."

Nyla had never met a man who was so quiet around her. Most of them chatted away like lovesick birds, trying to impress her with their careers, accomplishments, or money. Even the shy ones put forth an effort to make her laugh. She also had never met a man who didn't undress her with his eyes, at least secretly while she wasn't looking. Or so they thought. Women knew these things.

Yet, there was a peace about Calan. An authority and assurance that made her feel comfortable. Even in the silence in which they walked now.

It was hard to believe he was one of those crazy Deviants. He seemed quite sane, in charge of all his faculties, unafraid. And he had a good social score, which meant he had a VaxPass. What was up with that? Maybe Jennings' intel on this guy was wrong.

Nyla dug her toes into the sand, relishing the cool sensation. A tiny crab dove into a hole. A wave deposited a shell by her feet. She leaned to pick it up. What a beautiful, perfect shape— a fan of white and red. After the tsunami, the sea rarely brought any shells to the shore, as if it were still angry or holding a grudge. She smiled. What a rare gift. She glanced at Calan to show it to him, but he seemed distracted.

She knew that stance well. A warrior's stance. Alert, eyes focused on the surroundings. Then he whispered something, spun her around, and started the other way.

Strange.

Maybe the man was crazy after all.

A chill scraped over her. Odd. It had to be eighty degrees already. Nyla rubbed her arms. A shadow fell over them, and she glanced up, but no clouds covered the sun.

"Calan!"

A voice turned him around.

Down the beach, three men approached. Oddly, a small crowd followed after them. Calan stiffened beside her. Nyla wanted to ask him what was up, but she couldn't take her eyes off the man in the middle. Tall, well-featured, his light hair blew in the breeze. He walked with such grace, yet such power and confidence, much like Calan, but different. With more authority, assurance. His gaze locked upon Nyla, not in a sensual way at all, but in a determined, focused way.

The closer he came, the more Nyla felt like a thousand ants crawled over her body. Yet she couldn't move, couldn't leave.

Calan seemed to be motioning for the approaching men to leave, but the man in the middle paid him no mind. She could see his eyes now, blue as the sea, sparkling with life, a bursting vitality, and something she rarely saw in anyone these days. *Joy.*

The men stopped before them. The man smiled at Nyla and a chill coursed through her. "Introduce us to your new friend, won't you, Calan?"

The group of people following the men pressed in behind them, kept at bay by the two men circling him like a barricade.

Calan breathed out a heavy sign and gave the man a strange look. "This is Nyla Cruz. Nyla, Daniel Cain."

A shock wave rippled through her. So this was the infamous Daniel Cain! She had not expected to meet him so soon, nor to find him strolling about on a public beach. Wasn't he aware the entire NWU PK force was after him?

Apparently not, for without hesitation, he extended his hand and shook hers in a firm grip. "Miss Cruz, a pleasure. Any friend of Calan's is a friend of mine."

For the first time in her life—well, maybe the second—the words that screamed for release in her mind jumbled into a knot in her throat. She longed to arrest him on the spot, haul him off to Jennings, and end this stupid assignment. That was what she was here for, no?

Instead, she smiled and glanced at Calan. "Well, we aren't really friends. We've only just met. Calan saved my life a few days ago."

"Ah, the woman from the sea?" He winked at Calan, who shuffled his feet in the sand uncomfortably.

Jennings had been right. Calan *was* a very close friend of Daniel's. Now, what to do? Was Marco hearing this? If he was, he'd be calling for backup. Then all she had to do was distract Daniel and keep him here long enough for them to arrive.

They will take up serpents; and if they drink anything deadly, it will by no means hurt them; they will lay hands on the sick, and they will recover. Mark 16:18

Chapter 6

Walk with us awhile," Daniel said to Nyla before shifting his gaze to Calan with a smile.

Was he kidding? Nyla must be living under some serious good karma for this man to be handed over to her so quickly *and* so easily.

Calan, however, seemed uneasy, almost agitated, as he took her elbow and attempted to move her to the other side of the bodyguard standing beside Daniel. But Daniel was having none of it. "No, beside me, please. I'd like to get to know Miss Cruz."

Nyla was happy to comply even while Calan scowled and moved to his other side. They started on their way, and she tapped her com piece, wondering if it was working.

"Yeah, I see." Marco's voice rang loud. "I've already alerted Jennings. He's sending a team right away. Good job, babe."

Nyla smiled. Fastest undercover assignment she'd ever heard of. And now, with this successful mission, she was sure to be promoted. Maybe several rungs up the NWU PK ladder.

"Something pleases you, Miss Cruz?" Daniel asked, his blue eyes sparkling in a glance that held a knowledge he couldn't possibly possess.

She thumbed over her shoulder. "You have quite the following, Mr. Cain. Groupies?"

His laugh came out deep and strong. "No, just people in need."

She glanced at the dozen or so people who followed them. "In need of what?"

"You'll see."

No, it's you who will see, Mr. Cain. Crazy Deviant. Thoughts of her parents rose to prick her anger. It was exactly the beliefs of this man that had caused them to be taken away from her, away from Kyle, leaving them orphans and destitute. She had to get him off the streets, unable to deceive any more people. For her parents. For all the others who'd been taken to reformation camps. She owed them that.

Yet, when he looked at her, as he did now, why did she feel nothing but his concern for her, care even?

She snapped her gaze away. Better to stay angry. That way when her friends arrived, she would have no trouble joining them to arrest him.

Calan, however, might be a problem, along with the two other bodyguards. She glanced at him walking on the other side of Daniel, head up, eyes alert, scanning the area. He seemed more than able to handle himself. Still, without weapons, they'd be easily subdued.

A wave crashed ashore in front of them, foaming and bubbling, and Daniel splashed through it. Only then did she notice he wore no shoes and had his jeans rolled up halfway to his knees—holey jeans at that. Hadn't he been one of those rich preachers who'd had a mega-church that scammed ignorant people out of their money? She'd read up on him before her assignment. He'd owned a huge mansion in Boca right on the beach, a Porsche, and a wardrobe that would make a prince jealous. Yet here he was barefoot, in jeans and a tee-shirt. Served him right.

A couple of teens, surfboards clamped beneath their arms, dashed for the sea, and splashed into the surf in front of them. Down the beach, a barking dog chased a bird, a man shouted at his wife, and a siren blared from the city.

Rising sunlight warmed Nyla's cheek, and she drew a deep breath of sea air, trying to calm her nerves. Soon, this whole charade would be over.

"Tell me, Miss Cruz, how is your grandmother doing?"

Daniel's question tightened every nerve. "How do you....?" She gazed up at him in shock. She'd never told Calan about her grandmother, had she? She must have. Or maybe Daniel had done his homework on her, as she had done on him. That had to be it. Calan had given him her name, and he'd looked her up. Now he no doubt hoped she would think he was some prophet. No way she'd fall for that. "She's fine. Thanks," she replied in a tone of nonchalance.

Yet, if Daniel knew about Tata, then he surely knew that when she'd been a PK, she'd arrested many Deviants. "Listen, Mr. Cain, I no longer arrest your kind. I hope you know I got fired."

He laughed again. "My kind? And please call me Daniel."

"You know what I mean."

"Ah, here we are..." Daniel headed away from the water to a group of picnic tables set in rows beneath a thatched pergola. Several people milled about, some sitting, some standing, and all looking very excited when they saw Daniel approach.

He gestured for them to sit as he took a spot in the middle of the tables. The people following him mingled with the others.

Calan inched beside Nyla and leaned toward her. "Listen, you don't have to stay. Not sure why my friend is acting so strange, but he's busy now and won't notice if you slip out."

Slip out? Not a chance. "What is all this?" she asked.

"Something you won't like, I'm sure."

"Aren't you people supposed to convert me?" She raised a playful brow.

A hint of a smile curved his lips. "Is that what you want?"

Daniel cleared his throat, and the group of people—now about twenty-five of them—grew silent, giving Nyla an excuse not to answer Calan's question. What followed, however, completely baffled her. Daniel had the audacity to preach the

Gospel—how Jesus was the Son of God who died and rose again so that our sins could be forgiven...blah blah blah...and that whosoever repents and believes in him will live forever. She'd heard it all before. He added a little bit at the end about how even more difficult times were coming and the saints needed to be strong. She huffed to herself. There was no God. The arrival of the Neflams had proven that. Besides, what kind of God would allow all these tragedies to occur on a world He created? Yet, as she glanced around, these foolish people hung on Daniel's every word. A few even accepted his invitation to receive this fake god, whatever that meant.

She knew *exactly* what it meant. They would eventually be arrested and sent to reformation camps.

What baffled her most, however, was that Daniel seemed to have no fear of being arrested. She glanced around for one of the many cameras the NWU had installed after the war. Hmm. None in sight. They had chosen this spot well.

Calan remained beside her, listening to Daniel with a look of approval on his face. So much for the handsome bodyguard. He was just as crazy as the rest.

A hot breeze swept over Nyla, and she glanced toward the parking lot. What was taking her troops so long? The man was right here! If she had her weapons, she'd arrest him herself.

"Now, who would like to be healed?"

Daniel's question jerked Nyla's gaze back to him. *What?* She let out an unavoidable humph of disbelief that drew his attention for a moment.

Two people stood and helped another man walk toward Daniel. No, not walk. It looked more like a painful shuffle from the way he moved and by the look of agony on his face.

"He's got Multiple Sclerosis. Doc says he'll be unable to walk at all in a week." The two men hoisted him up as best they could.

Daniel asked his name and if he wanted to be healed

Nyla wanted to laugh. What kind of farce was this? Daniel was no Neflam with the power to heal.

Regardless, he laid a hand on the man's shoulder and spoke in a commanding voice. "Be healed in the mighty name of Jesus."

No trumpet sound, no chorus of angels, nothing met Nyla's ears but the crash and gurgle of waves and the distant call of a seagull.

"Now, let him go." Daniel gestured for the men to release their friend. They hesitated at first, but then at their friend's nod, they released him.

For a moment it seemed as though he would topple like an old tree, but then he took a step, followed by another and another, and he began praising God. The rest of the people joined in, singing praises and crying and hugging the man and each other.

Nyla wanted to barf. What a sham. Obviously, the man was a paid actor. She waited for Daniel to pass around an offering plate.

He didn't.

He merely gestured for more of the sick to come forward, and one by one, he laid hands on them. One lady had a withered hand, another suffered from stomach cancer, or so she said. One man's broken arm wasn't healing well, and a young girl had severe asthma. Nearly everyone in the crowd came forward, and after Daniel's touch and command, they all proclaimed they were healed and praised this invisible God.

Not all of them could be actors, could they? If so, where was the audience? And why wasn't money collected? She glanced down the beach, thinking surely the noise had caught the attention of others. But these days, most people kept to themselves to avoid trouble.

Standing beside her, Calan shifted his attention between the proceedings and the surrounding area.

The screech of tires blared from the parking lot. *Finally.* Three black SUVs pulled up, and at least thirty NWU PKs poured from within them like dark bees from a humming hive.

Some of the people screamed and dashed in all directions. Calan and the two other bodyguards stepped in front of Daniel, forcing him back as they formed a barricade around him.

Nyla recognized two of the officers and gave them a nod of approval, anxious to see this charlatan arrested. In seconds, they had Daniel, his guards, and the few people who remained surrounded. Dressed in full tactical gear, they leveled their AR-15s at the Deviants as she had done on many occasions. And apparently if all went well, she'd be doing so again soon—*very* soon.

"You did good, babe." Marco's voice rang in her ear.

"You are all under arrest by order of the NWU Florida Peace Keepers," Rick Myers shouted, if Nyla remembered his name correctly, the leader of Peace Team 45. "For an illegal gathering, spreading hate speech, and propagating false information. Where is Daniel Cain?" Myers peered behind the bodyguards. "If you hand him over, you won't be arrested with him."

"You will never touch him," Calan answered with authority.

Myers snorted and his crew laughed. Nyla would laugh too if she didn't suddenly care that these men would not be hurt. Stubborn man! Couldn't he see that resistance was hopeless?

"Calan, it's all right." Daniel's voice came from behind his bodyguards.

The guard advanced, weapon raised. "Step aside."

In a move too swift to see, Calan wrenched the man's gun from his grip, flipped it in the air, caught it, and leveled it expertly back upon him. "Back away or I'll kill him." Instantly, all the PK's weapons locked on Calan.

Whoa. Nyla couldn't help but be impressed. She knew he used to be a Navy SEAL, but she'd never seen anyone take out a man like Myers, not so easily.

"Put the gun down, Calan," Daniel said. "Our battle is not with flesh and blood."

The other two bodyguards raised their hands. "Come on, Calan. They'll shoot us all," one of them said.

Though fear appeared in Myers' eyes, he stood his ground, staring at Calan. "We've been trained to believe mission success is more important than the death of one or two. So, go ahead and shoot me."

Calan held a firm grip on the gun. Seconds passed that seemed like minutes as Nyla hoped he would make the right decision. Finally, he lowered the weapon and handed it back to Myers, who quickly spun him around to cuff him.

Daniel backed away from the men into a small cluster of people who had remained.

Nyla watched him intently. How did he expect to get away when they were surrounded? For a second, a millisecond, his eyes found hers, and he smiled. *Smiled?* A bright flash nearly blinded her as he backed into the crowd...and...disappeared.

What? Nyla dashed forward, shoving the people aside. He wasn't there. She darted past them, scanning the circle of armed officers behind them. They looked as baffled as she was. No sign of Daniel. No way he could have gotten past them.

Moving away from the crowd, she lowered her voice. "Marco, do you see him?"

"Who?"

"Daniel Cain! He got away!"

"What? No. No one has left that crowd. I would have seen him."

Nyla spun around to find the officers searching the area. Myers began barking angry orders to find him. Beyond them, Calan stood handcuffed while the remaining Deviants were being gathered.

Crud. Her job was not done. Not yet. She had to maintain her cover. "Tell them to arrest me."

"What?" Marco answered. "No can do."

"Do it. Now!"

They will lay their hands on you and persecute you, delivering you up to the synagogues and prisons. You will be brought before kings and rulers for My name's sake. Luke 21:12

Chapter 7

The worst part about being in prison were the looks Nyla received from people she'd worked with for years, fellow officers, guards, even clerks—all people she'd chatted with in the breakroom, greeted in the hall, some even trained with. All now glancing at her as if she were worse than the filth they dragged in on their shoes, fit only to scrape off and discard. The scathing looks, the disgust, the whispers behind raised hands, sliced deep into her heart. She'd worked so hard to become the best, a team leader, and to gain the respect of everyone around her.

She wanted to scream at them, tell them what she was doing.

But of course, she couldn't.

The best part about being in prison was she had fast-tracked gaining the trust of Calan Walker and his friends. After witnessing her treatment by other law officers, they would never suspect her of being a spy. Now, if she could just get Calan to tell her how Daniel got away and where he was hiding.

A putrid odor rose to curl her nose. Leaning forward, she dropped her head in her hands.

A warm touch on her back sent a pleasant shiver through her.

"It will be all right, Nyla. God is with us."

It was Calan's voice, deep, confident, reassuring. She sat up to face him, astounded by the peaceful look on his face. On *all* their faces as she glanced around at the other two bodyguards and the three people who'd been arrested with them. Several other lowlifes filled the large holding cell—men and women both—all awaiting their fate, but they paid no mind to the newcomers.

How many times had she tossed criminals and Deviants into this very cell, barely affording a glance at how dirty and nasty it was? Discolored patches stained the corners where no doubt vomit, feces, and urine had been hastily mopped up. The fluorescent light above them flickered off and on, pronouncing judgment on them in some sort of demented Morse Code.

Aaron, one of the bodyguards, shook his head. "Just don't get how they knew where we were." Tall, black, and bald, he reminded Nyla of a pro-wrestler, except for the tiny red rose tat on his right bicep.

"Yeah." Calan rubbed the back of his neck. "We switch spots every week."

"Then how do people know where to find you?" Nyla asked.

He shrugged. "Word spreads quickly from people who get healed, so they walk up and down the beach, hoping to find us." He smiled. "Daniel says God brings them."

"How you holding up, babe?" Marco's soothing voice filled her head, causing an unavoidable smile. At least she wasn't completely alone in this hell hole, but no way she could answer him.

She eased hair behind her ear. "Come on, now. Daniel didn't really heal those people. The Neflams are the only ones with that kind of power."

Aaron laughed and shared a glance with the other bodyguard, Jeff, who looked like a Ken doll on steroids. Calan smiled.

Why did the man always smile when it seemed the last thing he should do?

"God healed them through Daniel. You saw it yourself."

"I don't know what I saw." Nyla rubbed her temples where a headache brewed. She'd had Daniel right in her grip! So close. "So where is this miraculous healer then? Why has he left his friends to suffer in his stead?"

Marco spoke again. "That's it. Find out where the scumbag is. Then we can get you out of there."

"It wasn't his time," Calan answered.

"But it's yours, right? This God of yours doesn't mind sticking you in a prison, but not his golden boy." Anger sharpened her tone.

Calan and his fellow bodyguards chuckled.

Sighing, Nyla scratched her head. "I don't find any of this amusing." She shot to her feet.

Rising, Calan eased beside her. "God has a plan for each of us. We trust Him."

"Even to your death?"

"Even to my death," he returned with a seriousness that surprised her. She wondered what kind of God could inspire such loyalty in a man like Calan Walker. Or maybe he was just plain nuts.

"I don't think you'll be smiling when they toss us all in reformation camps." And that would be the least punishment they could get. Quite possibly their association with Daniel would get them thrown in the darkest hole of some prison. Either way, her mission would end in failure.

"Maybe." Calan turned to his friends and the other three people who were sitting as calmly as the rest. "Let's pray, shall we?"

Pray? Here? Nyla glanced at the other prisoners, then at the guard standing a ways off down the hall. Now she knew they were crazy. Praying in public would only increase their punishment.

"Nyla?" Calan gestured for her to join them as they grabbed each other's hands.

She needed to be trusted as one of them, but this was going too far. She shook her head, then took a step back just in case whatever they had was contagious.

With hands clasped together, they formed a circle, bowed their heads, and began taking turns praying out loud. Yet instead of pleading with this God of theirs to get them out of prison, all she heard were words of thanks, praise, and petitions for Daniel and their other friends still free.

Shaking her head in disgust, she sat back down, wondering how long Jennings intended to keep her here with these nutjobs.

"Sorry we had to put you in there, babe."

"I asked for it," Nyla covered her mouth and whispered. "Just don't leave me."

"Never."

A brilliant flash caught her gaze, and she looked up to see a fiery blaze of light, brighter than anything she'd ever seen. It swept through the air, lighting a swath of glittering gold around Calan and the others as they prayed. Then it was gone.

Nyla rubbed her eyes. She really did need a good night's sleep.

That at the name of Jesus every knee should bow, of those in heaven, and of those on earth, and of those under the earth. Philippians 2:10

Gripping the hands of his fellow saints, Calan led them in a prayer that surely was inspired by the Holy Spirit, because there was no way he was ever that eloquent. Besides, he'd felt the Spirit ever since they'd been arrested, a peace, and in particular, a power, as if heaven's warriors had been dispatched to their aid. Even now, he felt them standing guard around the saints as they prayed. Indeed, the Lord was with them, and whatever happened would be His will. Calan only wished Nyla believed that, believed in God at all. He said a silent prayer for her while the others took turns praying.

Loud shouts, stained with foul language, assailed them from the other prisoners. Ignoring them, Calan continued praying. He'd grown accustomed to being hated, insulted, and spat upon. He'd even grown accustomed to being physically attacked. Yet when he concluded all their prayers with an "Amen" and found them surrounded by at least ten other prisoners—ten of the largest male prisoners—every muscle in his body tensed.

"Deviants!" One man spat to the side. "The cause of all the world's mess!"

Others added their agreement with curses and blasphemies. One large man shoved Aaron. The bodyguard charged forward, but Calan leapt in front of him, holding him back, and faced the large man who looked more like a charging bull than a human.

"Back away," Calan said with authority.

The man looked him up and down as if he were a gnat. The others chuckled.

Aaron pushed against Calan's outstretched arm, but he held him at bay. In another life, Calan would not only release him, but join him in showing these punks who was boss. With his SEAL training, he could take them all on with no trouble and quickly put them in their place, albeit with several broken bones and smashed faces. Theirs, that was. But Calan was not that man any more. He was a new man in Christ, and though every ounce of him longed to fight, he stood his ground and tried to remember that Jesus loved these men too.

That part was getting harder as the men continued their insults and taunts.

A couple of the bigger ones pressed toward them, wafting a fetid malodor.

Demons had a smell. Much like sulfur, yet worse—rotten eggs mixed with sewage and a pinch of death.

Calan rubbed his nose, his hatred for the demonic beings rising. "I said back away."

"And who's gonna make us. You?" The leader of the pack said, taking a step forward in challenge. The all-seeing-eye tattoo on his forearm taunted Calan.

But it had no power over him. "Me and my God."

More laughter.

Power surged through Calan, a power not his own, followed by a peace not of this world. He released Aaron and stood his ground before the attackers.

"You will back away and leave us alone in Jesus' name."

Two of the men stumbled backward. The rest stared at Calan, blinking, as if they could not understand what he said.

"Whatever. You're not worth it." The leader finally cursed and waved a hand of dismissal over Calan before retreating to the other side of the cell.

Night in this godforsaken prison cell was far worse than day. Nyla found herself longing for the spastic fluorescent light to turn back on, if only to dispel the shadows that seemed to have a life of their own, slinking around her until she felt suffocated by their stink.

Godforsaken. She smiled at her adjective. It certainly didn't seem that way for Calan and his friends. Nor for the twenty or so other prisoners who at the mere mention of the name of Jesus had slunk back to their corners in defeat.

Nyla would not have believed it if she hadn't seen it for herself. She'd expected a full-fledged brawl to break out, actually looked forward to the entertainment, because she had no doubt Calan and his bodyguard friends would win.

Of course the bad guys retreating had nothing to do with the name of some dead prophet, a name these Deviants used as a weapon—or to heal. Strange cult.

Regardless, the guards would have probably come to break things up. Or would they? Except for an inedible bologna sandwich and bottle of water tossed their way at sundown, they'd hardly paid the prisoners any mind.

Which had Nyla slightly worried. Wouldn't Jennings have pulled her out by now, if only to find out if she knew where Daniel was? Not that she did. She'd asked Calan as many times as she could without giving herself away. And his answer was always the same.

"Daniel is safe in God's arms, Nyla. Don't worry."

Yeah, sure. Whatever, *crazy*.

To make matters worse, it seemed Marco's declaration to never leave her hadn't included his precious beauty sleep, because she hadn't heard from him in hours.

She snuck a glance in Calan's direction. He and his friends were praying again, only this time, they were singing. Softly, but loud enough so she made out the words of praise and worship to a God who had locked them up in this stink hole.

At least the other prisoners kept their distance. Which also made no sense. People hated Deviants. Deviants were the cause of the plagues, wars, climate change disasters, political upheaval, and most everything else that had brought so much pain and heartache across the globe. They held society back from evolutionary advancement, which was why the Neflams had been forced to take them from their homes and put them in reformation camps until they could be safely placed back in society. Like Nyla's parents. She couldn't wait to see them again.

A bright light caused her to slam her eyes shut. Had they turned on the lights again? She dared a peek. *What?* Rubbing her eyes, she looked again. A large figure outlined in light stood beside Calan as he bowed in prayer. No, not light...not any earthly light she'd seen. The figure, whose head touched the ceiling, slowly turned to glance at Nyla.

Before he disappeared.

"She sees you." Ranoss said to Anisian as he stretched out his hands over Calan and the other worshiping saints.

"Indeed." Anisian glanced at Nyla. "Unusual for one who is not in the Kingdom."

Crossbow flung over his shoulder, Ranoss inched closer to Nyla, desperate for her to open her eyes, longing for her to see him and know how much the Father of Spirits loved her. But she lowered her gaze to the filth-ridden floor. "Why would the Father give such a gift to one so unbelieving?"

Upon seeing the angel warriors distracted, a demon rose from the corner and dashed toward Calan and the saints. Anisian had his sword drawn before it reached them and sliced the specter in two. Screaming, it retreated, leaving a stench in its wake.

"The gift rests strong upon her," Anisian said, keeping his sword raised and his eyes on the forces of darkness. "When she comes into the Kingdom, the Father will use her mightily."

"*If* she comes in." Ranoss sighed. "She is so stubborn, so lost in the darkness." He knew he wasn't supposed to get attached to this daughter of Eve, but 'twas too late for that. She had such fire in her, such determination. He would hate to see her lost forever in the flames.

Anisian glanced up as if sensing something in the heavenlies. "You must have faith, my friend. She has much more to see, much more the Father wishes to show her."

"What is it?" Ranoss asked. "What do you see?"

"'Tis time." Anisian marched toward the iron-barred door of the cell.

"The Trumpets?" Ranoss glanced at the saints, who had finished their prayers. The one called Calan lifted his head and looked straight at Anisian, though 'twas obvious he could not see him.

"Aye," Anisian said. "It begins." The warrior angel's gaze followed Calan as he made his way to the cell door. "He has the gift of miracles. The Father has told him what to do."

Ranoss gazed down at Nyla. "And what of her?"

"She begins her training."

So the seven angels who had the seven trumpets prepared
themselves to sound.
The first angel sounded: And hail and fire followed,
mingled with blood, and they were thrown to the earth. And a
third of the trees were burned up, and all green grass was
burned up. Revelation 8:6-7

Chapter 8

A sound blared through the holding cell, so ear-piercing and soul-penetrating that it caused Nyla to jump to her feet and cover her ears. An alarm of some kind? Fire? War? Incoming missiles? Not any that she had ever heard. Still holding her ears, she glanced at her fellow inmates and found Calan and his friends crowded around the front of the cell, while the others were fast asleep in various positions on the floor, cots, and benches. What? Couldn't they hear it? Who could sleep through this noise?

Whatever it was, it went on for several seconds and then all went quiet. *Deathly* quiet.

"What the heck was that?" Nyla lowered her hands and walked toward Calan. "Did you hear it?"

"Hard to miss," Calan responded without looking at her. "The first trumpet has sounded."

"What are you talking abou—"

Calan waved a hand over the cell door, and the electronic lock clanked. Instantly the door slid open, creaking and clanking. "Let's go," he said as calmly as if they were all heading to the beach for a picnic.

Nyla's head spun. "How did you…?"

The Deviants rushed into the corridor as Calan faced her. "Never mind. Come on. There's not much time before it starts." He grabbed her hand, and before she could protest, pulled her behind him through the hallway and a series of locked doors, all of which instantly opened before them as if a magic button had been pressed.

Guards loitered up ahead, three of them, drinking coffee and chatting around one of the security stations housing all the cameras in this wing of the prison. Why had they not seen them escape?

Nyla pulled Calan's hand, halting him, while the other Deviants charged forward. "The guards!"

He smiled. "It'll be all right."

The next few minutes passed in a haze of shock and unbelief as the guards continued their conversations, completely oblivious to the escaping prisoners, not even once glancing in their direction. Instead, flashes of brilliant light in glittering silver and gold appeared and disappeared along the hallways and inside rooms as if the power was going on and off.

Past the final lock, they flew through the prison's front office and out the door, all the while Nyla marveling as Calan pulled her through the strangest dream she'd ever had. But then a blast of humid night air swamped her. She glanced up at a full moon and a red blazing object streaking across the sky, snapping her out of her daze.

Ignoring the odd sight for now, Nyla realized it must have been Jennings who arranged for their escape, unlocking the doors, ordering the guards to pretend they weren't there. Deviants were known to believe in miraculous nonsense, so it would be no problem for them to be convinced their God did this.

Calan and his bodyguard friends stared up at the dark sky. The streak grew larger, rounder, and a tail of flames curled behind it. He turned to the three people they'd met at the beach. "Come with us."

"No. We have families. We'll be all right," the older man said. "God be with you." He grabbed the lady's hand on one side and the young man's hand on the other, and all three darted through the parking lot.

A thunderous boom shattered the silence. The ground shook. The western sky lit up in a burst of orange and red. Above them, more red and orange flames streaked across the sky and struck the earth.

Nyla's heart did flips in her chest. "Are we being attacked?"

"No." Calan answered with a calmness that baffled her. "But we must get to safety."

"My apartment is nearby," Jeff said. "My truck is there. We can take it to Zion's Nest."

"Let's go, then." Calan turned to Nyla. "Can you run?"

Another missile hit not too far from where they stood, shooting fire into the sky and trembling the ground beneath her. "Yes, but—"

NWU officers and guards poured out of the building, shouting and pointing at the sky, paying the escapees no mind. Sirens screamed in the distance.

Calan grabbed her hand and the four of them bolted. She followed. For now. At least until they were away from the prison and out of danger, and then maybe she could figure out what the heck was happening.

But the fireballs kept coming, zipping across the sky like red-hot demonic fingers grabbing the world in their clutches. They hit the ground in fiery blazes, shaking the dirt beneath her shoes like quicksand. Screams, shouts, and curses joined the sirens as people emerged from homes and apartments to stare at the sky in horror.

Still, Calan pressed onward, face like flint, barely glancing at the hell raining down on them. They passed several dark stores and shops, a restaurant whose windows had shattered, before entering a neighborhood of run-down apartments. Flames engulfed two of the buildings that had been hit.

Dogs howled in fear, bringing back memories, horrid memories, of dogs barking and babies screaming and people sobbing—eerily familiar sounds from the recent past. What was wrong with her? She'd been through a missile attack, a tsunami, a smallpox plague, and still had not been this terrified.

Her breath came hard and fast. Her legs ached, but she would not be outdone by these men.

"What is happening?" she managed to yell at Calan running beside her, but he was silent.

They rounded a corner. Up ahead, a park was on fire. All the grass and trees were set ablaze, shooting sparks into the night sky.

Heat struck her as they passed, as if someone had opened a huge oven. She gasped for air.

Finally, Jeff turned into the parking garage beneath an apartment building, and before long, they all piled into what had to be a twenty-year-old Suburban. Their heavy breaths filled the air as Jeff started the truck.

"Wait." Nyla heaved out between gasps. "I'm not going anywhere until you tell me what's going on."

Calan turned to face her from the passenger seat in front, the light on the ceiling hardening his features. "The first trumpet. The judgment of God. Don't worry. You'll be safe with us."

Jeff backed the truck out of the spot and took off, wheels squealing.

Nyla wanted to scream. How could someone so kind and so handsome be so certifiably nuts?

"Babe, you okay?" Finally, Marco's voice filled her ear, the voice of sanity.

"Yes," she responded without thinking.

Calan turned toward her as Jeff sped out onto the street. "Yes?"

"Where are we going?"

"Should we risk taking her there?" Aaron asked from beside Nyla in the backseat.

Holding onto the dash, Calan studied her.

Where was *there*? Their underground hideout? Exactly where she needed to go. Where Daniel was no doubt hiding. But... what of Tata and Kyle? She glanced out the window where cars began to flood the road as people panicked and tried to get away from the fireballs. Those who didn't have cars were running down the street, dragging wagons behind them filled with their belongings. Where did they expect to go? Where would any of them be safe?

Not again. Tears burned her eyes. Hadn't the world suffered enough? Hadn't there been enough death and pain?

Up ahead, cars jammed the road. Horns rang. Above them, more fingers of fire streaked across the sky. Explosions boomed. Screams filled the air. A row of tall palms lit the night like candles on a cake. To the left, one of the fireballs hit an empty school bus, shooting sparks into the night sky before it exploded with a deafening boom. Jeff spun the truck to the right to avoid the traffic. Flames engulfed a house. Grassy fields transformed into lava beds.

"You're right," Calan finally said, facing forward.

The truck swerved, slamming Nyla against the door. Screams blared from outside. Tires screeched, and Jeff floored the vehicle past a field near the railroad.

A wall of fire met Nyla's gaze. Flames marched across the entire field. Beyond the railroad toward the west, orange and red lit the sky as if the sun were rising on the wrong side of the earth. But it wasn't the sun. The Everglades were on fire.

Nyla could only stare in shock. How could that be?

"Where can we drop you?" Calan shouted.

Crud. She needed to go to their hideout, find Daniel and be done with this charade, but she really wanted to make sure Tata and Kyle were safe. She opened her mouth to give them her address when something hit the truck, something big. Glass shattered, metal screeched....

And everything went dark.

Only after carrying Nyla's unconscious body—with Aaron's help—down the stairs into the basement of NeirLoom Corporation, a.k.a. Zion's Nest, did Calan feel the pain etching through his body.

"You're bleeding." Carolyn reached to touch his face with a rag, but he nudged her away. "Please, check on the girl first. I'll live."

One glance at Aaron and Jeff told Calan they looked as bad as he felt. Stars spun in his vision, and he closed his eyes, sinking into a nearby chair.

"All right," Carolyn conceded, "but you three stay put. I'll tend to you next."

It hurt to even smile, but Calan was thankful for the older woman, who had been a nurse before the Rapture. Her husband Max brought over bowls of water, rags, and a case full of what little medical equipment they had.

Others crowded around and began to pray.

There had been no time to pray before the hail, meteor, or whatever it was, had struck their truck. The force of it had flipped them over, crashing straight into a burning tree. Thank God Calan and Aaron had been able to pull Jeff and Nyla out before the vehicle exploded. Jeff had regained consciousness within minutes. Nyla hadn't been so lucky. The gash on her head still oozed with blood.

Oddly, fear rippled through Calan, not for the fiery hail, not for the city, not for the world...but for this stubborn, fascinating, warrior of a woman who lay on the couch unconscious and bleeding.

Kneeling before her, Carolyn went to work as Daniel approached from the back room, his gaze quickly taking in the scene. "What happened?"

More explosions outside shook the building, but they seemed far away now.

"Hit by one of them. Truck flipped," was all Calan could manage.

Glancing around, Daniel found a rag and tossed it at Calan, gesturing to his forehead.

He dabbed his skin, wincing. Blood stained the cloth.

"Praise God you are all okay." Daniel nodded to the other two bodyguards. "We were all praying God would get you out of prison."

"Thank you. He did. It was incredible." Calan pressed the cloth on his wound again, ignoring the pain and suddenly wondered why God allowed them to get hit after He had so miraculously freed them from prison. But he supposed there were no guarantees during the Tribulation.

Moving closer to Nyla, Daniel held out a hand over her, his lips moving in prayer. When he finished, he faced Calan, one brow rising. "Why did you risk bringing her here?"

Calan had come to hate that arched brow. It always meant he'd done something wrong. "She was out cold. We didn't know where she lived." He glanced at her. "I couldn't just leave her by the side of the road."

Daniel nodded his understanding, but Calan knew he'd made a mistake. Nyla was not one of them. In fact, up until recently she'd been a part of the very people who arrested them and tossed them into reformation camps. No doubt she had tracking nanobots inside her, as did everyone who'd taken the fifth booster. They'd managed to keep Zion's Nest hidden for over a year, and it had become a place of refuge for so many of God's saints, some of whom even lived here, having nowhere else to go.

And Calan had compromised all of that by his foolish decision, made from emotion. When would he ever learn?

Several hours later, despite Carolyn urging Calan to get some sleep, he couldn't pull himself away from Nyla. Though her wound had been bandaged and the rest of her checked for injuries, still she had not woken.

"A concussion, most likely," Carolyn had said. "She could be unconscious for hours. You should get some sleep too,

Calan." She pointed to the thick bandages binding his chest where she'd pronounced at least one cracked rib. Nothing too serious, but it hurt like heck. The cut on his forehead had not been too deep either, and Jeff and Aaron had not suffered any major injuries, praise God.

Calan glanced at the clock on the table. 2:00 a.m. The explosions had stopped, and the world seemed to be breathing a sigh of relief. At least for now. His thoughts drifted to their escape from prison, and he couldn't help but shake his head. Daniel had told Calan long ago that he had the gift of miracles. He'd not really known what that meant until last night when he'd heard clear directions in his spirit to pray for the locks to be removed in Jesus' name. He couldn't say he'd been surprised when they did, though now, as he thought back on it, shock filled him. It had all happened so fast and their escape so easy. God had not only opened all the locks, but He had made them invisible to the guards and NWU Officers.

He ran a hand through his hair. "What an incredible God you are," he whispered. "Amazing. Thank you for Your rescue." Sudden guilt pinched him that he'd not thanked God until this moment. Still, the loving Presence that instantly surrounded him was unmistakable.

For *him*? He still had trouble understanding how God could love someone who had made so many mistakes, one of them costing a precious life that had been entrusted to Calan—his brother.

He glanced at Nyla, lying there so peaceful and still, her curls spilling in chocolate waves over the pillow, her shallow breaths escaping her lips. An old scar in the shape of a diamond he'd not noticed before, marred the otherwise pristine skin of her neck. Daniel had prayed over her. She would recover. Still, Calan didn't want her to wake up in the middle of the night and not know where she was. He'd done that too many times in his life.

Leaning his head back onto the chair, he dared to close his eyes. Tribby leapt into his lap and began to purr. Smiling, he caressed her fur. He was a new man now, and more determined than ever to make up for past mistakes and succeed in everything Daniel—and God—handed him. Then, maybe then, he would feel worthy of the love of a Holy God.

If you were of the world, the world would love its own: yet because you are not of the world, but I chose you out of the world, therefore the world hates you. John 15:19

Chapter 9

S cenes fluttered through Nyla's mind, twirling, spinning, flitting about like stubborn pieces of a puzzle unwilling to assemble into anything coherent—Marco's handsome face, waves crashing ashore, a filthy holding cell, an angel of light, and a mad dash through burning streets. Some idiot was jack-hammering her skull. Pain radiated down her spine. Snoring. Someone was snoring, or was it the jackhammer? *Stop it*! She reached up to knock it away. Nothing was there. Her fingers touched something soft wrapped around her head.

The truck, the fire. Now she remembered. They'd escaped from prison!

The pain continued. So did the snoring.

She pried her eyes open.

Shadows, darkness. No, a lamp gave off a soft glow beside her. Blinking, she cleared her foggy vision. A man sat in a chair not a foot from where she lay, a black cat curled up in his lap. Rhythmic rumbling emerged from his mouth.

Calan. A large bandage was wrapped tightly around his bare chest. Muscles she had only guessed at before rounded his arms and rippled down his stomach.

She swallowed.

What was he doing here? Watching over her? And where exactly was *here*? Lifting her head, she attempted to push herself to a sitting position, but a sharp blade sliced from her head down her spine. Groaning, she dropped down to the pillow.

Calan jerked awake, blinked, and leaned forward. The cat leapt from his lap as he took her hand in his. "Nyla. How do you feel?"

For some reason, his deep voice and the concern within it delighted her more than it should. He was the enemy, despite his good looks, hunky body, and the kindness in his blue eyes.

"Like I got trampled by a herd of buffalo."

He chuckled.

"Where am I?"

Calan hesitated. "Someplace safe."

Memories returned. "My family!" She attempted to get up again. "The meteors. One might have struck my apartment." Fighting the pain, she managed a sitting position, but the shadowy room spun, her breath came fast, and she leaned her head on the back of the couch.

"Here. Drink some water."

She opened her eyes and took the glass Calan held out.

"You aren't going anywhere for a while." He leaned forward on his knees and studied her. "Not until you can walk without falling. You had a pretty good blow to your head."

She took a sip of water. "I've had worse."

He smiled. "My little brave warrior."

An odd warmth spiraled through her at the endearment. "I'm neither little nor yours," she returned.

His smile remained.

"What about you? You look worse than me." Nyla dropped her gaze to his bandage, suddenly regretting the effect his unclad chest had on her. Crud. What was wrong with her? Ah…must be the concussion.

Leaning back in the chair, he winced. "I've had worse."

Now it was her turn to smile.

"Can I at least try to call my family?"

He shook his head. "All cells are out."

The room tilted again, and she handed the glass to Calan. "Can you drive me over there?"

"When you're better, yes. Carolyn says you shouldn't move around too much."

Nyla groaned inwardly. She didn't like being told what to do, but then, she was having trouble remembering exactly how she got here. "What happened? What were those fire balls?"

"Hail and fire is my guess."

Her head began to throb. "The truck. One hit it."

"Yes, we flipped. Aaron and I pulled you out."

"I guess I should thank you."

"I guess you should."

She opened her eyes to find him grinning again, a very sexy grin, if she were honest. "Thank you," she said with sarcasm. "Though I wouldn't have been in that prison if you…" Memories returned, spinning a cyclone of nonsense in her mind. She rubbed her head where the pounding ache increased. "How did we escape?"

"That would be Almighty God's doing," he said matter-of-factly.

No, it must have been Jennings. But she couldn't tell Calan that, couldn't tell him that this mystical God he believed in was nothing but a fantasy.

She glanced around the large room. A warehouse of some kind? Couches, tables, and chairs were strewn about. A small kitchenette stood in the corner. Her heart nearly flipped. This must be one of the Deviants' hideouts. Most likely where Daniel Cain spent his time. What luck. *Marco!* She reached up to tap her ear, but the com piece was gone. *Crud.* Must have fallen out in the accident.

"Here, drink some more water. You look a little bewildered." Grabbing the glass, he handed it to her. "Carolyn said you might be dizzy for a while, feel tired, maybe nauseous."

Nyla gulped down the cool liquid. "Who is Carolyn?"

"Our resident nurse."

"Our?" She wanted him to admit where they were, to confirm her suspicions.

He was staring at her now, the light from the lamp highlighting the intensity of his gaze, as if he were trying to read her mind. Or dive into her soul. Not in a sensual way—she'd had a lot of experience with that kind of look—but more of a I-find-you-fascinating look which sent a shiver through her that wasn't at all unpleasant. She lowered her gaze.

"I promise we will check on your family as soon as we can, 'k?" He reached out and engulfed her hand in his. The warmth and strength of it nearly broke through her defenses, walls she'd erected after her parents left, the world collapsed, and she realized she could trust no one and nothing but herself.

"Thank you." Her vision blurred and nausea bubbled in her stomach. "I need to lie down."

Oddly, Calan stood, took her shoulders while supporting her head with his hands and gently laid her down. Within seconds, a blanket fell gently over her, and she thought she felt a warm hand brush over her cheek before she drifted into oblivion.

She should have stayed there because she woke to loud chattering, a TV blaring, someone singing, and the smell of fresh baked bread. Blinking, she opened her eyes and tried to focus. Two cats, one black, one white, sat on the edge of the couch, staring at her as if she were a freshly caught fish. Pushing up on her elbows, she slowly rose, tossed off the blanket, and swung her legs over the side. Her head felt as though it floated to the ceiling.

The cats still stared at her.

The room was full of people. A few smiled her way. One shouted to Calan, who stood talking with another man. He approached her with a strong, confident stride and a look of concern on his face.

"Welcome back, sleepyhead." He dropped into a chair beside the couch and leaned over to touch her forehead. "No fever. Good."

It had been a long time since anyone had taken care of her, not since her parents were here. She wasn't sure whether she liked it or not. She settled on not. Trust always led to heartache.

The cats leapt into Calan's lap. "How are you feeling?" he asked, petting both of the felines until their purrs rumbled through the air.

"Better." She lied, but she was worried about Tata and Kyle. The sooner she left, the sooner she could check on them while also informing Jennings of the Deviants' hideout.

And arrest these very people who were caring for her now.

A middle-aged woman came running over with a steaming bowl of something that smelled delicious. "Are you hungry, dear? Try some of my chicken soup. It cures all ills." She sat beside Nyla as if they'd been best friends all their lives. With short, graying hair, a plump figure, a round face, and a smile that would put anyone at ease, the mid-fifties woman exuded both joy and kindness.

"Nyla, meet Carolyn."

Ah, the nurse. "Thank you for taking care of me. And for this soup. It looks really good and smells wonderful, but I'm afraid my stomach is a little queasy."

"Of course. That's to be expected." Carolyn patted Nyla on the knee, then set the soup down. "Maybe you'll try some later. Oh, Max," she shouted, drawing the attention of an older man, who darted to her side.

"Meet Nyla, Calan's friend."

Friend? Was she? She glanced at Calan and found him looking at her.

"A pleasure, little miss." Max looked more bear than man with his thick gray hair and long grizzled beard, but the genuineness of his smile shocked her.

Actually, the genuineness of all their smiles shocked her, as one by one, the twelve or so people in the room came to meet her. But where was Daniel? He was the only one that mattered. Asking about him would give her away, so she'd wait. In truth, she wasn't feeling well enough to get up anyway.

Calan ran off to do something, while several others turned back to the TV to watch the reports of carnage left by the meteors. Horrific scenes passed over the screen of entire forests and grassy meadows on fire while people ran for their lives. All over the world? What? How could that be?

"This is a sad day for our planet," the newscaster said. "Nearly one-third of all earth's trees have been burned up, along with all the grass. There's not a green blade to be found on the globe, but amazingly, except for a building here and there, our cities remain relatively unscathed. Scientists from the NWU Space program are saying they've never seen anything like these objects." The camera switched to an older man with glasses and a lab coat. "It appears from our preliminary analysis that these fiery rocks consisted of a combustible liquid not found on earth. This particular liquid, which we are currently analyzing, not only explodes on impact, but appears to only burn plant life." He shook his head. "We have our top scientists working on it and will know more soon enough."

"Do you think this may be an alien attack?" the reporter asked the scientist.

"At this point, I wouldn't rule anything out."

The newscaster reappeared, and a small video popped beside his head of the two crazy old men in Jerusalem. "Some say the meteors were a result of these two men who have been calling for the world to repent or God would rain down fire."

Nyla huffed. Ridiculous. Those two old-timers? She and Kyle had watched them blather on and on just for the fun of it. They were harmless except for the nonsense they were spewing. Why the Israeli NWU forces had not locked them up yet was beyond her.

Someone switched off the TV, and a group formed, bowed their heads, and began to pray. Nyla switched her attention away. Praying wouldn't bring back the trees and grass. How many more disasters could earth handle? How many more could people handle? Surely Minister Aali and the Neflams would come up with a solution soon.

A few of the Deviants asked her if she needed anything. One young lady named Pam sat and tried to make conversation, but Nyla told her she wasn't feeling well. No sense in making friends with people she intended to arrest.

Unfortunately, an hour later when the group gathered for their morning Bible study and prayer, Daniel had not made an appearance. Ugh. How much of this nonsense would she have to endure? She wanted to check on Tata and Kyle. She wanted to get away from these wacky loons.

"Want to join us?" Calan's question drew her from her thoughts, and she gazed up at his outstretched hand. Did the man always look this good in the morning? Nyla eased hair behind her ear, suddenly realizing she must look a mess.

"No."

He smiled. "What are you afraid of? Come on. Let's see how you do on your feet. Then after the study, I'll drive you home."

She had managed a piece of toast and half a bowl of Carolyn's soup, and she was feeling better. Besides, maybe it would be good to learn what these people believed—gather intel on the enemy.

Grabbing Calan's hand, she allowed him to help her up, surprised when he eased an arm around her waist to support her. From the wince on his face, he was no doubt hurting more than she was, but he said nothing as he led her to another chair where people were gathering. Though still a little dizzy, she felt stronger. Her headache had subsided, and her stomach had settled.

Calan took a seat beside her and handed her a Bible—a real Bible. She shoved it back at him. "Do you realize I have put people in prison for having this book?"

She had whispered it, but several people must have heard because their gazes snapped her way.

Calan raised a calming hand. "It's okay. She's no longer with the NWU PK Teams."

"But if she took the booster, they could track her," said Madeline, a lady in her early forties who was covered in tats.

She was right, of course. Nyla had not been thrilled at taking the fifth booster, but after the doctor explained to her all the benefits, she felt better. The chip that assembled from the graphene nanotech monitored all body functions and alerted Medical whenever the slightest thing was wrong even before she knew it. It also ensured everyone was current on their vaccines. Such great advances in medicine could only be good for humanity. The fact that it tracked people had already drastically reduced kidnappings and other crimes. Yet these Deviants and others who held to archaic ideas of personal freedom had protested vehemently against it. Fools. Pure selfishness. There were too many people on the planet to cling to such outdated ideas. They needed to think of the collective good.

She glanced over the group, drinking coffee and chatting as if they hadn't a care in the world, and she suddenly wondered how they found employment or bought food and supplies without the vaccine and subsequent boosters. Not to mention a good social credit score. In fact, how had Calan purchased coffee the other day?

More importantly, why hadn't Jennings busted down the door and charged in? Certainly, they knew where she was. He must be waiting for her to confirm Daniel was present. Which she couldn't do without her com piece.

As if on cue, the infamous preacher entered the large room from a hallway in the back, illegal book in hand, grin on his face, and his intense gaze upon her.

Unnerved, she faced the group. "Why would they track me? I'm a nobody now."

Some people nodded, others remained skeptical as Daniel offered his greetings and took a seat across from her. "We will welcome Nyla as one of our own. She was willing to be put in prison and even sent to a reformation camp for us." He spoke to the entire group, but his eyes were on her with a burning, piercing stare that made her think he knew exactly what she was about.

But that would be impossible.

Then, opening his Bible, he began reading from some book called Revelation. Nyla wouldn't have paid attention except the words sounded eerily familiar, something about a trumpet and hail and fire, mingled with blood, and a third of the trees were burned up and all green grass was incinerated.

Conflicting thoughts ricocheted through her mind, only increasing her headache. No. Couldn't be.

Daniel looked up from the book. "Last night the first trumpet sounded."

Everyone nodded.

"We know what is coming." He held up his Bible. "The Lord in His mercy has told us so we can prepare."

"Amen. Praise His name!" an elderly lady named Violet shouted.

Just a coincidence. It had to be a coincidence. "That isn't in the Bible," Nyla said, drawing everyone's attention.

Calan held his Bible out to her and pointed to the verses.

She read them, soaking in each word, all the while wondering how they could have pulled this off. Is this how they fooled more people into joining their cult?

"No way." She shook her head. "Just a weird coincidence."

Calan sighed. Daniel smiled.

The woman sitting on the other side of Nyla showed her the same passage in her Bible. No way... No way would she believe this nonsense. Just a coincidence. Still, she had to pretend to be open to their fanatical ideas. She had to gain their trust so she would be invited back to join them, to call in the cavalry when Daniel was here.

When she glanced up, everyone was looking at her. She attempted a smile. "I admit to being intrigued. I want to hear more."

She could sense Calan's approval beside her. Everyone smiled. Everyone except Daniel, who looked at her as if he could see inside her mind.

But she *did* hear more—more than she wanted—from Daniel, from many of the others, about this book of Revelation, the two Jewish freaks in Jerusalem, the prophecies to come, and how wonderful Jesus was. By the end of the discussion as they all began to sing and praise God, Nyla longed to leave. These Deviants were truly insane. They spoke as if they had a one-on-one relationship with this invisible God they called Jesus. They spoke about miracles and healings that never could have happened and angels and demons and creatures called Nephilim. What had happened to make them all so crazy? Oddly, she felt sad for Calan as he joined in the discussion and now the singing, lifting his hands upward in praise of a God who didn't exist.

But one thing she knew for sure. She would have no misgivings about sending the lot of them to a reformation camp. Not only because people like them had ruined her life, but because in their mental state, it was the most compassionate thing to do.

And I will give power to my two witnesses, and they will prophesy one thousand two hundred and sixty days, clothed in sackcloth. These are the two olive trees and the two lampstands standing before the God of the earth. And if anyone wants to harm them, fire proceeds from their mouth and devours their enemies. And if anyone wants to harm them, he must be killed in this manner. These have power to shut heaven, so that no rain falls in the days of their prophecy; and they have power over waters to turn them to blood, and to strike the earth with all plagues, as often as they desire.
Revelation 11:3-6

Chapter 10

Calan sat on the idling Harley Sportster and watched Nyla slowly make her way up the cement walkway to her apartment building. She walked slower than usual, careful with her steps. Still dizzy, no doubt. In fact, she shouldn't be walking at all, but she'd insisted on checking on her family—a grandmother and brother. At least now he knew where she lived in case she needed him. Not that she would. Nyla Cruz was a capable young woman, independent, confident, brave, and strong. He'd never met anyone like her. Opinionated too. And stubborn. He smiled. Too bad she wasn't a believer. Not yet anyway. But would she ever be? She'd been indoctrinated by a propagandized media and a world system run by Lucifer. He'd seen her type all too often. And they were hard nuts to crack.

Yet, when Calan had asked Daniel about her, he seemed to harbor hope for Nyla. The man had a true gift of spiritual knowledge, and if Nyla had no chance of ever receiving Jesus, he would know it.

Calan's thoughts drifted to his last conversation with Daniel.

"I'm leaving for a few weeks, checking on the churches we planted," Daniel had told him. "You're in charge."

"Me? I should be going with you." Calan was Daniel's chief bodyguard. Rarely had they been separated.

"I need you here. The Lord wants you to run things."

Calan had tried to argue, but one look from Daniel stopped him. Surely the man had not heard correctly from the Lord. Calan was not fit to be in charge of Zion's Nest. He'd made too many mistakes, too many bad decisions. What would happen if he made the wrong one now with these precious souls under his protection and guidance? It was one thing to be on the Teams, where he relied on his training, physical weapons, and skills and quite another to rely on spiritual training, weapons, and skills— things he couldn't see or control. It wasn't just a matter of keeping the saints fed and safe. One wrong move, one tiny mistake, and they'd all end up in prison or dead.

Nyla disappeared into her apartment on the second floor and reappeared within minutes, giving him a thumbs-up.

Nodding, he put on his helmet, shifted into gear, and revved down the street. Ashes drifted down upon him like snow in hell. Glowing embers of once green grass sizzled on the side of the road. Charred remains of palms bent like weary black skeletons in the wind, reaching for him as smoke and soot slapped his face and stole his breath. Not only had much of the green plants burned up, but many people had lost their lives, some descending into everlasting torment. The First Trumpet had blown. The others that came after would bring worse disasters. The saints would have to be strong. They would have to be willing to die for the Lord. Many of them would be called to do just that.

During the short ride back to Zion's Nest, Calan remembered Daniel's final words. "The Lord is with you, Calan. He will be your strength and your wisdom. Rely on Him."

Yet, Calan couldn't shake the feeling that Daniel was training him for some future task. But what the man didn't realize was that Calan would most likely fail.

"Where you been?" Kyle rubbed sleepy eyes and ambled back to the couch, plopping down on the soft cushions where he spent most of his days and all of his nights. He reached for an old can of soda and took a swig.

Nyla shook her head. "Didn't you see the meteors? There were fires everywhere!"

He nodded. "Yup. All over the news."

Nyla's gaze traveled to a bottle of CBD pills, and she wondered if her brother could even assemble a rational thought.

"Maybe if you got off the drugs, you might have been a little bit concerned for me...for Tata. I was worried sick."

He flipped hair from his face and sighed. "That's the difference between you and me, Sis. You worry about everything, and I realize it don't matter. Life is hell, and it'll always be hell."

It was all Nyla could do to stop from slapping some sense into him. Instead, she started toward Tata's bedroom. She'd tried more times than she could count to get Kyle to quit the drugs and get a job, do something that interested him and grow up.

"What's with the bandage, Sis?" he asked. "And why don't you have your keys?"

A hint of concern tainted his tone, reminding her that somewhere beneath the drug-induced haze and the pain that scarred his heart, her little brother remained. She spun to face him. Her keys were back at NWU prison, but she couldn't tell him that.

"One of those meteors hit the truck I was in," she replied, but Kyle had already flipped on the TV and zoned out.

"I thought I heard my sweet Pajarito's voice." Tata entered from the hallway, her gray hair askew and a look of misplaced peace on her aged face.

Nyla swallowed her up in her arms, saddened by how frail she felt. "Tata. I was worried."

Tata chuckled. "*You* were worried? We are fine. But it was you who didn't come home last night. And this?" She reached up to touch Nyla's bandage. "What happened?"

"Long story, but one of those meteors almost hit me."

Tata gasped, then closed her eyes and whispered, "Praise the Lord!"

Nyla's forehead wrinkled. "You're thankful I was in an accident?"

"No, Pajarito," she reached up and cupped Nyla's chin. "The Lord told me you were in trouble, so I've been up all night praying."

Nyla didn't know whether to be grateful or angry. "Come, sit down." She led her to a cushioned chair beside the couch. "You shouldn't stay up all night, Tata. It's not good for you." Especially not to waste time praying to a nonexistent God.

"Spending time with God is the best thing for me." Tata eased into the chair. "Now sit and tell me of your adventures."

Nyla's head suddenly spun, and she plopped onto the couch beside Kyle, wondering what to tell her grandmother. Thankfully, something on the news had caught her brother's attention.

Tata's too, apparently, as her gaze was fixed on the flatscreen, an odd smile on her face.

Those two crazy old men stood preaching in Jerusalem. She'd seen them earlier that day on the TV back at the Deviant hideout, but night had fallen in Israel now, and they seemed to be shouting even louder. Floodlights draped them in sterile light as dozens of armed IDF surrounded them, keeping their distance.

"Repent, for the Kingdom of Heaven is at hand! Turn back to God before it's too late!" one of them said.

"Believe these guys?" Kyle laughed.

Nyla bit her lip, not answering. The Deviants had been glued to every word these old men had said, even talked about them being in the Bible. But how could you take two old men with long white beards wearing sackcloth and sandals seriously?

The other one spoke up. "According to the Word of the Most High, we have called down fire from heaven. We have stopped the rain and still you continue to pursue wickedness and defy the living God."

Nyla chuckled. "So these two are taking credit for the meteors. Figures." She shook her head.

"Do you have another explanation?" Tata gave her a knowing smile.

"Of course," Nyla returned. "It was a meteor storm. That's all."

One gray brow rose, scrunching the wrinkles on Tata's forehead. "Only burning grass and trees? Hmm."

She had a point. A point Nyla didn't wish to think about at the moment.

"And what about the current worldwide drought?" Tata continued.

"You both are crazy." Kyle rose and went to the kitchen.

Tata glanced back at the TV. "And when anyone tries to kill them, fire comes from their mouths?"

Nyla pressed a finger over the scar on her neck. "They must be Neflams. Evil ones. That's the only explanation."

"Not the *only* one, my Pajarito."

The news switched to another scene of several young Jewish men standing on top of a charred hill preaching to a crowd.

Nyla snorted. "What the heck is going on over there in Israel?"

"Oh, my dear, those are part of the 144,000 young Jewish men who are telling people about Jesus."

"What are you talking about?" Her grandmother was old, but Nyla didn't think she was going senile yet.

"It's all in the Bible." Tata smiled. "You should read it sometime."

Nyla laughed. Her grandmother had been trying to get her to read the Bible for years. "Good try, Tata."

"There's no food." Kyle slammed the refrigerator door.

Nyla rubbed her temples where her headache threatened to return. "That's because you eat it all." She glanced at her brother. A dark shadow cloaked his shoulders as if he wore a coat made of smoke. But that couldn't be. She rubbed her eyes and looked again. It was gone.

Kyle cursed. "Then I'll go get some."

"With what?"

"*Your* phone."

"You forget, I have no job. Therefore no money." Which wasn't true, of course, but she needed to ask Jennings how she could get food and supplies with her bad credit score. Not that she could buy much food if she had a good one. The bread lines were growing longer each day as food became increasingly scarce, brought on by the drought, climate change, and now these meteors—so many other things the Neflams came to fix. If it wasn't too late.

"What are we going to do?" Panic rang from Kyle's tone as he made a beeline for his bottle of mind-numbing drugs the NWU handed out like candy.

Leaning forward, Tata seemed to be having trouble breathing.

"Are you okay, Tata?" Nyla fell to her knees before her grandmother's chair and took her bony hands in hers.

"Yes. Just tired."

But Nyla knew it was more than that. Tata seemed to be aging before her eyes. "We should get you to a clinic."

"For what? So they can poke and prod me and inject me with their poison?" She squeezed Nyla's hand. "I'll be all right. I'm in the hands of the Great Physician."

Silly woman. "Let me help you to bed. You need your rest." Then Nyla would go find some food. Besides, she needed a new com piece if she was to continue undercover, ingratiate herself further into the Deviant group, get them to trust her. Then, when

Daniel returned from his trip, she had every intention of leading her fellow peace officers to arrest everyone at the hideout called Zion's Nest.

Zhaviel released a frustrated sigh as he watched Kyle return to the couch and turn on video games, his favorite pasttime, save taking his pills and eating.

"Why so glum, my friend?" Ranoss adjusted the crossbow strung across his back, his gaze on Nyla helping her grandmother to her bedroom.

"Can you not see it?" Zhaviel frowned. "He is so far from the truth. Behold the demons which surround him."

"Aye, we see them." Indira cast a look of sorrow toward Kyle. "I owe you many thanks for your assistance last night when they attacked Tata as she interceded for her granddaughter."

"Aye." Zhaviel gave a half-smile and gripped his spiked club. "We sent them scurrying, did we not?"

Indira chuckled.

"*She* saw them," Ranoss added.

Indira glanced toward Nyla and Tata as they disappeared into Tata's bedroom. "She has the gift."

Ranoss shifted his stance. "But she cannot use it fully until she surrenders to the King."

"She seems close. You are fortunate, my friend." Zhaviel moved to take a stance behind Kyle.

"Have faith," Ranoss said. "The Commander would not have you guarding him if there were no hope."

"Indeed." Zhaviel smiled at his friend.

Indira moved away. "I must watch over her as she sleeps. Many evil forces attempt to take her life, for she is a great witness to her two grandchildren."

"May the Father's power be with you, my friend," Ranoss said before facing Zhaviel. "The First Trumpet has blasted.

More evil has been released. We must be strong in the power of His might."

Zhaviel straightened his shoulders and nodded but said naught.

A dark presence drew Ranoss' gaze to Nyla, who was slipping from her grandmother's bedroom into her own, a book in hand. "Something is amiss. Her heart is searching. The enemy approaches." He glanced at Kyle, absorbed with his game. "Come, Zhaviel, I need your help."

Without hesitation Zhaviel joined Ranoss as they marched into Nyla's bedroom, blades drawn.

For the word of God is living and powerful, and sharper than any two-edged sword, piercing even to the division of soul and spirit, and of joints and marrow, and is a discerner of the thoughts and intents of the heart. Hebrews 4:12

Chapter 11

Nyla lowered to sit beside Spots' cage and stared at the illegal book in her hands. If anyone from the NWU saw her with it, she'd be arrested and most likely tossed into a reformation camp with her parents. Then why had she taken it from Tata's table after her grandmother had fallen asleep?

She set it on the floor and instead opened the cage and reached in to get Spots. "Missed me, eh?" She held the precious hamster up to her face, smiling at her pink nose and ever-vibrating whiskers. "If you weren't so cute..." She pressed her cheek against Spots' soft fur, then lowered her to her lap. After several pets, the hamster took off to explore, something Nyla allowed routinely. There was no way the hamster could get out of the room, she'd made sure of that, despite Spots' propensity for escape. Besides, creatures should not always live in cages.

Her gaze landed on the Bible again. Several minutes passed as she listened to the blast and boom of Kyle's video game and the scratch of Spots as she tested the strength of every inch of wall and floor. If she only knew she was safe and had all her needs met right here with Nyla. Out in the world, she'd die of starvation, get run over or eaten by a predator. Which reminded Nyla of something Pam, one of the Deviants, had said during their Bible study.

God is our strong tower, our provider. Those who run to Him are saved. If only people knew of His love, they would run into His arms.

Nyla huffed. If that were true, where was God when her parents had disappeared? They believed in Him. They followed Him. But He had not protected them.

She should just return the Bible to Tata. Better yet, she should destroy it before it got them all arrested.

Do it. Do it. Do it! The hissing whisper sounded so real, Nyla glanced around her bedroom. No one was there, of course. But the room seemed darker than usual. Hadn't she turned on all the lights?

A flicker of light, a swath of gold shimmered through the air. She'd seen it before. Must be something wrong with her eyes. A chill sped down her back.

Her gaze dropped to the Bible. Destroying it would kill Tata.

Sighing, Nyla opened her trunk, drew out her mother's blanket, and wrapped it around her shoulders. The smell and feel of it always soothed her. She picked up the Bible. "Okay, Mom. Let's see what you and Dad thought was so great about this old book."

Spots darted over to her, crawled up her leg and dove under the blanket. Odd. She never purposely gave up her freedom and came to Nyla. Something must have spooked her.

Shadows, drifting and hovering, stole light from the room.

What the heck was going on? Did a light bulb go out? Picking up Spots, she put her back in her cage and filled her food dish, snapping the door shut. The hamster dashed into her little house as if a cat were after her.

Nyla glanced over the room again. Her concussion must be worse than she thought. A chill enveloped her, and she drew the blanket closer and studied the book again.

The Deviants had been reading from the end, so she flipped to the final section called Revelation and it opened to Chapter

11. She scanned the first part about some temple and altar, but then read,

And I will give power to my two witnesses, and they will prophesy one thousand two hundred and sixty days, clothed in sackcloth. These are the two olive trees and the two lampstands standing before the God of the earth. And if anyone wants to harm them, fire proceeds from their mouth and devours their enemies. And if anyone wants to harm them, he must be killed in this manner. These have power to shut heaven, so that no rain falls in the days of their prophecy; and they have power over waters to turn them to blood, and to strike the earth with all plagues, as often as they desire.

"What?" Nyla's thoughts jumbled. She closed her eyes. Why would a book written thousands of years ago know about these two crazy Jewish men? *And* with such detail? There had to be an explanation. Maybe the crazy Deviants in Israel paid these guys to do this, to trick people into believing the Bible and its God were real. Yet, what about the miracles they performed? No human could do that. They had to be Neflams, as she suspected. But if they were, why would they want people to believe in a book the Neflams had denounced as evil?

She flipped a few pages back, wondering what had been written about the 144,000 Tata had told her about. One heading above chapter seven mentioned them.

Do not harm the earth, the sea, or the trees till we have sealed the servants of our God on their foreheads. And I heard the number of those who were sealed. One hundred and forty-four thousand of all the tribes of the children of Israel were sealed

Ridiculous. What kind of a trick was this? Nyla tossed down the book, angry and frustrated. The pages flipped forward as if by an invisible hand. Strange. Her window was shut. The AC was off.

They sang as it were a new song before the throne, before the four living creatures, and the elders; and no one could learn that song except the hundred and forty-four thousand who were

redeemed from the earth. These are the ones who were not defiled with women, for they are virgins. These are the ones who follow the Lamb wherever He goes.

Nyla slammed the book shut. Her head hurt. Her mind hurt. She rubbed her temples. She didn't want to read any more lies. Someone was going to a lot of trouble to make the prophecies in this book come true. But for what purpose? Yes, there had been a huge surge of Deviants after the Disappearance, but most had either been arrested or had gone underground. Why would anyone want to convince people the Bible was true when it would only lead to their death?

Or would it?

She'd not seen death in the eyes of the Deviants at Zion's Nest. She'd only seen life—more life and love than she'd seen in a long while.

"Marco." Nyla whispered his name as she spotted him—his perfect physique, his black wavy hair, tight jeans, and white shirt—standing several yards away by the shoreline. Had it only been nine days? She missed him, missed his touch, his scent, the sound of his voice, the way he made her body come to life. She lowered to sit on the bench perched beside an old lifeguard tower and drew in a deep breath of the sea, but instantly coughed from the smoke. Despite the sooty air, the sun's rays pierced through the haze and seared all those brave enough to be sitting on the hot sand. Was it her imagination or was the sun growing hotter by the day? Climate change, of course. She hoped the Neflams were working on a solution.

The meteors hadn't helped. Even the few palm trees lining the beach were nothing but smoking pillars of wood. Much of the greenery in the Everglades had burned up too, despite all the swampy water, and she'd heard on the news that the Amazon Rain Forest, the US National Parks, and forests everywhere were still burning. Hundreds of thousands of people worldwide had lost their lives, five hundred alone in Fort Lauderdale.

Nothing made sense anymore. Nothing but her mission to rid the world of those who had caused all of this—the Deviants.

As if sensing her presence, Marco turned, gave her that sexy smile of his, and gestured beneath her. Reaching under the bench, she yanked the small envelope stuck to the underside. Opening it, she found her keys and a com piece, which she quickly positioned in her ear.

"You're a heavenly sight," she said.

"Tell me about it, babe. I want to come over and swallow you up." He paused. "Hey, what's with the bandage? You okay? I was worried."

She reached up to touch her head. "Lost my com piece in the meteor shower." She glanced down the beach, wondering if it would be all right for them to come closer. She needed a hug. Badly. "Come over here and I'll tell you all about it." She smiled.

He didn't respond at first, merely looked around to see if anyone watched them. But why would they? These Deviants weren't sophisticated enough to have spies or access to NWU cameras. Besides, she'd given them no reason to doubt her.

While he slowly made his way toward her, she told him everything that had happened.

"So you found their hideout?"

"Not found. They brought me there. I got knocked out when one of those fireballs hit the truck we were in."

"Great luck, babe." Grinning, he stopped a few yards away, his dark eyes perusing her before he turned and pretended to be admiring the sea. "So you know where they are, where Daniel is?"

"Yes…well, not entirely. They blindfolded me on the way out. But it's a warehouse of some kind, and I think I know the general area. Come, sit on the bench. I can't take it anymore."

"Way too tempting, babe. I don't think I could be that close to you and not touch you."

"Yeah, you're probably right."

"How about meeting me at my apartment later?" He winked at her over his shoulder.

"I can't." She wanted to—desperately—but she also didn't want to muck up her assignment...*and* her promotion. "Believe me, it's killing me not to be with you. Hopefully, it won't be much longer. They are starting to trust me."

"Good."

"Hey, thank Jennings for me for getting us out of prison."

Marco spun to stare at her. "Jennings had nothing to do with that. It was the meteors. They hit the prison pretty hard."

Nyla bit her lip. "What?" She'd not seen anything hit the prison, at least not while she'd been there. "The door to our cell clicked open and all the other doors, and the guards ignored us."

Marco shook his head and raked back his hair. "That doesn't make sense. If Jennings intended to do that, he certainly didn't inform me. Far as I know, he said he would keep you in there until you found out where Daniel was."

A hot breeze coming off the sea tossed Nyla's hair behind her and scattered all rational thoughts, replacing them with other thoughts, bizarre thoughts—of prayers and angels and praises to a God who had delivered them.

She definitely needed some grounding in reality. She needed someone sane to tell her she wasn't losing it. "What do you think of those two crazy old Jewish men?"

He shrugged and stooped to pick up a shell. "They're nuts. Why do you ask?"

"I don't know. Something the Deviants read from their book."

He chuckled. "You aren't letting them get to you. You're the last person I thought would get tangled up in their crazy ideas."

"I'm not. I'm just saying...well, they read about the meteors. The book predicted it, knew it would happen. And the two crazy Jews too."

Marco tossed the shell toward the water, then approached and plopped down on the other side of the bench as nonchalantly as he could. "The meteors are just meteors. They hit the earth from time to time. Anybody could predict that. And those two crazy Jews are just two crazy Jews who are taking credit for tragedies caused by Climate Change. The Deviants either changed that book of theirs to match current events or they are orchestrating the events themselves." He dared a glance her way, giving her one of his irresistible smiles.

The wind fluttered his jet-black waves and brought her a whiff of his aftershave, tantalizing her senses. She wanted nothing more than to scoot over and fall into his arms.

"As the Neflams have told us," he continued, "there is no God. Everything has a rational explanation." He started to reach for her but then pulled back. "I miss you. The team isn't the same without you."

"I'm sure you're leading it just fine."

He shook his head and stared out to sea. "I'm not you, that's for sure."

Nyla longed to grab his hand and give it an encouraging squeeze. "You're just as good a leader as I am. If not better." She'd told him that a thousand times and would tell him a thousand more until he believed it. "Just because your parents emigrated from Brazil and your mom was a maid and your father a janitor doesn't make you unable to achieve your dreams and be successful."

He nodded. "I know you're right. Besides,"—he laughed and gestured to his body—"who can resist such looks and charm?"

She smiled, but pain tugged at her heart. "That's not all you are, Marco. You're much more than a pretty face."

"You're the only one who has ever thought so."

"I doubt that." She faced the sea again, always amazed that someone like Marco, who had everything—charm, skill, looks, and intelligence—could still feel so insecure.

"I need you, Nyla. If the undercover work is too much for you, I can have Jennings—"

"No, I'm fine." She pressed a hand on her bandage. "It's just been a long couple of days."

"I wish I could hold you."

"Me too." Every inch of her fought for his touch.

His dark eyes scanned her in that way of his that made her feel special, loved, desired. "So, what's the plan from here?" he asked.

"Daniel is out of town for a while, so I'm going to wait and see if they contact me. I think I made friends with his bodyguard."

Marco's lips slanted. "The handsome one?"

She smiled. "Jealous?"

He looked at her. "Maybe."

"He's got nothing on you." Though even as she said it, she remembered Calan's gentle care and concern for her when she'd been injured. "Hey, I need some food. We are running out at home."

"Okay, let me remind Jennings. He has a QR code you can use."

"Thanks, Marco. I better go." Before she flung herself into his arms. "I'll let you know when they make contact."

Rising, he nodded, gave her a sensuous grin, and strolled away. Missing him already, she watched him until he disappeared from sight.

The ten horns are ten kings who shall arise from this kingdom. And another shall rise after them. He shall be different from the first ones and shall subdue three kings.
Daniel 7:24

Chapter 12

Nyla was going nuts—stir-crazy, batty, certifiable, whatever you called it when someone who hated being unproductive was bored off her behind. And it had only been a week since she'd last seen Marco. Aside from the occasional flirting over the com piece—which they weren't supposed to do—Nyla had no contact with any of her old friends or colleagues and no purpose to each day as she dragged herself out of bed. How Kyle could live such a meaningless life was beyond her, and she began to wonder if they were even related.

Yet there he was, passed out on the couch when she came out to get a cup of coffee at 9:00 a.m.

Grabbing a mug, she whispered a thanks to Tata, who must have gotten up early to make it, and then went over to turn off the TV Kyle had left on all night.

Immu Aali's handsome face filled the screen as he stood behind a podium. Behind him, sitting in highbacked chairs were at least seven of the NWU's regional presidents, while behind them, the Tall Whites, representing the Neflams, stood in regal display. Though she had to admit they were quite attractive—tall with hair as white as an Arctic fox, gorgeous bodies, and striking blue eyes—something about this particular brand of Neflam creeped her out. The tape running at the bottom of the screen said, "Breaking News. Presidents of the North American Union, the Middle East Union, and European Union have been removed from office on charges of conspiracy to commit treason against the New World Union."

"Whoa." Nyla sat down, cupping her mug in her hands.

President Aali began telling the world that they had suspected the three leaders of plotting to evict the Neflams from the planet and return earth to its former state of free nations.

"Evidence was gathered," Aali said with all seriousness. "A trial was held, and they were convicted on all charges. I'm sorry to bring you such unhappy news." He stopped for a moment and seemed to be having trouble speaking. "These men and women were my friends," he continued. "Or so I thought. However…" He glanced behind him at the other leaders and the Tall Whites before facing the camera again. "I am honored to be chosen to step into their positions, to become the eighth president of their combined regions."

The audience clapped so loud, he had to wait before continuing. "Thank you. Thank you. I am humbled to have been chosen by both the Neflams and my fellow presidents." His smile was so alluring, so mesmerizing, that all Nyla could do was stare at him as he conceded the podium to one of the other presidents and stepped aside.

So, their North American President was a traitor. Nyla shook her head and took a sip of her coffee. Thank goodness they caught him and the others in time before they started another world war. That was just what the planet didn't need right now.

Kyle snored, and Nyla got up to turn off the TV and check on Tata. She peeked in her bedroom to find her sleeping peacefully in her chair, open Bible in her lap and empty coffee cup on the table next to her. With the QR code Jennings had sent Nyla, she'd been able to purchase enough food to last them a few months. She'd lied and told Kyle she gave a friend money to buy the food for them, but regardless, she was glad to provide for her family. Would Mom and Dad be proud of her? She hoped so. If only she could talk to them, see if the reprogramming was working. But of course that was not allowed.

After getting dressed and finishing her coffee, Nyla grabbed her keys and cell and went out for a run to the beach. Better to keep in shape than hang out in the apartment with nothing to do. Tata would not approve. Since food shortages were on the rise and now most of the farmland had been burned up, people were beginning to riot—more than usual—and it wasn't safe to be walking alone through the city. But how else could she find Calan? She had no way to contact him except to run across him and his crazy Deviant friends healing people—or whatever they were doing—on the beach. If she never saw him again, her assignment would be a failure, and she could not accept that. Too much was at stake—for the world and for her family.

She started down Commercial Boulevard, squinted in the sun rising above the buildings, and slipped on her sunglasses. Angry shouts, horns, and sirens blared from the east, prompting her to make a turn and take side streets around the madness. People peered at her from behind curtains and locked windows as she passed homes with charred lawns. Florida used to be so pretty, with its tropical flowers and lush green lawns. But now, it seemed as if all the color had leached from the world and along with it, all the joy and kindness. Hopefully, now that President Aali was in charge, things would change.

Ahead, a large group of people, mostly young men, assembled, some in trucks, some riding motorcycles, others walking. Shouting and curses stung her ears, and she turned left down a smaller street. The rumble of motorcycles brought Calan to mind. She'd thought they'd had a connection. She'd sensed his attraction to her, but maybe she'd been wrong. Unlikely, but maybe. She smiled.

Shouting filled the air, followed by cursing as footsteps pounded. "Hey, sweetheart." A voice drew her gaze up. She'd been distracted, thinking of Calan. Foolish girl. Five young men surrounded her.

"I'm not your sweetheart." She kept jogging, all the while assessing the situation as she'd been trained. Two of the men were well-built, the other three mere boys. Still, she doubted she could take all of them if they jumped her at once.

One of the large men moved in her path. "Not so fast. Where you going?"

He reeked of beer and sweat and hatred. Halting, Nyla lifted her chin and stared at him with an authority she'd learned on the job. "Step aside."

"Why should I?" He laughed and glanced at his friends.

"Because you don't want a broken nose?" She gave a tight smile.

The men laughed.

"Why don't you run along with your little friends and go riot somewhere else. I'm busy." She shoved him out of the way and kept jogging. Nyla had been in dangerous positions before, but she'd always had backup. This time, in this narrow, vacant street, she was on her own. She tapped her ear. Shoot! She'd forgotten her com piece. Her heart raced.

Adrenaline pumping, she continued running, ready to fight to the death if she had to. She knew exactly what these men wanted. And she'd rather die than give it to them.

A thick hand pinched her arm and spun her around.

Nyla went into battle mode.

Flinging his crossbow in front of him, Ranoss lit an arrow with his breath and positioned it to fire. At what or who, he wasn't sure, for the dark spirits remained within the fallen sons of Adam.

"Nay!" Anisian appeared out of nowhere and held his arm in front of Ranoss. Two other warriors of light appeared with him.

"They will do her much harm!" Ranoss argued, refusing to lower his bow.

"'Tis the Commander's will," Anisian said with the authority of his station. "You are not to harm the humans. We cannot interfere, save when the dark ones come out of them to attack us or at the Commander's order."

Ranoss knew he was right. Every muscle within him twitched, longing to engage. He studied his ward. She was outnumbered, and the humans who were infested with darkness began their attack. "But…she will be harmed and never come to the knowledge of the truth!" He heard the doubt in his own voice and shame caused him to lower his weapon.

Anisian gripped his arm. "You must have faith. Remain strong. Stay by her side but do nothing. The Commander has sent another."

Calan swung his leg over his Harley, put on his helmet, and started the engine. He glanced back at Nyla's apartment. The young man who answered had been none too happy about being wakened from his sleep, though it was near 10:00. He left Calan at the door to look for Nyla, but then returned within seconds.

"Not here. She's probably out running on the beach or something," he said before slamming the door.

Not the friendliest guy. Must be the brother she spoke about. Calan had been wanting to visit Nyla for several days, but the needs of Zion's Nest in Daniel's absence had stolen his time. He'd wanted to see her to evangelize her, of course. She had shown interest in the Lord and the things of God, and he wanted to follow up with her. But if he were truthful, he missed her, longed to see her gentle smile and the wisdom in her stunning eyes.

The sounds of an angry mob penetrated his helmet, a familiar noise in the city these days. The beach was so close, Nyla must have walked…or run. Yet things had become much more dangerous after the meteors and this mess with three of the regional presidents being removed. People were confused, hungry, and filled with fear. Despite Nyla's training, she was still a woman alone.

Fear buzzed through him, and he put the bike in gear and thundered down the street. He sensed danger in his spirit, danger for Nyla. *Which way, Lord? Which way?* He started down Commercial but saw the mob ahead and heard *turn right* in his spirit. He meandered through a quiet neighborhood, seeking the Lord's guidance within.

Left.

He had nearly passed the street when he sensed he needed to turn. That's when a woman's scream speared him in the gut. Turning, he sped the bike forward, scanning each street he passed.

There. Up ahead. *Nyla!*

She was battling two men while three stood to the side laughing. She kicked one in the privates, sending him backward with a moan. The other struck her across the cheek. Hard. Instead of falling, she swung her legs out and struck his feet. He toppled to the ground with a curse. The other three swarmed her, while the first man picked her up by the shoulders and slammed her to the ground on her back.

Calan was off his bike before it fully stopped. Charging toward the thugs, he had already struck one of them and tossed him to the pavement before any of them knew he was there. One by one, he yanked them off Nyla, striking one across the jaw, another in the gut. The largest one, a man at least 6'2" with pulsing gym-made muscles, charged Calan. He swung at him, right and left, up and down, but Calan dove out of the way each time before landing a blow across his jaw that knocked him to the ground. The other large man stared at Calan, glanced at his friends who lay moaning on the pavement, then turned and dashed away.

Nyla, chest heaving, sat up, and stared at him as if he were some strange creature from another world. He held out his hand to her. Two of the punks attempted to stand.

"We'd better go," he said as she gripped his hand and he yanked her up. Without another word, he rushed to his bike, picked it off the street, and started it while she slid behind him.

The engine roared, and he took off, nearly knocking the men over again as they passed.

Nyla wrapped her arms around his waist. Tight. She had not done that on their ride before, and for some reason, it meant the world to him, having her trust him, cling to him, even though she removed her arms by the time they pulled into the beach parking lot.

Leaping off the seat as if it were on fire, she moved toward the sand, faced the sea, and bent over, hands on her thighs.

Calan stopped the bike, took the key, and slowly approached, unsure what to do. He'd never met a woman like Nyla. Did she want to be held, comforted? Did she need a shoulder to cry on?

She spun around, anger on her face. "I didn't need your help. I had everything under control."

For a moment, shock zigzagged through Calan.

Wind shifted a strand of her unruly hair across her face, shielding him from her fury. She flipped it away and let out a sigh.

Now it was his turn to be angry. "Sorry. Guess I've been trained that when I see five people attacking one person, I should help."

She stared at the sea, her jaw tightening. "I should have been able to handle myself better. I've been trained too, you know?"

"I know. And believe me, I was impressed with your effort. Hey, you're trembling."

She hugged herself and looked away.

He reached for her, and despite her resistance, drew her close. At first she kept her arms up, fists clenched against his chest. This one had pride, pride in her skills, her independence, and for some reason, she'd built a wall so high, no one could breach it.

"I'm not some damsel in distress who needs a knight in shining armor." She mumbled into his shirt. Still, she made no effort to push away.

"Good, 'cause I left my armor at home."

She laughed, a small chuckle, but it was something. He felt her start to melt against him when someone shouted.

"Calan!"

Tyson and Pam, two people from Zion's Nest, approached them from the shore.

Instantly, Nyla stepped back, wiped her eyes, and straightened her shoulders.

And Calan felt the loss immediately.

What was she thinking? Nyla wiped the moisture from her eyes as Calan's friends approached. How embarrassing. How weak. She was not some wimpy female who needed a man. She was a trained PK, a *leader* of men. Yet there she was, allowing Calan to hold and comfort her.

Boy, it sure had felt good, his strength and warmth surrounding her, his distinct masculine scent and the deep rumble of his voice in his chest. She'd felt safe, like someone cared...for the first time in years. Not to mention the man had skills. But what did she expect from a SEAL? He had dispatched those hoodlums quicker than anyone she'd ever seen. It was impressive, and she was not easily impressed.

But to fall into his arms like some feeble, needy female was humiliating. And in front of his friends.

She took a step away from Calan and pasted on a smile. The good news was, she was back into the Zion's Nest fold, back to her assignment, back to finding and apprehending Daniel and getting on with her life.

"You remember Tyson and Pam," Calan said, still looking at her with tenderness.

Nyla nodded, though she had trouble putting names with faces. Pam, a woman around Nyla's age with short blond hair and attractive features, looked at her curiously.

"Are you all right, Nyla? You seem upset."

Nyla glanced at Calan. "I'm fine. Thanks."

"The others are waiting," Tyson said, gesturing over his shoulder. The African-American man could be no more than twenty, tall, fit, with dark hair and sharp eyes—eyes full of humility and wisdom, not the lunacy one would expect from a Deviant—and Nyla wondered how any of these seemingly normal people could become so deceived.

Calan gestured toward the shore. "Join us, Nyla."

"For what?"

"Just walking down the beach, allowing the Lord to lead us to anyone who needs help or is ready to hear the truth."

Restraining a snort, she smiled and nodded. In truth, she'd rather go for a jog, eat rocks, or better yet, visit Marco. Wait. She'd forgotten her com piece, but what did it matter? Daniel was no doubt still away or he would be here.

At the shoreline, they met up with Clarisse, Tyson's wife, Max and Carolyn, and Madeline. They all welcomed Nyla warmly. Max even gave her a bear hug that squeezed the air from her lungs. She wasn't used to being hugged, touched at all, for that matter, and she wasn't sure she liked it. Weren't these people afraid of spreading viruses?

They began walking, Calan in the lead with Max by his side, and the others behind, eight of them, seven Deviants and a spy, all meandering down shore as if the world weren't ablaze and they weren't wanted by the NWU authorities.

Stopping for a second, she removed her shoes and continued, smiling at Pam who walked beside her. A foamy wave spread over her bare feet, its bubbles tickling her toes as they sank into the sand. The Deviants continued onward, laughing and chatting and enjoying each other's company. Brilliant rays from the sun warmed her cheek, and a humid breeze swept over her from the sea, along with it the oddest sense of belonging. She shook it off, but at that very moment, Calan glanced at her over his shoulder and smiled, that smile of his that held promise and hope and...

"Beware the servants of the most high!" A shout came from behind Nyla.

Halting, she spun around to see a woman close to Tata's age, pointing a bony finger at the Deviants. A shadow hovered over her, but when Nyla looked up, there was no cloud.

Calan appeared beside Nyla as the woman continued. "Beware these servants of the Most High, for they tell you how to be saved from the punishment of sin!"

And as you go, preach, saying, 'The kingdom of heaven is at hand.' Heal the sick, raise the dead, cleanse the lepers, cast out demons. Freely you have received, freely give. Matthew 10:7-8

Chapter 13

"Our enemy has many gathered against them." Ranoss stood his ground between the saints and the witch.

Anisian drew his blade and glanced at the other warriors doing the same. "But we are strong."

Grabbing his crossbow, Ranoss positioned it against his chest as a demonic horde advanced over the beach toward them.

"They think the saints are weak without their leader," Cassian said.

"But little do they know," Anisian snorted. "Their power comes from the Most High, not any son of Adam."

"May His name be praised," one of the angels shouted. "The name of Jesus!"

The dark horde shrank back for a second, uttering foul curses, but then quickly advanced.

Ranoss drew an arrow from his quiver, blew a flame onto its tip—a holy flame—and positioned it in the crossbow.

Snakes poked their vile heads out of the witch's mouth and hissed at the warriors. "Lucifer is the god of this world. Your lord was defeated long ago."

Ranoss aimed his arrow for the snake, but Anisian held his arm. "Not until the sons of Adam grant us authority."

The angels waited, eyes focused, muscles pulsing, and weapons drawn.

Nyla couldn't tell if the old woman was crazy or if she was one of the Deviants. Her words, though spoken in anger, were words of praise, at least from the Deviants' point of view. Yet there was a darkness about her, a sense of despair and evil—if there were such a thing.

"You are correct," Calan said as the other Deviants gathered around him. "Why not join us?"

"Join you?" The woman spat. "I follow the true god."

Behind her, people approached over the sand, drawn by the altercation.

Calan crossed arms over his chest. "There is only one true God."

Nyla ground her teeth. If someone believed what the woman had called them and reported it, NWU officers would arrive and arrest them again, and that would only delay finding Daniel.

A burst of light caused her to blink. Wind slapped her face, and for a second, the glowing outline of a tall man with a sword formed in her vision. She shook it off. Just a trick of the sunlight reflecting off the ocean.

"I'll put a curse on you!" the woman's eyes flattened into slits as spit flew from her mouth. "On you all!"

Max began muttering something in another language.

"Let's go, Calan." Nyla tugged on his arm, but he would not be moved.

The crowd was almost there. One of them spoke on his phone. There was a reward for any tip leading to the arrest of a Deviant.

Calan's eyes never left the old woman. "Come out of her in the name of Jesus," he said with the authority of a judge pronouncing sentence.

Ranoss fired his crossbow. The flaming arrow sped straight into the snake's mouth and down the woman's throat.

The vile reptile flung this way and that, screaming in agony and forcing the woman to the sand.

"Go back to hell, where you belong!" Anisian shouted.

The thick, massive snake slithered out of the woman's mouth. Dropping onto the sand beside her, it coiled upward, raising its head high, high, high above the mighty warriors, its black eyes slits of hatred, its reptile smile foaming with evil.

Anisian swung his blade at the snake's neck, severing it in two. The head exploded in a burst of black ink. The body fell to the sand, writhing in death throes, splashing in the surf. One of the angel warriors picked up the gyrating body and tossed it into the sea.

Ranoss spun to face the rest of the demonic horde. His fellow warriors lined up beside him, blades glittering in the sun, golden shields impenetrable.

Ready to fight. Ready to battle for their King.

Instead of waiting for the enemy to reach them, Anisian gave the order and the mighty warriors rushed the demons.

If Nyla hadn't seen it with her own eyes, she would never have believed that just one command from Calan would have sent the old woman falling to the sand, screaming in agony, and shouting curses and threats to the Deviants. Even stranger, the voice coming out of her wrinkled, frail body was not that of a woman, but a man's voice, deep and malevolent.

She started forward to help the woman, but Calan held her back with his arm.

"Come out of her in Jesus' name!" he said one more time, and an eerie hissing seeped from the old woman's mouth—like the last bits of air in a balloon—before she fell silent.

Calan dropped his arm, and Nyla, along with Madeline, rushed to the woman's side. They got her to her feet, but she jerked from their grasps and stepped away, staring at the

Deviants with more hatred than Nyla had seen. And she'd seen a lot.

A flash caught Nyla's eye yet again, and she turned toward the street. A wall of blinding light stood between her and the people who had been approaching. A shout, like a trumpet, echoed in her ear.

"Come join us," Calan's tender appeal brought Nyla's gaze back to him as he held out a hand to the old woman. "Give your life to the one true and only God."

The woman blinked, swallowed, stared at the sea and then back to Calan, confusion and fear firing from her eyes.

"Before it's too late," he added.

"No!" Screaming, she held both hands to her ears and took off as fast as she could hobble down the beach.

The wall of light evaporated. Most of the people who had been heading toward them had turned back. Only a few continued.

Nyla drew a breath and rubbed her eyes. Why was it every time she hung out with these Deviants, weird, unexplainable things happened? She wanted to ask Calan about the old woman, but he started speaking with the five people who approached. Leading them away from the water, he gestured for them to sit in the sand while he answered their questions and preached the Deviant Gospel in hushed whispers so as not to alert NWU ears. At least four of the five sat in rapt attention, though one finally shook his head and stomped away. Just plain stupid of Calan. Why take the risk? Why speak of forbidden things right out in the open, things that, at best, could land them all in a reformation camp, but at worst, on death row?

She didn't want to hear the Deviant heresy, but neither did she want to leave, not until she had an invitation to return to Zion's Nest. Dropping to the sand a few yards from where the others sat, she repressed a sneer in their direction. Christianity had caused nearly every war on earth and more deaths than any other cause. On the other hand, the New World Religion had united all philosophies and beliefs into one system that could benefit all mankind and lead to peace and safety. Not that she adhered to it or any religion. They all led to false hope, and she'd had enough of that to last a lifetime.

"Mind if I sit?"

Shielding her eyes from the sun, Nyla glanced up to see Pam standing beside her. "Sure." She lied, but she needed to make friends with these people.

"So, what was up with that old lady?" Nyla asked as Pam sat down and drew her knees to her chest.

"She was possessed."

Nyla couldn't help but laugh. "Like by the devil?"

Pam gave her a gentle smile. "Demons... a powerful one, from the way it reacted."

Nyla ran her fingers through the fine silt at her feet. A blast of wind tore over her, tossing her hair, and she eased a strand behind her ear, wishing she'd not forgotten her com piece.

"I know it's hard to accept at first," Pam continued. "Been there, done that, but I can assure you, that is exactly what you witnessed."

Right. *Freaks.* "So, what is *your* deal? Were you demon possessed too?"

Pam laughed. "No, but you should hear Madeline's story." She nodded toward the dark-haired woman with the multiple tats. "Daniel cast at least a dozen out of her."

Nyla wanted to puke. Just when she started to think these people weren't so bad, they proved how insane they truly were.

Pam gazed over the sea, its foam-capped waves glittering in the sun. "I lost my whole family in the rap—disappearance. Husband, two kids..." Hesitating, she swallowed. "Parents and two siblings." Her voice emerged raw and shaky.

Nyla could relate, at least a little, though she could not imagine being separated from a spouse and children. "I'm sorry. I lost my parents too. But they aren't really lost, are they?"

Pam wiped moisture from her eyes and smiled at Nyla, her blond bob blowing in the wind. "No. I'll see them again, but I hate that I was so dumb, that I didn't listen to them."

"You wish you'd gone to a Reformation Camp too?" The question came out before Nyla realized that Pam was not referring to a camp. *Stupid girl.* She was supposed to fit in, pretend she believed as they did.

Pam chuckled and dug her bare feet deeper in the sand. "They are in heaven now, Nyla, not some FEMA camp. They tried to warn me over and over, and at one time I *did* believe. I gave my life to Jesus and started following Him." She sighed and gazed over the sea again. "But I drifted away, got caught up in the pleasures of this world. We were rich, you see. We lived well, had two yachts, and took lots of expensive vacations." She gave a sad smile. "My husband wanted to give all our money to the poor, but I was adamantly against it."

Nyla frowned. Another reason to hate religion. Christianity was all about following rules—what you could and couldn't do, and making people feel guilty if they fell short. "You had money. You wanted to be happy. There's nothing wrong with that."

Pam looked at her with such love and also....*pity*? She picked up a shell, a beautiful white shell with one side chipped away. "Truth was, I wasn't very happy," she said. "Yes, there were fleeting moments, but knowing Jesus, loving Him and following Him has brought me more joy and peace than any of those pleasures I experienced." She smiled. "They tried to warn me, you know...told me Jesus was coming to get them, begged me to repent and come back to Him so I could join them." She tossed the shell. "I didn't listen. Now I'm here in the Tribulation."

Tribulation. What a bunch of crap. Yes, earth had gone through some tough times, but most of them had been caused by religion, war, climate change, and Christians like these who had spread hate and division. Nyla wanted more than anything to tell Pam the truth, to pull her out of this Deviant cult, to tell her that she'd see her family and her children again after they'd been reformed. The Neflams had promised.

Pam closed her eyes as a visible shudder ran through her. "And my kids. Six and three years old. I miss them so much."

Nyla placed a hand on her arm. "I can't imagine. I'm so sorry."

"Thanks. And you, too. You must miss your parents."

Nyla dropped her gaze to the sand. "More than you know."

After what seemed like forever, Calan urged Pam to join him, and together the Deviants prayed with the four people, all except Tyson, who stood to the side with head bowed. Odd, but the area around them seemed brighter than the rest of the beach, almost like a halo of gold circling them as they prayed. Astronomers said the sun was growing brighter, and it was definitely playing tricks on Nyla's vision.

Finally, the Deviants gave the newcomers hugs and sent them on their way. Good thing, because some people were beginning to stare at them, and it would only be a matter of time before someone called the NWU. Deviants or not, it was illegal to meet in groups of more than ten.

"Wanna lift home?" Calan approached with a rather pleased look on his face.

"You look like you won the Nobel Peace Prize or something."

"Better. Two souls just got yanked from hell and are on their way to heaven."

Crud. The man was far too good-looking and masculine to be so naive, but looks were deceiving.

She attempted a smile. "Sure, I'd love a ride."

The look of delight in Calan's eyes took her by surprise. He was interested in her. He was attracted to her. And if she were truthful, there was some attraction on her part as well. Not that he held a candle to Marco. But perhaps she could use his interest to her advantage, flirt with him, get closer and get more information on Daniel's plans.

So, on the way home, she wrapped her arms around his waist and hung on tight. By the time he pulled in front of her apartment building and got off the bike, he had a pleased but shocked look on his face. He stood there, awkward as a schoolboy on his first date, staring at her as if he'd never seen a girl before. He started to say something but then laughed, and she thought it was the sweetest thing she'd ever seen.

When Marco looked at her, there was no question what was on his mind. When he spoke, it was with the practiced tongue of a charming seducer. But this man, a Navy SEAL, a warrior, stood tongue-tied before her.

"Thanks again for your help today." She still refused to admit that he had rescued her. Turning, she started up the path to her apartment, using the playing-hard-to-get bait that had worked so well in the past.

"How about you come for Sunday services at Zion's Nest?"

Yes! She spun to offer him a smile. "Sure."

"I'll pick you up. Around 8:00 in the morning."

Caught him. Now all she had to do was reel him in.

I know your works, that you are neither cold nor hot. I could wish you were cold or hot. So then, because you are lukewarm, and neither cold nor hot, I will vomit you out of My mouth. Because you say, 'I am rich, have become wealthy, and have need of nothing'—and do not know that you are wretched, miserable, poor, blind, and naked— Revelation 3:15-17

Chapter 14

Calan had always been awkward with women, but with Nyla, he seemed to sink to new moronic levels. Good grief, he was thirty years old, and in his pre-Jesus days, he'd been with many women, too many, in fact. Once they learned he was a Navy SEAL, his charm and social skills didn't seem to matter. They flung themselves at him. He'd eaten up the attention—and the sex—believing it was okay with God. After all, didn't God invent sex? And what was wrong with loving someone, anyway? That was his philosophy as he'd sat week after week in Daniel Cain's church where, honestly, he never heard anything to the contrary.

Not until the Rapture, when suddenly most of the church remained, and Daniel began to preach the *real* Gospel. Unlike many people in the church, Calan had not lost anyone in the disappearance. Growing up an orphan who was cast from one foster home to another, he'd had trouble forming close relationships. But he witnessed firsthand the devastation of those left behind, people who believed they would be taken, believed they were saved, even though their belief in Jesus had merely been a mental assent, not a true belief of the heart.

At first, he'd felt abandoned by God, like everyone else in his life, but it was Daniel and his persistent friendship and encouragement that had saved Calan from a very dark path. Angry, feeling betrayed, Calan had not been easy to deal with back then, but Daniel never gave up on him.

And neither did God.

A knock on the door brought his gaze up and his thoughts back into focus. He'd been praying, praying for strength, for wisdom, for Nyla.

"There you are." Daniel slipped inside the private office at Zion's Nest and shut the door.

"You're back!" Calan leapt to his feet and gave his friend a hug.

"Yeah, just now." Daniel returned his embrace. "Terrance and Max tell me you did an excellent job in my absence." His smile was genuine, but there was a seriousness in his blue eyes. "Didn't mean to disturb your prayers."

"It's okay. I want to hear everything. How are the churches doing?"

Daniel lowered into one of the cushioned chairs and released a sigh. Calan sat across from him, elbows on his knees, anxious for some good news for a change.

"Most are doing well... As good as can be expected in these times." Daniel rubbed the back of his neck. "The St. Augustine church lost their meeting place. One of the meteors hit it and burned it to the ground."

Calan gulped. "Was anyone hurt?"

"No. Miraculously, God had sent each one out on various missions. No one was there."

Calan dropped his gaze to the concrete floor. "Guess the Lord is not done with them yet." There were no guarantees in the Tribulation, especially the last half. Daniel had taught him that. Jesus plainly said that the gates of hell would not overcome the church, but in the Tribulation, the Antichrist would be given power over the saints. It was a different time. He glanced up at Daniel and saw the same sorrow Calan was feeling. They had missed the age of grace, the opportunity to escape, due to their foolish hearts.

"And the rest of the churches?"

Daniel smiled. "Growing. Adding to their numbers every day. It's amazing." He picked up a Bible sitting on the table and held it up. "It's like the church of Acts all over again. Miracles, healings, deliverances, many coming to the Lord." Excitement sparked from his eyes as he laid the book in his lap and ran a hand over it. "If only I had known before the Rapture that the church was supposed to be this way, the good I could have done."

"You're doing good now, Daniel. A lot of good. Look at all the churches you've planted...all the teachings you share with them, how they are all growing."

Daniel nodded. "For such a time as this."

"Yes." Calan studied his friend, sensing there was more to tell. "There's something else bothering you."

"You know me well, my friend."

A few moments passed before Daniel spoke again. "The Spirit told me that my time is almost up."

"What?" Alarm pinched Calan. "What do you mean?"

"I am soon to go home."

"So it appears that President Aali is truly the Antichrist," the man called Terrance Gonzales stated as the Deviants spread out on comfy chairs and couches, preparing for a Bible Study.

If it weren't for seeing Calan again, Nyla would rather be shoveling horse manure in hundred-degree heat than to sit here and endure more lies and deception. Still, she had to admit when Calan had ridden up on his Harley, looking all manly and handsome and smiling at her as if she were a precious ruby, she couldn't help the leap of her heart. Now, however, at Zion's Nest, surrounded by these lunatics—and enemies of the NWU—

she just wanted to be done with this assignment and return to her normal life.

Calan squeezed between her and another lady on the couch. Their thighs pressed together, and her body warmed at his closeness. Ridiculous. He was just as crazy as the rest. Besides, she had a boyfriend, a handsome, *sane* one, so what was her deal with Calan? It was that look in his eyes, the same one in them right now as he gazed at her—like she was something to be cherished, adored, saved. Bah! He was the one who needed saving, not her.

A white cat leapt into his lap and glared angrily at Nyla before curling in a ball and starting to purr. Odd. Regardless that people couldn't afford pets anymore, she would never have pegged Calan as a cat lover.

"Yours?" she asked.

He scratched the cat's head. "Apocalypse, meet Nyla. Nyla, this is Apocalypse."

She chuckled. "You named your cat Apocalypse?"

"Calypsey for short."

He continued petting the cat and the cat continued to purr and push her head against his stomach. Nyla reached out to touch her, and after she sniffed Nyla's hands—no doubt smelling Spots—she allowed Nyla to caress her fur.

"She likes you." Calan's tone was one of surprise. "She doesn't allow just anyone to touch her."

Nyla was about to tell Calan about Spots when Daniel entered the room from the back.

He was here! All she had to do was notify Marco to send troops to her location, and they'd arrest the famous preacher. Easy peasy!

Smiling, Daniel made a beeline for her with that knowing look in his eyes. "Good to see you here, Nyla," he said as he passed by her, oddly waving a hand over her head.

He took his seat in a wooden chair across the way and initiated a prayer. As everyone bowed their heads, Nyla tapped her com piece. She and Marco had decided on the code word

"Spots" to indicate when she'd found Daniel. No sound entered her ear. Usually Marco responded to her tap.

"Spots," she whispered.

Nothing. She said the word again, unfortunately drawing Calan's gaze.

Nothing.

Daniel finished his prayer, then turned to Terrance. "You are correct about Aali, though we all assumed he was the Antichrist when he strengthened the accords with Israel."

The Antichrist? Ridiculous. Immu Aali has done wonderful things for the people of the world. He had stopped World War 3, brought peace to the globe, and then assisted in the formation of ten world regions to avoid further wars. In addition, he'd been the liaison with the Neflams when they'd first arrived, extended earth's hand of friendship, and worked with them to incorporate their technological advances. Since then, he'd offered wise counsel to the ten presidents of the NWU—and now had become one—helping them initiate reforms to stop climate change, instill racial and social equality, and create a more just society. *The Antichrist?* She wanted to laugh.

"I see you are skeptical, Nyla." Daniel's voice brought her gaze up to him. *Crud.* She'd forgotten to temper her expression.

She shrugged. "Maybe. I just don't get what you all are talking about."

Daniel gestured to Madeline, the tat lady. "Could you read Daniel 7:23-24 to us, Maddy."

Smiling, she opened her Bible, found the page, and began reading.

"The fourth beast shall be
A fourth kingdom on earth,
Which shall be different from all other kingdoms,
And shall devour the whole earth,
Trample it and break it in pieces.
The ten horns are ten kings
Who shall arise from this kingdom.

And another shall rise after them;
He shall be different from the first ones,
And shall subdue three kings."

"This is a prophecy made three thousand years ago," Daniel began, glancing over the crowd. "It concerns a final world kingdom that would arise and be ruled by ten kings, just as we are witnessing today."

What? Nyla rubbed her eyes. That didn't make sense.

"And, as we can all see, this passage is about the Antichrist, who will come up and take out three of those kings."

Nyla's world tilted. How was that possible? It was one thing to pay a couple of old Jewish men to act nuts in Jerusalem to trick people into believing the Bible was true. But how could these Deviants create a final world kingdom, let alone force a particular world leader to get rid of three presidents and take their place?

Yet wasn't that what had just happened?

Her thoughts jumbled into nonsense in her head. Nor could the Deviants have added this information to a Bible that—which she'd been taught had been altered over the years—could not have been changed just last week.

"So, without a doubt," Carolyn, the lady who had taken care of Nyla, spoke up. "He is the one."

Daniel nodded, and all seemed to be in agreement. Even Calan, who remained silent beside her, a somber expression on his face as if they'd just made a suicide pact.

"So, what is this Antichrist supposed to do now?" Nyla blurted out, longing to catch them in a lie, trick them into seeing their own deception.

Daniel and an older Hispanic man named Terrance both started answering, but Daniel deferred to him.

Terrance looked her way. "He will become the single world leader and will one day enter Jerusalem, sit down in the Holy Temple, and proclaim that he is God."

"Then," Madeline continued, "he will demand everyone worship him and submit to his kingdom by getting some kind of microchip implanted."

"Like the quantum dot technology they have now," Pam said.

"And they won't be able to buy or sell without it," Terrance added.

Nyla flattened her lips. "So what? They are already doing that now if you aren't vaccinated." Which reminded her. How the heck did these people buy anything?

"Yes, but it will be much worse. The tech injected into people, perhaps through one of these vaccines they are requiring, will change a person's DNA and make them no longer human."

Nyla raised a brow. Like she said, nutjobs.

"We can show you the Scriptures," Pam said.

"That's okay. I'm on overload at the moment." Nyla attempted a smile and a few of them chuckled.

"Can you read our text for today?" Daniel asked Pam.

Glancing down at the open *illegal* book in her hand, she began, "Then the second angel sounded: And something like a great mountain burning with fire was thrown into the sea, and a third of the sea became blood. And a third of the living creatures in the sea died, and a third of the ships were destroyed. Revelation 8:8-9."

"This is what we can expect next, Saints. This is what we must prepare for." Daniel glanced around the group with all the seriousness of a judge pronouncing a death sentence. "Though we don't know exactly *what* this will be, it sounds like an asteroid."

"But what can we do? How can we prepare the world for something like that?" one of them asked.

"We can't in the natural. But we can pray for God's mercy. We cannot stop the things that must come, but our prayers can help save the lost. We must always be in prayer for people to come out of this great deception and turn to God."

"Amen," several said, including Calan.

Nyla touched her com piece again, desperate to get out of there, but things had gone too quiet for her to say the code word.

Daniel continued to read other Scriptures, mostly about patience, endurance, and how much God loved them, but Nyla felt like a cyclone ravaged through her brain, leaving any rational thought in a pile of rubble. None of this made sense, but then again, crazy people weren't supposed to make sense.

Shifting uncomfortably in her seat, she longed to excuse herself, go topside and try to reach Marco. Finally, just as Daniel seemed to be wrapping up the ridiculous meeting, he glanced her way.

"How about we all introduce ourselves to Nyla and tell her how we came to be here."

"That's not necessary." She smiled as she started to rise.

"I think it might help you understand us better." Daniel's tone was insistent.

She eased back onto the couch. Calan gave her hand a squeeze, which didn't help her resolve to leave. Quite the opposite, in fact.

One by one, each person gave their names and welcomed her with genuine smiles. Though she expected to be bored, she had to admit each of their stories touched her deeply.

Carolyn and Max, the nurse and the big hugger in their fifties, had been caught up in politics, in what they called Dominionism and the New Apostolic Reformation, whatever that was.

"We put all our hopes in America, in patriotism, in getting a good man in office, rather than in God."

"Trouble was," Max added, "the movement was deceptively Christian, but in the end, it was just a front for the New Age religion."

"So, we," Carolyn glanced at her husband, "were deceived, lukewarm in our love for God, and left behind."

Tyson, the young African-American man from the beach, spoke up from his spot next to his wife, Clarisse, a beautiful dark-skinned girl, who obviously adored him. "We were living together. We had plans to get married, but life got in the way. We had a son." He lowered his head and took his wife's hand in his. She shut her eyes and even from across the room, Nyla could see a tear slip down her cheek. "We have a son," he corrected. "We thought we were Christians. We never thought about the Rapture or End Times."

Calan leaned to whisper in Nyla's ear. "Their son was taken."

How horrible. Yet she'd heard similar stories. The Neflams had taken children all over the world, deeming it necessary to educate them properly and not take the risk they would be indoctrinated by deceived, yet well-meaning parents. At the time, it had made sense to Nyla. Nationalists, conservatives, and religious nuts had caused all the problems of the world, and if they were allowed to brainwash their kids, the cycle would go on forever. Yet, seeing the pain on this young couple's face made the agony real, and Nyla couldn't stop the moisture filling her eyes.

Madeline, the plump, brown-haired woman Nyla had met before, spoke up next. "I was a lesbian. Had been all my life. Or at least I thought I was." She glanced at Daniel and smiled. "Until Daniel delivered me of too many demons to count."

Nyla wanted to vomit. What was wrong with one's sexual orientation? Religion. Always judging, always condemning, always making someone feel guilty. Enough of this nonsense! She tapped her com piece again. Nothing.

Javier and Elena were next, a middle-aged Hispanic couple Nyla had met briefly before.

"We were worship leaders at our local church." Elena glanced at Javier with a loving smile. "Oh, how we loved to perform, hear the applause and the praise of the congregation."

Javier snorted. "But we didn't actually believe the words we were singing. We thought we did. But we were living for ourselves."

When it was Pam's turn, she merely smiled at Nyla and said, "I've already shared my sad tale with Nyla."

Others spoke, Aaron and Jeff, the other bodyguards, an older lady named Violet, Beth a schoolteacher, and Ephraim a landscaper. One by one, each of them shared how they had either never been religious or how they'd thought they were "saved," as they put it, only to find themselves "left behind," another weird phrase they kept saying. All had lost loved ones in what they called the Rapture, which Nyla realized was when the Neflams had taken them for reprogramming. If only these people understood why this had happened, they wouldn't have followed in their loved ones' deluded footsteps.

It was sad.

Finally, the man Nyla assumed was from Mexico, Terrance Gonzales, spoke up. "I was a famous preacher. I had a global ministry that reached every nation. Perhaps you've heard of it? World Kingdom Ministries?"

Nyla shook her head. Why would she have?

He sighed and rubbed his short-cropped gray beard. "I was a fake. I did it for money. I had six mansions all over the world, a private jet, and a yacht." Tears filled his eyes, and he bowed his head.

Daniel, who sat next to him, put a hand on his back. "You are not that man, anymore, Terrance."

He looked up. "No. The Lord has made me new."

"And you've done incredible work since then." Daniel looked at Nyla. "Terrance is an evangelist. The Lord pops him all over the world when there is a soul searching for truth."

Pops? Nyla pursed her lips. She didn't want to ask.

Instead, she wanted to shout, tell these people that their loved ones were safe in reformation camps, and they'd see them again. But only if they stopped believing this nonsense. How foolish!

She tapped her com piece. Grr. Why wasn't Marco answering? "And what is your story, Daniel?" she asked him, hoping for some dirt on the man she could use later if necessary.

A sudden sorrow gripped his expression, like a vise of gloom, and for a moment his gaze wandered to another place. Then, as quickly as it had left, it snapped back to the present. "For another time," he said. Which only made Nyla more curious. She was also curious why Marco wasn't answering. She glanced up at the low stone ceiling. Perhaps they had some sort of signal jammer? No, these Deviants were not that technical. Or were they? Somehow they managed to get food and supplies without a VaxPass or good social credit score.

She asked Pam that very question after the study disbanded and everyone went to do other things.

"God provides," Pam said as she opened the fridge and pulled out a jug. "Some of the people have friends who get supplies for us. Tyson has taken the fifth booster, so he has a vaxpass and buys food and other things we need. He has not been labeled a Christian, so his social credit score is still good too, by the grace of God. Also, he's a bit of a geek"—she smiled, her glance finding him across the room—"who works for one of the big tech companies, and he was able to replicate a VaxPass and credit score on Calan's mobile… something about Calan having been employed by the government making it easier. But he couldn't do it on anyone else's. That's how Calan got the job here at the warehouse." She poured what looked like orange juice into a glass and handed it to Nyla. "And this we squeezed from the oranges I picked off the tree in my backyard. Not that we'll be doing that anymore since it burned up."

Nyla hadn't had fresh oranges in years. The sweet citrus taste exploded in her mouth. "Thanks. But if Tyson has the fifth booster, can't they track him?"

Pam sipped her orange juice. "Daniel prayed over him, and God deactivated it."

She said the words as if that sort of thing happened all the time. But of course it was ludicrous. Maybe these Deviants had harnessed some of the Neflams' power to heal, but no way they could disrupt their technology.

Nyla's gaze found Calan across the room talking to Terrance. As if he knew she was looking at him, he glanced her way and smiled.

"He likes you," Pam said.

Snapping her gaze down to her cup, Nyla ignored the thrill speeding through her. "Who?"

"Oh, stop it." Pam shook her head. "Calan, of course." She nodded toward him. "I've never seen him act so weird around any other woman."

Nyla laughed. "He is a little shy, isn't he?" She continued staring at him, unable to look away. "Why is he so intense all the time? Do you know his past? Does he have any family?" She had no idea why she asked so many intrusive questions, but the man never spoke about himself, and she was curious to know more.

Pam slanted her lips. "No, he's an orphan. But I have heard he once had a brother. Geesh, sorry, I shouldn't tell you, anyway. It's his place."

"You're right. I'm sorry," Nyla said as a black cat leapt into Calan's arms. "But at least tell me what's up with the cats?"

Pam laughed. "I don't know. They sort of follow him. Weird. He's like the pied piper of cats. They love him."

"What's the black one called, the one he's holding now?"

"That's Tribby."

Before Nyla could ask what Tribby stood for, Javier began tuning a guitar in the far corner.

"We are going to worship," Pam said, excitement in her eyes. "Want to join?"

Not in a million years. "I can't. I have to be somewhere." Anywhere but here. Anywhere she could contact Marco. "You go ahead. I'm going to go above and wait for Calan."

A flash of skepticism crossed Pam's eyes before she smiled and walked away.

Nyla touched her com piece. Still nothing. Keeping her eyes on Calan, she inched her way to the stairs that led upward into the warehouse.

The glowing outline of a large man appeared beside Terrance. She stopped to stare, unable to pull her gaze away. He had one hand on the hilt of a giant sword and the other he put on Terrance's shoulder. Terrance immediately stiffened, said something to Calan...

And then disappeared. Gone. Completely.

Nyla stumbled backward, tripped over a footstool, and would have fallen had Calan not rushed over and caught her.

He causes all, both small and great, rich and poor, free and slave, to receive a mark on their right hand or on their foreheads, and that no one may buy or sell except one who has the mark or the name of the beast, or the number of his name. Here is wisdom. Let him who has understanding calculate the number of the beast, for it is the number of a man: His number is 666. Revelation 13:16-18

Chapter 15

Nyla stormed into her apartment, tossed down the keys, scowled at Kyle passed out on the couch, and headed straight for her bedroom. Shutting the door, she leaned back against it and closed her eyes. When she'd accepted this assignment, she'd hoped to capture and put away the most notorious Deviant in the North American Region. What she hadn't expected was to catch whatever insanity the Deviants suffered from.

A man had disappeared! Nyla slid down to the floor and drew her knees to her chest. Completely and utterly vanished. And not a single Deviant seemed shocked. In fact, quite the opposite. Several formed a circle and began to pray, while others started singing. And what was that glowing creature she saw? More importantly, why did she keep seeing him?

Calan, who had caught her in his arms—a sensation she would have enjoyed if not for the shock spiraling through her— merely smiled and asked if she was okay.

Okay? No, she was not okay! What had Pam put in that orange juice?

She'd immediately demanded Calan take her home, which he did without argument and very little conversation.

"I know that was a shock, Nyla," he said after he shut off his bike and she'd leapt off. He removed his helmet and smiled at her. Smiled? As if nothing unusual had happened.

Though everything within her told her to run, she could only stare at him.

"God can instantly translate people from one location to another. It's in the Bible at the end of Acts 8."

"Okay. Whatever. I have to go." It was a stupid thing to say, but she couldn't conjure up an intelligent response to such lunacy.

Now as she sat in her bedroom, she wouldn't be surprised if Calan never wanted to see her again. He was no dummy. He had to know she wasn't buying into their religious nonsense. Which meant her assignment was over. *Wait.*

She touched her com piece. *Come on, Marco, come on!* She'd been so shocked by Terrance's disappearance, she'd completely forgotten to alert the authorities.

Nothing.

Digging it out of her ear, she stared at it. Stupid thing. It must be broken. Fighting back tears, she threw it across the room. Her one chance to get Daniel Cain and her piece-of-crap com piece went on the fritz. Of course she knew now where Zion's Nest was. Calan had not blindfolded her this time, so she could call in the troops anytime.

But Daniel wasn't always there. Calan said he often traveled to other Deviant hideouts. Sure, the others would be arrested, but Daniel was the target. She had to wait. Be patient. Get a working com piece and try again.

If she was ever invited back.

Her phone sat idle on her dresser. Against the rules or not, she should call Marco. If the Deviants had any way to trace her calls, her cover would be blown. She'd seen nothing at Zion's Nest to indicate they had that kind of technology, but she'd not been permitted in the back rooms. Pam had said Tyson was a tech wizard. Maybe he'd installed a jammer of some sort, not because they knew she had a com piece, but because of the tracker in the vaccine she'd taken. That would also explain what had happened to Tyson's tracker. If so, they were smarter than she'd given them credit for.

"Grr." She growled and ran fingers through her hair.

Spots poked her head out of her wooden house, causing Nyla to smile. Wiping her eyes, she crawled over to her cage, opened the door, and picked up the warm ball of fur. "You're not crazy, are you?" Nyla pressed the hamster to her cheek.

A rap sounded on her door. "Pajarito, is that you?"

"Yes, come in."

Tata opened the door and slipped inside as Nyla put Spots back in her cage.

"You and that hamster." Tata smiled.

Rising, Nyla gave her grandmother a hug.

"Sweet Pajarito, what is the matter? You are trembling, dear."

"I'm okay." Nyla withdrew and helped Tata to sit on the bed. "Just had a rough day."

"A rough day? Are you back on the force?"

"No." Nyla sat beside her grandmother. Should she tell her what happened? Her Tata was one of them, but certainly not as crazy, right?

"Tata, can God move people from one place to another? I mean like make them disappear and then reappear somewhere else?"

Tata chuckled and placed a hand on Nyla's knee. "Oh, dear, sounds like you've been spending time with all the right people."

Nyla snorted. If she only knew.

Tata coughed, a deep cough that concerned Nyla. Finally, she gathered her voice. "But to answer your question. Yes. Let me show you."

Before Nyla could protest, Tata struggled to rise, left, and returned with her Bible. Flipping it open, she sat beside Nyla and read from Acts 8.

"Now when they came up out of the water, the Spirit of the Lord caught Philip away, so that the eunuch saw him no more; and he went on his way rejoicing. But Philip was found at Azotus. And passing through, he preached in all the cities till he came to Caesarea."

"You see, Nyla, Philip was an evangelist. His job was to tell people about Jesus so they could be saved. Sometimes it was necessary for God to translate him to various places to meet with people who were seeking the truth."

Hmm. The same thing Calan had told her. Nyla dropped her head in her hands. What was happening? Why did nothing make sense anymore?

Kyle poked his head inside her door. "Hey, you gotta see this." His tone was full of excitement, but a scowl appeared on his lips when he saw Tata's Bible. "We're gonna end up in jail because of that book."

Closing the Bible, Tata pointed a finger at her grandson. "This book is the only thing that will save you."

Uttering an unintelligible curse, Kyle stormed away. After heaving a sad sigh, Tata went to return the Bible to her room, while Nyla followed her brother into the living room. A group of NASA scientists appeared on the TV screen beside a picture of a large rock in space—an asteroid.

Nyla's knees gave way. Gripping the arm of a chair, she sank onto the soft cushion.

"Scientists have been tracking this asteroid for decades. Up until a week ago, its trajectory posed no danger to earth. However, something in outer space caused it to alter course, and it now appears to be heading straight for our planet. The Neflams have been informed and are currently devising a way to divert its course by using…"

But Nyla wasn't listening anymore. All she could think of was the Scriptures she'd heard that morning about an asteroid hitting earth. Impossible.

"Cool, huh?" Kyle ran a hand through his dark hair.

"Cool? No. What if they can't fix this?"

"They're Neflams. They can do anything. You worry too much, Sis."

Nyla slanted her lips. "What have you done with my grumpy, negative brother?"

Kyle shrugged.

Tata appeared beside Nyla. "Trumpet two."

What? Nyla stared at her grandmother, then shut her eyes. No sense in arguing with her. "Are you hungry, Tata? Let me make us some dinner."

"Sounds good to me." Kyle leaned his head back on the couch.

"That would be lovely, dear."

Nyla leapt up and headed toward the kitchen while Tata sat in her chair. Better to keep busy than to think about all this craziness.

The scene on the TV switched to local news. But the words "NWU Peace Keepers" caught Nyla's attention, and she spun to watch.

Video played of members of a PK team raiding a Deviant hideout. She looked closer at the insignia. It was 88—her team! That should be *her* in the lead. "Three this week," the newscaster said. "A remarkable success for the New World Union."

She fisted hands at her sides. She wanted to be with them! Instead she was wasting her time being brainwashed by a bunch of Deviants. Stifling a curse, she reached for her phone to call Jennings and quit. No! She had to follow through. It was the only way to get promoted and keep Tata and Kyle safe *and* well fed.

Biting her lip, she opened the freezer to see what she could cook.

"The Deviants will be sent to reformation camps," the announcer said, "where professional doctors and psychologists will remove the brainwashing and reprogram them to become normal, productive members of society."

She'd heard the words before, but for some reason, they sounded more sinister now. Were her parents being programmed? What did that entail? And why didn't it sound like a good thing? More importantly, why did the Neflams insist they receive no visitors during the process?

She pulled out a frozen pizza, set it on the counter, and turned on the oven.

"And in technical news, President Aali announced today that the scientists in his company, Medical Access Renewal Kontrol, in association with the Neflams, have nearly perfected the ETN-666 vaccine. If what he says is true, this vaccine has the technical capability to merge human and machine to eradicate all known diseases, prolong human life by a century, and enhance both muscular and mental capacities to a level only dreamed of before. The age of the superhuman has come."

"Wow," Kyle whistled. "Doesn't that sound great? Can't wait to get it!"

"It's the Mark of the Beast," Tata responded calmly, "And you will do no such thing."

Kyle cast her a scathing glance but remained quiet.

It actually *did* sound good to Nyla. The Neflams had promised this kind of progress when they first arrived. Soon mankind would not only be free of war and famine but disease as well. And they would live longer, maybe forever, in healthy, strong bodies. This was the progress Nyla hoped for with the NWU. She must keep her thoughts on that and not on the strange happenings of the Deviants.

She unwrapped the pizza, placed it in the oven, and made up her mind. She would get a new com piece, and maybe a backup one, contact Calan, and somehow get back to Zions' Nest.

Her phone was ringing, distant, echoing, clanging like a runaway train on the peaceful tracks of her sleep. Groping for it on the table beside her bed, Nyla picked it up and punched the button. "Hello."

"Nyla?"

"Calan?" She rubbed her eyes and sat up, searching for her clock. 5:00 a.m. "What is it? What's the matter?"

"It's about Terrance. I'm sorry to wake you." His voice broke slightly. "I'll let you get back to sleep."

Exhaustion tugged at her, luring her to lie back down, ignore the rude interruption. No. This was her assignment. "It's okay. What's going on?"

"I'm outside your apartment. Want to go for a ride?"

At five in the morning? Nyla let out a ragged sigh. "Sure. Be down in a sec." Rising, she flipped on a light, leapt into her jeans and tossed a tee-shirt over her head. She peered into a mirror, attempting to tame her wavy hair, then finally gave up. Dark circles framed her tired eyes, and she didn't have a lick of makeup on. But who was she trying to impress? Calan? Ha. Ludicrous.

After guzzling down a couple gulps of yesterday's coffee, Nyla crept past a snoring Kyle, grabbed her keys, and slipped out the door.

It was rarely cool in South Florida, even at this time of morning, but a refreshing breeze whipped around her as she descended the stairs and took the walkway to the street. The gentle rumbling of Calan's Harley brought an odd comfort to her. When her eyes met his, the streetlight reflected sorrow and pain within them, not the usual hope and kindness.

"You okay? What's up with Terrance?"

"Hop on. Let's go watch the sun rise." He handed her a helmet.

Strapping it on, she slid behind him and reached her hands around his waist. He patted them gently with his own before he put the bike in gear and drove off. For some reason, that small act of affection touched her deeply. Only then did she remember she'd forgotten her com piece. After she'd called Marco and explained what had happened, it finally started working again by the time she went to bed. Even so, she set up a meeting with him at eight that morning in their same spot to get a backup com piece just in case.

Calan spun around a corner and revved the bike faster down the nearly vacant street. Most of the rioters had either given up, passed out, or been rounded up over the past few days. Wind, ripe with the smell of soot and the sea, blasted over her face, spinning her hair behind her. Another scent filled her nostrils...Calan's unique scent—masculine, raw, and spicy—that had no rival to any aftershave she'd smelled. She felt free on this bike with this man, flying through the dark streets of a broken city as if they could ride forever through the dismal world until they found a place of light with no fear, no war, no danger.

A utopia that didn't exist.

What was she thinking? The Neflams were here to create such a world. The man in front of her was fighting against it. But right now, she didn't care. Didn't want to care about anything.

He roared into a parking lot at the beach, locked his bike, set the helmets on top, and before she could protest, took her hand in his and led her to the water. His hand was rough, calloused, and harbored a restrained strength she'd not expected. It engulfed hers in a shield of warmth and safety she was unaccustomed to feeling. She enjoyed it and hated herself for it.

A few streetlamps spread crumbs of light over the sand but enough to see that the beach was vacant except for a few homeless curled up in sleeping bags. Normally the NWU rounded up anyone out past curfew, but they always missed a few.

They walked along the shore for several minutes, the light of a half-moon painting silver over the edges of incoming waves. All the while, Calan never said a word, neither did he let go of her hand.

She tugged, stopping him. "What is it? Tell me." She strained to see his face in the shadows.

"It's Terrance." He frowned and stared over the black sea, where the faintest hint of gray lit the horizon. Then, leading her away from the water, he plopped down in the sand.

She sat beside him, waiting for him to continue.

"They caught him evangelizing in France."

France? Nyla drew her knees to her chest. Impossible.

"They are going to broadcast his execution over all media at 7:00 a.m. our time."

Nyla was still stuck on *France*. How could he have gotten from Florida to France in less than a day? "Wait. They don't kill people for that. We...they put them in camps."

"There's a new edict from NWU, coming down from Aali himself. All Deviants found proselytizing are to be put to death immediately."

Nyla hadn't heard that. But of course, she wasn't in a position to be informed of any new edicts.

"Everyone at Zion's Nest is praying for him. I just couldn't stay there anymore. They are all going to watch it on the TV. I couldn't. Couldn't do it. I had to get away...out of there... I wanted to see you. Watch the sun rise. It always reminds me of God's faithfulness." His jaw stiffened, where she could now see the faintest shadow of morning stubble.

God's faithfulness? In allowing his friend to die? Nyla had no words...no idea what to say. Of course, it was great Calan thought so much of her that he wanted to share his pain...trust her with his feelings. That played well into her assignment. On the other hand, her heart went out to him. He and Terrance seemed close, and she knew the agony of losing a friend.

"I still can't believe they would kill him," she mumbled.

Calan snorted. "We knew it was coming. Either out in the open or secretly in the camps."

"Come on. They don't kill people in the camps. They help reform them, get them ready to go back to society."

Calan glanced at her, his blue eyes coming into focus in the pre-dawn light. "You still don't get it."

Nyla slipped her hand into his and squeezed. "I'm trying. I want to." She lied, but even as she thought that, she found a part of her wanted it to be true, wanted to understand this man.

"If only I could take you to a camp to see what goes on." He shook his head but gripped her hand tighter. "Do you ever wonder why they never let you see your parents?"

Nyla raised a brow. "I thought you said they weren't even there."

"Precisely. But for those who've been arrested since the Rapture, it's a living hell. And they don't last long. They line them up to have their heads chopped off with a guillotine."

Nyla laughed. "That's ridiculous and barbaric. The guillotine hasn't been used since the French Revolution." She tried to determine from his expression whether he'd been kidding, but he remained serious. "How do you know?"

"Daniel had a vision."

Yeah, right. Just when she thought he might have some actual proof. "Well, one thing is for sure. With the new edict, you and the others need to stop preaching here on the beach."

"Not going to happen. Not if I know Daniel."

"Then you're going to get arrested. Just like we were before. Only this time, you'll all be killed."

"Then God will set us free."

She felt like screaming at his ignorance. "And if He doesn't?"

"His will be done." He smiled, that boyish smile of his, and lifted her hand to his lips.

She hadn't expected his kiss. It hadn't exactly been a romantic moment, but the warmth of his lips on her skin did odd things to her body, things that went beyond physical pleasure.

Crud. What was wrong with her?

He dropped her hand, suddenly awkward. "Sorry, don't know what made me do that."

"No. I liked it." She grabbed his hand again and smiled.

A sparkle of delight appeared in his eyes before he grew shy again and stared out to sea.

At that very moment, the sun peeked over the horizon as if the creator of the bright orb was pleased with them. Restraining a chuckle, Nyla pressed the scar on her neck. How silly of her to even think such a thing. These Deviants were rubbing off on her.

Is that a bad thing? A voice, deep and calm, spoke from within, so clear, so loud, that she tapped her ear, thinking Marco was there.

But of course, she'd forgotten her com piece.

Wind tossed her hair every which way, and Calan moved a strand from her face and slid it behind her ear. His fingers dropped to her neck, to the scar she hated.

"What happened?" he asked.

Removing his fingers, she covered it up with her hand, suddenly self-conscious. "It's nothing."

"Looks like it might have hurt, though."

"Yeah." She studied him for a moment, then dropped her gaze to the sand. The story wasn't exactly flattering, but what did she care about what this man thought? "When I was a rookie PK, I thought the officer with me had my back. We were checking out an abandoned shop, and this creep came out of nowhere and sliced me with a knife. Like I said, no big deal." She hated to talk about it, to bring back memories of her failures, of trusting people who always let her down.

"And your partner didn't come to your aid?"

"I don't know. He took off. Left me to fight my attacker." Abandoned a new PK out on her first assignment. And he was never reprimanded.

Calan smiled. "My brave little warrior."

She raised one playful brow. That's the second time he'd called her that, but this time it didn't seem to bother her. She touched the diamond-shaped scar yet again. "I should get it fixed."

"Why?" Calan gripped her hand and pulled it away. "It's part of you. Like a badge, it shows your courage."

Shocked, she stared at him. Marco had told her it was ugly, had asked her to get it removed.

Calan grew quiet again, his eyes closed, his face basking in the sun peeking over the horizon. A wave of peace seemed to wash over him so strong Nyla could sense it too. Strange. How could anyone find peace when their good friend was about to die and an asteroid was heading their way?

They sat there hand in hand for several minutes, eyes closed, listening to the waves lap and the seagulls squawk, feeling the warm rays of the rising sun. For the first time in her life, Nyla felt calm, unhurried, untroubled. As if sitting there with Calan, she was transported to another place where nothing bad ever happened, where there was nothing but love, joy, and peace.

And she found she never wanted to leave.

But of course, they couldn't stay there all day. People began to arrive, joggers, picnickers, surfers, and vendors.

Rising, Calan extended his hand and led her to the parking lot.

"You helped me, Nyla. Thanks for being there."

"I didn't do anything."

"More than you know." He brushed the back of his hand over her cheek, so gently, so lovingly, she closed her eyes. When she opened them, he was staring at her with those piercing blue eyes, a slight upward curve on his lips, strong jaw peppered with stubble and dark hair blowing in the wind. He was like a hero of old, a man of courage, honor, dignity who lived by a code of morality and decency he would never break. She had no idea men like him existed.

Of course, just her luck, he had to be crazy.

He wanted to kiss her. She could see it in his eyes. He wouldn't, of course. Most men she'd dated would have already tried to sleep with her. Not Calan. He was too honorable, too moral. For some reason, she loved that about him.

Standing on her tiptoes, she kissed him straight on the lips. Just a quick peck to show her interest. What happened next, she hadn't expected. Calan eased a hand behind her head and drew her lips back to his. Instantly, Mr. Awkward became Mr. Expert kisser, exploring, loving, caressing. Her toes tingled—toes that *never* tingled—and a flush of heat swept through her, swirling a pleasurable dance in her belly.

She never wanted him to stop.

Disappointment flooded her when he did. Breathless, he ran his fingers through her hair, then handed her the helmet.

The ride home was as magical as the ride to the beach. After he walked her to her door, he kissed her on the cheek and said he'd be in touch. Nyla stood there in front of her apartment, watching him ride away on his bike and all the while wondering if she'd finally lost all touch with reality.

And I saw thrones, and they sat on them, and judgment was committed to them. Then I saw the souls of those who had been beheaded for their witness to Jesus and for the word of God, who had not worshiped the beast or his image, and had not received his mark on their foreheads or on their hands. And they lived and reigned with Christ for a thousand years.
Revelation 20:4

Chapter 16

Nyla glanced down the aisle, searching for a bag of flour Tata had requested. Her grandmother loved to bake fresh bread when she had the energy *and* when Nyla could find flour and yeast. That would not be today, however, because except for a few boxes of crackers, the baking aisle was empty. Two years ago before the war, grocery stores were full of everything anyone could ever want. Nyla had taken it for granted, as had so many.

She swerved her cart into the next aisle, grabbed the last two cans of soup, and headed toward the checkout. Above the stations, a huge screen flashed news of the day, which she normally ignored, but nearly everyone in the store had stopped to stare.

Nyla had to grip the cart to keep from falling. It was Terrance. She was sure of it. Five NWU European Regional Peace Officers restrained him, while another man read the charges against him.

"For the crime of proselytizing the forbidden false religion of Christianity and hence committing treason against the New World Union, you will be beheaded. May our Creators have mercy on your soul."

What? Beheaded? So, Calan had been right. The camera zoomed in on Terrance. It was him all right. He *was* in France. But...how? Even if he'd taken a jet...which he couldn't do without papers...wait. A look of perfect peace and joy beamed from the old man's face. He glanced into the sky and smiled. "Forgive them, Lord." His words came out clear and strong. Two men gripped his arms and dragged him to a guillotine in the middle of a city square. An angry mob of people circled the spectacle, held back by armed officers.

"I see heaven open and my Lord standing at the right hand of God!" Terrance shouted over the noise as the two men forced him to his knees and shoved his head into the holder.

Nyla's heart seized. Her thoughts flew, finding no rational place to land. She'd just seen this man not three days ago. Whoa. What? Standing on either side of the guillotine, two bright figures appeared, towering over everyone, their massive wings spread out in glittering array. These were not the glowing warriors she'd seen before. Those had no wings, at least none she could see, and these beside Terrance had no weapons. She glanced around at the crowd in the store. Did they see them too? But though some looked horrified at the scene, no one seemed shocked.

The order was given. The blade dropped. The crowd on the scene cheered. Instantly, the bright figures shot up into the sky, so fast she could hardly see them. Was it her imagination or were there three instead of two?

The scene switched to the incoming asteroid and people went back to their shopping.

Heart pounding, Nyla passed her cart though the scanning arch, swiped the QR code on her phone that Jennings had sent her, and left.

A numbness overcame her as if she were stuck in a reoccurring dream. No, a nightmare and one from which she could not escape. Maybe she *was* going crazy. Only one cure for that. Seeing Marco. He would set her straight. He was her rock, her grounding in reality.

"So, you falling for this guy?" Marco's angry voice blared over her com piece.

Nyla sat on the bench, stunned. She'd been so excited to see him, to talk to him, that she'd gotten there early, retrieved the com piece in the small package under the bench and quickly inserted it in her ear. She hadn't seen him until he stepped from behind a lifeguard station.

A flutter passed through her at the sight of him.

Until she heard the fury in his tone.

"What are you talking about?"

Marco stood roughly twenty yards away, handsome as ever, his black wavy hair tossed in the wind. Too far to see his eyes.

"I saw you."

Nyla swallowed.

"I saw you," he repeated. "With him on the beach earlier. You kissed him!"

Horrified, Nyla thought back to that magical moment. She hadn't seen Marco there. In truth, she hadn't seen much of anything but Calan. "What were you doing here so early?"

"What does it matter? I saw you."

"Listen." Nyla bit her lip and tried to make out the expression on his face but couldn't. "It's just part of my role. I have to get close to him, get him to trust me, so I can get to Daniel."

Marco crossed arms over his chest and faced the sea. "You enjoyed it. I could tell. I know you, Nyla."

He was right, of course. She *had* enjoyed the kiss. "I'm sorry. It's not what it looked like," was all she could think to say. "You know you are the only one for me, Marco."

"Humph."

If she knew one thing about Marco, it was his enormous vanity and his volatile insecurity. "Why would I want someone like him when I already have the best thing going?"

"True." He shook his head, then turned to face her. "I just hate seeing you with him. I miss you. I want this to be over."

"Me too. I'm working on it. I'm close to them now. I just need to go back to their hideout when Daniel is there. Only a few more days, I promise."

"Then I want you back in my bed, babe."

Whenever he had spoken so seductively in the past, her entire body would react. For some reason, she felt nothing now. Odd. She was probably just tired, or maybe she was still in shock from Terrance's beheading. Not the beheading itself, but the look on his face, what he had said...what she had seen.

"Soon enough. We'll be together again," she said with less enthusiasm than she intended. "So, there's a new beheading edict for proselytizing?"

"Yeah, about time. Maybe that will stop these Deviants from spreading their dangerous propaganda."

"Why the guillotine? So archaic?"

"It's clean, effective. More humane than electrocution or poison. I'm coming closer. I want to see you." He started for her when her phone rang.

It was Kyle's ring tone, the Imperial March from Star Wars. He never called her.

She pressed the green button. "What is it?"

"It's Tata. She's sick."

Indira stood beside Tata, a look of sorrow on his face.

Ranoss laid a hand on his shoulder. "Never fear, Indira. This is all part of the Father's plan."

"I know." Indira nodded. "I do not enjoy watching her suffer. She has endured so much in her life."

Zhaviel approached the two angels. "Much by her own doing."

"Indeed." Indira stared down at Tata lying feverish in bed. "But not since she joined the Kingdom. She has done much good. She can still do much good."

Ranoss gripped the hilt of his sword and glanced at the salivating demons they kept at bay around the room. "Indeed. The Father's plans are always good. This illness has a purpose."

Indira glanced up at him. "It will not take her?"

Ranoss shook his head. "I know not. The Father has not said." He spun to see Nyla enter and rush to her grandmother's side. He smiled. "She loves her so much."

The dark spirits growled at the mighty warriors.

Zhaviel growled back and raised his club at them. "We will keep the spirits of death from her as per the Father's orders."

"Aye." Ranoss studied Nyla, then snapped his gaze to the demons, a rare sense of unease traveling through him. "They want her as well. They seek her death while she still remains in the darkness."

"You must not lose faith." Indira gripped Ranoss' arm. "We will do as the Father wishes, and all will be well."

"Would that I shared your optimism," Ranoss said. "Nyla has seen much already and still she does not believe."

A trumpet sounded, loud and long. All three angel warriors glanced up, their faces stern, their bodies tight, ready to battle.

"Am I doing the right thing?" Calan leaned back on the couch and crossed arms over his chest. "She's not a believer."

Daniel sat on the edge of the table that doubled for his desk and studied Calan with that intense gaze of his.

Calan hated that gaze. He felt like a bug under a microscope, having every inch of his insides dissected and analyzed. He had told Daniel about the kiss. He wanted Daniel to tell him not to see Nyla again, to warn him away from danger. That would be the only way—except a direct word from God from a burning bush—that Calan would be able to resist the charming lady.

"You have feelings for her." Daniel smiled.

Calan frowned. "You know my past."

"What does that have to do with anything?"

Stunned, Calan raked back his hair. "It has everything to do with it. I don't want to make the same mistake. My weakness, as you know, is beautiful women."

"And is that all Nyla is, a beautiful woman?"

No. If he were honest, she was different, special—strong, courageous, yet feminine, smart, witty, kind. She intrigued him. She surprised him. He couldn't get her out of his thoughts.

Calan leaned forward, arms on his knees. "I can't afford another mistake. There's too much at stake."

"You are referring to the woman you trusted with your brother."

Claire. Just thinking her name made his gut churn with rage. "She had me completely fooled. I was so taken with her."

"You aren't that man anymore."

"Then why am I falling for a non-believer? Didn't the Apostle Paul tell us not to mix with non-believers?"

"He said not to marry them, yes." Daniel grinned. "Are you thinking of marrying Nyla?"

Snorting, Calan hung his head. "No. But why start something I can't finish?"

"Have you prayed about it?"

"Yes. I'm just not hearing an answer. So, I come to you. Tell me what to do. I feel like I should cut things off." He flattened his lips.

"I won't tell you what to do, Calan. You need to hear from God yourself. It's part of growing in your faith. Just follow the leading of the Spirit."

"Part of my training, huh?" He shook his head. "And I thought SEAL Team training was hard."

A trumpet blared from above.

Daniel stood, the muscles in his face stiffening. "Here we go."

Then the second angel sounded: And something like a great mountain burning with fire was thrown into the sea, and

a third of the sea became blood. And a third of the living creatures in the sea died, and a third of the ships were destroyed.
Revelation 8:8-9

"Nyla!" Kyle shouted, hysteria in his voice.

Now what? Nyla kissed her grandmother's feverish forehead and rushed into the living room. She barely glanced at her brother before her eyes snapped to the TV where the video of a massive burning asteroid filled the screen.

"Oh my gosh, where is it?"

"It's here!" Kyle screamed, his voice cracking. "Just broke through our atmosphere!"

"What you are seeing is a live picture," the announcer blared. "The New World Union's top astronomers, along with the Neflams, have been unable to deflect this monster. By all projections, it will hit us within seconds." The newscaster stopped talking and stared into the screen as if he was too frightened to talk. The colleague beside him took over.

"It does appear, however," the attractive blond said, "that it will strike the sea." She pressed a hand to her ear. "What's that?" Her eyes grew big. "I am hearing that it has hit the Atlantic Ocean. Oh, my God, it has hit!"

The screen went black for a moment before a video reappeared of the asteroid striking the sea, causing a towering wave that spread out in all directions. The water churned and bubbled around the impact spot where the huge rock yanked the sea down with it like a massive sink hole.

Nyla lowered to sit. Kyle stood, panting as if he couldn't breathe. He took up a pace. "I can't believe this! I can't believe this! Are we going to get hit by another tsunami?"

"Calm down. Let's just wait and find out."

"We should go! Get Tata." Kyle rushed to the door, searching for Nyla's keys. Thankfully, they were still in her pocket.

"If it's another tsunami, where are we going to go?" Nyla said. "It's too late to evacuate. Come on, Kyle, sit down."

"Sit down! Are you nuts?" Kyle grabbed his bottle of CBD pills, opened it, and downed a handful.

Great. Now if they needed to evacuate, her brother would be useless.

"The water appears to be turning red," the announcer was saying, drawing Nyla's attention back to the screen.

A red film rose from where the asteroid had struck and spread out in circular waves like a drop of food coloring in a bowl of water.

Nyla leapt up and dashed into her grandmother's room. Grabbing her Bible, she opened it to Revelation and skimmed the pages. Her heart nearly stopped beating as she read the words that confirmed what had just happened.

Can't be. It just can't be.

Tata was so warm, *too* warm. Nyla gently brushed her grandmother's hair from her face as she leaned on Nyla's shoulder in the waiting room of the NWU's health center.

"Pajarito, you shouldn't go to all this trouble for an old lady."

"Don't be silly, Tata. You have a fever. It's best to get checked out and see what's wrong."

She had waited to hear of any tsunami warnings, but when they cleared Florida from any danger, Nyla had been quick to get Tata downstairs into her Jeep. Unfortunately, the waiting room was packed, and since all Tata had was a fever, they put them on a list and told them to sit. And sit...and sit...another change brought on by the NWU that didn't seem to be working as well as they hoped. But at least everyone's health care was free now.

A TV hanging on the wall showed video after video of the asteroid hitting the sea in the middle of the North Atlantic. Due to its size and weight and the location of the strike, the resulting tsunamis that were predicted to hit the northern coasts of the North American and European Regions would be dangerous only to those near the shore but would not bring complete devastation. Even so, major evacuations had begun for all coastal cities north of Virginia Beach. Worse, however, were the ships that seemed to drop off, one by one, from satellite view as the tsunamis traversed the sea in a giant wave of red that was killing off all sea life in its path.

Tata lifted a shaky finger to the screen. "A third of sea life will die and a third of ships will be destroyed."

Exactly what Nyla had read in the Bible earlier. "It's okay." Nyla took her hand in hers and squeezed. "Don't worry about such things."

Tata let out a sigh, too weak to respond. The newscaster continued. "Scientists have yet to determine exactly what this red tide is, but they are saying that it is quite deadly."

Of course. Exactly what the Bible had said. Nyla wanted to scream. She could make no sense if it, and honestly, didn't want to. She had a job to do, and she intended to complete it with success.

Thankfully, the nurse finally called them back to a small windowless room that smelled of bleach and something sour. After a thorough examination and several tests, the doctor, an aged man with a hawk nose and black-rimmed glasses that refused to stay in place, drew Nyla aside.

"I'm afraid it's not good news, Miss." He scribbled something onto the chart in his hand.

Nyla's blood raced, making her dizzy. "What is it?"

"I believe it's melioidosis, a rare tropical disease we don't encounter very often."

"Tropical…"

"Yes." He continued making notes, never once making eye contact. "Unfortunately, we have not caught it early enough for successful treatment."

Sterile white walls and fluorescent lights spun in Nyla's vision like a nightmarish cyclone. She needed to ask intelligent questions, but she couldn't think of anything to ask except, "What are you saying?"

"You can expect pneumonia-type symptoms, cough, shortness of breath, fatigue, nausea, fever, and an irritating rash. Keep her as comfortable as possible."

"But you have medicine for her, right?"

He stopped scribbling and stared at her with a look of bewilderment. "Of course. I will prescribe what she needs, but like I said, the disease is quite advanced, and it may be too late."

Nyla gripped his arm, her emotions oscillating between hysteria and confusion. "But there's still hope."

Jerking from her grip as if she had a contagion, he emitted an annoyed grunt, signed the papers, and handed them to the nurse. "I wouldn't cling to any if I were you. She's eighty, after all."

And with that, he stormed out of the room, the nurse following close behind.

And fear not those who kill the body but cannot kill the soul: But rather fear him who is able to destroy both soul and body in hell. Matthew 10:28

Chapter 17

Flames the color of blood leapt toward a sky of charcoal—snakes of lava bubbling and oozing in a demonic dance of death. Heat, hotter than the hottest day in Florida, baked Nyla. Sweat streamed down her back and matted hair to her head. Hideous screams for help punctured her ears and spiked terror through her. In the distance, jagged mountains of coal stood like sentinels. Where was she?

A creature more reptilian than human crossed in front of her. It stopped, stared at her as if she were an oddity, then hissed so forcefully, she nearly fell backward. The stench of sulfur and feces suffocated her. Bending over, she gasped for air. But there was little air, most of it being consumed by the fires blazing all around her. The creature darted away.

Human shadows moved between the fires. Screams and moans continued, accompanied by curses of rage. A burst of flame shot into the sky, firing red, burning balls.

A man in singed clothing and soot on his face darted up to her, his eyes wide with terror. "Have you come to get us out?" He gripped her arm and squeezed so tight, Nyla let out a yelp.

"I'm not supposed to be here. There's been a mistake!" Terror streaked across the man's gaunt face as he tightened his grip.

Pain lanced up Nyla's arm into her neck. She tried to tug from him, but he refused to release her. "Let me go!"

"Did He send you to get me out?" He screamed. "Did He? Did He? Take me out! Get me out of here!"

Nyla woke with a start. Her breath came hard and fast. She stared into the dark room, trying to focus on anything, anything that would tell her she was home in her own bed. Finally, her ceiling came into view, her mother's painting of a tall ship at sea formed on the wall, along with the edge of her dresser. A strip of morning sun speared through a crack in her curtains, landing on a stuffed monkey hanging on her bed post.

A dream. Just a dream.

Then why was she so hot? Flipping back her covers, she sat up and wiped sweat from her neck and arms. What was happening to her?

Maybe the dream meant something. Tata!

Leaping to her feet, Nyla opened her door and rushed into Tata's bedroom. Her grandmother had fallen fast asleep last night after taking her medicine, so Nyla had left her alone. But could the fever have gotten worse during the night? Nyla knelt before the bed, careful not to wake her, but Tata's eyes slowly opened. A smile formed on her lips.

"My Pajarito…" She raised a hand to caress Nyla's cheek.

Thankfully, it was not too hot, at least no hotter than it had been yesterday and no more than a week ago when she'd taken her to the doctor. Maybe that meant she would recover, that the medicines were working, or the doctor had been wrong? Nyla hoped so with all her heart.

She took Tata's hand in hers. "How are you feeling?"

"Good." Her words came out breathless.

"I don't believe you."

Tata squeezed her hand. "Please, don't worry about me. You have too much to concern yourself with these days, too much for one so young."

"But I cannot lose you. I *won't* lose you." Moisture burned in her eyes. "Besides, you can't leave me alone with Kyle."

Tata laughed. "God will take me when it's time."

Nyla scowled. "Well, in the meantime, I'm going to take good care of you." She reached for the digital thermometer on the table. "First, I'm taking your temperature, and then I'm going to make you breakfast and give you your medicine."

"And then you're going to go about your day as normal," Tata began, but started coughing as Nyla took her temperature.

A hundred degrees. Down a little from yesterday. Good.

Tata continued, "I don't wish to be a burden. I don't want any extra care."

"We'll see about that." Nyla stood, then helped Tata to sit.

"Hand me my Bible, will you, dear?"

Nyla grabbed it from the table and gave it to her grandmother. "I'll be back with breakfast."

Out in the living room, Kyle was in his usual spot on the couch. However, this time he was awake. So early? Nyla glanced at the clock. 7:00 a.m.

Instead of asking him, which would only elicit a sarcastic response, she snapped her gaze to the TV, where President Aali spoke from behind a podium.

"Asteroids have been hitting our planet for years. This is nothing to fear. I encourage you all to remain calm in the face of these minor catastrophes." He smiled that smile of his that spoke of peace and hope. It always had a calming effect on Nyla's nerves. Apparently it did the same for Kyle, who sank into the cushions with a sigh.

"Rest assured, the Neflams are sharing technology that will not only give Earth ample warning of any dangerous incoming asteroids in the future, but that will be able to easily divert such massive rocks away from our planet."

Reporters in the audience began shouting questions.

President Aali lifted a hand to quiet them. "Since the Neflams arrived, we have learned much from them. They are more than willing to teach us everything about their advanced civilization. However, in this case, we had not gotten to that chapter in the book yet." He laughed at his own joke and others in the audience joined him. "But we will be more prepared in the future."

The camera panned to the thousands of people who had gathered to listen to him.

"We are working hard, along with the other leaders of the New World Union, to create a new world for us all, a better world, a world of social and economic justice, an advanced civilization where we live longer, happier, healthier, and better lives."

The crowd cheered.

"As with any great and historic endeavor, there will be bumps along the road, but I assure you that in the end, it will have all been worth it, both for us and for our descendants. We have entered a new age, the dawn of a great awakening! So, be at peace, my fellow earthlings. Be at peace!"

The crowd went wild with shouts of praise and approval.

Nyla stood there, mesmerized. This was just what she needed to shake off the hypnotic influence of the Deviants and ground herself back in reality, back to her real purpose, to aid the NWU in making the world a peaceful and prosperous utopia.

Smiling, she headed toward the kitchen as the newscasters switched to other news. Riots had broken out in several cities due to food shortages. NWU troops were having a hard time containing the angry mobs, who now realized that with the asteroid's strange red tide, seafood would be in short supply, along with the lost cargo on many destroyed ships.

Nyla opened the fridge, found a couple of eggs and a carton of orange juice, and set them on the counter before she started the coffee.

"Despite tsunami warnings, crowds of people line the shores on both sides of the Atlantic to offer sacrifices to the asteroid gods," the newscaster was saying, and even Kyle chuckled.

Nyla glanced at the TV to see people, with hands raised, kneeling in the sand, crying with loud voices. Every incoming wave deposited more dead fish, adding to the piles already lining the shore. She couldn't make out what they were saying, but a reporter stopped one to ask.

"The asteroid is a sign," the elder lady said. "A sign that the end is near! You see the bloody water? There is no forgiveness without the shedding of blood! We must pray to the god of the asteroid for forgiveness and beg for his mercy."

The reported slanted her lips. "And who is this god?"

"He is Lucifer, the prince of the power of the air."

The reporter scrunched her face. "Wait, isn't that Satan?" But the woman had gone back to worshipping.

"And there you have it. Doomsayers on both sides," the blond newscaster said from the studio. "Those who follow the mythical God of creation and those who follow his adversary. Both say the end is near."

The man beside her shrugged. "Then why not arrest these people as well?"

"They are harmless, Pete. The Deviants, however, preach against the NWU, which is traitorous."

Weird people everywhere. Nyla scooped the coffee into the filter, poured in water, and turned on the pot.

"What you doing up so early?" Kyle finally spoke to her.

"I was going to ask you the same thing." Nyla cracked open the eggs in a bowl.

Kyle stood and grinned. "I have an interview."

Nyla dropped an eggshell on the floor and turned to stare at her brother.

"Yes, I know. A shock," he said.

Only then did she notice he had shaved and wore a clean pair of jeans and a decent shirt. "For a job, as in *working*?"

He cocked an eyebrow. "I know you think I'm a loser, just like Dad did, but yes, as a guard in one of the reformation camps."

"A guard?" Excitement buzzed through her. "Maybe where Mom and Dad are?" Nyla bent to pick up the eggshell, trying to process what her brother was saying.

"Probably not." Kyle shoved hands in the pockets of his jeans. "Who knows where they sent them, but we'll see."

"I think that's great." Nyla turned on the stove and slapped some butter in the pan before facing her brother. "I'm proud of you."

He gave her a skeptical look and then shrugged. "Anyway, gotta run."

It wasn't until after he'd slammed the door that Nyla realized she'd have to find someone to watch over Tata if she went anywhere, especially with her being sick now. But, wow, her little doped-up brother was finally growing up. Amazing.

She finished the eggs, poured some coffee and orange juice for Tata, and started for her bedroom when the loud blare of a trumpet shook the building.

Oh no, not again.

Then the third angel sounded: And a great star fell from heaven, burning like a torch, and it fell on a third of the rivers and on the springs of water. The name of the star is Wormwood. A third of the waters became wormwood, and many men died from the water, because it was made bitter.
Revelation 8:10-11

"Pam, thank you for having me over so quickly." Nyla smiled at the young woman standing at the doorway of a very modest, single-family home in what once was a middle-class neighborhood.

"Of course, come in." Pam stepped out of the way and led Nyla into a living room stuffed with old but comfy-looking couches and chairs. The smell of some kind of fruity tea and baked bread made Nyla's mouth water. After the comet struck, she'd been so shocked, she'd forgotten to eat, and here it was nearly 2:00 in the afternoon.

"It isn't my home. It's actually Maddy's. But after my family left, I had nowhere to go. Have a seat. I'll get you some tea." Pam disappeared around the corner as Nyla sank onto a chair beside front windows that took up nearly the entire wall. Outside, afternoon sunlight turned the charred remains of what once was a rose garden into gray, thorny skeletons. With all the grass and trees burned, South Florida had transformed into a black and white world—the way TV shows looked before color.

Nyla had served Tata breakfast, and together they'd watched the news. A massive comet had entered the atmosphere, broken up into dozens of smaller comets, and struck fresh water sources all over the earth—lakes, ponds, rivers, even penetrating in some cases to ground water. What remained of the Everglades was hit too, though by the time Nyla had gone outside to look at the sky, the comets had already landed. Tata had read to her the prophecy from Revelation, which only made Nyla more confused and angry. Yes, angry, though she didn't know why exactly.

So, after Kyle returned from his interview—which went well, he said—Nyla called Pam. She wanted to call Calan, but he would just feed her the same garbage Tata was spouting. And although Pam was one of them, she seemed a little more normal, if one could call any of these Deviants normal. Nyla wanted answers, needed some rational explanation or even a hint of one to keep her from going nuts.

Pam returned with two steaming cups and took a seat beside Nyla on the couch. "No cream or sugar, I'm afraid."

"That's fine." Nyla took the cup and smiled.

"I hope you don't mind, but I called Daniel to ask about the third trumpet, and he is heading over with a few of the others."

Nyla sipped her tea. Did she mind? Not if Daniel was coming. Madeline's house was much closer to NWU quarters, and she had her com piece tight in her ear. Maybe all this nonsense would finally be over. Yet, instead of feeling excitement, her thoughts immediately drifted to Calan, wondering if he was coming. Crazy girl.

"I don't mind at all. It will be nice to see them." Nyla set down her cup. "But first I want your opinion on the comet and the third trumpet. I can't make sense of it."

The low rumble of a Harley sparked Nyla's heart, and she turned to see Calan and another car drive up and park in front of the house.

Pam sipped her tea. Concern and something else…almost like love, not a sexual kind, but a real care, filled her blue eyes. "I hear you, Nyla. I've been where you are. I always believed in God, but the rest of this stuff? I know it seems crazy." She reached out and placed a hand on top of Nyla's. "But it's true. It's all true. Surely you can see that now."

Nyla bit her lip and sank back on the couch, staring at her friend. Could God be real? All this time? The thought ignited hope in every cell, every fiber of her being. But then a chill passed over her, prickling her skin.

Shadows dimmed the room. Pam closed her eyes. A bright flash swept through the air, shoving the darkness away.

A knock on the door brought Pam to her feet.

Nyla didn't have to see Calan to know he'd entered and was standing right behind her. There was a presence about him that stirred something within her like no one ever had. She hated it. She didn't want to like these people.

Daniel hugged Pam and took a seat across the room from Nyla. Smiling, he gave her a look as if they'd known each other all their lives. She didn't want to like him either, because one way or another, she intended to see him locked up.

"I didn't expect to see you here." Calan attempted to keep the delight out of his voice as he sat in a chair beside Nyla. He'd not seen her since their kiss, and he wondered what her reaction to him would be. Would she push him away, disgusted, or would she draw closer as he hoped?

Her gorgeous brown curls were as unruly as ever. She slid one wayward strand behind her ear in that cute gesture of hers that made her seem almost shy. But that couldn't be the case. Not for this brave warrior. She lifted those creamed coffee colored eyes to him again, and what he saw within them was anything but disgust.

"I wanted to ask Pam about the comet," she said.

Calan glanced over at Pam, who was talking with Tyson and Madeline. "I'm glad you're friends."

"I wouldn't say that, though I do like her." She smiled. "She's the only one who gave me her number."

Calan chuckled. He'd given her his number, but he wouldn't mention that. Maybe she needed a woman's perspective. "Well, I'm glad you're here."

She glanced over the people hugging and greeting each other as if she'd never seen such a sight. Maybe she hadn't. After the virus hit, people rarely hugged. Even after it dissipated, it seemed like people thought it was far too dangerous to be affectionate.

"Daniel will talk about the comet soon, and what's coming next." He drew back Nyla's gaze.

Her eyes widened and a disingenuous smile graced her lips, which startled Calan. He'd never known the lady not to be up front. She rubbed her ear.

"He's also going to talk about new churches he's planting," he continued. "And lead a small Bible study."

She dropped her hand from her ear. "Good."

Good? Hmm. He attempted a smile. He needed to be patient with her. All this was new to someone who'd been in the opposing camp.

The noise of chatter rose, accompanied by Javier, who had begun to play guitar. Poor Nyla. She glanced around like a chicken in a fox den. She pressed fingers over the scar on her neck, as she seemed always to do when she felt uneasy, out of place, insecure.

"Well, I better get to it." Calan slapped hands on his knees and rose.

"Get to what?"

"Cooking dinner. Wanna help?" Standing, he extended his hand, happy when she took it.

What is happening to me, Lord? He prayed as he led her to the kitchen, his body and soul reacting to her touch. "Don't let me trust the wrong woman again. Don't let me make another mistake."

Bless the Lord, you His angels, who excel in strength, who do His word, heeding the voice of His word. Psalm 103:20

Chapter 18

Nyla had never seen anything like it. The kitchen was packed full of Deviants, each performing their assigned task for dinner. Nyla's job was to cut up vegetables for the salad. There weren't many, of course, but at least they had some fresh lettuce from Madeline's indoor hydroponic garden, along with a few tomatoes and carrots. Still, Nyla had not seen fresh produce like this in years, nor real meat *or* so many potatoes. Where had they gotten all this food? Sure, Calan and Tyson had jobs and VaxPasses, but even so, the grocery stores had very little food.

Every once in a while, she'd look up and find Calan staring at her as he assisted Tyson forming patties from hamburger meat. Something was surely wrong with her, because the man became more and more handsome each time she saw him. Of course it didn't help that she'd enjoyed his kiss. A lot. Marco had been right. She had no business allowing such intimacy. She was getting too involved.

She had to stay on task.

Which reminded her of her com piece. She'd been about to call Marco to alert the troops to come get Daniel, but then Calan had said Daniel intended to talk about the location of new Deviant hideouts. If she could not only get Daniel as prize, but several other Deviant locations, that would go a long way for her promotion up the NWU PK ladder. Besides, why the rush? Why not enjoy a good meal first?

Only they didn't get to enjoy it, at least not much of it. After it was prepared, they packed it up and drove it to the poorest section of town to distribute to the needy. Nyla got out of the car and stayed in the background, both her stomach and her disposition growling. Not that she didn't care about the poor. She did. But handing out a few meals wouldn't do much good in the long run. Only the NWU's plans to use Neflam technology to grow an abundance of food for equal distribution would see a world without hunger. That took time, President Aali had explained, but they were well on their way. Besides, Nyla could hear Daniel and the others forcing their Deviant ideas on the poor unsuspecting people who received free food. Always a price. There was always a price for everything.

No sooner was the food gone, than the crowd turned on the Deviants. Some shouted obscenities, others cursed the God they preached, while others took up stones to toss at them. A few threatened to report them to the NWU for proselytizing. Nyla couldn't have that. After all she'd gone through, she couldn't let the capture of Daniel Cain go to anyone but her. Besides, the penalty now was immediate beheading, and for some reason, that thought terrified her. Dashing forward, she tried to reach Daniel to convince him to leave, but Calan was not allowing anyone near him, particularly a few of the angriest people who advanced with rocks and baseball bats.

Nyla's fury rose, and she turned to face the mob with all the authority of her position, or her *former* position. "These kind people give you free food, and this is how you repay them?" she shouted at them over the noise.

Calan glanced at her, a look of fear *and* approval on his face.

"It's all right, Nyla," Daniel said. "God will protect us."

"We really should leave," Calan urged him. "Now."

"Not yet." Daniel's gaze swept over the mob as if he were searching for someone.

Pam yanked on Nyla's sleeve. "Let's go wait in the car."

"Everyone, back to the cars!" Tyson shouted, obvious terror in his voice. Odd, since none of the other Deviants seemed afraid at all. A glaze of fear covered the young man's eyes as he took one last look at the furious mob before racing back toward their vehicles.

Nyla agreed. They should leave. She'd seen groups like this quickly turn into violent mobs. Besides, they were greatly outnumbered.

A man in a wheelchair appeared out of the crowd and rolled toward them. A large, ruddy-faced woman with gray bushy hair pushed him, looking very determined.

A rock flew toward the Deviants. And another and another. All missing them by inches. More people emerged from the surrounding apartment buildings.

Nyla should leave, join Tyson, who appeared to be the only Deviant with common sense. But she couldn't keep her eyes off the chaotic scene.

Calan, Javier, Max, and Aaron formed a barricade in front of Daniel.

Daniel lifted his hands in the air and closed his eyes. "I thank You, Lord, for every soul here and pray they come to know You. I thank You for the miracle You are about to perform so that they may know that the one true and living God loves them beyond measure."

Nazare, sword hefted before him, charged the hoard of demonic spirits advancing toward the sons of Adam, Anisian and Ranoss by his side.

Halting, Ranoss snapped a flaming arrow in his crossbow and aimed it toward their leader, a reptilian-looking beast with a snaked tongue and four arms, each hand carrying a long knife.

He fired. The arrow struck the monster in the chest. With an agonizing roar, he gripped the arrow, trying to pull it out. The fire spread over his torso, his arms, his legs, and quickly consumed him. He toppled to the ground, the stench of his burning skin filling the air.

"Good shot," Anisian said as he advanced upon two smaller demons.

For a moment, the dark spirits seemed confused after their leader fell, but soon, they regrouped and continued their assault, shoving the humans they controlled toward the sons and daughters of God, floating in and out of them, filling them with hatred and rage.

But none of God's children were to be harmed this day. The word had come down from the Commander of Heaven's Armies.

Nazare swung his blade and sliced one of the devils in two, then quickly tossed his sword into his other hand and stabbed another demon coming up on his left.

Standing in front of Nyla, Ranoss deflected bricks and stones with his massive arm, then thrust his blade into the mob of vile beasts. Shrieks of agony emerged, along with the foul stench of sulfur and hatred.

"We need help! There are too many!" Ranoss shouted to his companions.

Nazare glanced up. "The Commander has sent reinforcements. We are to hold them off until they get here."

A large demon crept toward them, his elongated face and bulging eyes a testament to his eternal agony. He grinned, spit dripping from his mouth, and stared at Nazare as if he were a bug to be squashed. "You are no match for us, warrior of heaven."

"Come and see." Nazare hefted his blade in the air and swept it down upon the demon with a mighty clang!

Anisian glanced at Calan, his ward, proud that he was such a brave, strong warrior. Still, he could not know the totality of what he was up against—the growing mob of devilish spirits advancing in a raging wave of hatred. Anisian struck a charging demon, quickly dispatching him. More and more came. The humans were few compared to the dark spirits controlling them. So many! A spike of what humans might call fear shot up his spine. Nay, not fear, but a warning. He glanced toward the west.

Out of a bank of dark clouds, two winged beasts appeared, heading their way.

"Nazare, two fallen ones are fast approaching!"

Nazare followed his gaze to the west and stiffened at the sight.

"Why?" Ranoss fought off two demons at once, swinging his blade to the right and then quickly shooting a flaming arrow at another vile spirit on his left. "Why send the fallen ones for such a small battle?"

"There are many to be saved here today," Nazare responded just as a human in a wheelchair appeared in the crowd. "Some now, some later when the seeds planted are watered."

Ranoss positioned another arrow in his crossbow, blew a flame onto the tip, and aimed it toward the incoming fallen ones, angels as powerful as they, but filled with the evil of the master they followed.

"Surround the son of Adam in the chair!" Anisian shouted. "Protect him at all costs!"

The fallen ones landed behind the mob and drew the long swords at their sides. Wings that had once shimmered with golden filigree were now faded and hung in shreds. Garments that once reflected the majesty of their Holy Commander now reflected the depravity of their new commander, black, torn, and tattered. Yet their bodies remained strong, their countenances fierce, their eyes full of rage.

Ranoss fired. The tallest one ducked just in time, a vile grin on his face.

Now, what to do?

Calan spoke, drawing Anisian's gaze. The son of Adam prayed. He prayed for angelic protection, for God to intervene. He spoke Holy Words of the Most High, invoking promises of miracles and safety.

Finally.

A shout came from above. Nazare glanced up to see at least twenty of heaven's warriors descending, weapons drawn.

"Praise be to the Commander of Heaven's Armies!" Ranoss shouted.

The demonic hoard shrank back, hissing and moaning. The two fallen ones charged forward, ordering them back to task.

Nazare, Ranoss, Anisian and the new warriors formed a barricade between the sons of Adam and the forces of darkness.

Nyla felt like she was watching a movie, a mere spectator intruding on a scene that wasn't hers to watch—a fantasy film filled with actors who'd forgotten their part to play and instead, were just going crazy. Like a fast-growing mold, the angry crowd grew and grew, swelling and surging, a sea of raging fists in the air, spitting up foaming curses that pricked Nyla's ears.

Rocks flew through the air, bricks even, yet none of them struck the Deviants. Pam kept tugging on Nyla's sleeve, but she couldn't seem to move. Something crackled in the air, a power, an intensity, something that told her more was going on here than what she could see, which made no sense whatsoever.

That's when she saw them. The shadows. Only they weren't shadows. They moved and had limbs and faces—hideous faces frozen in expressions of pain and horror. They swarmed around the mob, whispering in people's ears, shoving them forward, churning them into a furious brew. Nyla shrank back, heart racing.

Pam gripped her arm. "What is it?"

The vision disappeared and in its place, light shone—bright, white light in human shapes, tall, muscular, armed with swords.

Clearly she was losing her mind. "Maybe we better go to the car," she mumbled and started to turn when she heard Calan praying, not a begging prayer, not a plea for safety, but a prayer of authority and power.

She halted. The glowing figures formed a wall between the Deviants and the mob. Then as quickly as they had appeared, they vanished from her sight.

Daniel pushed past Calan and the others, then knelt before the man in the wheelchair.

"He's not walked his whole life," the woman shouted over the roar of the crowd. "Can you help him?"

"Not I, but God can." Daniel took the man's hand in his and looked at him with more love than Nyla thought possible for a complete stranger.

"Do you want to be healed?"

The man nodded, desperation in his eyes.

"Do you believe Jesus can heal you?"

A moment passed. The woman squeezed her eyes shut as if she couldn't bear to watch.

"I do," the man said.

"Then in the name of Jesus, I command you to get up and walk."

Now the multitude of those who believed were of one heart and one soul; neither did anyone say that any of the things he possessed was his own, but they had all things in common. Acts 4:32

Chapter 19

The trip back to Madeline's house was a blur, like an out-of-body experience where you see everything that's happening but somehow aren't really there.

Smiling, Madeline handed Nyla a cup of tea. "Kinda crazy, huh?" The plump forty-something lady covered in tats sat beside her. "When I first joined, I was sure all those drugs I took had done a number on my brain."

Nyla's hands shook, and she set the tea down. "I'm still not even sure what happened."

Madeline touched Nyla's arm. Life and love beamed from her brown eyes. "You'll see soon enough."

"Did they really cast demons out of you?" Nyla wouldn't normally be so bold, but after everything that had happened, what did it matter?

Oddly, Madeline smiled. "They did... Dozens of them. I was a mess."

"What did they look like?"

Her brows rose. "The demons? No idea. I never saw them, but I felt them leave." She glanced over at Daniel talking with Calan. "One by one, I felt them leave, like thick chains falling off me."

Someone called her from the kitchen, and she promptly excused herself and left.

Shaken, Nyla picked up her cup again and took a sip. After Daniel had ordered the lame man to stand, he'd done just that. He rose, took a few steps, and then began praising God. The woman, who must have been his wife, flew into his arms so forcefully, he nearly fell back down.

Instantly, the crowd settled, staring at the miracle. Apparently most of them had known the man, knew he'd been crippled.

While the man and his wife embraced with tears of joy, Daniel took the opportunity to tell them what the Deviants called the Gospel. Nyla had heard it many times before, but for some reason, when Daniel spoke it this time, it didn't seem so absurd, so unbelievable, so crazy and religious. It made sense. If there was a God, and He wanted to reunite with His creation, to have a relationship with them and love them, but couldn't because of their sin, why not send His only Son to pay the price if that was the only way?

Nyla shook her head and glanced over the room. Others had joined the group after they'd returned. Javier was tuning his guitar, while his wife, Elena, sat beside him. Tyson, who looked as shocked as Nyla, sat on the couch next to Clarisse. Carolyn, Max, Pam, and Madeline were in the kitchen preparing a snack. Aaron and Jeff conversed about something in the corner, and Beth and Violet, a woman who looked as old as Tata, prayed together by the front door.

Finally finishing his talk with Daniel, Calan headed her way.

She should tap her com piece and alert Marco that Daniel was here. She should...

But she needed to make sense of what had happened. It was a miracle. She could not deny it. And what about the creatures she'd seen, light and dark? Perhaps there *was* a God these Deviants worshipped. But hadn't the Neflams said the God of the Bible was evil? That He wanted to enslave people in cages of rules and regulations, that He was a narcissistic tyrant who demanded worship and obedience to His restrictive laws?

At the time, she'd blown off such discussions. God or no God, religion had destroyed her life, and surely the Neflams were the most knowledgeable about any lifeforms beyond earth.

Yet...why would an evil God heal a man who was poor and unimportant? A nobody. Wasn't that a good thing? A *kind* thing?

Calan sat beside her and studied her with those piercing eyes of his. "You okay? You look like you've seen a ghost."

The way he was looking at her, his closeness...his scent and warmth, once again, it did weird things to her, *nice* things. She smiled. "I think I have. Lots of them."

Calan took her hand in his, engulfing it in his strength. "I know it can all seem crazy, but I'm here to answer your questions."

She shouldn't allow him to hold her hand, to sit so close, but after all that had happened, it felt good to have him near. It felt right. But of course she had to play along, pretend she had feelings for him in order to infiltrate deeper into the group.

Yeah, keep telling yourself that, girl. She frowned. *Whatever.* She *did* have questions, one in particular that rushed to her tongue. But just then, snacks were brought out from the kitchen, and Daniel called the meeting to order.

He started out in prayer and then spoke about the comets that had just struck earth. Madeline read a few news reports from the web saying that some of earth's fresh water sources had become poisonous and people were dying.

Dying? Nyla drew a hand to her mouth. Yet no one else seemed shocked by the news.

Daniel must have noticed her expression. "We read you the Scriptures that prophesied this, Nyla. Remember?"

Yes, she did, but...to see it come true, well, that was more shocking than the news. "How did you know...?"

"We didn't," Calan responded. "God did."

"And you'll soon hear," Daniel continued, "that a third of earth's fresh water supply is contaminated."

Nyla huffed. All eyes rested upon her. She squirmed in her seat. "Okay, so what's next?"

Tyson snorted. "What's next is that we're going to have a hard time finding fresh water to drink."

"With God, all things are possible," Carolyn added. "Don't worry, Tyson."

After smiling her way, Daniel nodded to Max, who already had his Bible open. "Then the fourth angel sounded: And a third of the sun was struck, a third of the moon, and a third of the stars, so that a third of them were darkened. A third of the day did not shine, and likewise the night."

Daniel glanced around the group as a solemn spirit fell over them. "So, that's what we need to prepare for."

Nyla remained silent. A third of the sun and moon? Ludicrous. That would destroy most of what was left of the crops on the planet and plunge the world into an ice age. Besides, what could cause such a catastrophe? Yet...if the first three trumpets had come true... She rubbed her eyes. Nothing made sense. Not these prophecies, the trumpets, the strange figures she was seeing, the demon deliverance of that woman on the beach, or the lame man walking. Nothing. Parlor tricks, that's all. Illusions meant to trick her, trick others into joining their cult.

But for what reason? They didn't want money or power or much of anything. From what she could tell, they required nothing from new converts.

"God will keep us safe." Calan spoke beside her. "And if He doesn't, we will go home."

"Amen! Praise His Mighty Name!" others shouted.

"Nyla." Daniel's voice drew her gaze to him. "You seem troubled. Is there a question or maybe something you need prayer for?"

Prayer for? She certainly shouldn't express any more of her doubts. "Well, yes, my grandmother is ill." It was the only thing she could think of.

Everyone expressed their sorrow at the news.

"Thank you." Attempting to smile, Nyla slid a strand of her hair behind her ear. "She shouldn't be alone, but my brother might have a job now, so it's hard for me to get out…to find another job, that is."

Carolyn perked up. "I can help. I was a nurse before I got fired for not taking the vaccine."

"I don't want to be a bother."

"No bother, Nyla. I'm happy to come over anytime you like and help out."

"Me too," Pam added.

From the look in both their eyes, Nyla knew they meant it. "Thank you," was all she managed to say. She'd never met such kind people.

"We would be happy to come over and pray for her," Daniel added.

No. She didn't want these people near her brother, and though Tata would adore them, there was no sense in feeding her fantasies. "Thank you. I'll let you know."

Javier began strumming his guitar, and soon everyone in the room rose to their feet, hands in the air, praising their invisible God, Calan included. He tried to get her to stand with them, but she remained sitting, mesmerized by the emotion these Deviants displayed toward someone they couldn't see, hear, or touch. Some of the women even had tears streaming down their cheeks. Ridiculous. Yet Nyla could not deny the atmosphere in the room had changed. Somehow it seemed brighter, as if a cloud had moved aside, allowing the sun to fully shine. Hope was in the air. And joy. So strange.

That's when she saw them.

Immense creatures of light dancing around the Deviants, joining in the Deviants' praise toward God. *Dancing?* Though she could see right through them, they radiated light, their faces aglow with adoration. Nyla slammed her eyes shut, willing them away. Yet when she opened them, the light beings were still there.

She was going insane. Completely and utterly insane. She glanced at her cup of tea. Had they put something in it?

Jumping to her feet, she slipped through the crowd and made her way out the back door into the garden.

The sun sank in the west, casting fading rays through the remaining branches of trees. A small oval pool took up most of the yard, and Nyla flicked off her sandals, rolled up her jeans, and sat, dipping her legs in the cool water. Thankfully, the music and singing could hardly be heard from out here.

She tapped her com piece. "Marco?"

After a few minutes, he responded. "Babe. How are you? I was getting worried."

"I'm good. Just been busy. I need a sanity check."

"A what?"

"Tell me I'm not going nuts."

"You're many things, babe. Smart, strong, brave, gorgeous, sexy, but never nuts."

She smiled. "I miss you."

"Me too." He hesitated. "You hanging out with that Calan guy?"

"I have to. He's Daniel's bodyguard."

"But you don't have to enjoy it."

She gave a nervous laugh. "Give me a break. I'd rather be with you." Only then did she realize that wasn't completely true. Not anymore.

"Well, let me know when you are with Daniel. I've got the troops on standby."

Nyla glanced back toward the house. Calan emerged from the sliding glass door and headed her way.

"Will do. Gotta go." She tapped the com piece and faced Calan with a smile. She should turn it back on and give Marco the go-ahead. She should! But all these kind people would be arrested. They were crazy, yes, but they didn't deserve to die, did they? Did Calan?

Calan took off his shoes, rolled up his pants, and sat beside her. "You okay?"

"Yes, just needed some air."

"I know the worship can get a little overwhelming for someone not used to it."

She didn't want to talk about worship or God or miracles, so she blurted out the dumbest question in her mind. "How do you all survive? I mean all that food. I haven't seen fresh food like that in a long time. I know Tyson and you have the proper credentials, right? And you have a job, but you all eat better than most people I know."

"Yes, two of us can buy things. Javier and Elena sold their home in Boca for a pretty penny before the war and gave the money to the church, so we live off that mostly. But Maddy has a hydroponic garden here in her house. She used to grow pot." He laughed. "Oh, and Max had tons of emergency food stored before all this happened." He shrugged and swirled his legs through the water. "Besides that, God just provides. We've never lacked for anything."

Amazing. She'd never seen such a group of loving people. "So you all share everything?"

He nodded. "We take care of each other. If someone has a need, someone else can always provide. It's how God wanted His children to live."

Nyla drew a deep breath. "Sounds wonderful in a way." She snuck a peek at him as he stared at the water, deep in thought, his dark hair going this way and that, the light stubble on his determined jaw, the way his black tee-shirt tightened over his biceps.

Wind spun around them, tossing her hair and bringing the scent of burnt grass to her nose. She wiggled it, longing for Calan's scent to return. Ah, there it was. It filtered through her, dispelling the scorched stench and easing her nerves. Silence settled comfortably around them as if they'd known each other all their lives. Odd. She'd never felt that way with Marco.

Turning toward her, Calan brushed a wayward strand of her hair from her face. "I'm glad you're here."

Oddly, she was too. "It was a crazy night. A lot for me to see."

"But you're still here. You haven't run away." He looked at her, his stark blue eyes barely noticeable in the deepening shadows. "I'm sorry about your grandmother. I hope it isn't serious."

It was.Very. Emotion clogged her throat, preventing her from answering. She shifted her gaze to the water, not wanting him to see the moisture in her eyes.

He put a finger under her chin and lifted her gaze back to his. "God can heal her, you know. It's going to be all right."

He said the words so confidently, so full of concern, that she actually believed him for a second. Against all her resolve, she lowered her head to lean on his shoulder. "Thank you."

Swinging an arm around her, he brought her close and kissed the top of her head.

No man had ever been so caring and gentle with her. Most had just wanted sex. Even Marco. Whenever he looked at Nyla, it was always with desire. She hadn't minded. It made her feel wanted, sexy, attractive. But Calan looked at her differently.

"I want to get to know you better, Nyla. I hope you'll let me."

He wanted to know her? The *real* her? No one had ever said that to her before. She didn't quite know how to answer, but she found that she wanted to know more about him as well.

"On one condition," she responded, teasingly. "That you go first and tell me about your brother."

For to one is given the word of wisdom through the Spirit, to another the word of knowledge through the same Spirit, to another faith by the same Spirit, to another gifts of healings by the same Spirit, to another the working of miracles, to another prophecy, to another discerning of spirits, to another different kinds of tongues, to another the interpretation of tongues. But one and the same Spirit works all these things, distributing to each one individually as He wills. 1 Corinthians 12:8-11

Chapter 20

Stunned, Calan had no idea how to respond. How did she know about his brother? Part of him was angry at whoever told her, part of him wanted her to know, wanted her to understand events of his life that had drastically impacted the rest.

Part of him wanted to hold her in his arms until he could break through the shield she formed around herself, a shield of stubborn independence he longed to pierce.

Maybe telling her his story would help.

"It is not very flattering," he began, still pressing her against him, not wanting to move his arm from around her.

But she wiggled out of his embrace and met his gaze, searching his eyes. "I have a ton of those too." She smiled. "You share yours. I'll share mine."

He loved the way her nose wrinkled when she smiled. Wind blew a strand of hair across her face, and he reached up to brush it away, realizing he was being forward. But it couldn't be helped. He was falling for her. Hard. And he hated himself for it. She was an unbeliever, an ex-NWU PK, and they were in the Tribulation! Heck of a time to fall in love. Especially with his track record with women. Was he just being used? Played for a fool like all the other women he'd fallen for?

Yet when he looked into those eyes the color of creamed coffee, he saw nothing but sincerity, a desire to know the truth, intelligence, and dare he hope, some interest in him. He'd never met anyone like Nyla, opinionated, stubborn, smart, courageous, yet so full of life and love. She was a warrior like he was, yet with the tender heart of a woman. He hadn't thought such a creature existed.

He released a heavy sigh and ran a hand through his hair. "Okay, yes, I had a brother once, a younger brother."

"Calan!" A voice called his name from the house, and he turned to see Daniel heading his way. "You're needed inside. Max needs help with a security issue."

"Now?" He tried to nod nonchalantly toward Nyla to let Daniel know they were in the middle of a conversation, but Daniel's eyes remained locked on him. "He has to leave soon. It will only take a few minutes."

"To be continued." Calan stood. He could tell she was disappointed, but maybe this was God's way of saying it wasn't the right time.

Crud. Nyla had finally gotten Calan to start opening up. She watched him roll down his jeans, smile her way, and disappear into the house.

"Wanna go back in?" Daniel remained standing a few feet from her.

Night had invaded the backyard, making it difficult to see his expression. Drawing her feet from the water, she stood. A thousand questions welled in her throat, begging release. How did he heal that man? Was God real? Why did they risk their lives for a God they couldn't see? And who were the creatures of light she kept seeing?

But none made their way to her tongue. Something was off. The man, this Deviant, who was on the NWU Most Wanted List, seemed suddenly sad, off his game.

"You go in. I need to be alone for a minute," he said.

Why wasn't he trying to convert her? Why wasn't he offering to answer her questions? No, instead, he lowered to sit in a chair and stared into the darkness as if a thousand weights had been added to his heart.

She should signal Marco.

"Is something wrong?" She dragged a chair beside his and sat down. "Can I help?"

Shock brought his gaze to hers as a sad smile lifted his lips. "No, but thank you, Nyla."

"You are always so filled with hope and joy, even when"— she shrugged—"in my mind, there isn't much to be happy about." She sighed. "But I bet the weight of your responsibility must be difficult at times."

It was the only thing she could think to say to get him to open up. Here was the man she was supposed to arrest, sitting and talking to her one-on-one. Maybe before she called in the troops, she could discover the locations of the other churches or even where he hung out when he wasn't at Zion's Nest.

Hot wind swirled around them, and he leaned forward, elbows on his knees, staring at the dark ripples in the pool. "The Lord sustains me, Nyla."

"Then what is it?"

When he didn't answer right away, she sighed and started to rise. "Sorry, I'm being rude. You want to be alone."

"It's okay." He flattened his lips and gestured for her to stay. "It's just that I miss someone. Very much."

Nyla could relate to that. "They were taken in the disappearance?"

He swung his gaze to hers, his eyes searching. "The Rapture of the saints. And yes, *she* was."

Nyla swallowed. "Your wife?"

"As close to one as I'll ever have." He hesitated and looked down. Another blast of wind tossed his light hair and fluttered the edge of his tee-shirt. In the distance a siren blared. "She was my love, the mother of my son. Angelica." He spoke her name as though it hurt him to say it. "But I called her Angel because she *was* an angel."

Against everything in her, Nyla's heart ached for this man. She had not expected him to be a romantic. Not at all. "I'm sorry."

Daniel rubbed the light stubble on his chin. "She tried to warn me, but I wouldn't listen."

"She knew the Neflams were coming?"

"Nyla, sweet Nyla." He gave her a look of disappointment. "The Neflams didn't take our loved ones for reprogramming. God took them to heaven for the wedding of the Lamb."

A lamb getting married? Okay, sure. Nyla eased hair behind her ear, trying to figure out a way to change the topic from crazy town to the things she needed to know.

"The Wedding of Jesus to His Bride," Daniel added, no doubt sensing her skepticism.

Music and laughter drifted from the house, spinning about them in the evening breeze. A gunshot echoed in the distance, accompanied by car horns and yet another PK siren, reminding her she had a job to do.

"So, why didn't *you* get taken? You were a famous preacher, right?" Actually, now that she thought about it, why *hadn't* the Neflams taken him? He'd been a huge part of the archaic religious system holding back man's evolution.

Daniel hung his head with a sigh. His jaw tightened. "I was a fake. Sure, I believed in God, in Jesus, and the Bible, but I preached a different Gospel, a Gospel of prosperity and hyper-grace that had nothing to do with Jesus and His sacrifice for us." He shook his head. "I didn't love God with all my heart. I loved myself, my fame, and money, and I taught those following me to love the same."

Nyla heard the disgust in his voice, shocked by his self-loathing. "I don't understand. Didn't you have a huge church with thousands of members? It couldn't have been all that bad."

He snorted. "And I led nearly all of those members astray, caused them to be left behind to endure the Tribulation."

"But things will get better." For some reason, Nyla longed to cheer him up. "Now that the world is united, we can finally achieve peace and prosperity for everyone."

One brow arched. "Look around you, Nyla. Is that what we are witnessing?"

"It takes a while to work out the kinks."

He laughed.

Moments passed as the sounds of the city's nightly mayhem drifted on the humid breeze—shouts, screams, gunshots, sirens. Yet, the sweet tingle of a wind chime in the distance offered a sliver of hope.

"So, tell me about Angelica. And your son?"

"Isaac." He smiled. "He was just ten. Great kid. I had only just met him." He closed his eyes. "Angel, well, it's a long story, but we'd only recently reconnected. She was beautiful inside and out. I loved her with all my heart. I intended to marry her, make a life together."

"I'm sorry." She really was. Daniel might be wacky, and he might be preaching illegally, but he'd always been kind to her. In fact, she'd only ever seen him be kind to everyone, heal people, pray with people. Crud, she was supposed to hate this man, to hate all Deviants who had led so many astray.

"She disappeared right before my eyes," he continued. "In a flash of lightning. Just as she was warning me."

Same thing had happened with Nyla's parents. Her mother had reached out her hand toward Kyle and Nyla, pleading in her eyes, as if she knew she was about to leave. The memory haunted Nyla in her worst nightmares. Anger returned. Good. She would need it when she betrayed this man. "And you believe they are in heaven now?"

"With all my heart."

"Then you will see them again."

He smiled. "Yes. I sense them waiting for me."

Nyla repressed a snort. Regardless of whether Angel and her son were in a reformation camp or in heaven, that was true enough.

"As your parents wait for you."

Nyla nodded. She hoped so with all her heart. Despite her anger, moisture filled her eyes at the thought of her mom, and she blinked it away, needing to change the subject before she broke down in front of this man.

"I've been meaning to ask you something."

"Yes."

"Sometimes I see things," she began, but then bit her lip, unsure whether he would think her as crazy as he was. "Beings made of light."

Instead of acting surprised, Daniel nodded. "Really? What do they look like?"

"Most are tall, muscled, different shapes, and all outlined in light with sort of a glow coming from inside them. And they have weapons too, archaic ones."

Smiling, he shook his head.

"What?"

"You have the gift."

"What are you talking about?"

"Tell me what else you see."

"Dark shadows with hideous faces. I especially saw them today all around the mob that was attacking you."

"Yes, the forces of evil were strong today. I felt them."

"Am I going crazy?" She realized that asking an insane person if she was going nuts was probably a crazy thing to do, but who else could she go to? These people seemed to understand things beyond this world.

"Quite the opposite. You have the same gift Angelica had. Spiritual sight."

"I don't understand."

"You can see into the spirit realm. It's a gift from God."

Yeah. Sure. Like God would give *her* anything. "What are these creatures?"

"Demons, angels. They exist in another dimension outside our own. They are there, but we can't see them. Unless, of course, God allows us, or we have the gift." Laughter from within the house drew his gaze for a moment. "The large angels with the weapons are God's warriors, fighting the forces of darkness on our behalf."

Nyla was sorry she asked. She dropped her head into her hands, feeling a headache rising. Still she could not deny that she had seen something. But angels, demons? Then that would mean that God....

"So your girlfriend saw things like this?"

"All the time."

Fear squeezed her heart. Was she somehow transforming into one of these Deviants? Maybe they had a brain virus and she'd inadvertently caught it. She needed to get out of here. And fast, before she was completely taken over and her life ruined.

She pressed her com piece to turn it back on. "Well, you've given me a lot to think about, Daniel. I appreciate it. So, tell me, how many churches have you planted so far?"

She should have asked him earlier in the conversation, but she'd wanted to know about the beings she'd seen before her undercover assignment came to an end.

"I hear you, babe," Marco said in her ear. "We're tracking your location, and we'll be there soon."

"At least thirty," Daniel responded, rising to his feet. "Why do you ask?" Light from the house shone on his face, highlighting the look of skepticism in his eyes.

"Just curious. I mean, I really am starting to like everyone here. Everyone's so friendly, and I can see why people"—*fall for your nonsense*—"join your group. I've learned a lot from you and Calan, and I'm starting to believe."

"Are you? I'm glad to hear it, Nyla." He cocked his head slightly.

Then why did she get the impression he knew she was lying?

"Thirty churches? Wow. All over the state?"

"Various places." He studied her. "More will come. People are hungry for God and for the truth."

"We're on our way," Marco chirped in her ear. "Be there in ten."

"Thanks for the conversation, Nyla, but I better get back inside," Daniel said.

"Sure, I'll be right in." She wanted to verify the address with Marco and needed a moment alone.

Smiling, Daniel turned and headed toward the back door, his gait confident, his tall and well-built figure evident even in the shadows. He was nearly at the door when he stopped, smiled at her over his shoulder, and then completely vanished.

And for this cause God shall send them strong delusion, that they should believe a lie. 2 Thessalonians 2:11

Chapter 21

Nyla blinked, staring into the darkness. Where had Daniel gone? She hadn't seen him open the door and enter the house. No way. Besides, the sliding door had a characteristic squeak that she hadn't heard.

Her breath heightened. Her heart grew tight. *Calm down, Nyla. It's dark out here. Your eyes are playing tricks on you, that's all.*

Dashing forward, she flew into the house and glanced around. Madeline and Clarisse greeted her from the kitchen. No Daniel. She moved into the living room where Javier and Elena played music and sang as others joined them. Calan and Max stood in the corner, deep in conversation.

Pam approached. "You okay, Nyla?"

"I'm looking for Daniel."

"I thought he was with you."

"He didn't come in? Did he go to the bathroom? Can you check?" Nyla hated the urgency in her tone. She was being ridiculous.

"Sure." Pam gave her a curious look then left and returned in a few minutes. "He's not here, Nyla. Maybe he went home."

No, he didn't go home. He had disappeared! Completely. And right before her eyes.

"Thank you." Nyla walked out the front door and peered down the sidewalk in both directions. No one was in sight.

"Marco."

"I heard. What happened to him?"

"He just disappeared. We were talking and then he walked away and vanished into thin air."

Marco shouted a cuss word. "Okay. We'll stand down."

"Sorry. He was right here."

"I don't like you spending time with these Deviants. It's taking too long."

"Me too. I'll be in touch." She snapped him off.

Nyla couldn't sleep. After Daniel disappeared, she decided it was best to make a quick exit. Without even saying goodbye, she drove home, doing her best to make sense of her conversation with the Deviant leader. Could they be putting something in her drinks that made her hallucinate, even see those light and dark creatures? Either way, she would have to be careful whenever she spent time with them. They could be brainwashing her somehow, though she'd been trained to recognize all the modern methods.

But to what end? She had no money. Nothing to offer them except another body to add to their numbers. For what purpose would they be trying to recruit others? They would never gain enough converts to be able to defeat the Neflams and the New World Union.

Groaning, she sat and flung her legs over the side of her bed, staring into the darkness. Silver light from the moon pierced her window to parry with the night. One particularly bright shard landed on Tata's Bible, which Nyla had borrowed when she'd gone to bed.

She'd intended to read it, but couldn't bring herself to open it, sensing if she did, the words might drag her into a pit of insanity.

Rubbing her eyes, she settled the Bible on her lap. Flipping on a light, she carefully opened the book that, if anyone saw her reading, would get her tossed in prison.

Her gaze focused on the word "angels" on the page.

And He will give His angels charge over you, to guard you in all your ways. They will pick you up in their hands, lest you strike a foot against a stone.

So, here was a reference to the angels Daniel told her about, how God sends them to protect people. Interesting.

"Okay, God, if you exist, show me some other angel stories in this book of yours."

Ranoss knew he wasn't supposed to become attached to his ward, but in Nyla's case, it was far too late to avoid. Hence, the smile on his face as he watched her flip through the Scriptures in search of truth.

He turned to Indira, who stood beside him. "She is on the right path at last."

"So 'twould seem." Indira gripped the Book of Blessings tighter to the silver chain mail covering his chest. "Let us pray it continues."

"I am hopeful, but perhaps I should not be premature, for she has a long way to go." And just like that, his hope of only a minute ago evaporated...as it so often did with Nyla Cruz. 'Twas a bumpy ride with this one, but he was more than determined to keep her safe and on the right path—as much as he was allowed. He had lost his last ward to the enemy, and he would not suffer another defeat.

"Do not frown, my friend." Indira gripped his arm. "'Tis a promising first step toward the light."

The stench of sulfur invaded the room. Shadows stole the light. And before Ranoss could see them, he had his crossbow gripped in both hands, arrow lit, and aimed at the demons slinking in through the walls and window.

Indira drew his silver blade. "They come to stop her from reading the Holy Text."

"But they will fail!" Zhaviel appeared beside the two warriors, spiked club in hand. He glanced at Ranoss. "I sensed you might need some help."

Ranoss fired his arrow at a particularly large dark spirit. The demon exploded in a volcano of black oil even as it howled in agony. "You sensed correctly, my friend." Lighting and positioning another arrow, he smiled at Zhaviel.

"If you two are done talking, can we get to work?" Indira sliced a demon in two with his blade.

"Indeed." Zhaviel charged toward the black mass, swinging his club right and left, leaving a trail of dark ooze and shrieks of pain.

Ranoss fired at another distorted black demon crawling in the window, hitting his mark perfectly. He glanced down at Nyla. She read through the Word as if it were bread, and indeed it was—the Bread of Life.

Spinning around, he joined his friends, and soon, with their help and the power of the Almighty, they chased the dark spirits away. Zhaviel nodded and returned to Kyle, while Indira stiffened, uttered a "she needs me" and left for Tata's bedroom.

Shouldering his crossbow, Ranoss remained standing beside Nyla, keeping a vigilant eye out for any further trouble.

Light flashed over the open Bible, and Nyla glanced up, but nothing was there. She began searching all the "angel" references found in the glossary. Flipping through the paper-thin pages, she finally landed on Isaiah 37.

Then the angel of the Lord went forth, and smote in the camp of the Assyrians a hundred and fourscore and five thousand: and when they arose early in the morning, behold, they were all dead corpses.

Wow. So, angels are warriors, just like Daniel had said. She turned more pages to the book of Daniel.

My God hath sent his angel, and hath shut the lions' mouths, that they have not hurt me: forasmuch as before him innocency was found in me; and also before thee, O king, have I done no hurt.

Hmm. And angels protect from lions, apparently.

Flipping forward to Acts, she read about an angel who helped Peter escape from prison, much like she and the Deviants had done. Wow. In fact, in every passage she read, angels were either giving messages, protecting, or fighting. Interesting. But what about demons? Were they in the Bible too? She found the word in the glossary and read the reference found in Mark 5.

When he saw Jesus from afar, he ran and worshiped Him. And he cried out with a loud voice and said, "What have I to do with You, Jesus, Son of the Most High God? I implore You by God that You do not torment me." For He said to him, "Come out of the man, unclean spirit!" Then He asked him, "What is your name?"

And he answered, saying, "My name is Legion; for we are many." Also he begged Him earnestly that He would not send them out of the country.

Now a large herd of swine was feeding there near the mountains. So all the demons begged Him, saying, "Send us to the swine, that we may enter them." And at once Jesus gave them permission. Then the unclean spirits went out and entered the swine and the herd ran violently down the steep place into the sea, and drowned in the sea.

Nyla couldn't take it anymore. She slammed the book shut, tempted to toss it across the room, but instead laid it gently beside her. If it *was* holy, she didn't need to add to her crimes. Mind jumbled, she dropped her head in her hands, wanting to cry, but unable to. What was happening? According to this God book, angels helped people all the time, even delivered messages. And the dark creatures—the demons—even Jesus had cast them out.

Just fairy tales and myths, a voice spoke, yet not audibly. But... she had seen... she had seen proof, hadn't she?

She really needed to stop spending time with the Deviants.

A bright light lit the room behind her eyelids, and she opened her eyes. Nothing.

Yes, she really needed to get this assignment over with. And soon.

What she really needed was to see Marco, to do something normal, something from her old life, to talk about regular things, to snuggle up beside him and hear his words of love.

The first glow of dawn crept over her windowsill and spilled into the room. No doubt, that was the brightness she'd seen. Just the rising sun. Grabbing the Bible, she made her way to Tata's room to return it and check on her grandmother. She'd been sleeping well last night, but now she sat on the edge of her bed, long gray hair askew and face pale.

"Tata." Nyla slid the Bible onto her nightstand and knelt before her. A palm to her grandmother's forehead told her the fever had returned. "You're burning up, Tata. Lie back down."

"Oh goodness, Pajarito, don't make such a fuss. I'm tired of lying in bed." Despite the pain etching lines on her face, she managed a smile. "Been reading God's Word, I see."

"Don't get too excited." Nyla helped her to stand. "I was only checking on something. Now, let's get you to the living room, and I'll get your medicine and a cool washcloth."

"Did you feel my prayers, dear?" Tata groaned as she hobbled out the door to the living area. "The good Lord woke me up and told me to pray. You must have been under attack."

"Attack? Don't be silly."

"Never you mind, dear." She breathed a sigh as she sank into her favorite chair. "The good news is, the Lord answered and protected you, showing you verses as you read."

Nyla bit her lip. How would her grandmother know such a thing? Regardless, it was way too early in the morning to deal with such nonsense. She moved to the kitchen where she started coffee, assembled Tata's medicines, and ran a cloth under cold water in the sink.

The lock on the door jangled. Kyle, in his new NWU guard uniform, burst in, an unusually happy look on his face for someone who hated work of any kind.

"How is your first week at work going?" Nyla knelt before Tata, handing her the pills and a glass of water.

"Hmm. Is that fresh coffee?" Kyle tossed his keys to a table and made for the kitchen. "Great. It's going great!"

"Whoa, I never thought I'd see you so happy about working."

Tata frowned as she swallowed her pills, then leaned back.

Nyla laid the cool cloth on her forehead.

"I never thought I'd enjoy working, but this place is cool." Kyle poured himself a cup of coffee. "The other guards are nice and, hey, guess what? The Tall Whites are there too."

Tata started coughing.

Nyla stared at her brother, noticing he'd shaved and combed the unruly mass of black waves he called hair. "You mean the Neflam Tall Whites, who so rarely make an appearance anywhere?"

"They're evil," Tata choked out.

Kyle cussed. "No way. They're beautiful, smarter than anyone I've known, and well, there's something about them. They really...affect me."

"They are demonic." Tata started to rise, unsettling the cloth.

Nyla retrieved it, urging her to lay her head back. "Tata, you must rest. Don't let him upset you."

Though she had to admit the Tall Whites were more appealing than their reptilian friends, no one knew much about them, they so rarely appeared in public. Even as a NWU PK, she had yet to encounter one, but she'd heard stories of women and men who found them extremely alluring, almost captivating, and not necessarily in a good way.

"I don't care." Kyle gulped his coffee. "I like them, and I may even have a chance to talk to one soon."

"And why is that? You're just a new guard. Why would you have such a privilege?"

He shrugged. "'Cause I've been invited to join a group."

Nyla rose and headed toward the kitchen, an uneasy feeling stirring in her gut. "What group is that? Like a club?"

"Yeah I guess. Kinda like Freemasons, but it's called Kabal."

Gripping the sides of her chair, Tata pulled herself to sit and faced Kyle with more determination than Nyla thought she had the strength for. "You will do no such thing, young man. Those groups are pure evil. Satan worshipers! I rebuke the mere thought of them in Jesus' name!" Then as if she'd spent all her energy, she released a sigh and sank back into her chair.

Snorting, Kyle turned away. "Whatever."

Nyla speared her brother with a look that had caused the most hardened criminals to shrink back. "Why would you do that? You've never been one to join anything."

For a moment, softness stole the steel from his gaze and a sweeter version of her brother appeared—the old Kyle. But then he quirked his lips and huffed. "'Cause they have power. Lots of it. At least that's what I hear. Don't you want me to be successful? You always told me to find something I like and am good at. Can you imagine if I had some authority and power in the NWU? Especially now that you are disgraced, we're gonna need someone to support the family."

Though she knew it wasn't true, the word disgraced caused a lump to form in her throat. Yet his words didn't ring true either. When had her brother ever worried about helping out with money? Maybe he was changing. Maybe he'd found his niche. Still, Nyla didn't like the sound of clubs. In her experience, most of them brainwashed their initiates, promising them huge rewards while using them for their own gain.

She poured a cup of coffee for Tata, then gripped Kyle's arm. "Just don't talk about it in front of Tata. She's weak and shouldn't get upset."

Kyle's brown eyes narrowed. His jaw bunched as if it would explode, but instead the pressure released in a seething whisper. "I finally find something I love and a purpose, and I can't even talk about it in front of our loony grandmother." He thumbed toward Tata. "You never approve of anything I do. I've always lived in your shadow. Dad's favorite. I could never live up to his expectations, and now you are taking his place. Great." He slammed down the mug. "I'm going to bed."

"That's not true, Kyle." Yet even as she said the words, she knew there was some truth in them. "Hey, I need you to watch over Tata for a few hours today."

"No can do." Without turning, he waved at her over his head and disappeared down the hall. "I have to work the graveyard tonight. I need to sleep."

Nyla leaned on the counter and released a heavy sigh. What was she to do now? Grabbing Tata's coffee, she found her grandmother asleep. No, not asleep. Her lips were moving. Praying?

"Here's your coffee, Tata." Nyla whispered to see if she were awake or only dreaming.

Here eyes popped open, full of more life than a sickly eighty-year-old should have. "Thank you, my Pajarito." Taking the mug, she placed a hand on Nyla's arm. "Don't worry. God has everything under control."

Though Nyla wanted to laugh, she merely nodded and returned to the kitchen to make Tata's breakfast. Maybe God had things under control where *He* was, but in Nyla's world, everything seemed to be falling apart.

And this gospel of the kingdom will be preached in all the world as a witness to all the nations, and then the end will come. Matthew 24:14

Chapter 22

Nyla shut the car door of her Jeep and pressed the fob to lock it. She'd been lucky to find parking, yet she hesitated to leave her car unattended, even in the daylight. She knew from experience that most of the crimes in Fort Lauderdale occurred in this seedy neighborhood. In fact, PKs rarely responded to emergency calls from the area, where drug lords, gangsters, and prostitutes thrived, which only gave the criminals more freedom to do their lawless deeds. So, imagine her surprise when Calan invited her to a "street revival," as he called it, and gave her the address.

Not that she was into street revivals, but she was definitely curious, and if Daniel was present, perhaps she could put an end to all this madness. Which was why she'd allowed Carolyn to sit with Tata while she was away. The kind lady even brought over a pot of chicken soup—fresh chicken soup, a rarity these days—and seemed more than happy to stay while Nyla attended the revival. Such kindness still baffled Nyla. In fact, it made her suspicious. Everyone had an agenda.

She glanced both ways down the busy street, but no group of Deviants was in sight.

Homeless tents packed alleyways and vomited onto the sidewalks. Beggars sat hunched in filthy corners. Gang members strolled the streets like lords and ladies of the realm, and here Nyla was without her Glock. Taking a deep breath, she started down the street toward the address Calan had given her, just a block away. He'd insisted on picking her up and bringing her here himself, to protect her he'd said, but she'd wanted her car in case she needed to make a fast getaway. Besides, it was only two in the afternoon, and most of the lowlifes would be asleep.

Not to mention, she could take care of herself.

A man loitering in front of a burned-out store followed her with lustful eyes as she passed.

The acrid stink of urine, rotten food, sweat, and hopelessness bit her nose, and she hurried her steps, shielding her eyes from the afternoon sun.

A man suddenly appeared beside her.

Her reflexes kicked into gear. Without facing him, she slammed her elbow into his ribs, then leapt behind him and pounded him across the back with both fists. Groaning, the man bent over just as she went in for the kill with a kick to the back of his legs to topple him. Before she could do so, he spun on her. Instinctively, she raised her fist to clip him on the jaw, but he caught it in his grip, twisted her around, forced her back against him and locked both her arms together across her chest.

Crud! Anger, followed by fear, sizzled through her as she strained against the barricade of his meaty arms. She was about to execute a back kick on his shins when he leaned to whisper in her ear.

"It's me, Nyla." That voice…and now that familiar scent that swept away the stench in her nose.

He released her, and she whirled to face Calan, both relieved and embarrassed when she saw him grinning at her. He pressed a hand over his ribs. "You pack quite the jab, princess."

"I'm no princess, and you know it." She started walking, irritated that she'd let him get the best of her. Irritated that she hadn't seen who it was. But she'd been trained to react first, think later.

He fell in beside her. "I saw you pull up and didn't want you to walk through this neighborhood alone. It's not safe." When she didn't say anything, he continued. "But I see you can handle yourself."

MaryLu Tyndall

She stared up at him, squinting in the sun. "Obviously not. You got the best of me."

One brow arched as his lips slanted. "Navy SEAL."

Good point, she supposed.

A car passed, blaring music that made the sidewalk shake.

He brushed a lock of hair from her face. "I didn't mean to scare you. Sorry." The intimate gesture, along with the look of concern in his eyes, swept away her anger and caused a rush of warmth to flood her.

She smiled. "Just don't surprise me like that again."

He pressed his chest again. "Lesson learned, believe me."

She had learned a lesson too, two of them. One, there was no shame in being beat by a Navy SEAL. And two, chivalry was not dead. At least not when it came to Calan. No one, not even Marco, had ever been so protective of her. The feminist side of her should be mad. The woman in her found it alluring.

"Truce?" she asked.

"If you say so, but I won fair and square," he joked, his eyes sparkling with mischief.

"You're impossible." She punched his arm and started walking.

He fell in beside her again, gently steering her around a man lying beside a dumpster strung out on drugs.

"Lovely place for a revival," she said.

"The perfect place, actually. We come here once a month."

A drunk stumbled out of a bar, his glazed eyes latching upon Nyla. "Hey, baby, can I buy you a drink?"

Grabbing Nyla's hand, Calan led her to the other side of him, away from the man, and placed a palm on the drunk's chest. "Back off."

Thankfully, the man offered no argument, but instead growled and stumbled away, unraveling a string of foul words behind him.

The stench of alcohol and old greasy carpet emanated from the place as they passed. Up ahead, a neon sign of a naked woman blinked off and on, announcing that "Real live naked girls" were inside.

Nyla didn't know whether to laugh that they advertised "live" girls instead of dead, or be sick to her stomach. She did neither as something caught her eye. Shifting shadows drew her gaze to the roof of the club. She froze, blinked to clear her vision, but they were still there. Greyish-blue creatures, some thin, some fat, some tall, others short, all perched on top of the strip club like lifeless gargoyles. But they weren't lifeless. They moved, scratched themselves, and shifted black empty eyes toward her, seemingly as shocked that she could see them as she was.

"What is it, Nyla?" Calan halted beside her and followed her gaze above.

"What are they?" She reached for her gun, but of course it wasn't there.

"Who?"

"You don't see them?" All the breath fled her lungs, but she couldn't pull her eyes away. She stumbled, and Calan gripped her arm and brought her close.

"What do you see, Nyla?"

"The ugliest creatures ever, like out of a horror movie. At least thirty of them sitting on the roof."

"So, it's true, then."

"What?"

"Come, let's go." Allowing no argument, Calan turned her around and hurried forward.

A group of young teens hung out in front of a convenient store with bars on the windows. With one look from Calan, they shuffled away.

Daniel's voice echoed down the street.

"What do you mean, it's true?" Nyla asked as they approached Daniel and a small group of the Deviants standing in front of a nightclub called The Mermaid Den.

"You can see in the spirit realm."

"So Daniel said. But what were they?"

Stopping, he faced her. "Demons, Nyla. Demons, waiting for the strip club to open is my guess."

Nyla searched his eyes, seeking any hint of insanity, any speck of madness that would put her at ease, but instead she found intelligence, wit, strength, and clarity.

Part of her wanted to ask him more questions, part of her didn't want to know. Surely there was another explanation. Thankfully, Daniel leapt onto a crate and began preaching. Wearing jeans and a gray tee-shirt, he looked more like a model for casual men's clothing than a preacher.

At first only one or two people stopped to listen, but soon a small crowd formed—a couple of teenagers covered in tats, an old, clearly-drunk man, a woman pushing a shopping cart filled with trinkets, another woman with an infant in her arms, and a few very large men who stood listening with arms crossed.

If anyone would cause trouble, it would be these men. Calan noticed them too but made no move toward them.

Beside Daniel, Madeline, Javier, Elena, Pam, and Max were handing out cups of water and fresh baked rolls from behind a table. A sure way to draw more people in and force them to listen to Deviant nonsense.

A few people passed by, hurling curses toward the Deviants and blaspheming the Jesus whom they preached. But it made Daniel preach all the louder. Calan went off to guard him, urging her to join them, but Nyla refused. Best if she hung back to keep an eye out for trouble, a job she could well do on her own. Even so, she watched as Calan spoke to Tyson and nodded toward her.

The young man made his way to stand beside her. Tall, dark, and handsome, the phrase fit Tyson to a T. Though now that she studied him, even beneath a Miami Dolphins baseball cap, he definitely had the body of an engineer rather than an athlete.

"Sorry," she said. "I guess you're on bodyguard duty."

He smiled and crossed arms over his chest. "He just cares about you."

Against her will, that statement settled happily in her heart. "Where's your wife?"

"Home. Missing our little boy."

"I'm sorry."

"It's okay. She has good days and bad days. Today was a bad day."

Nyla bit her lip. Maybe when she returned to her duties, she could try to find out where the children went, maybe even locate Tyson and Clarisse's little boy.

Hot wind filled with unsavory odors blasted over them, and Nyla glanced up at the sun. With all the ash still filtering through the air, she would not expect it to be so hot. But the sweat on her neck and arms told a different story.

"There is only one way to be saved, only one way to find peace in this world, and joy in the next," Daniel shouted.

"Yeah, a bottle of Jack Daniel's!" one man yelled, causing laughter through the crowd.

"You could try that, sir." Daniel smiled at the man. "By the looks of you, you already have, many times. But I bet you that it gave you neither peace nor joy. At least not lasting joy. Not eternal joy."

The man shrugged but remained to listen.

In fact, most of the people remained, and as the crowd became larger, more and more people joined them.

Nyla had to agree. There was something mesmerizing about Daniel Cain, the man himself *and* the words he spoke. Both were filled with life and hope and peace, things most people desperately lacked. Yet they were also filled with promise, not empty, but *real* promise and a love, an unconditional love that no longer seemed possible in this world. Daniel's zeal and confidence supercharged every word and sent it out with the ability to enter someone's soul. Nyla could easily see how he'd once pastored a church that drew tens of thousands of members.

Oddly, Tyson gave a cynical huff.

She stared at him. "You don't agree with Daniel?"

His eyes widened as his gaze snapped to hers. "What makes you say that?"

"I don't know. I guess it takes one to know one."

He sighed, flipped up his baseball cap, and scratched his hair before replacing it. "Well, just not sure. My wife, though, man, she's really into this, believes all of it. Prays, reads her Bible. Sings songs all the time."

"And you?"

One shoulder lifted. "Don't know. I've seen a lot of things that should convince me, I guess. But who knows where the power comes from with all the new tech out there, you know, virtual reality, robots…and now with the Neflams' arrival? But honestly, I'm just here 'cause it makes Clarisse happy. That's all I want in life."

Nyla nodded. They had a skeptic among them. Interesting.

A knot of concern threaded across his forehead. "You won't tell them, right?"

"Of course not." Crud. Why had she not alerted Marco? She pressed her com piece and finally heard his sexy voice respond.

Daniel continued preaching, glancing over the crowd. "Do you want to be healed? Do you want abundant life, purpose, joy, and meaning?"

"Heard him," Marco said. "On our way."

"This is nothin' but a bunch of crap and lies!" one man yelled.

More shouts, followed by curses fired from the group.

"There ain't no God, and we ain't givin' you no money!"

"We didn't ask you to come here. Get out of our neighborhood. Take your garbage and leave before we call the PKs!"

"I want to be healed!" a woman yelled from the back.

"Come forward!" Daniel strained to see where she was as Calan left his post beside him and made his way through the mob.

The woman cried out again, and all eyes shifted her way, causing groans of disgust to wave across the mob as many backed away from her. Even Nyla flinched. Around sixty years of age, the poor woman's face, neck, and arms were covered with blisters, red, pustulating blisters.

Calan, however, did not even flinch, did not hesitate to gently take her arm and help her move to the front. Nyla had never seen anything like it, especially the kind and loving look on his face as he assisted her, without a care at all that she might be contagious.

That's when she saw them. Not the nasty beings she'd seen on top of the strip club, but worse, *much* worse—darker, larger, and well-armed.

And one of them was heading straight for Nyla.

The angel of the Lord encamps all around those who fear Him
and delivers them. Psalm 34:7

Chapter 23

Ranoss drew his blade and leapt before Nyla, instantly meeting the sword of his opponent with a mighty clang.

The dark beast with fangs hissed and growled as he dipped to the side and charged Ranoss from the left. Anticipating his move, Ranoss tilted his sword down in defense, then swung it back up, snagging the demon's blade hilt to hilt. Metal grinding against metal, Ranoss forced him back.

"I will have her," the demon spat. "You'll see. She is marked by our master."

"You will do her no harm!" Ranoss fired back. "Ever! By the order of the Commander of Heaven's Armies!"

Smoldering, vacant eyes glared at Ranoss. The demon leapt back, reached inside his cloak, and pulled out a star-shaped object. Ranoss had little time to recognize the lethal weapon before his opponent hurled it at him. If it struck, he'd be severely wounded and unable to assist his companions.

An arrow flew in from the right. The tip struck the death star and ripped it from the demon's hand. Ranoss charged him and plunged his blade into his heart.

Sputtering, the dark creature dropped to his knees, hands reaching to remove the blade. Black ink poured from his mouth as he looked up at Ranoss. "This changes nothing," he gurgled, spewing droplets of death.

Ranoss jerked his blade from the demon's chest with an eerie swish. "By the command of the Lord of Heaven's Armies, go to the abyss where you belong."

Instantly, the demon disintegrated into a cloud of black dust.

Ranoss looked over at Nazare to give him a nod of thanks. But the mighty warrior was already rushing to protect his ward Daniel from several demons attempting to stop the man of God from healing the daughter of Eve.

Anisian fought off three more demons trying to attack Calan. Cassian was busy with two others, and three additional warrior angels kept other dark ones at bay. They knew this would be a difficult fight. The Father had warned them that two souls would be saved this day and many more healed as seeds of light were planted in darkened hearts. Hence, the need for twenty of the Commander's best warriors.

Circling around Nyla, Ranoss took a position behind her. His orders were to guard her at all costs. But that didn't mean he couldn't help the others.

Drawing his crossbow over his shoulder, he plucked out an arrow, lit and positioned it to fire. One by one, he sent flaming arrows speeding, each one hitting their mark in the demons' hearts. For now, the enemy retreated.

A beam of light fell from heaven onto the daughter of Eve who was bound by Satan with a spirit of infirmity. Daniel commanded the spirit leave and the woman be healed. With an ear-piercing screech, all darkness left her and she began touching her face, shouting for joy.

The demons howled in agony as if the victory tortured them with pain.

Yet, they were not done yet, for the son of Adam, Daniel, was not done yet.

Calan couldn't help the burst of joy that overcame him at the woman's healing. He'd seen such miracles a hundred times before, but they never failed to excite him, to prove to him that he served an all-powerful, loving God.

The middle-aged lady kept thanking Daniel, and Daniel kept telling her it was Jesus who healed her. The crowd had been stunned into silence, some pressing in to see the woman's clear skin, others with confused expressions as if they were trying to find a logical explanation.

Daniel led the woman in a prayer to give her life to the Lord, and as she began praising God with tears rolling down her cheeks, he leapt back atop the crate.

"What you witnessed here is God's love for you all. There's no one outside of His loving reach. He wants all of you to know Him and to live with Him forever."

"Can you heal me too?" someone from the mob yelled.

"God can heal anyone," Daniel answered.

A chill scraped over Calan's back, an icy wind, a foreboding of evil with which he was very familiar. Uttering the name of Jesus, he eased closer to Daniel. He'd been sensing the dark forces since they arrived, sensed a battle had occurred or *was* still occurring. Scanning the mob, he sought out Nyla standing at the back. He'd been watching her off and on, intrigued by her expression, as if she were horrified by something yet too fascinated to look away. Tyson looked bored beside her. Did she see the battle that Calan sensed? He would have to ask her later.

Daniel turned to Calan. "We have to leave soon. The authorities are on their way."

Calan nodded. He'd long since stopped asking how Daniel knew things. He was rarely wrong.

The famous preacher gave one more appeal for those who wanted to know Jesus and have eternal life, and two more people came forward. While Calan prayed with them, hecklers assembled around the group, shouting obscenities, while a few brave souls in the crowd told them to stop, proclaiming that these were men and women of God.

Tension filled the air, strung tight. A dark void collapsed upon them. Shuddering, Calan stood his ground. The battle intensified.

"We should leave. Now," he urged Daniel.

"But you didn't heal me!" a man shouted.

"My mother's sick. Let me go get her!"

"I'm blind in one eye. Can you help me?"

More desperate shouts filled the air.

Daniel faced Calan, that familiar look in his eyes that said he'd received other orders—orders that defied Calan's . "I feel the power of God on me, Calan. Strong. I'm going to walk through the crowd and touch them."

"I don't like it."

"Then pray and stay close. You're God's warrior."

Was he? If something happened to Daniel, it would be the worst failure of his life.

And he'd already had too many to count.

And believers were increasingly added to the Lord, multitudes of both men and women, so that they brought the sick out into the streets and laid them on beds and couches, that at least the shadow of Peter passing by might fall on some of them. Acts 5:14-15

Demons and angels, light and dark, fullness and emptiness, Nyla had seen glimpses of something she could not explain. Ancient swords, glowing armor, fiery arrows, and hideous specters all clashing in some otherworld battle.

There was an explanation, of course. There had to be. The Neflams had opened human eyes to other worlds, to powers that, before they arrived, would have been labeled miracles. Surely this was just part of that.

But deep inside, she knew it wasn't. A totally buffed figure of light stood guard over her. Once, in the briefest of seconds, she saw his face as he glanced at her. She remembered every feature, every detail. Firm jaw, golden eyes, a pointed nose, and long, light hair. The look in his eyes was one of a fierce warrior but also something more...concern. For her? She thought she saw him smile at her. Right before he vanished.

Daniel stared her way above the bobbing heads of the mob, above the noise, the clamor, the cussing—he looked at her with a sorrow, a disappointment as if he knew she'd contacted the NWU PKs.

Crud, she had! Only then did she remember. And for some reason, she suddenly regretted it.

A dark spot on the ground caught her gaze, and she stooped to touch it, rubbing it between her fingers. Soot? No. Not oil either. Or ash. She'd never seen the likes of it. Where had that come from?

"We gotta go, Nyla." Calan grabbed her arm and lifted her up. "Come with me. I've got to stay near Daniel."

Still stunned by the odd soot, she merely nodded and followed him. Unfortunately, so did most of the crowd, clawing their way to Daniel as he started down the street, waving his hands over the people, touching as many as possible. The other Deviants abandoned the food on the table and pressed behind him, trying to keep the people from crushing their leader.

Calan rushed forward, pulling her along. "In Jesus' name, I banish and bind all demonic spirits attacking our group, attacking Daniel."

A light that wasn't from the sun spilled over the mob.

"I'm healed!" a young man shouted, emerging from the crowd. Others stopped to stare at him. "I had a club foot. Now look!" He marched in a line, his gait perfect. "All I did was walk in his shadow."

This set off a mad rush to get near Daniel. Releasing her hand, Calan ordered her to stay there and shoved his way through the mob, disappearing among them. But soon, Daniel's voice rose above the mayhem, calm and caring, announcing his return in a week.

Another person emerged from the throng, eyes wide and tears streaming down her face. She kept glancing down at her hands, flipping them over and over as if she hardly recognized them. "I had rheumatoid arthritis," she finally squeaked out, glancing over the few who had stopped to question her.

In shock, Nyla watched as person after person got healed. She watched, until her mind raced, seeking another explanation, any explanation besides the one that stared her straight in the face.

The thief does not come except to steal, and to kill, and to destroy. I have come that they may have life, and that they may have it more abundantly. John 10:10

Chapter 24

The last thing Nyla should be doing is having dinner with Calan. She should be home, praying, or whatever people did when they came head-to-head with proof that there actually might be a God, a creator of all things, and that He was good and loving. But she supposed she hadn't come quite far enough to pray yet. She needed to think, to ponder what she had seen, maybe even pass her thoughts by someone sane, someone like Marco.

Yet when Daniel and the others had safely driven off, Calan took her aside and asked her on a date. For some reason, she'd been unable to say no. Besides, she needed to get rid of him before Marco and the PKs arrived and made her look suspicious. Why Marco wasn't answering her, she didn't know, but no sooner had she gotten into her Jeep and pulled onto the street, than her troops arrived. Thankfully, Calan had already sped off on his Harley.

The same Harley he'd picked her up on for their *date*—if that's what you called it. Oddly, deep down, she wanted it to be, and that only added to her confusion.

They entered the Mai-Kai, one of the few original restaurants still open after the tsunami, and Nyla suddenly felt underdressed. Everyone in South Florida knew about the Mai-Kai, an elaborately decorated, fun, and expensive place to get great Polynesian food and even better entertainment. Nyla had never been. Not only had her family been too poor, but now that she looked around, neither had she ever owned a fancy skirt or a pretty sundress like most women were wearing. She frowned down at her best pair of jeans and her favorite lacy peach shirt.

"You look beautiful," Calan said just as the hostess arrived to show them to their table.

How did the man always seem to know what she was thinking? "I can't believe you can afford this place." Nyla could hardly keep her eyes on the host as he wove around tables and down aisles decorated with Polynesian statues, masks, Tiki lights, and tropical plants. Brightly colored lamps hung from a thatched roof held up by poles carved with native figures. The host stopped at a white-clothed table beside a window overlooking the gardens.

Calan pulled out her chair. "I know the owner."

Nyla stood there a moment, unsure what to do. She'd never had a man pull out her chair before. She imagined most of them worried that she would slug them for such a demeaning act. Which she might well have.

She sat. "Thank you."

"How is your grandmother?" Calan asked after he sat across from her.

"Hanging in there. Not getting better but not worse. Kyle, my brother, is with her now." Carolyn had gone home when Kyle woke up, and Nyla had promised him she would be home before he went to work. She only hoped he would take good care of Tata in the meantime.

"I'm sorry to hear that. You really should have Daniel come pray for her."

The waiter arrived and they both ordered a fruity drink and an appetizer.

Candlelight flickered over Calan, making him even more handsome. Or maybe just more interesting, stronger...the way it highlighted the light stubble on his firm jaw and sparkled in his blue eyes as he looked at her. Or maybe it was just the *way* he looked at her that caused her stomach to flutter.

She was hungry, that's all. She hadn't eaten since this morning.

"Wanna talk about what happened today?" he asked.

"No." She smiled and took a sip of her drink. "I don't know. I… I don't know what I saw."

"I could tell you saw something, probably whatever it was I was sensing."

"Hmm, so you sense it and I see it. We make quite the pair." The words were out there before she realized what they could mean.

"We make a great pair." Calan grinned. "So, do you believe now?"

She flattened her lips and slipped a strand of hair behind her ear. "I believe something powerful is happening at these meetings. Something not of this world. But what, I'm not sure."

"It's the power of God." Calan leaned back in his chair, staring at her with a knowing grin. "Sometimes it's pretty intense, I agree. Especially when Daniel really senses God's presence." He chuckled. "He loves preaching in front of that mermaid bar."

"But a bar?"

"Yeah. It's where his…well…it's where the woman he loved worked."

Angelica? Daniel had made her sound like a saint. "She worked at a topless bar?"

"Before, it was just a normal bar."

Nyla withheld a chuckle. The famous pastor's story just got stranger and stranger. "What I don't get is how people can be healed if he doesn't even touch them? Doesn't pray or command or whatever he does."

"It's in the Bible."

"Really?"

"The Apostle Peter did the same thing. The power of God was on him so strong, people would be desperate just to get in his shadow to be healed."

Nyla swirled her drink with the umbrella stick. She must have looked skeptical because Calan reached for her hand. "I wish you'd believe. It's obvious God has given you a gift, and He has a purpose for you."

She huffed. "What, to go to prison? I already have a purpose." Not that she would tell him.

Withdrawing his hand, Calan frowned and glanced over the restaurant. And for some reason, Nyla felt bad that she'd upset him. Thankfully, the waiter came and, after they ordered their food, conversation lightened a bit. Savory scents from dozens of meals swirled beneath Nyla's nose. Her stomach growled. Calan smiled.

"Sorry," she said. "I guess I'm famished."

"That makes me happy." He looked away awkwardly.

"That I'm hungry?" she teased.

"No, that I can give you a good meal." He glanced back at her, gazing at her as if she were...what? a princess? He seemed to want to say something, then stopped. Finally, he smiled sheepishly, and she could tell he was feeling awkward again. "The tsunami only wiped out part of this place, so the owner was able to rebuild most of it to the original specs. It's one of a few decent restaurants still running around here." He ran a hand back through his hair and shook his head. "Of course, you know that. Still, with all the shortages, the menu isn't what it used to be, but I'm sure the meals are still delicious."

She didn't want to talk about food. She wanted to talk about Calan, to learn more about this man. But he suddenly seemed so out of place, like a teenager on a first date. So, she asked him about his job at the warehouse and how they started Zion's Nest, to which he happily responded with zeal. He then asked her what it was like being a PK and was the training difficult? Talking about it only reminded her of her duplicity, so she was thankful when the food arrived.

She didn't hesitate to dive into her plate of sea scallops and rice. "Tell me about your brother. You were about to the other night, and then we got interrupted."

With a heavy sigh, Calan gripped his fork and stared at his plate of Mai-Kai beef. "It's not a good story, but I'll share it." He took a bite and then sat back. "My brother and I were orphans. Both our parents were killed in a car accident shortly after he was born. I was nine. My brother just a few months old."

The food in Nyla's mouth soured. She swallowed. "I can't imagine how horrible that was. I'm so sorry."

"We were separated in the foster care system. I hopped around a lot, causing trouble in every home I was placed."

Nyla smiled. Now *that,* she could imagine. She slipped a spoonful of scallops covered in lobster cream sauce into her mouth, the taste exploding into tiny droplets of pure enjoyment. It had been a long time since she'd had food this good. "So you never knew where your brother was?"

"No." Calan sipped his drink and took another bite. "Not until I turned eighteen, got out of the system and found him. As soon as I got custody of Chris, I got a job and took care of him. I was working days and going to school at night."

Such a hard life. One she could well understand since she had done much the same after her parents disappeared.

"I couldn't make ends meet. I couldn't care for Chris like I wanted. He was emotionally scarred from his years in foster care. He'd had a run-in with drugs, was in juvenile for a short time. I needed money to send him to a good school, get him counseling. So, after I finished college, I joined the Navy, got into pre-BUD/S, and then made it onto BUD/S for SEAL training. It was good money, better than I'd ever made, and I guess I found my calling." He smiled. "I loved it."

He sat back, closed his eyes, and squeezed the bridge of his nose before continuing. "And the women loved it too. You might as well know that I've had trouble with women in the past."

She set down her fork and stared at him. Actually, it did shock her. He didn't seem the philandering type.

"When I got my first overseas deployment, Chris was only fourteen. I was involved with a woman at the time. A lawyer.

We were engaged. She knew Chris well and offered to look after him while I was gone. I foolishly agreed."

As if a heavy drape had closed, Calan's light demeanor darkened. He swallowed hard as if he were trying to swallow down the memory. Nyla wanted to reach across the table to him, but she wanted him to continue, to get it all out.

Picking up his fork, he shoved the remainder of his food around his plate. "She found some other guy and abandoned Chris. He hooked up with a gang and was shot on the street. The coroner said he was full of MDMA."

Nyla's appetite fled. Setting down her spoon, she leaned back on her chair, finding no words to say. What a horrible story. What a horrible burden to bear. He blamed himself for his brother's death. She could see it written all over his face as plain as on the pages of any tragic novel.

He released a sigh and rubbed his chin. "It's my fault. I should never have left him. I shouldn't have trusted Claire…that woman." He stared into the room, his thoughts far away. "She had me convinced she loved me. She swore on her life to take care of Chris. And I left him to die."

"You couldn't have known."

His stern gaze snapped to hers. "I *should* have known. But I've always had a weakness for…for women, I guess."

Several minutes passed as the waiter returned to clear their plates. In the distance, drums and music began for the night's entertainment. Finally, she reached for his hand. Thankfully, he gripped it. "I'm sorry that happened to you."

He caressed her fingers. "You aren't going to try to convince me that I'm not to blame, that I didn't kill my own brother?"

"You have to work that out with yourself. Nothing I, or anyone, says will help. Listen, we all make mistakes. My past is full of them. The key is to get beyond it and do better."

"You sound like Daniel."

"Whoops. I don't want to do that!"

They both laughed.

"You're a special lady, Nyla. You know that?"

Marco had called her special, too, but the look in Calan's eyes spoke of something deeper, more meaningful, and it made her tingle all over.

"Wanna get out of here and take a ride down by the beach?"

She'd love nothing more.

After he paid the check, he led her out through the gardens, always with that touch to her back that spoke of protection and ownership. She should mind it, should tell him she didn't need either. But she didn't want him to stop.

The Mai-Kai had once boasted of gorgeous Polynesian gardens filled with thick tropical foliage, lit by green lights, complete with small bridges over ponds, and gushing waterfalls. Athough all of it was plastic and fake now, it appeared nearly the same as Calan escorted her down a small stone path that wove through the lush tropical paradise. Lanterns lit their way as gentle music created a romantic atmosphere, and Nyla drew a deep breath of air, pretending that it smelled of earth and loam and freshness instead of plastic and ash, pretending that, for just this moment, that the cruel world outside didn't exist. That there weren't wars and Neflams and reformation camps, lost loved ones, and food shortages, and disasters.

Calan gripped her hand and held it tight as he stopped before a backlit waterfall. Blue light flickered over cascading water that bubbled and frothed in a small pond. "I had fun tonight."

"Me too. Thanks for dinner."

Turning toward her, he brushed hair from her face as he was prone to do, then ran a thumb down her cheek. She covered the scar on her neck, suddenly self-conscious, but he removed her hand and kissed it. Before she knew it, his lips lowered to hers. Gently at first, caressing, exploring before passion enveloped them both, and she clung to him, allowing him a full kiss. And my, my, my, her entire body buzzed from head to toe with an electric shock of pleasure and longing she'd not felt before.

They parted breathless, their lips still inches from each other.

When a very familiar voice resounded, "Nyla, what are you doing here?"

Every sense, every nerve instantly tightened as she turned to see Marco, a gorgeous blond on his arm.

Then the fourth angel sounded: And a third of the sun was struck, a third of the moon, and a third of the stars, so that a third of them were darkened. A third of the day did not shine, and likewise the night. Revelation 8:12

Chapter 25

Calan dropped into the cushioned chair in Daniel's office and heaved a frustrated sigh.

"Your date went that good, eh?" Daniel walked over to put a book back on the shelf, then turned to face his friend.

"It *was* going great. I even told her about my brother."

"Bet that was hard for you."

"Yeah. Besides you, no one else knows. I felt I could trust her, you know? There's something about her." He leaned forward, elbows on his knees. "Maybe I'm fooling myself. What do I know about trustworthy women?"

Daniel took a seat across from him and waited, as he usually did when Calan was sorting through his thoughts out loud.

"Food was good, conversation great. I could tell what she witnessed this afternoon at our revival had affected her. For the best." He slanted his lips. "Then I kissed her."

Daniel smiled.

Calan nodded. "Yeah. A good kiss, one of those mind-blowing, body-jarring, wow kisses." He leaned back with a huff. "Then some couple came up to us. Nyla went stiff on me. Even though the lighting wasn't good, I watched all the color drain from her face."

Daniel's brow furrowed. "She knew whoever it was."

"Yeah. Told me she used to work with the guy." Calan shook his head. "But something changed. She was quiet on the way home. Barely said a word."

"Hmm."

Tribby leapt into his lap and began to purr. He caressed her, happy for the comfort. "I met her brother again."

Daniel cocked his head, studying him. "What is he like?"

"A kid, really. I don't know, maybe twenty. Works at one of the NWU concentration camps. He stared at me as if I were a cockroach he longed to step on."

"What did you sense about him?"

"Darkness. Confusion, drugs."

Daniel nodded.

"Tell me what to do." Calan closed his eyes for a moment and squeezed the bridge of his nose. "I don't want to make any more mistakes. If God has given her a gift to see into the spirit realm, doesn't that mean she'll join the Kingdom eventually?"

"I would think so, Calan," Daniel said with a shrug. "But honestly, in the Tribulation, I'm not sure how things work. Of course God wants her saved, but just because He gives someone a gift, doesn't mean that person will make the right choice."

Calan huffed. "Then I shouldn't see her anymore." He set Tribby down.

"I didn't say that. There's still hope."

"I'm falling for her."

Moments passed in which Daniel lowered his gaze, as he often did when he was deep in thought. Finally, he looked up. "The Lord is going to give her visions soon."

Calan couldn't hide his shock. "Visions? Of what?"

"Possible futures."

"Okay." Calan had no idea what that meant or whether these visions would do any good. He was a here-and-now kind of guy, and in the here-and-now, he feared he was making a huge mistake. "I don't trust myself. She was a Peace Keeper. She knows where Zion's Nest is. What have I done?" Shaking his head, he leaned forward and stared at the floor. "Have I gone and compromised us? Have I put you in danger just because of my stupid romantic notions?"

"You give yourself too much credit, Calan. Isn't God the one in control?"

"Of course. But He won't always protect me from my own foolishness."

"Give it to Him. Ask Him to guide you. If your heart is in the right place, you can't go wrong in that." Reaching out, Daniel gripped Calan's shoulder. "Besides, we have other concerns. The fourth trumpet is about to blow."

Calan sat up straight. "Then I need to check the supplies. Get more as needed."

"It's wise to prepare, Calan, but remember God is our provider." Daniel stared at him with the seriousness of a college professor. "There may be times when there is nothing to prepare, nothing to store. That's when your faith must be the strongest it has ever been."

Calan nodded, remembering that Daniel said his time was coming to an end. Was he telling Calan all these things—all the lessons he had taught him over the past year—preparing him to carry on without him? Calan couldn't think about that now. Didn't want to even talk about it.

"Thanks for listening. I don't know what I'd do without you."

Daniel smiled—that knowing and wise smile that made Calan feel so unworthy of his friendship.

After glancing both ways, Nyla opened the Audi R8 car door, slid onto the passenger seat, and slammed it shut. Marco's spicy aftershave filled her nose with its alluring scent and her mind with tantalizing memories even before she dared to face him.

He wasn't looking at her. Instead, he stared at the steering wheel as if he wanted to tear it from the dash and toss it out the window. She shouldn't be meeting him like this in public, but after what happened…well, whatever needed to be said had to be said in person. Especially since he'd hardly spoken a word to her over coms. Finally, after a week of trying to get him to talk, she pleaded with him to meet. Of course he'd been mad when he'd shown up at the location she'd given him and the Deviants were gone. She'd tried to explain that they'd just left, that she'd tried to keep them there, but he'd shut her off, angry. But this? Cheating on her?

Glancing out the window, she waited for him to say something, thankful for the sliver of moon which barely pushed back the dark night, thankful also he'd found a private place to park. Though she desperately wanted to hear his side of the story, neither did she want to jeopardize her assignment.

"So…"

"What…"

They both spoke simultaneously.

"Listen, Marco," she began with a sigh. "Just tell me if you've moved on. I'm a big girl. I can handle it."

He swung those bedroom eyes her way. Normally a sheen of seduction covered them.Tonight they were filled with anger. "Me? Moved on? What was up with that kiss?"

"No way. No, you aren't changing the subject. I'm on assignment. You aren't."

"Ah, that's what you call it! I don't remember Jennings telling you to sleep with the guy!"

"I'm *not* sleeping with him!" Not that she hadn't wanted to, especially after that kiss—a kiss she relived over and over in her dreams. "Why are you so angry with me? You're the one with the busty blond on your arm."

Releasing a low growl, he faced the windshield. "She's just a friend."

Nyla gave a cynical laugh. "Give me a break, Marco. You forget, I know you better than anyone."

"It's nothing." He swung his gaze to her again, but this time pain and pleading filled his eyes. "She means nothing to me. I just…I just have needs since you've been gone."

Needs? Nyla's anger broiled. "So that's all I am, someone to fill your needs?" She reached for the door handle. "Forget it, then."

He grabbed her arm. "No, you're much more than that. You know that, babe. I love you. Why else would I be so jealous over seeing you kissing that *Deviant?*" All anger fled his eyes, and once again his love for her returned. Or was it lust?

Still, her anger refused to abate. "Let me get this straight. It's okay for you to be jealous, but not me? It's okay for you to sleep with someone else, but I can't kiss someone? For an assignment? Is that it?"

"I'm sorry." He released her and seemed to shrivel in his seat. "You're right. I just went crazy when I saw you with him."

She'd had the same reaction when she'd seen him with that blond. Yet that was a week ago, and in all honesty, Calan's kiss, along with what she'd seen at the revival, had consumed her thoughts more than Marco's infidelity. In fact, she was well aware of the way women looked at Marco and the way he looked at them. It was one of the reasons she liked being with him. It made her feel special he had chosen her.

She stared down at the pristine floor mat and smiled. Marco always kept his car buffed and spotless. "I have to get close to Calan so I can find out where Daniel is. I told you that."

"But you don't have to enjoy it."

"And neither do you," she shot back.

"True." He gave her that charming boyish grin. "I won't see her again, okay?"

She wanted to believe him. She did. But deep down, she didn't trust him. She never really had. If there was anything she'd learned over the years, it was that no one could be trusted.

"Hopefully, this will all be over with soon," she said.

He leaned toward her, and before she could protest, he consumed her lips with his. His scent, his taste, so familiar and usually igniting an urgent need for more.

Only not this time. The kiss fell flat. Confused, she withdrew, hoping he didn't notice. Thankfully, he didn't appear to. Instead he smiled. "I've missed you so much, babe."

"Me too." Though she wondered at his sincerity, especially when once again the vision of the gorgeous blond popped in her mind. "Hey, why didn't you ever take me to Mai-Kai?"

His phone rang. He answered, his eyes growing more intense as he listened. Finally he said, "On my way." Hanging up, he stared out the window.

"What is it?"

"Yellowstone has blown. And three other active volcanoes across the globe."

"What?"

"Yeah, gotta run, babe. We good?"

"Sure." Nyla gave him a peck on the lips and got out of the car. He sped away, leaving her alone in the dark in a bad part of town. Something Calan would never have done. But no matter. If what he said was true, the world was in a really bad way.

The sound of a loud trumpet echoed across the night sky.

A week later, videos of lava spewing into the air continued to fill the TV screen.

"Yellowstone in Montana, Kilauea in Hawaii, Mount Etna in Sicily, Mount Merapi in Indonesia, and Ambrym in Vanuatu continue to erupt, though there are signs of each one slowing down," the newscaster said, horror pinching his normally handsome features. "Yellowstone's plume of ash, lava, and volcanic gases has reached ten miles into the sky, where it is being blown coast to coast. At least two feet of ash has fallen in the Rockies thus far."

The lady newscaster, a blond that looked much like the one Marco had been with, took up the narrative as the video shifted to a busy emergency room. "Hospitals are full of victims, coughing up blood as the silicate in the ash slashes their lungs. It is recommended that you wear a mask outside at all times, even in locations where there isn't much ash. Also beware of acid rain. Scientists project it will kill off a good portion of sea and freshwater life."

The screen pictured what was left of a crushed barn and an open field covered in soot. The newscaster continued. "The heavy ash has collapsed roofs, contaminated water supplies, downed power lines, prevented some air travel, and still might take out electrical transformers, bringing the nation's power grid to its knees. Worse still, ashfall will possibly wipe out the Midwest's crop of corn and soybeans. Much of America's rich farmland might be poisoned for a generation. Combine this with a likely worldwide volcanic winter, in which global average temperatures could plunge as much as eighteen degrees Fahrenheit for a decade, and you have a recipe for a global starvation event that could endanger hundreds of millions of people."

Nyla dropped her head in her hands. A numb horror crept over her, stealing all hope and joy. It had only been a week since the eruptions worldwide and already the sky was darker, and the temperature had dropped ten degrees. Floridians who normally only wore tee-shirts, shorts, and flip-flops walked around in sweaters, long pants, and shoes.

Kyle opened his prescription bottle of CBD and downed another pill.

"That won't help, Kyle." Tata muttered from her easy chair. "It only dulls the brain and the senses."

"Exactly," Kyle snorted back.

"We expect to see even more food and water shortages in the near future," the newscaster said. "Best to prepare now. Scientists are saying that one-third of the light from the sun, moon, and stars will not reach earth for quite some time."

"Ha!" Tata exclaimed, drawing Nyla's gaze. "Get my Bible, will you, dear?"

Kyle growled. "We should burn that thing. I could get fired if they knew I had it in my house."

"Dear boy, it is neither your house nor a thing, but the living Word of God Almighty."

"Whatever." Kyle cussed.

Nyla returned with the book and handed it to Tata. "Respect your grandmother, Kyle. You know she doesn't like that kind of language."

He frowned. "Since I'm the one making the money now, I should have a say," he grumbled.

Tata opened the Bible and flipped over a few pages. "Here it is. And the fourth angel sounded, and the third part of the sun was smitten, and the third part of the moon, and the third part of the stars; so as the third part of them was darkened, and the day shone not for a third part of it, and the night likewise."

Nyla swallowed. She could no longer deny this book was telling the future. And quite accurately. Did the Neflams have the power to tell the future? Not that she had heard. Nor would they put their predictions in a book they arrested people for possessing. Her head hurt trying to figure it all out.

"What does that prove?" Kyle spat out. "That's just some old book that people could easily alter."

"It proves there is a God," Tata's voice came out shaky and scratchy. "It proves He is in control, and you had better listen to Him." She pointed a crooked finger at her grandson.

"Now, Tata, calm yourself down." Nyla went to the kitchen to get her some water, but the dirty dishes piled up in the sink reminded her that it was shut off, at least for eight hours a day. The smell of rotten food curled her nose, and she reached for the jug of water on the counter and poured some in a glass.

Tata had been on the medicine nearly a month now and had not gotten better. Her fever came and went, along with her appetite, and she often complained of shortness of breath and joint pain.

Kyle slouched back onto the couch. "Well, you can thank me and not Him when we have enough food to eat. I am making powerful friends at the Broward Reformation Camp. Powerful. And people who align with them have everything they need."

"The devil's people," Tata said as Nyla handed her the cup.

"You don't know them." Kyle stood, adjusting his uniform. "They are beautiful, wise, and kind."

Immediately, Nyla saw a dark cloud slithering around him. Frozen, she watched it slink and slide around Kyle's chest, arms, and head. A face suddenly lunged at her from within the hideous mist, teeth baring, eyes red.

She leapt back. And then it was gone.

"What's *your* problem?" Giving her a look of disgust, Kyle pushed past her toward the door.

"Tata is right," Nyla said. "We don't know much about these Tall Whites except that they rule over the Neflams on their planet. What if they are evil? What if they are tricking you?"

"That's crap. Like I said, you don't know them. They are the only ones who have ever believed in me. They think I have great potential and will quickly rise in their organization to a position of authority." Anger flared from his eyes, but also pain, *tremendous* pain. "You never believed in me. And neither did Mom or Dad. They only criticized me. Like you and Tata. I never measure up."

Nyla's heart broke. "I'm sorry, Kyle. It's just that we love you. We all want the best for you. Tell me you didn't join their club. What was it called, Kabal?"

"I'm joining today. The initiation is tonight."

Tata moaned.

Nyla opened her mouth to try to talk him out of it, but he raised a hand to silence her and slammed out the door.

For He shall give His angels charge over you, to keep you in all your ways. In their hands they shall bear you up, lest you dash your foot against a stone. Psalm 91:11-12

Chapter 26

Nyla plopped down on the sand, removed her shoes, and shoved her toes into the cool grains. Cool, yes, because, though it was nearly noon, the sky was a dark grey, as if a storm blew in. Yet there was no storm. The beach was unusually empty for this time of day, except for several body surfers wearing wet suits and a few families wrapped in blankets having a picnic. Though only about sixty degrees, it felt like winter to most Floridians.

She was thankful for the peace and quiet. She needed to think, clear her head, figure out what to do. Normally she ran full steam ahead with whatever life brought her, but things she'd witnessed over the last couple of months had shoved her train off track.

After a fitful night of tossing and turning, playing with Spots, and flipping through Tata's Bible, Nyla had spent the morning trying to get her grandmother's fever down. Kyle had burst through the front door, said not a word, and stomped to his room to sleep. The living area seemed to darken as he swept through, leaving a foul odor behind him. Maybe she was just imagining things. She'd finally gotten Tata to eat something, and the woman had fallen fast asleep in her bed.

A gust of wind, ripe with the scent of sea and smoke, flipped Nyla's wayward curls behind her and trickled goosebumps down her arms. She hugged herself. On the way to the beach, she'd encountered traffic jams and long lines of people trying to stock up on what food and water remained in the stores, which wasn't much. Homeless encampments had sprouted up everywhere, and of course, rioting had broken out. Oh, how she longed to join her fellow PKs in helping maintain control...do anything normal again that had purpose.

Not live in this state of constant confusion and fear. It just wasn't like her.

She hadn't seen Calan in over a week, though he had called a few times. Each time she saw his name on her phone, her heart leapt. In a good way, and she hated that. She didn't want to fall for this Deviant! For *any* Deviant! Closing her eyes, she tried to rekindle her fury and hatred for the people who had misled her parents and so many others, the people who had caused so much agony in the world. But she found only a spark remained. Crud! How was this any different from Kyle joining his cult?

No. There was definitely something evil going on with Kyle. That much was obvious.

Then there was Tata. Nyla could only sit and watch her sweet grandmother fade a little more each day—slowly slipping out of this world and into the next bit by bit, and there was nothing Nyla could do about it.

Her eyes burned. She rubbed them. Another thing she rarely did. Cry.

What would she do without Tata? Without her calming love and care, her wisdom? She'd be all alone in the world.

Not alone.

Nyla pressed her ear. Had Marco spoken? Couldn't have. She'd not put her com piece in before she left.

Marco. The love of her life. Or was he? She had thought so once. Yet seeing him with that bimbo hadn't affected her as much as it should have. She *was* jealous, sure. But it was more her pride than her fear of losing him. She did love him in a way. But maybe she was simply using him for her own prestige just as he was using her for...what? Sex? Who knew, when she could so easily be replaced?

No, her thoughts focused more on Calan, the way he treated others with such kindness and care, even strangers, the way he treated her as if she were a priceless crystal vase to be protected, his strength and skill, his dedication to Daniel. There was so much to admire about the ex-Navy SEAL.

But the main thing causing her mind to tie into knots was this God of the Deviants. Surely He must be real. There was no other explanation—not for the angels and demons she saw more and more frequently, not for the love the Deviants had for everyone, not for the words of an ancient book that came true on a daily basis.

Waves crashed on the shore, spewing up foam. A baby cried in the distance, and Nyla grabbed a handful of sand and let it slide through her fingers.

If this Creator in the Bible was real, then this Jesus guy was real, and that meant that what was happening in the world was not at all what she believed.

That was the hardest part of all. Believing in this God would mean her entire life had been a lie.

A *caw, caw* overhead drew her gaze to a black bird circling above her. A raven? There weren't ravens in Florida. Yet it continued to circle and was soon joined by another and another, until their screeches drowned out the crash of the surf.

An icy chill enveloped her. Rising to her feet, she glanced down the beach. No one else seemed to hear or see the dozen or so birds hovering and shrieking above her head.

A large figure outlined in sparkling white stepped in front of her. Her heart thundered against her ribs. Standing at least two feet above her, his body reflected the surroundings like a shimmering pool. His hair was the color of the sun. Golden armor covered his shoulders. He raised a crossbow above his head.

Then he was gone.

So were the ravens.

Nyla's head swam. Her breath clogged in her throat, and she nearly collapsed to her knees. Instead, she crept down to the shore's edge and bent over, leaning her palms on her knees. Foamy, cold water swept over her bare feet as she tried to collect her thoughts. Calan had said God assigned angels to protect them. Was that hers? He looked an awful lot like the one she'd seen at the revival.

She wanted to pray but had no idea how.

Instead, she straightened and gazed over the leaden sea. Something appeared on top of the water several yards out, like a mirage, or a projection of a scene. It was her! She and Calan stood in front of a huge crowd, maybe hundreds of people. Calan was preaching, and Nyla was praying for people who stood in a line, laying hands on each one and smiling.

The wind blew, and the vision vanished.

And I looked, and I heard an angel flying through the midst of heaven, saying with a loud voice, "Woe, woe, woe to the inhabitants of the earth, because of the remaining blasts of the trumpet of the three angels who are about to sound!"
Revelation 8:13

Ranoss smiled up at the sky where he'd sent the demons fleeing with one command and an array of flaming arrows. These were the lowest level of demonic beings that always appeared to humans in raven form. Possessing very little power to do much of anything but annoy the sons of Adam, they often sped off at the sight of one of the Commander's mighty warriors.

She saw me again. For some reason, he was pleased when Nyla could see him. He knew her so well, had been with her since her birth, that it felt good when she noticed him. Then again, the Commander had warned him not to get involved. Something he must work on.

He glanced at her, standing down by the shore, and knew her mind was troubled by all she'd seen and experienced. If only he could pray for her as humans could, but his job was to protect and nothing more. Perhaps later, he'd be told to bring food, water, and other things to her, things she would have need of as the world grew darker, as his fellow angels did for their wards. But for now, until she was transferred from the kingdom of darkness into the kingdom of light, he must only protect—and then only when commanded to.

Something alerted him, a strong sense of coming doom and destruction. Dark spirits roamed the beach as usual, but nothing out of the ordinary. 'Twas difficult to watch these sons of Adam suffer, but the judgments of the Almighty were just and necessary. If they only knew of the mercy and love of the one true God, they would turn from their wicked ways and bow before Him. If they only knew the eternal pleasures that awaited them, they would find nothing in this realm of any value but knowing the Lord Almighty. Praise be His name forever! Many had already turned to Him. Many more would come. His gaze dropped to Nyla making her way back to her car. Hopefully, her name would soon be found in the Book of Life.

A booming voice thundered above Ranoss, and he looked up. Ah, 'twas Duzar, one of the Commander's heralds.

"Woe, woe, woe, to the inhabiters of the earth by reason of the other voices of the trumpet of the three angels, which are yet to sound!" Duzar shouted in a bellowing, trumpet-like voice, then flew onward.

Nyla halted and stared at the sky, her expression confused. Ranoss glanced over the beach, noting that only one of the sons of Adam lounging on the sand looked up. Only those with ears to hear ever heard the Commander's warnings. Praise His name that Nyla had.

Shaking her head, she started back toward her Jeep.

Ranoss followed close behind, drawing his blade.

After Nyla responded with the secret phrase, Max opened the door to Zion's Nest, wearing a huge smile. No sooner had she stepped inside than the bear of a man swallowed her up in yet another of his huge embraces. Normally she didn't like to be touched, but for some reason, Max's hug made her feel welcome, even loved.

"Don't squeeze the life out of her," Calan said as he approached, both the grin on his lips and the expression of delight on his face taking her by surprise. It had only been two weeks. Had he missed her that much? He walked up to her and took her hand in his, and for a moment she thought he intended to bring it to his mouth for a kiss like the gallants of old. But he released it, eased a lock of her hair behind her ear, as was his way, and said, "I'm so glad you called and decided to come."

For a moment, she merely stared at him, noting the care in his blue eyes, trying to sort through her own feelings of joy at seeing him. She *had* missed him. She already knew that. But to have her entire body react at his presence was quite another thing.

"Me too." She nodded, wanting to fall against him, feel his arms around her.

Instead, a swarm of people surrounded them, flooding her with kind greetings. Not plastic hellos and "nice to see you again," but real heartfelt welcomes.

Pam eased up beside her. "How's your grandmother?"

"Still feverish, but she's resting now. Kyle is with her."

"Well, I'm available any time to help." She smiled, her short blond bob shaking.

Nyla put a hand on the kind woman's arm. "That means a lot. Thank you."

The scent of buttery baked bread swirled beneath Nyla's nose, causing her stomach to rumble. "Fresh bread?" She looked up at Calan as everyone went back to their tasks.

His brows rose. "Want some?"

"Are you kidding me?" Nyla glanced over at the kitchen where Carolyn had returned to take something out of the oven.

"Where did you guys get flour, milk, and butter? The stores are empty." Not only that, but tap water was being rationed, and nary a bottle of water could be found for purchase anywhere.

"When are you going to believe that God provides for His people?" Calan's brows rose. "It just shows up, bags of flour, butter, other things. Some of it we find on our doorsteps. Other supplies are sent to us in boxes. I can't explain it except to say we trust God and His Word."

One more mystery to join the spinning cyclone in her mind. But she hadn't come here for that. She'd come to talk to Daniel about the angel and the vision she'd seen. And of course to see Calan. She hoped seeing him again would make things clearer, but how could she think straight when he stood so close?

"He's on!" Javier shouted, luring everyone to join him to watch the only TV in the room.

She recognized the voice coming across the screen before she saw his face. Immu Aali, the NWU Premier. She'd forgotten he was addressing the world today.

"Fellow World Citizens." He glanced over the crowd assembled before him then nodded at the camera. He stood atop a stage set before the ruins of the Colosseum in Rome with the other seven regional kings and the pope standing behind him.

"This world has recently endured many tragedies, all of which have been out of our control. Fires have devoured a third of our crops and a third of our forests. Asteroids and meteors have polluted a third of our seas and a third of our fresh waters. And now with the recent volcanic eruptions blocking out the sun, we face a shortage of food and water that will, no doubt, bring further diseases. While I know many of you are suffering, I'm here to offer good news, news that will bring back hope, restore life, and advance mankind."

Calan slipped beside Nyla, but his eyes were riveted on the premier. She wondered if the Deviants still thought he was evil, this Antichrist they spoke about. Glancing around the room, she found not a single Deviant was smiling. Instead, all wore somber expressions as they watched the TV, especially Daniel, who had emerged from the hallway to stand beside Calan.

"As I have previously announced, the NWU regional kings have been working closely with the Neflams to incorporate new technology that will prevent incoming debris from space from entering our atmosphere—both defensive and offensive measures that will protect our wonderful planet."

Applause roared as the camera panned over the crowd, which had to be in the thousands.

"I only regret," he continued, "that we didn't have such capabilities sooner." True sorrow clouded his handsome Middle Eastern features. "In addition, we are working closely with the Neflams to clean our atmosphere from the soot and ash presently blocking our sun. Their knowledge and technology are amazing, and I expect to see our skies blue and clear within a few months."

More applause broke out as the people lifted hands in the air, their faces filled with joy and wonder.

"Unfortunately, the eruptions of these volcanoes have caused considerable damage and loss of life. The NWU has spared no expense in sending emergency teams to each location to assist survivors in either rebuilding their lives or to move to more habitable locations. Their universal incomes will be increased to cover further expense until they are settled and on their feet again."

Cheers bounced through the crowd as people began chanting, "Aali! Aali! Aali!"

With a huge smile on his face, the premier raised his hands to silence them.

"As premier of the NWU, I promise we will do our best to distribute food and water to each region as needed, but I assure you that soon we hope to install new agricultural technology that will double the food production of the globe!"

Again the crowd exploded in cheers and praises.

"But I save the best news for last," Aali shouted, quieting them. "Imagine a world free of disease, free of war, free of conflict. A world that uses sustainable energy and preserves the natural balance of the planet, reduces global warming, and thus prevents the earthquakes, storms, and volcanoes that have plagued us of late. A world where social, economic, and racial equality are the rule of law and the impoverished and the outcasts are a thing of the past. A world in which all beliefs are combined into one religion, a faith that promotes love, peace, and unity, not rules, restrictions and bias."

Nyla smiled, astonished at the man's mesmerizing charisma. Truly this was the leader the world had waited for, someone to unite all of mankind and solve the earth's problems.

Applause filled the air. It took several minutes for Aali to be able to speak again.

"This is the goal of the NWU under my and the other regional kings' leadership." He glanced behind him at the seven kings before nodding at the pope.

When he faced forward again, his eyes held a gleam, a dark gleam, that Nyla had never seen before. "But even better," he continued, "a world where no one ages and no one dies."

The audience grew silent. Wind tossed the premier's black hair behind him as he gazed over the mob, then stared into the camera. "A world in which everyone will live forever!"

More applause and shouts of praise blared across the screen, along with looks of wonder on many of the people's faces.

Calan groaned. Daniel's jaw stiffened. Pam dropped her head in her hands, while Madeline sank to her knees on the rug in prayer. Javier and Elena hugged each other. Carolyn approached from the kitchen, dish towel in hand. Aaron, Violet, Beth, and Ephraim, along with the others, stared blankly at the screen. What was wrong with them? Wouldn't living forever be a good thing?

When the audience settled, Aali continued. "We are developing an injectable device using nano and gene-editing technology to reprogram human DNA, combining the most advanced biotechnology with lifesaving vaccines that will enhance human agility, brain power, strength, and longevity. Imagine a world without sickness or aging, a world where every one of us could become superheroes."

The crowd went wild, leaping and jumping and reaching toward Aali as if he were god himself.

Daniel nodded to Max, and the large man picked up the remote and turned off the TV.

"So, the Mark is almost here," Pam said to no one in particular.

Grabbing a Bible off a nearby table, Daniel gestured for everyone to sit. Calan took Nyla's hand and led her to a sofa in the corner as Daniel opened the book and started reading.

"And whereas thou sawest the feet and toes, part of potters' clay, and part of iron, the kingdom shall be divided; but there shall be in it of the strength of the iron, forasmuch as thou sawest the iron mixed with miry clay." Daniel looked up. "As we all know, the prophet Daniel is speaking of the final kingdom on earth, the one in which we now live." He started reading again. "And as the toes of the feet were part of iron, and part of clay, so the kingdom shall be partly strong, and partly broken. And whereas thou sawest iron mixed with miry clay, they shall mingle themselves with the seed of men: but they shall not cleave one to another, even as iron is not mixed with clay."

Stopping, Daniel frowned, glancing over the group. "We now know what the prophet Daniel was speaking about when he said iron and clay. It is the forging of human and technology. Transhumanism."

Nyla flinched. Of course she'd heard about transhumanism. They were already doing marvelous things with it. But wasn't it a good thing, a way to enhance human life? Calan must have noticed her uneasiness because he grabbed her hand and gave it a squeeze.

Daniel continued. "One more verse, and it's the most important one. 'And in the days of these kings shall the God of heaven set up a kingdom, which shall never be destroyed: and the kingdom shall not be left to other people, but it shall break in pieces and consume all these kingdoms, and it shall stand forever.'"

Every Deviant in the room shouted "Amen," with a few adding "Hallelujah."

But Nyla had questions. "Why is transhumanism a bad thing?"

"Very bad," Daniel answered. "It changes us from human to something not human. It changes our DNA, whether by adding tech or by fallen angel DNA."

Fallen angel DNA? Whoa. Nyla slanted her lips. "But if it eradicates disease and gives us strength, makes us smarter, isn't that good?"

Instead of answering, Daniel began flipping pages in his Bible. "'And he causeth all, both small and great, rich and poor, free and bond, to receive a mark in their right hand, or in their foreheads: And that no man might buy or sell, save he that had the mark, or the name of the beast, or the number of his name.' This is the injectable Aali is talking about."

"But isn't it already like that? No one can work without a VaxPass or a positive social credit score. This would just be another step."

"Listen to this in Revelation 14," Daniel continued. "'And the third angel followed them, saying with a loud voice, if any man worship the beast and his image, and receive his mark in his forehead, or in his hand, the same shall drink of the wine of the wrath of God, which is poured out without mixture into the cup of his indignation; and he shall be tormented with fire and brimstone in the presence of the holy angels, and in the presence of the Lamb.'"

"Oh, come on." Nyla wanted to laugh. "Fire and brimstone? Seems a rather harsh punishment. What if you got this mark by accident?"

"That's where the DNA changing comes in. If a person has been changed from human into something not entirely human, he or she cannot be saved. Jesus died and rose again for humans, not for angels, not for demons, not for anything other than humans."

Nyla's throat burned with an emotion she could not name. She swallowed it down. "So, if you take this thing, you go to hell? Is that what this is saying?" She was about to mention that she didn't believe in hell, but then she remembered her nightmare, and a cold sweat rose up her spine.

"Yes," Daniel answered matter-of-factly.

"So what are you supposed to do if you can't buy or sell anything or even get a job?"

Max smiled her way. "What we are doing now. Trusting in the Lord to supply all our needs."

"Many of us will die." Daniel's words held not an ounce of fear.

"To live is Christ, to die is gain!" Madeline said, glancing up from her prayers and causing all to utter. "Amen!"

Nyla rubbed her temples.

"You don't seem convinced, Nyla." Pam's voice drew her gaze to her.

"I don't know what I think anymore." And that was the truth. "So, tell me what's going to happen next? What does your Bible say?"

"The fifth trumpet brings great pain on the lost for five months." Sorrow claimed Daniel's expression. "It is unclear exactly what causes this, but I suspect demonic creatures will be released from the bottomless pit to infect people with painful sores."

This was all too much. Too much to process. Too much to believe. "Why so cruel? How can you worship a God who inflicts so much pain?"

"God warns people over and over," Pam said. "But there comes a time when He must judge evil, Nyla. He is just and cannot be otherwise. Besides, often these punishments are the only way some people will turn to Him."

"Let's worship the King of Kings!" Daniel gestured to Javier and Elena, who promptly went to get their guitars.

Releasing Calan's hand, Nyla stood and moved away. She'd come here to become less confused, not more, to unravel her knotted thoughts, not tangle them further.

Calan followed her. "You all right?"

Javier began strumming his guitar.

"Yeah. It's just a lot to take in." She attempted a smile. "How about some of that bread?" Better to distract Calan than have him see the doubt and confusion in her expression. She had yet to talk to Daniel about her vision. Now she wondered if it wouldn't be better just to contact Marco and have him arrested.

What was she thinking? She obviously had no intention of having Daniel arrested, or any of them. Which was why she kept purposely forgetting her com piece.

Confused, worried, alarmed, and even amazed, she took the bread, slathered in butter, Calan handed her. Delicious! A treat she hadn't had in months. Calan was slicing himself a piece when a knock on the door echoed through the room. The Deviants were too busy singing to hear it, leaving Calan to give the inquiry and receive the expected response.

Clarisse darted inside, wiping tears from her eyes, her normally pretty face a swollen mask of sorrow and despair.

Nyla gripped her arm. "What is wrong, Clarisse? What happened?"

The music stopped and Madeline, Pam, and Beth approached and led her to one of the couches.

Daniel knelt beside her.

Tears streaming down her face, Clarisse looked up at him. "Tyson and I fought. It was horrible."

Pam eased beside her on the couch, while Madeline took her hand and sat on the other side. "Every couple has fights, dear. It'll be okay."

Clarisse shook her head. "Not this time."

Pam handed her a tissue. After attempting to pat her face, she crumpled it in her hands and began sobbing again.

"What happened?" Max said. "I'm happy to go talk with him."

"No. It won't matter. He's not one of us. He's only been pretending."

Though shock rolled over all their expressions, Daniel remained stoic, as if he already knew.

"I guess I suspected all along." Clarisse closed her eyes as tear after tear spilled down her cheeks. "I just hoped...hoped he wasn't faking it for my sake." She dropped her head in her hands. Pam eased an arm around her and drew her near.

"Now I've lost my baby *and* my husband," she sobbed.

Daniel took her hand in his. "You haven't lost either. They've just been misplaced for a time. Trust in the Lord. All things work together for good."

Nyla knew these Deviants were tight, knew they cared for each other, but it still astounded her how, when one of them was in pain, the others rallied around, crying, as if they, too, felt the same agony.

In fact, she wanted to help Clarisse as well. If there's one thing she was very familiar with, it was loss and heartache.

Calan suddenly jerked. His body stiffened. His alarmed gaze snapped toward the door before he faced Daniel. "We have to leave. Now."

Daniel stared at him for a moment, but then stood and began barking orders for everyone to gather their things and follow him.

"What is it?" Nyla searched Calan's eyes.

"Someone gave us away. The NWU PKs are on their way to arrest us all."

But before all these things, they will lay their hands on you and persecute you, delivering you up to the synagogues and prisons. You will be brought before kings and rulers for My name's sake. Luke 21:12

Chapter 27

Mind and heart whirling, Nyla followed Calan out the door of Zion's Nest. She stopped to glance back over her shoulder, oddly sad to never be returning.

Carolyn and Max had insisted on remaining behind and now scrambled through the kitchen to pack up as many of the pots, pans, bowls, and silverware they could.

"Only for a few minutes," Daniel had instructed them. "Don't wait too long to leave."

"We'll be right behind you," Max had said.

"Come on, Nyla." Pam urged her from the other side of Violet as together they assisted the older lady to walk.

Calan, a black cat in his arms, glanced back at them, an urgency in his gaze she'd not seen before. Was he right? Were the NWU PKs on their way? She certainly had not alerted them. Of course they could probably see where she was, but surely they would not come without knowing Daniel was here.

Without so much as questioning Calan's declaration, Daniel had gathered up his people with a calm confidence that defied their situation. If he knew, as Nyla did, the expert skill and weaponry of the PKs, along with their determination and unwillingness to fail, maybe he'd be more frightened. As it was, Calan had a hard time getting the man to leave. Finally, with a backpack full of Bibles and notes flung over his shoulder, Daniel disappeared up the stairs in front of Calan.

"We haven't much time." Calan urged as Nyla and Pam hurried poor Violet onward as fast as the eighty-something woman could go.

One by one, the Deviants bolted up the stairs, scurried around crates and boxes, avoiding cameras as they'd been taught to do, finally to emerge into an empty parking lot, a setting sun blurred by ashen skies, a blast of humid air smelling of charcoal and gasoline, and the sound of sirens growing closer.

Daniel assembled everyone. "Get to your cars and go home. I'll be in touch about where we will meet in the future. Let's pray."

Pray? Was he kidding? Nyla well knew the sound of those particular sirens. The PKs would be here in minutes. A battle raged within her. Should she warn them or delay them? With Daniel arrested, her assignment would end, and she could return to her normal life. Wasn't that what she wanted? What the heck was wrong with her?

Leaving Pam to hold onto Violet, Nyla charged forward, unable to stop herself. "There's no time. We must hurry."

"She's right," Calan said. "I need to get you out of here. Fast!"

Ignoring them, Daniel closed his eyes. "Lord God Almighty, we ask for Your protection over us now. We ask for angelic escorts to usher each one of us to safety. We ask You to allow us to remain free so that we may help more people come into Your Kingdom. In Jesus' name, Amen!"

But it was too late.

Three black SUVs roared into the parking lot, sirens blaring. Nyla's heart felt like it crashed into a wall. She should be happy. Instead, she felt like screaming, "Run," to her new-found friends. But there would be no use now as the PKs poured out of the SUVs like bats jarred from their sleep, armed with enough weapons to confront an army.

Setting Tribby down on the pavement, Calan took her hand in his. "Stay still, everyone. Stay perfectly still."

What?

That's when she saw them.

Bright glowing figures, tall, muscular, wearing long flowing robes encased in armor and strapped with all manner of weapons. Some were massive, others thin, some had long hair, others no hair. All stood with their backs to the Deviants and their drawn swords facing outward.

Nyla's breath fled her lungs. Her knees gave out and she began to topple.

Grabbing her arm, Calan caught her, and after staring at her a few seconds said, "You see them, don't you?"

Nyla blinked. "I don't know...I see...."

"They were just there!" Marco dashed toward them. His fellow officers followed, their gazes scanning the parking lot.

"Didn't you see them?"

"Where they'd go?"

Marco stood mere yards from Nyla as his team—her team, all friends of hers—moved to scour the area. Part of her wanted to shout, to run and join them. This was her team, the team she'd worked so hard to lead. She should be with them. She should end this now!

But...how could she? In light of what she clearly saw—the beings of light cloaking the Deviants, making them invisible. Though she sought a rational explanation, some technological advancement the Deviants had in their possession, she knew better. She could see angels, which meant they were real, which meant...

Daniel glanced over them with a smile and gave her a nod. Did he know she saw them? Probably. He seemed to know everything. Still, the Deviants remained quiet, each one's initial fear melting off them like snow off mountains on a sunny day. Some of them lifted hands to God in praise. Others bowed their heads in prayer. Calan flung an arm over Nyla and drew her close.

The PKs dashed into the warehouse. Daniel began praying. But there was little they could do when Carolyn and Max were hauled out in handcuffs, tossed into one of the vehicles, and all three SUVs raced away.

One of the angels turned to face her—the same one she'd seen on the beach. A smile appeared on his lips...ever so slight...before they all vanished.

"Nay, my friend." Nazare faced Ranoss. "The Lord of Heaven's Armies told us to protect only these sons and daughters of the Most High, not the two who chose to remain behind."

Ranoss flung his crossbow over his shoulder with a scowl. It would be easy to defeat the demons surrounding the PKs, rescue the son of Adam and daughter of Eve, and bring them inside the circle with the others. But the Commander knew best.

Anisian nodded at Ranoss. "I am of the same mind, Ranoss. But it is enough we keep our wards safe." He jerked his head toward Nyla. "She is close now. Very close."

Ranoss smiled and glanced her way. "Indeed. I am most pleased. Alas, that only means the enemy will attack her at every opportunity."

"Then you must be ever vigilant, my friend." Nazare slid his sword back in its scabbard as the vehicles drove away. He heaved a mighty sigh and turned to face Daniel. "His time is almost at an end."

"Do not be sad, Nazare." Anisian gripped his friend's shoulder. "You have been privileged to guard such a mighty warrior of the Most High. He will get his reward."

"Aye, 'tis the manner of his death which upsets me. But what must be, must be. The Father of Spirits knows best."

"Where did they take them?" Nyla sat on the bench at the beach, her gaze on Marco standing several yards away near the old lifeguard station.

"What's it to you?" His voice bore none of the sultry affection she'd grown accustomed to.

A chilled wind blew in from the steel-gray sea, and Nyla hugged herself, wishing the Neflams would get busy clearing the skies. "They are not Deviant leaders. They are nobodies. Innocent followers who have harmed no one." She'd checked with one of the guards at the prison, and they weren't there.

"What are you talking about, Nyla? Everything they believe is a harm to society and a threat to human evolution. You know that." Huffing, he kicked the sand. "Maybe you've been hanging out with them too long."

True enough. But she couldn't help but be worried about two people who had been nothing but kind to her. "I'm just curious why they aren't in prison, nor at the Broward Reformation Camp." Yes, she had Kyle check, just to be sure.

"New rule. All Deviants are to report immediately to the NWU Containment Center in D.C." His voice softened. "If you were back on the job, you'd know such things."

Containment center? That was not a good sign. She'd heard such places were not really so much for containment as for elimination. A shiver etched down her back.

Though it was nearly noon, the beach was vacant except for a group of teens in wetsuits preparing to boogie board. Dark clouds—or was it still ash?—hung so low, it seemed you could reach up and swipe a hand through them. "I'm trying," was all she could think to say. "Daniel is just never around long enough for me to contact you." She cringed at the lie, but it couldn't be helped.

He snorted, and she knew him well enough to know he didn't entirely believe her. "It doesn't matter. We got a tip from someone who said Daniel was there. So, how did you know who was arrested?"

"I know these people, Marco. You should have waited until I was there with Daniel."

Marco crossed arms over his chest, his gaze remaining on the sea. "Jennings is getting impatient."

"I wish he *and you* would just let me do my job." She huffed at her hypocrisy.

"Why weren't you there?" Marco asked. "Your tracker said you were, but when we arrived, you disappeared off my screen."

She couldn't help but smile. He had no idea. "I left before you got there."

Finally, he turned to face her, and even from this distance, she could see the pain in his expression. "Jennings wants me to tell you that you only have a few more months before he pulls you out."

The words struck her in the gut like a fist. Pulled out? Never to see the Deviants again? Never to see Calan?

As if Marco could read her mind, he added with sarcasm, "Unless you'd rather stay with your boyfriend."

"He's not my boyfriend." Yet her tone did little to convince even herself.

"Listen, babe. I'm sorry. I just want you back."

She glanced at him, almost able to see his smile. Handsome Marco with his fit physique, gorgeous Hispanic looks, and black hair blowing in the wind. A part of her really missed his touch. "Soon." And even though she said the word, she knew she could never go back to Marco.

She could never go back to her old life.

Calan knocked on the door, excited to see Nyla, excited to talk to her about what she'd seen at Zion's Nest, excited to talk to her about Jesus. She was coming around. He could sense it. And it delighted him, not only because he could formally date her, but more importantly because she would be saved for all eternity. Another soul snatched from the enemy's clutches.

Her brother opened the door—a young man with curly dark hair, strong features, and a perpetual scowl on his face. A chill scraped over Calan as if a host of demons had just been released from hell. "Nyla here?"

Without saying a word, the man stomped away, leaving the door open and shouting. "Nyla!"

Calan entered and shut the door just as the lady herself emerged from a back bedroom. Wearing a white sleeveless tee-shirt and tight jeans and with her wild hair spiraling down over her shoulders, she appeared more lioness than human—a *gorgeous* lioness. But it was the delight on her face that made the trip worthwhile.

"Calan!" She cast a nervous glance at the young man who'd since plopped down on a couch and put on virtual reality goggles to play some sort of game. *Or* look at something he shouldn't. "Sorry about him. Kyle!" She headed toward him and punched him on the arm. "We have company. Be polite."

Ripping the goggles off, he stared at Calan. "Who's this, your boyfriend?"

Nyla rolled her eyes. "Kyle, you remember Calan, my friend."

Calan thought to extend his hand for a shake, but something told him it would not be accepted. In fact, Kyle merely stared at him with more animosity than one should a stranger.

Perhaps Calan should speak to him, break the ice, get to know the brother of the woman he lo…wait. Did he? Love her? He glanced her way, and she smiled, and in that smile he found such promise, his heart nearly broke through his chest. Turning back to Kyle, he sat down on one of two easy chairs across from him.

"Can I get you something to drink?" Nyla asked nervously, confusion twisting her expression. She, no doubt, wondered why he'd come, but that could wait.

"No, thank you." He glanced up at her, only then noting how tiny the apartment was with kitchen, dining room, and living room all together in one small space and a hallway leading toward the back. Though the furniture was modest, everything was clean and tidy. But he would expect no less from Nyla.

Calan returned his attention to the young man—a man who seemed somehow empty, alone, lost. He asked a few trivial questions, to which Kyle grunted out answers as if it pained him to respond. Finally, Calan asked him what he did for work.

At this, the young man came to life. "I'm a guard at the Broward Reformation Camp." He scooted to the edge of the couch and pointed to a badge on his arm. "Been there a little over a month and already been promoted to NWU Second Correctional Officer."

Nyla slid onto the arm of Calan's chair. "He's made friends with the Tall Whites, joined some club they run."

Calan stiffened. Ah, the explanation for the darkness he felt when Kyle had opened the door. He glanced at Nyla, wondering why she didn't see what he felt so strongly, but then again, people were often blind when it came to loved ones.

Should he say anything? He cleared his throat. "That's so great about your success. You should be proud."

Kyle smiled.

"However, these Tall Whites…" Calan schooled his voice to contain no reprimand, but merely concern. "I would stay away from them and any club they run if I were you. They are not who they seem." Calan knew he walked a very narrow rope. Still, he could hardly let this young man continue without a warning, but neither could he give himself away.

Kyle's lips slanted in disgust. "What are you, one of those crazy Deviants?"

Nyla gave a nervous laugh. "Don't be stupid, Kyle. You should listen to Calan. He knows about such things."

But Kyle wasn't listening to his sister. Instead, he stared at Calan with narrowed eyes, eyes that now seemed black and vacant. A dark spire shot from within them to Calan.

Calan's lungs collapsed. The air turned to syrup, and he struggled to breathe. Gripping his throat, he whispered, "Jesus, Jesus, Jesus! Demons, I command you to leave."

Immediately, his breath returned.

Though no way Kyle had heard him, the young boy glared at him with pure hatred. "Yeah, right. Well, nice to meet you." Standing, he gathered his goggles and headed toward the hall.

"I'll leave you two to do whatever you two do." The way he said it gave no room to doubt what he meant.

A red hue blossomed on Nyla's checks.

Despite the fact demons had just tried to strangle him, Calan grinned. "You're blushing."

Slapping her hands to her face, she turned away. "I am not."

"I think it's cute."

"I apologize for my brother. He's been through a lot. Can I get you something?" She headed toward the small kitchenette in the corner.

"You already asked me that." He lowered his voice. "I came to tell you where we are meeting now."

She spun around, a worried look on her face. "Is everyone okay?"

"Yes, we are all safe...Well, except..."

"Yeah. That's horrible." She glanced down the hall. "Let's go somewhere else to talk."

"Pajarito!" A woman's voice echoed from the back. "Who's here?"

"Pajarito?" Calan asked.

Nyla shrugged. "My grandmother's pet name for me. It means little bird."

Calan smiled.

"Wanna meet her?"

"Sure."

Calan followed Nyla down a short hallway, past two rooms whose doors were shut, and into the third, where instantly the weight Calan had felt since entering the apartment lifted. The room was cluttered with all manner of knick-knacks, vases, trophies, pictures, and crosses. An elderly woman with long gray hair, chubby cheeks, and a smile like an angel sat in a chair, a quilt on her lap and a Bible in her hands.

"So, this is the young man who is helping you see the truth."

"What are you talking about, Tata? This is Calan, my friend."

"I know. I've seen you before."

"You have?" Calan asked.

"The Lord has shown me a vision of you and my Pajarito here."

Calan approached, knelt before her, and took her hand. "You are a believer?"

The woman smiled, revealing one row of crooked teeth and another with several missing. "Takes one to know one."

"Praise the Lord," he said, a bit confused how Nyla could still be a skeptic with such a grandmother.

"Hallelujah!" the elderly lady exclaimed with more strength than he thought possible.

Nyla's eyes couldn't be wider as she swept her gaze between the two of them. "Tata, you must not tell Kyle about Calan."

"Ah, don't worry about him." Tata swept a bony hand through the air, but then started coughing uncontrollably.

Grabbing a glass of water from a table, Nyla knelt before her. "See, you've gotten yourself too excited."

"More than worth it," Nyla's grandmother choked out as she took a sip. "Now you two run along. I'm tired."

Nyla laid the back of her hand on her grandmother's forehead. "Good. Your fever is gone for now."

"A pleasure to meet you," Calan took the old woman's hand and kissed it.

She giggled. "We will meet again."

"I have no doubt, young man."

Though from the look on Nyla's face, she had more than enough doubt for them both.

"Want me to pray for her?" Calan asked after they left the room. "I'm happy to."

"No, not now. Not with Kyle here."

Calan nodded. "Can you spare an hour? I'll give you a ride and we can talk."

She smiled, causing her nose to wrinkle slightly, something he'd come to adore.

And once again, he found himself thoroughly enjoying her arms wrapped around his waist as he drove his Harley down to the beach. On the way, he'd been forced to take a few back streets, to avoid the growing food lines where FEMA trucks handed out daily rations to those in need.

It broke his heart. If only people would turn to God, their Creator, their Provider, they would have everything they needed.

After he parked, he took Nyla's hand in his and led her to the shore, where they both took off their shoes and started walking.

Through the ash and smoke, the afternoon sun cast an orange hue over the beach, creating a surreal scene as if they walked on some alien planet. Perhaps they did. Calan no longer felt at home on earth, hadn't for quite some time. This was not his home. At least it wouldn't be until Jesus returned to rule and reign. Things would be very different then, like the Garden of Eden God had planned for mankind in the first place. A return to the beginning before the fall of man. Calan couldn't wait. But for now, he was here in the Tribulation. For now, he felt led to save this woman beside him, along with her family.

"We have to get your brother away from the reformation camp and those Tall Whites," he finally said.

"No way. It's the first steady job he's had since our parents disappeared. He's super excited about it." She flattened her lips and stared out to sea. "I hate to come down on him when he finally has a goal."

"What club did you say he joined?"

"Kabal something. I don't remember exactly."

Calan cringed. "Listen, Nyla. I'm going to speak plainly to you now since you've seen so much. The Tall Whites and the Neflams are not from another galaxy, as they say, but from another dimension. They are demonic beings who work for Satan. The Tall Whites, in particular, have supernatural sexual skills and allurements which entrap people. This club is nothing more than a form of Satan worship, which is what the entire

Tribulation is about. Satan's time to rule this planet before Jesus returns."

A wave washed over their feet, bubbling and foaming, much like it seemed Nyla's mind was doing as she stared ahead, her expression perplexed.

"Even if that's true," she said, "what can I do? He's a grown man and rarely listens to me."

"We can pray. And you and your grandmother need to pray together against the demonic forces Kyle brings home. I know you know what I'm talking about. You've seen them."

Wind tossed another wayward curl across her face, but this time he stopped and slipped it behind her ear. She smiled. "Yes."

"And you saw the angels who shielded us from the PKs?"

Wonder filled her eyes. "They were amazing. One of them even smiled at me."

"Your guardian, no doubt."

"I can't believe God would care enough to assign *me* a bodyguard." She swallowed and moisture glazed her eyes. But then she grabbed his hand and started walking again.

They approached a pier where several homeless lay asleep in the sand. The PKs would move them at night, but for now, they found rest, since most of the beach was deserted. It was a dangerous life out in the open where people committed violence for no reason at all. Calan noticed a young family, mother, father, a newborn and a teen among them. Heart sinking, he made a mental note of the location so he could return with food and blankets.

He turned Nyla around to return the way they'd come.

"Do you know who alerted the PKs about Zion's Nest?" she asked.

"Clarisse thinks it was Tyson, unfortunately. When she got home that night, he had packed his bags and left."

Nyla sighed. "I just don't see how he could hang out with you guys and yet...."

"Not believe? Like you?"

She laughed. "I admit I didn't in the beginning."

"And now?

"How can I help but believe?"

"Then how about you put your trust in Jesus once and for all? I can lead you in a prayer."

Behold, I give you the authority to trample on serpents and scorpions, and over all the power of the enemy, and nothing shall by any means hurt you. Luke 10:19

Chapter 28

Halting, Nyla stared up at Calan. Should she give her life to this invisible God who obviously cared about her? Why He did, she still could not understand. Was she ready or even willing to release all control of her life to this God? To trust Him with everything? He'd given her a gift, to see into His realm, and it humbled her and brought tears to her eyes. Why her? She'd done nothing but deny Him her entire life, speak out against Him, even hunt down His followers, probably gotten many of them…

The realization hit her like the round of an AR-15. "Oh, my God." Jerking from Calan's grip, she stomped away from the water and fell to her knees in the sand.

Calan dropped beside her. "What's wrong?"

Wiping tears from her eyes, she shook her head. "I've put Deviants in prison, gotten many killed! I've done terrible things, Calan. God won't accept me now. Why would He?"

Calan gently cupped her chin in his hands, bringing her gaze up to his. "That's just it, Nyla. None of us are worthy. That's why Jesus had to offer Himself as a sacrifice on the cross to pay for all of our sins. When He rose again, it was to victory over sin, death, and hell. It doesn't matter what you've done. When you receive Him, it is all washed away!"

"No." She jerked her chin from his grip, more ashamed than she'd ever been. "It's too much to forgive."

"Nothing is too much for God."

The words sounded too good to be true, which meant they must be. Moving from Calan, Nyla drew her knees to her chest, wrapped her arms around them and stared out at the sea. Oh, how she longed for the sun to shine again and turn the sky blue and the sea turquoise and the sand to golden glitter. Without it, everything seemed so dull and lifeless.

Just like life without Me, the one and only Son.

She glanced at Calan, who had cautiously sat beside her. But he stared at the water same as her. The voice had clearly come from within her, yet not from within.

Either way, it brought tears to her eyes again, but she forced them to dry. She was not some weak, weepy female. She was an NWU PK team leader.

Or was she? She didn't know what she was anymore.

"You know the Apostle Paul arrested and even killed Christians before Jesus appeared to him and he got saved," Calan announced. "And look what he ended up doing."

For some reason, in all the Bible studies her parents had tried to cram down her throat, she hadn't remembered that. "For real?"

"For real."

Waves rolled ashore one after the other, some large, some small, some agitated and spitting up foam, others calm and serene. And each one spreading over the sand, only to retreat back into the sea. Much like each human life, here for only a moment, trying to be noticed, leaping for value, for meaning, only to fade away. What was the point of it all? Apparently the Apostle Paul had finally figured it out. The point was Jesus. Grabbing hold of Him and allowing Him to lead His children through this fallen world into eternity. Her parents had often quoted Paul. He'd been a great evangelist.

She huffed. "I'm no Apostle Paul."

"How do you know? We never know what God has in store for us."

Oddly, Nyla remembered the vision of her and Calan ministering to people. She'd wanted to talk to Daniel about it but hadn't had the chance.

"So, what do you say? Want me to pray with you?"

A gust of wind blew sand onto her jeans. Nyla bit her lip. "I don't know. I'm not sure I'm ready."

Calan grabbed her hand. "Do you think God would give the gift of seer to someone He didn't intend to forgive?"

Nyla dug her toes into the cool sand. Good point. She smiled. "You're good at this, you know."

"What?"

"At preaching, teaching, telling others about Jesus."

He shrugged. "Not really. I bumble my words a lot. That's Daniel's gifting."

"I don't know."

"Now, look who needs encouragement," she teased, staring at him, his dark, short-cropped hair tossed by the breeze, the look of admiration in his blue eyes, the way the wind sped along the cut of his strong jaw. And before she could control herself, she leaned in and kissed him. She'd intended only a peck, but Calan wrapped his arms around her and drew her close, intensifying the kiss, caressing her mouth with his own, until finally they both fell onto the sand in each other's arms.

Marco halted, every muscle, every nerve in his body set aflame with jealousy, anger, rage, betrayal. Which one he couldn't tell. Maybe all four! Either way, it was a horrible sensation, and one he never wanted to feel again. Still, he could not tear his eyes away from Nyla and Daniel's bodyguard making out in the sand.

Finally, the man called Calan pulled away and helped her to sit. Laughing, they both rose and continued strolling down the beach, fingers entwined.

Fisting his hands, Marco spun and headed the other direction. He'd spotted them both as soon as they'd parked. Nyla should know he often came to this spot to think, to jog along the shore, to babe-watch. When he'd seen her approaching on his scanner, he foolishly thought she might be coming to see him. Instead, she drove up on the back of that Deviant's bike. Already angry, he'd followed them just in case they might be meeting Daniel.

"Witch! Liar!" He added a few more colorful names as he kicked up sand. Obviously, she felt something for this Deviant. No way she was that good of an actress. She'd lied to him, tricked him. Cheated on him! He'd never had a woman betray him before. He'd always been the one to break things off, to find someone new, someone better. But this! He swallowed down a lump of agony. So, this is what a broken heart felt like—like his world had just been blown to bits, like life wasn't worth living. Fighting back tears, he marched into the parking lot.

What was her game? What did she hope to accomplish? Once they captured Daniel, they'd probably arrest her new boyfriend too. Stupid girl. Risking everything, her career, her life, for what? A fling with a Deviant, of all things, the very people she'd sworn to eradicate from the earth.

He opened his car door, jumped inside, and started the engine, still fuming. He needed to talk to her, call her out on her betrayal, hear what she had to say. If she was being brainwashed by these Deviants, he would go to Jennings and get her pulled out immediately. Either that, or Marco would arrest her himself.

Tata coughed. Blood dribbled from her lips down her chin. Nyla wiped it with a damp cloth. "I'm going to call an ambulance."

"No, dear Pajarito. Please. I refuse to die in one of those NWU hospitals. Please."

"But the medicines aren't working." Fighting back tears, Nyla dropped the cloth in the bowl of cool water and wrung it out. Just when it seemed her grandmother was improving, she'd grown far worse this last week. Her fever leapt and plummeted like a bucking horse, but at its peak, it was always too high. She wasn't eating much, was coughing all night, and now the appearance of blood. All signs that the melioidosis was advancing. Rapidly.

Tata's breathing sounded raspy, but finally it smoothed out as she fell asleep. Good. Sleep was good at least. Sleep without coughing.

"I can't lose you," she whispered. Not after losing both parents. Nyla would truly be an orphan with no family except an antagonistic brother. Were her parents really in heaven now and not some reformation camp? If so, they were happy and together. But that also meant they were not coming back in this life—that she truly was all alone.

She was being selfish.

"Rest, dear Tata." Nyla rose from beside her grandmother's bed, her eyes landing on the ever-present Bible on the table. Maybe Nyla should try praying. What harm could it do? She'd seen Daniel heal people with a word.

Kneeling beside the bed, Nyla reached out to lay a hand on Tata's arm when Kyle entered the room.

"You weren't praying, were you?" He laughed. "What's wrong with you?" He gazed down at Tata with more affection than Nyla expected.

Shooting to her feet, she eased back onto the chair. "I'm willing to try anything, aren't you?"

"Not something that stupid." He sighed, then took another step toward her. "Sorry. Listen, what can I do to help? I don't want to lose her either."

Shocked, Nyla stared at her brother. He'd never offered to help before. Neither had he expressed the concern she now heard in his voice. "Just care for her while I'm gone. Get her to eat something, keep her fever down, and try to convince her to go to the hospital."

"We should just force her."

"I don't want to do something against her final wishes, you know?"

Kyle frowned and ran a hand through his brown curls. "I heard you and that Calan guy talking."

"Oh, yeah." A spark of alarm wormed its way through her.

"He's a Deviant, isn't he?"

"Why do you say that?" Nyla searched her memory of what Calan had said when he was here, but nothing came to mind that would incriminate him.

"A hunch, a feeling, something Shamesh said." The emptiness had returned to her brother's eyes.

"Who's Shamesh?"

"One of the Tall Whites who has befriended me. He's really cool." He glanced over the dimly lit bedroom. "He said I would know the Deviants because I could sense their evil."

"Evil. What are you talking about, Kyle?" Nyla picked up the bowl and headed out of the room to the kitchen.

"They worship God, right?" Kyle's voice followed her.

"Yeah. But that doesn't make them evil."

"Have you ever read the Old Testament? Or even parts of the new?"

Setting down the bowl, she stared at him. "No, not most of it. Have you?"

Kyle leaned a hip against the kitchen counter, arms crossed over his chest. "This God of theirs, the one the Christians worship, the God of that Bible Tata carries around, it's Him who is the evil one, not Lucifer. They've got it all backwards. All these centuries, all those dumb Christians were tricked. Just read for yourself. Their God kills, maims, and destroys entire cities and countries. He sends fiery sulfur on them, tells the Israelites to butcher every man, woman, and child in all the towns. Then in the New Testament, He orders people to worship him, obey his every command, and if they don't, he throws them in hell."

Nyla had never heard such things, nor did she want to. She'd finally come to believe there was a God and that He was good, kind, and loving. "How do you know so much about the Bible?"

"Shamesh is reading it to me, explaining it."

"Even though it's illegal?" She gave him a sarcastic smile.

"For educational purposes only," he returned sharply.

"So you're telling me that this Lucifer, the Satan in the Bible, is the good guy, not the evil one?"

"Exactly. Think about is, Sis. He's the one who freed Adam and Eve from slavery in the Garden. He opened their eyes to real life, not following a bunch of dumb rules from their God. Lucifer gives us freedom. Freedom to do whatever we want. No rules. No restrictions. Just enjoyment."

Sounded like anarchy and chaos to her. "I thought you never believed in religion or any of this stuff."

"I didn't. But the Tall Whites have opened my eyes." Kyle's voice held more excitement than it had in years. "The God of the Bible is not actually a God. He is just a powerful being from another world, just like Lucifer. They have been battling for years. God wants to enslave mankind, and Lucifer wants to free them."

Nyla closed her eyes for a second, *God, if you're there, help me.* What Kyle was saying made a little sense, but it couldn't be true. "I don't know, Kyle." She finally dared look him in the eyes and leapt back. Dozens of vaporous serpents spun around her brother, slithering into his nose, mouth, and ears and emerging from the same. Hideous laughter filled the air. Red fiery eyes glared at her. Forked tongues hissed.

She blew out a breath. *Keep cool, Nyla. Keep cool.* She mustn't let on to Kyle what she saw, or he'd probably report her to his new friends. Yet she could not deny the thrashing of her heart and the terror that gripped her. She'd been trained to appear calm during harrowing situations, and she leaned on all that training now.

Greater is He who is in you than He who is in the world. She remembered a Scripture Daniel had read and another one about how God grants His people authority over all the power of the enemy, and nothing will harm them. She had to believe that. *God, I'm trusting You to protect me, to protect Kyle and Tata.*

Ranoss lit an arrow and positioned it in his crossbow, his anger rising at the falsehoods Kyle was telling Nyla. 'Twas just like the enemy to use Scripture, to use bits of truth mixed with a host of lies to lure the naive into darkness. After Nyla had nearly given her life to the Commander, Ranoss knew the battle would intensify. She was right on the precipice of eternity, but 'twas a dangerous place to reside. One lie, believed, could drag her back into the darkness. One prayer of faith could surround her with light forever.

He pointed his crossbow at the hoard of demons leaping from Kyle onto Nyla, churning up doubts in her mind.

"Nay, my friend." Zhaviel laid a hand on the crossbow, forcing Ranoss to lower it. "You must wait for her permission."

Growling, Ranoss lowered the weapon. "'Tis far too difficult to stand by and watch."

Zhaviel huffed. "I can well relate, for look at my ward. He moves further into the darkness every day."

Indira appeared beside them, Book of Blessings in hand, his glance taking in Nyla and Kyle. "Tata prays. She senses the battle."

"Good." Ranoss nodded. "Mayhap the Commander will grant me permission to fight."

"Wait." Zhaviel said excitedly. "Look, Nyla prays. She remembers Scripture."

Ranoss smiled and lifted his crossbow once again.

Zhaviel drew his blade and joined him.

"Now we fight!" Ranoss said.

A spark flew through the air, followed by a streak of gold, and instantly the dark spirits retreated. Unfortunately, they slunk back inside Kyle. If Nyla had seen these things three months ago, she would have committed herself to an asylum. But now she knew exactly what had happened.

Placing a hand on her hip, she stared at Kyle. "And you believe this stuff about God and Lucifer?"

He nodded, his eyes wide with excitement. "You bet. You should see what the Tall Whites can do. The power they have. I've seen so many awesome things."

Nyla had seen what God could do. And everything He did was good—healing, delivering, protecting, providing. Would an evil being do such things?

"I've seen the God of the Bible do incredible things too, good things."

Kyle cussed. "So that guy *is* a Deviant. I should call him in. And you too." One of the demons lunged toward her, his black bony hand reaching for her throat.

Closing her eyes, Nyla whispered the name of Jesus as she'd seen Calan do so often.

A light flickered through the air and the hand was gone.

"No, Kyle, you don't understand. I'm on assignment. I'm still with the NWU PKs." She had to say something to keep him from reporting Calan or her, and it was the truth, after all.

It took him a minute to settle, but even so, tiny demons taunted her from his eyes. "Cool, like undercover?"

"Exactly."

"So you're going to bring them all down?" He grinned.

"They just want the leader. When I hand him over, I'm done."

Nodding, Kyle headed back to the couch. "Glad you told me, Sis. I was getting worried about you."

Releasing a deep breath, Nyla silently thanked God and turned to fix some tea for Tata when the sound of a mighty trumpet blared across the sky.

Then the fifth angel sounded: And I saw a star fallen from heaven to the earth. To him was given the key to the bottomless pit. And he opened the bottomless pit, and smoke arose out of the pit like the smoke of a great furnace. So the sun and the air were darkened because of the smoke of the pit. Then out of the smoke locusts came upon the earth. And to them was given power, as the scorpions of the earth have power. They were commanded not to harm the grass of the earth, or any green thing, or any tree, but only those men who do not have the seal of God on their foreheads. And they were not given authority to kill them, but to torment them for five months. Their torment was like the torment of a scorpion when it strikes a man. In those days men will seek death and will not find it; they will desire to die, and death will flee from them. Revelation 9:1-6

Chapter 29

What do you mean, you can't heal them?" Nyla stormed up to Daniel, who sat with Bible open in his lap, preparing for a Bible Study hosted at Madeline's home. She'd been invited, of course, but had turned them down. How could she enjoy time with friends when everyone she loved was in great physical torment? Well, not everyone she loved. Calan stood behind Daniel, looking both happy to see her and concerned. It was the same look he'd worn when he'd shown up at her apartment during the past two weeks after the trumpet had sounded, begging her to come to the Deviant meetings or at the very least go walk with him on the beach.

But she'd refused. Just when she thought the God of the Bible was the real deal, that He was pure love as Daniel and Calan so often told her, He'd unleashed a horde of demonic creatures half animal, half machine that flew through the earth like crazed insects stinging everyone within range. Those who got stung were instantly tortured with extreme pain, the source of which no doctor could determine. Neither was there any medicine that numbed it. The worst part was that it only affected non-Deviants, such as Marco and Kyle and all of Nyla's friends at the PK headquarters.

Thank God, Tata was not affected, and for some reason neither was Nyla, although she didn't consider herself a Deviant. Maybe she was at heart, for she did believe in Jesus. She had thought about following Him, wanted to make that commitment.

But then the trumpet had sounded, and she remembered what was coming. When it hit, it was worse than what she imagined, and she began to wonder how the God she'd come to believe in could be so cruel?

In the meantime, though Tata was not one of the afflicted, she had grown even worse.

A meow sounded, and Nyla's gaze snapped to Calypsey stretched across the back of the couch where some of the other Deviants sat. Tribby was curled in Elena's lap. Nyla would ask how they'd managed to find the cats, but it really didn't matter. Not now. All that mattered were the people she cared about who were suffering.

Daniel set the Bible on the coffee table. "Good to see you too, Nyla. We've missed you."

"Yes, we have." Everyone agreed, and soon Pam, Madeline, Elena, and others surrounded her.

Swallowing down a burst of emotion, Nyla glanced over them all, her anger abating. "I've missed you, too. But I just…well, so many of my friends are in agony." She glanced at Daniel. "Calan says you won't pray for them. I've seen people healed by your touch."

Standing, Daniel gestured for her to sit. When she didn't, he sighed. "This is a judgment from God on the unbelieving and unrepentant. I cannot heal it nor stop it. I wish I could."

"So, I'm supposed to just stand by and watch people I care about suffer. My own brother!"

"I'm sorry, Nyla," The tone and look in his eyes told her he meant it.

Calan came to stand beside her. "Won't you stay and pray with us? Many of us have family and friends who are afflicted as well."

"I don't know. Why would God do this? My brother says God is evil and Satan is good."

"An age-old lie, Nyla," Daniel said. "From the pit of hell. Same lie Satan told Eve. God is keeping you in a prison, keeping something good from you, keeping you from being a god like Him. No, Nyla, you've seen too much, heard too much truth, to fall for such a lie. You've felt the love of God."

She had. Or she thought she had. She pressed a hand over the scar on her neck. "I'm just so confused. I don't know what to believe."

"Then sit and pray with us, Nyla." Calan took her hand in his. After two weeks without him, his touch felt so good, so right. Maybe she should stay. Maybe she should listen to the Bible study, pray with these kind people. But she needed to get back to care for Tata and Kyle and help her PK friends, including Marco.

"Sorry, I can't. I have too much to do."

Pam approached. "Let us help. I can come by tomorrow."

"I can bring some food," Madeline added.

Others joined in with offers.

Nyla held up her hands. "No. Thank you. I need to think, to figure things out."

"At least let us come pray for your grandmother?" Daniel asked, pleading in his gaze.

"Maybe…I'll let you know. Sorry, gotta run." She'd come here angry, ready to fight, ready to challenge their beliefs, and now, she left more confused than ever.

Storming out the door and onto the front driveway, she heard Calan's heavy footsteps behind her.

"Nyla, Nyla."

Pretending not to hear him, she leapt into her Jeep, slammed the door, and drove off. She didn't want to hurt him, but she couldn't be a part of his life until she figured out what she believed. It wouldn't be fair to him. Or her.

Shadows dove at her car. She swerved to avoid them and nearly hit a mailbox. At least the hideous locust drones were no longer flying around. She supposed they'd stung everyone they intended to sting. Of course, Premier Aali and the Neflams were taking credit for defeating them with their advanced laser system. She wondered if that was true. She'd not seen any lasers shooting through the sky. Regardless, Premier Aali said it was an attack by the Neflams' enemy, a powerful being from another world that some people called God.

The black figures lunged at her again as they had been doing for the past two weeks since the trumpet had sounded— vapors, misty shadows, not black exactly, but more absent of all light. The visions had started out small, fleeting, but with each passing day, she saw more and more of these demonic creatures surrounding her friends and hovering in the sky above the city. Lucifer's legions. Yet always there were the creatures of light too, pushing back the dark ones with otherworldly weapons— the warriors of God. Kyle had been right about one thing. God and Lucifer were in a battle, an *intense* battle, and the prize appeared to be the souls of men. Which side was evil and which side good? She was determined to find out for herself, though in all honesty, she had a pretty good idea.

Every time the dark shadows overwhelmed her, the brilliant blaze of a golden sword, the zip of a flaming arrow, or the glitter of a fast-spinning weapon would flash in her vision, and the demons would disappear. The warriors of God protected her. Why? She'd done nothing to deserve it. Yet when she cried out to this God for answers, only silence replied.

Night cloaked Cypress Road as streetlights did their best to pierce the still sooty air. Seeing little to no traffic, Nyla punched the accelerator, confused and angry, wanting to get away from everything and everyone, not caring that she sped way past the speed limit. Instantly, fog enveloped her car and the headlights flipped on. Strange. She slowed, unable to see.

A huge Mack truck jackknifed across the road in front of her.

She had no time to stop. No time to even pray.

"Ranoss!" Butho, the immense angel who fought beside him, looked his way. "Your ward!"

Ranoss fired off ten arrows in rapid succession, each one hitting their intended mark. Snapping his gaze to Butho. "What say you, my friend?"

Butho withdrew his blade from the blubbery paunch of a foul creature and wrinkled his nose at the stench. "Cassian says your ward is in danger. The Commander calls you."

"Wind and wings!" Ranoss had been so occupied in battle, he'd not heard the King. "Thank you, Butho."

But Butho was already engaged with two more demons, who attacked him from both sides. Ranoss would stay to help, but the burly warrior seemed to have the situation well in hand.

Ever since the Shofar's fifth blast, the battle across earth had intensified. Legions of depraved and noxious creatures with all manner of powers had been unleashed. Their mission? To prevent the afflicted from turning to God.

Ranoss had never been so busy, nor so tired from the constant fight. Drawing his blade, he moved forward, swinging it left and right like a machete in a thick jungle of demonic vines, slicing the blasphemous spirits advancing upon him.

At the call for help from Cassian, he'd only left Nyla for a moment. She was, after all, safe with the saints at the daughter of Eve Madeline's home. He plunged his blade into a particularly rank demon, who laughed at him like a sick hyena. Finally, he spotted Cassian ahead.

"Go to her now, Ranoss!" Cassian shouted while battling off a demon that was more slime than solid.

Only then did Ranoss hear the Commander's orders, loud and clear. "Make haste!"

In an instant, Ranoss appeared on the street, assessed the situation, and then dove in front of Nyla's car, slamming both hands on the hood. A force as strong as one of the four winds of Heaven struck him, shoving him back a few feet. He groaned beneath the strain, his muscles bursting, but finally the car came to a stop. He glanced through the windshield at Nyla, and for the briefest of seconds, recognition, along with shock, appeared on her face.

Relieved, Ranoss nodded her way, then glanced at his fellow warriors who had followed him and were holding back the demonic horde attacking Nyla. The Commander had informed Ranoss that these attacks would get worse now that Nyla was nearly in the kingdom, but he hadn't expected them daily. Nor so violent. But this was the Day of the Lord, the seven years of judgment in which the forces of the enemy were unleashed at unprecedented levels. These were the days he and his fellow warriors had been training for. He would not be caught off guard again.

Grabbing Cassian's arm in a strong grip, he nodded his thanks for the assistance.

They were up to the task. They would not let the Commander down.

Yet, as he watched Nyla drive off and prepared to follow her, Ranoss couldn't help a spark of fear, perhaps even sorrow, at the possibility that in the end she would make the wrong choice.

For the Father of Spirits never removes free will from these sons of Adam.

Nyla's phone chirped. Calan's name lit the screen. She sighed and stared at it for a moment. Part of her longed to answer, to hear his deep comforting voice, to make plans to see him, but part of her knew she couldn't. Not yet. Not until she knew the truth. The last thing she wanted to do was break both their hearts. Funny how she no longer thought of herself as being undercover, waiting for an opportunity to arrest Daniel. Of course, all law enforcement had ground to a halt anyway with everyone so sick, even the criminals, so Jennings applied no more pressure on her to complete her assignment. In fact, she'd not spoken to the man at all. The entire world economy had collapsed, food production, shipping, manufacturing, everything. Along with the Deviants, only those at the very top of the pyramid—Premier Aali, the seven regional kings and their governments, and the Neflams—remained able to function. Why? She had no idea except perhaps they had been able to take shelter from the locust drones. The streets were mostly bare except for those who came out to forage for food, hunched over in their agony. How long could this go on? How long before people starved to death? The Bible said five months, which meant they had one month to go—a month that seemed an eternity for the afflicted.

Slipping her cell back in her pocket, she entered the elevator of Marco's apartment building. During the past months of physical torture for most of the world, Nyla had done her best to provide food and what comfort she could to her PK friends and Kyle. Marco, however, had not wanted to see her, had not wanted *her* to see him in this state, he had said. But finally, after months of pestering him, he agreed. Most likely because he'd run out of food.

The elevator door opened. She stepped onto the plush carpet in the hallway and started down the right to apartment 6B. Memories swarmed her, happy memories, fond memories of the two of them, arm in arm, stumbling to his apartment after a night on the town, ready to spend the rest of the night in bed in each other's arms.

She stopped before the door and took a deep breath, unsure how she felt about those times now or about the man behind this door. She'd been the envy of every woman in town, but had she ever really loved him?

Inserting the key, the one he'd given her long ago, she opened the door and slipped inside. Setting the bag of food and jug of water atop the kitchen counter—supplies she'd gotten from the Deviants—she glanced over the dark living area as familiar scents brought more memories. Shaking them off, she started toward the bedroom. "Marco?"

"Nyla." His scratchy voice echoed down the hall, and she stepped inside the room to find him lying on his bed, stripped to his undershorts, blistering sores covering his once perfectly tanned skin.

Heart aching, she made her way to him. "Marco, I'm so sorry. I know what kind of pain you're in."

"Do you?" He pried his eyes open, eyes that had once looked at her with admiration and desire but were now filled with pain and horror. They widened slightly. "Why aren't you afflicted?"

"Do you want me to be?"

"No. Sorry, babe."

"Let me get a cloth and hydrogen peroxide. Be right back."

"Don't bother," he called, stopping her. "It doesn't help. I've tried it."

"How about just some cold water to soothe your sores? It seems to help Kyle."

He nodded, and Nyla moved to the bathroom, found a washcloth, and turned on the faucet. No water, of course. It must be rationing time for this part of town. Back out in the kitchen, she opened the jug of water and poured some in a bowl, then returned and began pressing the wet cloth gently on the blisters, wincing every time Marco cringed.

"I didn't want you to see me like this," he said. "I want you to remember me as I was."

"You're not going to die, Marco. This will be over soon."

"How do you know? I watch the news. The doctors and scientists have no idea what sort of bioweapon these enemy drones have inflicted on us. Nor who sent them. Except God."

Shocked, Nyla stared at him. Marco had always been an atheist. "God?"

"Yeah, that's what the Neflams say." Marco moaned in pain and closed his eyes. "Apparently," he ground out, "the God of the Bible is the archenemy of the Neflams."

He gripped her hand. "Thank you for coming. The pain is so horrible. It never goes away. I hate to admit it, but I took a bunch of sleeping pills, hoping to die." His handsome face scrunched tight in pain before he gasped out, "but I woke up still here."

"Oh, Marco, why didn't you let me come before?"

"What could you do? What can anyone do?"

"I can offer company and comfort." Which was what she'd been doing for her other friends. "And food. Let me get you some."

Tears filling her eyes, she left to heat up a can of chicken soup in the microwave. It wasn't much, but at least he wouldn't starve. Although despite the massive food shortage, no deaths from starvation had been reported.

It was just like the Bible said. *And in those days shall men seek death, and shall not find it; and shall desire to die, and death shall flee from them.*

Returning with the soup, she helped Marco sit and then spoon fed him what she could before he raised a hand for her to quit, cried out in pain, and plopped back onto the bed.

"What's going on with the Deviants?" he muttered. "Just talk to me. Help me get my mind off this pain."

"Nothing much. The world has come to a stop with most people in such agony."

"But the Deviants, are they afflicted? How about *Calan*?" He said the name with such spite, it startled her.

"For some reason, they were not attacked by the drones or whatever they were."

His breathing grew labored, and his forehead wrinkled. "Neither were you."

She shook her head. "No idea why."

"Don't you?"

Setting the bowl on the stand beside his bed, she avoided his gaze. "How would I know?"

"Because you're one of them," he hissed.

"That's insane. You know me, Marco. You know better than anyone."

"That's why I didn't want to believe it!" Closing his eyes, he moaned. "But I saw it happen right before my eyes. You fell for that bodyguard. I saw you on the beach. You're sleeping with him!"

He saw them on the beach? She swallowed. "I am not!"

"You believe like they do. That's why their God didn't attack you. He only attacks people who don't worship Him!" Marco gripped his belly and writhed in pain.

She reached for his hand. "What does it matter now, Marco? I'm here to help. Let me help you. You've never been one to believe in God or any of that religious stuff."

He jerked away from her. "I didn't, but the Neflams have me convinced." His breath came hard and fast as eyes filled with rage scoured over her. "I can't believe it! You are never going to turn in Daniel! That's why he always slips away."

Rising, Nyla took a step back. She'd seen the same hatred in her brother's eyes and knew there was no point in arguing. Still, she wanted to help Marco, longed for him to know the truth of what was really going on in the world. "Not at first. I tried hard to get him captured. He always seemed to slip away."

"And now?"

"Listen, Marco. I've seen things. Miracles, people healed, saved. I see demons and angels. God is real."

He laughed—a laugh filled with pain and remorse. "You've lost it, babe. Completely lost it! And I'm going to turn you in. I'm reporting you to Jennings."

Nyla's mouth went dry.

"You're done, Nyla. Done. Your career is over."

"I'm telling you the truth. Please, Marco. Listen to me. I don't care if you turn me in. But please, turn to God instead."

Moaning, he tried to get up, but sank back onto his pillows. "I can't believe you. I've worked too hard to get where I'm at, achieved too much to have it ruined by associating with you."

Nyla should be insulted, but all she felt was pity. Pity and an urgent need to help him see the light. "Life is so much more than fancy cars, luxury apartments, and prestige, Marco. I know you've fought your entire life to be someone, to rise above your poor beginnings, but has any of it made you happy?"

He merely stared at her with disgust before squeezing his eyes shut again. "I loved you, babe. I really did."

Emotion clogged Nyla's throat at the pain in his voice. She'd always thought he would be the one to break her heart, not the other way around. But none of that mattered now. "There's a God, Marco, and He loves you. He wants to give you meaning and purpose and life beyond anything you can get from this world." Even as she said the words, she wondered where they came from. When had she turned into an evangelist?

"Get out! Get out of my apartment. And never come back." Clearly taxing his remaining strength, he gripped the bowl of soup and hurled it at her.

Leaping out the way, Nyla watched it crash against the wall and shatter into pieces on the carpet.

Tears flowing down her cheeks, she turned and raced through the living room, left her key on the coffee table, and slipped out the door. Wiping her face, she drew a deep breath. Well, now she'd gone and done it. If Marco followed through with his threat, she'd not only lose her job, but she'd be sent to a reformation camp, or worse, a containment center. Then what would happen to Tata?

He has redeemed my soul in peace from the battle that was against me, for there were many against me. Psalm 55:18

Chapter 30

"I'm losing her," Calan said. "I sense it."

"Do you?" Daniel smiled as they jogged side by side along the seashore.

Calan glanced at his friend. "You know something. Something about the future."

"Only God knows the future."

"And He's told you a part of it."

"I won't deny it." Daniel leapt over an incoming wave. "But I wouldn't give up on Nyla just yet."

Calan rubbed sweat from the back of his neck and glanced toward the water. A giant orange sun hung low over the horizon, turning the sea red and the sand peach. They'd all told Daniel it was best not to make a public appearance, but he'd insisted he needed a run. Besides, the PKs were in too much pain to bother with him.

Apparently, he'd been right. The beach was as deserted as Calan had ever seen. He skirted around a pile of fly-infested garbage. The stench wrinkled his nose.

"She won't answer my calls. She was so close to receiving the Lord." He remembered the very moment he asked her to pray and commit her trust to Jesus. She'd said she wasn't ready, but he sensed that wasn't true. "Now she's confused and far away."

"There is a battle for her soul, Calan." Daniel glanced upward as if he could see it raging above him. "A huge battle. For her and for many others right now."

Calan nodded. "I've been praying for her."

"Good. That's the most important thing. We are enduring the last of God's easier judgments. He is pleading with the lost to turn to Him before Aali takes full power and institutes the Mark. Then it will be much, much harder. We must fast and pray, not only for Nyla but for all the lost."

"I know you're right." Calan hesitated, catching his breath. "I don't want to make another mistake with a woman. One that will cost lives. Especially your life, which you have entrusted to me."

"You are not that man anymore, Calan." Daniel glanced his way with a smile. "You have Jesus to lead you, to give you wisdom." He splashed through a wave, kicking up foam. "You must have faith, confidence in who you are now, in the man the Lord has made you to be."

Trouble was, Calan still felt that old man inside of him, tugging on him, luring him. Was he really a new man? God help him, because the last thing he wanted to do was make another mistake, trust another woman, and end up hurting Daniel and his friends.

Nyla was tired. So very tired. She was tired of tending painful sores, tired of seeing people she loved in agony, tired of the glimpses of a spiritual battle she could not enter, could not grab her Glock and engage in the fight.

And on top of everything else, she feared she'd soon be arrested and tossed in prison. Marco was not one to make idle threats. But, with the tracker inside her, she had nowhere to run. Even if she could, she would never leave Tata.

She ran the laser over her forehead. 103. Too high. Moaning, her grandmother reached for her hand and Nyla gripped it. "I'm here, Tata."

"How is Kyle?" she mumbled.

Wasn't that just like her grandmother? She was clearly dying, and yet she worried about Kyle.

"He's doing better. The pain is nearly gone, and the sores are healing."

Tata nodded. "It's been five months, then."

"Yes." Obviously, Tata would know the prophecy well. She longed to ask her about God, Satan, the Neflams, and every other crazy thing that had spun through her mind these past months, but she dared not cause her further anxiety.

Eyes burning, she looked away. With her grandmother refusing to go to the hospital and her medicine all but gone, it wouldn't be long now. She'd tried everything, from herbs to vitamins to healthy food—what she could find of it—and even prayer. Yes, she'd prayed over Tata just as she'd seen Daniel do. But of course nothing happened.

Well, at least now that the plague or attack or whatever it was had left, she could focus more time on Tata's care and not have to run back and forth from Kyle to her as well as look in on her other friends in the city. The news announced that everyone across the globe was recovering, thanks to the Neflams, who had sprayed something in the atmosphere to counteract the bioweapon from the drones. Drones they still blamed on the God of the Bible.

"You must believe, my dear Pajarito," Tata said in a shaky voice. "Satan is a liar and the prince of lies. God is good. He only sends judgment as a last resort to get people to turn to Him."

"How did you know what I was thinking?"

"The Lord keeps me informed." She squeezed her hand. "Do not be deceived. There is great deception in these days, far more than most will understand until it is too late."

"I know, Tata. I've been reading your Bible."

"You have?" Her smile was weak but there, nonetheless.

"Yes, to you while you are asleep. I hoped it would make you well."

"If God wishes to heal me, He will. Don't you worry."

"But why wouldn't He? I need you."

"You don't need me, my dearest."

"*I* need you." The voice came from the doorway, Kyle's weak voice. It was so good to see him up, even though he leaned against the door jamb for support.

"My beloved grandson. Come here." Tata waved him in, and Nyla rose and moved another chair closer to the bed for her brother.

Before he sat, she hugged him. At first, he stiffened beneath the unusual display of affection, but finally he embraced her back.

"I'm so glad you are feeling better," Nyla said.

"Me too."

Kyle took a seat and laid the back of his hand on Tata's forehead. He jerked it back. "She's burning up."

"I know. I'm trying to bring it down."

Tata waved them both away. "Stop fussing over an old lady. Tell me how you are, Kyle. I heard the sores were painful."

"They were." He shook his head, his expression gnarled just by remembering. "Excruciating. Never felt such agony." He frowned. "But I heard you say it was a judgment from God."

"Only to bring you to Him." Tata reached for his hand, which thankfully he took. "He doesn't enjoy inflicting pain. But what is five months of misery compared to an eternity of joy, peace and love?"

"Seems He could find another way." Kyle placed her veiny hand back on the bed and leaned forward in his chair, clearly exhausted.

Tata struggled to find her breath but finally said, "He did. He came here and He died for you."

Nyla bit her lip. Should she say something? Give herself away? But how could she not try to help her brother. "God is the one who is good, Kyle. The Tall Whites have lied to you."

Kyle shot her a skeptical glance. Her poor brother. He'd lost nearly ten pounds and dark shadows circled his eyes. But at least he was not raging at her.

Tata smiled. "God loves you so much, Kyle. There's only a short time left to turn to Him. Once you do, you'll see. He has a great eternity planned for you."

He drew a deep breath and released it slowly, leaning back in his chair. "I don't know. Sounds crazy to me, but after the disappearance, the Neflams, and those psycho drones, lots of things seem crazy." He looked at Nyla. "You said you've seen this God heal. Why doesn't He heal Tata?"

"I don't know, but I'd love to have my friends come and pray over her."

"Heck, if they can heal her, go ahead and call them. I won't say a word. Not if Tata gets well."

Nyla searched his eyes for a speck of insincerity, then glanced around him for the dark shadows that had made their home with him lately. She saw neither. Was her brother finally softening to the truth? Her heart nearly burst with joy. Maybe, if he saw a miracle, he too would believe.

"Thank you. I'll call them right away."

An hour later, at a knock on the door, Nyla rushed to open it, smiling when she saw Daniel, and Calan standing there.

"Thank you so much for coming." She ushered them inside, shut the door, and spun to face Kyle coming out of Tata's room.

Hesitant at first, and with slight suspicion in his eyes, Kyle finally shook Daniel's hand as Nyla introduced him. She forced back a laugh as it suddenly dawned on her. If anyone had told her just eight months ago that she would be inviting Deviants to her home to lay hands on Tata and heal her, she would have thought they were stoned, drunk, kidding, or certifiably insane.

She glanced up at Calan. Man, it was good to see him standing there so strong, confident, and looking at her as if she had dropped out of heaven itself. She'd only seen him a few times the past five months, and she had no idea until this moment how much she missed him.

"I'm glad you called," he said, squeezing her hand.

And suddenly she was too. "Come, my grandmother's in here." She led the way down the hall.

Daniel sat on one of the chairs beside the bed. Calan took the other.

Tata pried open her eyes and smiled at them. "I sense the Spirit in you," she said.

Daniel nodded. "I've come to pray for you, dear saint. Will you allow us?"

"Of course, but be advised," she coughed out, "I'm not opposed to going home."

At the sight of blood spilling from her mouth, Nyla started forward, but Daniel grabbed the cloth and wiped it. "Do you have faith to be healed?"

"I have faith for many things, young man."

Kyle slipped inside the room and leaned against the back wall.

Daniel bowed his head and seemed to be praying silently for a moment as Calan put a hand on Tata's leg.

"Lord, You said in Your Word that You heal all our diseases," Daniel began, "that You desire that Your saints live long and healthy lives. Therefore, in Jesus' name, I command this precious woman to be healed."

Nyla added a silent prayer, and when she opened her eyes, a figure of light stood next to Tata. In one hand, he held a thick book and with the other, he forced back two dark creatures that were reaching for her grandmother. Nyla's heart raced. She had to do something, but just as she started forward, they disappeared.

Calan sensed great power flowing over Nyla's grandmother.

Tata coughed, blinked, and shifted her gaze to Daniel. "Thank you, young man."

Pushing forward, Nyla laid a hand on her forehead. "Her fever is gone! It's gone!'

"Praise God!" Calan said, thrilled once again to see God's love and power in action, thrilled even more to see Nyla happy.

Daniel rose and smiled down at Tata. "Be well and may the Lord bless you."

"And you, my dear young man. We shall see each other soon." Tata winked at him.

For a moment, Daniel gazed at the woman as if they shared a secret. Then, after nodding at her, he faced Calan and said with all seriousness, "We must go." He left the room as suddenly as he'd come.

Strange. Calan sensed no immediate danger. Besides, he could hardly pull his eyes off Nyla kneeling before her grandmother's bed, caressing her hand and kissing her face, both of them crying tears of joy. He turned to Kyle, wondering at his reaction, praying he would see the light, but the boy remained against the wall, looking as if he'd seen a ghost.

Rising, Nyla dashed to her brother. "We've been wrong. There is a God and He's good and powerful and He heals!"

Still Kyle said nothing. Didn't move. The only indication that he heard her was the slight moisture covering his eyes.

"Come, talk with Daniel," Calan urged Kyle. "He'll explain it."

"Naw," Kyle said, his expression bearing more sorrow than it should at this joyous event. "I want to stay here with Tata." He faced his sister. "You go with your friends."

Out in the living area, Nyla hugged both Calan and Daniel. "Thank you. I should have trusted you, called you to pray for her long ago."

"We've missed you, Nyla," Daniel said, attempting a smile that Calan could tell also held a little sorrow. "Everyone has been asking about you."

"I've been busy. And honestly, I guess I was mad at God for being so cruel to people I care about."

Daniel nodded. "He's a father, we must remember that. He will do whatever He can to get people saved."

Nyla nodded, her eyes still moist. "I see that now."

"In fact, that's where I need to go now." He glanced at Calan. "After this last trumpet, the harvest is ripe. The Lord sends me to speak to those who are finally seeking."

Ah, so *that* was the hurry. The Lord must have given Daniel a word about someone in need.

Nyla bit her lip. "Before you leave, would you mind speaking with Kyle? I think he may at least be open to hearing the truth."

"Next time. Okay?" Daniel headed toward the door.

Odd, the man never passed up an opportunity to witness.

Calan hung back. "Can we get together tomorrow? I've missed you."

"Yes." She gave him a peck on the cheek. Her unique Nyla scent flooded him, and his body *and heart* reacted. Oh, how he longed to stay and spend time with her, Kyle, and her grandmother, but his job was to protect Daniel.

Slipping a curl behind her ear, he brushed the back of his fingers over her cheek. "I'll see you soon."

She leaned into his hand and smiled.

Ripping himself away, he left and shut the door, catching up with Daniel, who had already descended the stairs. "What's up, Daniel? I know you. Something is wrong."

"I'm afraid Nyla's grandmother won't make it through the night."

Blessed be the God and Father of our Lord Jesus Christ, who according to His abundant mercy has begotten us again to a living hope through the resurrection of Jesus Christ from the dead, to an inheritance incorruptible and undefiled and that does not fade away, reserved in heaven for you, who are kept by the power of God through faith for salvation ready to be revealed in the last time. 1 Peter 1:3-5

Chapter 31

Nyla crept down a dark alley between two broken-down brick buildings, Calan by her side. A blast of icy wind slammed her, and she pulled a threadbare sweater closer around her neck. Still, the chill knifed through rips in her jeans and the holes in her shoes as she trudged forward in haste, avoiding sewage-laden puddles. Flickering streetlamps offered glimpses of crumbling walls and piles of rat-infested garbage.

"This way," Calan whispered over his shoulder at the thirty or so people who followed close behind, huddled together. A baby cried and his mother quickly comforted him to silence. Fear hung over the group like a band of evil specters. Nyla shivered.

"Do you know a place?" she asked Calan.

A beard had overtaken his chin and jaw and his hair was longer, but his blue eyes bore the same clarity, love, and power they always had. "Yes. Don't worry, Nyla. God has shown me where to bring these saints, a place where we can rest and be safe for a time."

Saints. Nyla glanced over the group behind them, and she knew, she knew that she and Calan, by the power of God's

Word, had yanked these precious souls from hell's grip. But now, the NWU hunted them down. No place was safe.

"Pajarito, I love you." Tata's voice drifted through the alleyway, and Nyla turned, stood on her tiptoes, and scanned the mob, looking for her grandmother.

She jerked up in bed, sweat beading over her neck and face. Tossing off the covers, she swung her legs over the side and tried to settle her breath. Something was terribly wrong. The dream had been weird but certainly not terrifying. Then why was her heart beating like a rock band's drum?

Dropping to the floor, she knelt before her mother's trunk, opened it, and sought out the cross necklace. She gripped it close to her heart. "God, if You are there, Jesus, if You are there, what is happening?"

When she opened her palm, her nightlight shimmered over the silver symbol that had once represented everything she hated. "You went through such a painful death, suffered so much torture and rejection, just so we...so *I* could be saved." She finally understood what her parents had seen in this invisible God. Invisible to her physical senses but becoming more real to her every day.

Tata!

Alarm raced through her veins. Tata!

Dropping the necklace, she darted to her grandmother's bedroom. Tata lay in her bed with the most peaceful look on her face. Nyla smiled. Just sleeping. Good. But where was the slight snore her grandmother always had? Why wasn't the blanket rising and falling with each breath?

Kneeling by the bed, Nyla reached for her hand. Cold. It was cold! Numb with fear, she put a finger beneath her nose. No breath.

Nyla dropped her head onto her grandmother's chest and sobbed. "No, God, No!"

Six hours later, a numbing daze overcame Nyla, a sort of aloof callousness, as if she'd leapt out of her body because it was too painful to remain. At least by then she'd been able to take the necessary steps, call the morgue, make arrangements for Tata to be taken away to be prepared for cremation, as she'd wished, set a date for a service.

She should call someone, friends or family? But there was no one to call. Kyle was the only other living relative. And he was in worse shape than Nyla. He hadn't even wanted to see Tata. When Nyla came out of the bedroom crying and told him Tata was gone, he'd downed several pills and curled up in a ball on the couch.

She wanted him to scream, to cuss even, to be angry or sad. Something! *Anything.* But he just laid there, eyes open, as if he'd transported to another place.

If only they could.

After the undertakers left, Nyla stood in the kitchen intending to make coffee, but instead she stared at the coffee pot as if it were a million miles away. How long she stood there, she couldn't say. At least long enough for her legs to ache and what was left of the sunlight to fade from outside the window.

"They killed her. That's what they did." Kyle's angry voice startled her from her morbid daze. But she had no answer. No defense for a God who healed some and allowed others to die.

Rap rap rap. Someone knocked on the door. She didn't want to see anyone, didn't want to talk to anyone, but maybe it was the morgue or…

"Calan, what are you doing here?"

"I heard about Tata."

That made no sense. She hadn't called anyone.

"I'm so sorry, Nyla."He took her in his arms, and she allowed it. For now. She needed the comfort. She needed the love. But deep down, anger fumed for this man and for Daniel. She pushed from him.

"Why didn't Daniel heal her?" She shot out, taking a step back.

Calan's expression fell. "It's not Daniel who heals. You know that. It's God."

"Then why didn't He? She was a good woman. She believed in God, followed Him!" Fisting her hands, she pounded him on the chest, wanting to hurt him, wanting him to feel a portion of her pain. "Why? Why?"

Gripping her wrists, he held them tight. "He must have wanted her home. There's always a reason. A good reason."

Tearing from his grip, she batted the moisture from her face, embarrassed at her weakness in front of this man. "I needed her. *We* needed her." She gestured toward Kyle, who had managed to sit up when Calan entered. "She was all we had."

Pain lanced across his moist blue eyes. "I'm sorry, Nyla. I came as quickly as I could. What can I do? What can I do to help?"

Nyla turned her back on him, afraid she'd give in to the urge to fall into his arms again. "You've done enough."

"Yeah. Just leave, *Deviant*." Kyle stood and gave Calan a dark stare, an *evil* dark stare she didn't think possible coming from her brother.

"I know you both are hurting," Calan said. "I'll leave if you want me to. Call you later, okay?"

Kyle took a step toward Calan. "No, she won't be talking to you again. In fact, she'll be calling the NWU PKs."

Nyla's breath seized. Darkness encased her brother, thick and heavy like a coffin.

"Oh, you didn't know?" he continued with sarcasm. "My sister was sent undercover into your little Deviant cult in order to arrest your crazy leader."

"Enough, Kyle!" Nyla shouted, but the dark specters only laughed at her.

Shock and pain twisted Calan's expression.

"Yeah, that's right. She's been playing you for a fool all along."

"Nyla?" Calan's gaze swept to her.

Too stunned to move, too stunned to speak, and too heartbroken to do anything about it, Nyla merely gestured toward the door. "I think it's best you leave."

The firm hand on Calan's shoulder jerked him from his misery, and he looked up to see Daniel standing beside him, his outline dark against the noonday sun, but his features distinct.

"You okay?" Daniel took a seat beside him in the lawn chair in Madeline's backyard. The same place where Calan and Nyla had shared such a tender moment together.

No, he was not okay, nor did he want to talk. Yet as he watched the wind send ripples of light across the swimming pool, he wondered if he was even worthy to talk to such a Godly man as Daniel. Even so, he needed to warn him of the danger Calan had put him in.

"Nyla is still an NWU PK." There, he'd said it. Not wanting to look at Daniel's expression, he waited to hear the shock, disappointment, even anger in his tone.

All he heard was, "Hmm."

"Hmm? Is that it?" Calan glanced at him and found not an ounce of fury or fear on his face. Instead, he smiled.

"Don't you see?" Calan raised his voice. "She's a spy. She was sent to infiltrate our group to have you arrested."

Still Daniel just stared at him with that knowing look in his eyes.

Anger burned. "Maybe you're not hearing me. I brought a spy into our group! She tricked me, and I believed her. I put all of us…I put *you* in danger!" He lowered his head. "I'm such a fool."

Daniel leaned forward, elbows on his knees. "You are no fool, Calan. You are a mighty man of God, a warrior for the Kingdom, and God has great plans for you."

Punching to his feet, Calan glared at his friend. "What are you talking about? Because of my weakness for women, my stupidity, I nearly cost you your life. How can God use me, how can He trust me, if I can't even trust myself?"

Daniel shrugged. "Do you see me in prison?"

"No, thank God. I found out in time. Don't you see? I almost did it again. Just like with my brother. I trusted a woman, thought she was being sincere...fell in..." He stopped, his throat suddenly clogged.

It was bad enough he'd put Daniel and the others in danger, but he'd also allowed his heart to be crushed. Facing the pool, he crossed arms over his chest. "I loved her. I wanted to make a life with her. And she played me for a fool."

"Did she?"

"You're not listening to me."

"I've heard every word. I just don't agree."

Calan stared at his friend, baffled by him, as usual. Then it hit him. "You knew about her?"

Daniel smiled.

Calan huffed. "She's probably over at PK headquarters reporting us now." Alarm sped through his veins. "We shouldn't be here! We need to find a new place. She knows where Madeline's house is." He headed toward the back door. "Come on."

Daniel grabbed his arm as he passed, stopping him. "Calm yourself. It's going to be okay. Listen, Calan. When you were tricked by women before, you didn't know the Lord. You weren't following Him. Things are different now. You walk in the Spirit and are led by the Spirit. As long as you remain in the Spirit, the Lord is the one who leads you."

Calan pulled from Daniel's grip. "Then why didn't I hear Him about Nyla?

"Maybe you did." Daniel stood, the ever-present smile on his face.

Closing his eyes, Calan rubbed the bridge of his nose.

"Maybe you were supposed to meet her," Daniel added, "to bring her here."

"For what? She never truly got saved. At least not that I know."

Daniel sighed and raised a scolding brow. "As long as you follow Jesus and heed His voice, He will never steer you wrong.

It may not always make sense, but let Him work out His will, and you'll see how it always ends up for good."

Calan shook his head. "Doesn't matter. She hates me now, hates us for her grandmother dying."

Daniel rubbed the back of his neck and watched as a cold wind tossed the charred fronds of a nearby palm. The ashes floated to the ground like black snow, a telling scene of the times in which they lived.

"My time here is almost done," Daniel said.

Burning ignited behind Calan's eyes, and he hung his head. "I don't want to hear it. Not today. Please."

Daniel gripped Calan's shoulder and shook him. "You have been a good friend, the best friend a man could want. And God has told me you are to take over for me."

Terror raced like ice through his veins, along with doubt and a host of other strangling emotions. "Me? No way. I can't do that."

"You can and you will, by the power of Almighty God."

How did one sleep when their entire world crashed down around them? Nyla lay on her bed in the dark staring up at a ceiling she couldn't see. In a single day, she had lost everything, her career, her future, the man she loved, her faith—little as it was—all her friends, and her grandmother—the only person who really loved her.

She glanced at the clock. 2:00 a.m. Kyle wouldn't be home for another four hours. Not that it mattered. Marco and *her* team would, no doubt, be knocking on her door soon after that. The perfect ending to her disastrous life—tossed in a reformation camp with all the other Deviants. Disgraced, forgotten, alone.

Never alone.

If that was God, she didn't want to hear it. Couldn't get past the anger and pain to even entertain the idea that God cared. Finally, after another hour passed with bouts of tears and growls of fury, Nyla felt herself drifting off…

A green meadow spread before her. Flowers in every color—some colors Nyla had never seen before—waved in a light, warm breeze. Music, gentle, soothing, and pure filled the air each time the wind blew, as if the flowers themselves were singing. Birds and butterflies flitted about across a golden sky, their wings etched in silver. Majestic mountains rose in the distance upon which an imperial city sat.

Where was she? How did she get here? She should be frightened, but all she felt was joy and peace. Songs rose from the city, drifting upward in glittering spirals to form diamonds in the sky before disappearing. Laughter and voices lured Nyla to start walking toward a set of gates that shimmered like an ivory sea. For some reason, she wanted more than anything to get to that city, to enter it and never leave. There was life there, purpose, peace, and a joy like she'd never known. If she could just reach it.

"Pajarito."

The voice, the name, spun her around. Tata stood behind her, though it wasn't Tata as Nyla remembered her. She was young with plump, firm skin and gorgeous wavy hair tumbling over her shoulders. Her eyes were clear and bright, her face bore not a sag or wrinkle, and her body was fit and strong. Nyla had seen pictures of her grandmother in her youth, but the vision before her now, far surpassed them all.

Breathless, Nyla darted toward her and flew into her arms. "Tata!"

Her grandmother's embrace consumed her in strength and love. "Yes, it's me, my Pajarito!"

Nyla buried her head in her grandmother's hair, never wanting to let go of her. It smelled of sweet incense. "Where are we? What is this place? You died!"

"Only my body died, my sweet Pajarito." She eased Nyla back and gripped her face between both hands. "I am in heaven and so are your parents. We are well. You will join us one day." She smiled.

Her parents? "I will join you now, Tata. I want to stay."

Tata kissed her on the cheek and stared at her, overwhelming love pouring from her eyes.

And then she was gone.

"I want to stay! I want to stay..." Nyla screamed, jerking awake, heart thrashing in her chest.

Breath panting, blood racing, she sat up and glanced around. Her bedroom. She was still in her bedroom. Dropping her head in her hands, she gathered what was left of her mind. A dream. Or was it a dream? She'd never seen such a place, never seen her grandmother so beautiful and so happy.

"God?" She glanced around the room. "Is Tata really with You, really there in that wonderful place?"

No answer. Sighing, she rubbed her eyes, feeling silly for asking. Instead, she just sat there, unable to move, trying to make sense of it all. How long she sat there, she didn't know, but the cross necklace she'd dropped on the floor began to glow—a soft silvery glow. How? No moonlight came in through the window, and her nightlight wasn't on. Yet still it glowed off and on, like a lighthouse during a storm, bright, low, bright, low.

Falling to her knees, she crawled over and picked it up. It felt warm in her hands. "Lord, was that really heaven?"

You know.

She did know. It was heaven and Tata was there. Tears pooled in her eyes. "You showed me! You let me see her...I don't know how to thank You." It was the most incredible gift she could have hoped for.

There is a heaven! The realization whirled through her, sparking every cell to life. *And people who follow You, who trust in You, go there.* There was a reason for all this madness, for everything that happened. A purpose to life, and an eternity worth all the suffering in the world.

Her breath came fast. Her heart skipped with more joy than she'd ever felt.

She'd heard it from her parents and the Deviants, but for some reason, until this moment, it had not sunk deep into her heart.

Yet, along with it, her failures, her sins, her mistakes and weaknesses—every horrible thing she'd done—hit her in a tidal wave of regret.

"I've been terrible. I've done terrible things. I've been selfish and ambitious, and I was so cruel to my parents. I hunted down and tossed in prison people who love You, I slept around, I drank too much."

Gripping the cross, she sank to the floor and curled into a ball.

Two dark spirits, Doubt and Unworthiness, weapons drawn, circled Nyla.

Positioning his crossbow, Ranoss lit an arrow and aimed for them, but a mighty arm spread across his chest.

Growling, Ranoss lowered his bow, casting an angry glance at Cassian beside him. "She's so close. Behold, the light of the Kingdom!" He gestured to the half of the room glistening in Heaven's gleam—the light that had begun to force back the darkness as soon as she began talking to the Father of Spirits.

But it had stopped when the enemy whispered all her sins in her ear. It had stopped just a handsbreadth from Nyla, leaving her in darkness.

Guilt, a rather corpulent demon, covered with venom-dripping spikes, looked at Ranoss and uttered a hideous laugh.

Ranoss returned his sneer. "Your days will soon be over, demon!"

The spirit belched and sped away.

Doubt and Unworthiness continued their assault, stabbing and slicing Nyla, who had fallen to the floor in agony.

Ranoss ground his teeth. Tears slipped down Nyla's face. If she succumbed to the words Guilt had told her, if she held onto a shred of doubt, a hint of unworthiness, the light would fade, and she would miss her chance. This time. Mayhap forever.

"I know, 'tis maddening," Cassian said. "The Commander sent me to assist you, but for now, there is naught we can do."

He was right, of course.

Still, Ranoss kept his arrow lit, his crossbow in position.

Cassian drew his long blade and took up a fighting stance beside him.

Nyla sat, wiped away her tears, and stared at the cross in her hand.

The light advanced.

Ranoss smiled. Leveling his crossbow at the two spirits, he fired. The flaming arrow struck Doubt in the chest. Quickly reloading with a precision honed from thousands of years of warfare, Ranoss fired again. The arrow zipped through the air, piercing Unworthiness in the back as he fled. Both demons dissipated into puffs of ash.

More demons hissed and growled from the shadows. Flipping his crossbow over his shoulder, Ranoss drew his sword.

Do not think that I came to bring peace on earth. I did not come to bring peace but a sword. For I have come to set a man against his father, a daughter against her mother, and a daughter-in-law against her mother-in-law and a man's enemies will be those of his own household. Matthew 10:34-36

Chapter 32

Nyla glanced up. The heaviness she'd felt had vanished, as if someone had lifted an immense weight from her back and set her free. A brilliant sword of sparkling gold formed above her head, held by an invisible hand.

Yet, she knew who held it. Her guardian angel.

Bowing her head again, she released a sigh and repented, one by one, for all the horrid things she'd done in her life—at least the ones she could remember. "I'm so sorry, Lord Jesus. I've been blind, dumb, and stubborn. Thank You for not giving up on me. Thank You for forgiving me." She'd have to work on forgiving herself later. But for now, she had no other choice but to submit to this wonderful Savior who had given His all for her. She hated losing control, hated trusting someone, but Jesus was not someone. He was everything, and He'd more than proven to her that He could be trusted. "I submit to you, my Lord and my King. I'll follow You always."

Light enveloped her, shimmering off the cross in her hand. Warmth seeped through her, touching every part of her soul. Love, like she'd never felt before, bubbled in her throat until she found herself giggling. And she was not one to giggle. But she couldn't stop. Rising, she raised her hands in the air and thanked God for His mercy and kindness, all the while wondering why she had waited so long. She'd never felt anything so freeing, so wonderful.

She'd never felt so loved.

Taking the cross still in her hand, she slipped it around her neck and clipped it in the back. "Mom, I'm finally going to wear it. Thank you." She smiled, remembering Tata in heaven, knowing she'd see her and her parents again.

She had to tell Calan. She had to ask him to forgive her. Quickly jumping into some jeans and tossing a shirt over her head, she ran a comb through her unruly hair. Out in the living room, she looked at the clock. 6:35 a.m. Why wasn't Kyle home? Frowning, she grabbed her keys and sped out the door. She'd talk to him later. As far as she knew, the Deviants who didn't have homes were staying at Madeline's house. Which was where she hoped to find Calan.

Twenty minutes later, she *did* find Calan, Calan *and* Daniel, in fact, both shocked to see her. No, only Calan seemed surprised. Daniel, on the other hand, merely smiled at her as she dashed through the front door.

Slamming the door, Calan spun to face her, torment and sorrow twisting his normally handsome features. She'd hurt him. Terribly. Would he ever trust her again?

Moving to the front window, he shoved the curtains aside to look out. "Where are your friends? Why aren't they here to arrest us?"

The spite in his tone shot straight into her heart. She deserved it.

"Calan, I'm sorry." She bit her lip. "Yes, I was sent to infiltrate your group." She glanced at Daniel, expecting his scorn, but all she saw was approval. What an odd man.

Facing her, Calan crossed arms over his chest. "I don't care, Nyla. You lied to me, to us."

Nyla lowered her chin. "Guilty as charged." She stared at the worn carpet, avoiding Calan's gaze. She couldn't bear to see his anger and hatred. "But I didn't turn you in. I didn't. I came to care..." She swallowed, glancing between them both. "To care for all of you. I wanted to know more about your God."

Daniel finally stood. "And what did you discover, Nyla?"

She smiled, sensing once again the joy and love of God's Spirit within her. "I finally see! I finally understand! I gave my life to Jesus!"

"Praise God!" Daniel approached and gave her a hug. Gripping her shoulders, he held her back, beaming with joy. "It is what we have been praying for, isn't it, Calan?" He glanced toward his friend.

Calan's lips quirked. "If it isn't another lie."

How could Nyla be so happy, so filled with joy but at the same time feel like her heart broke in two?

Daniel fingered the cross around her neck. "Yours?"

"My mother's"

"Ah. Do you know what your name means, Nyla Cruz?"

She shook her head.

"It means Champion of the Cross."

Nyla blinked. "It does?" She had never known.

Daniel took a step back. "It is who you are now, Nyla. Your new beginning." Then, raising his hand, he waved it over her.

Her heart seized. "My tracker." She raised both hands to her mouth. "I forgot. I'm sorry."

Daniel shrugged. "It's disabled now. And will remain so."

She stared at him, confused. "But why didn't you do it before?"

"God's timing is perfect."

But before Daniel got the last word out, the screech of tires—many tires—sounded from outside.

Calan glanced back out the window. "The PKs are here!"

Calan entered battle mode. He'd been trained for high-stress, dangerous situations, and he knew what to do. Blocking out fear from his heart and mind, he focused on the best plan to get Daniel to safety.

Had Nyla turned them in? No. The poor woman stood frozen in place, terror blazing in her eyes, repeating, "It's all my fault. It's all my fault."

"Come," Calan ordered. "Out the back."

"Is there anyone else here?" Nyla asked.

"No," Daniel answered with a calmness that defied logic. "Everyone is either at work or out collecting supplies."

Grabbing Daniel by the arm, Calan gestured toward the back door. "We can slip into the neighbor's backyard and make it to my bike parked down the street." Yet even as he said it, he realized he could only take one of them.

Nyla must have realized it too. "I'll stay, hold them off. I know them."

Daniel stepped out of Calan's grip and shook his head. "No, Nyla, they know you betrayed them."

"I don't care. It's my fault. Go!"

Love and sincerity filled those gorgeous eyes of hers, along with a spark, a light that had not been there before. All of Calan's anger instantly fled, but there was no time to think about it. "No one stays. We all go together. Come on! They'll have us surrounded soon."

Dashing past the kitchen, Calan opened the back door, glanced around to make sure the coast was clear, then gestured for them both to follow. Nyla stepped out beside him, her eyes scanning the area, her body tense and alert.

Daniel stopped in the doorway. "Get Nyla to safety."

Someone pounded on the front door. "NWU Peace Keepers. Open up!"

"No," Calan seethed. "I'm taking you both!"

"You know you can't. There's only one bike, and they'll have the neighborhood sectioned off and surrounded within minutes."

"He's right about that," Nyla said. "I'm staying. Get Daniel to safety!" Her frantic eyes shifted between his.

How could Calan choose? The woman he loved but who betrayed him or the man he loved, whom he'd promised to protect with his life? If Daniel was lost, how could Calan ever live with another failure?

Daniel gripped his shoulder. "Trust God."

Nyla attempted to shove past Daniel to get back in the house, but the man stood like a steel barrier at the door.

"Let me through!" she cried.

"It's my time," Daniel said. "Now, go!"

Lord? Calan sought the still small voice within.

Nyla, was all he heard…along with commands coming from PKs who were heading into the backyard.

A loud crash resounded through the house.

"They're in." Nyla said.

Trust Me.

Calan pulled Daniel into an embrace. "I'll see you soon, my friend."

"God is with you." Daniel nodded and finally stepped out the door.

Casting a last glance at the man who had taught him everything that mattered, Calan grabbed Nyla, raced across the yard, slipped behind the burnt trunk of a tree, and squeezed through a hole in the fence, all while fighting Nyla, who tried her best to pull away from him.

"Let me go! Let me go!" she cried.

On the other side of the fence, he slammed her back against his chest and covered her mouth. "Shh."

Finally, she stopped struggling. Her tears dripped over his fingers.

The PKs flooded Madeline's backyard. Daniel stepped toward the pool, hands raised.

"We got him!" one man shouted, and the cock of a dozen guns snapped through the air.

Heart breaking, Calan took Nyla's hand, and together, they tore through the yard, climbed a fence, and darted across two more backyards until they emerged onto the sidewalk where Calan's bike stood against the curb.

He unlocked it and leapt on, finally glancing at Nyla. Tears spilled down her cheeks as she glanced toward Madeline's house.

"It's my brother!" She sobbed.

Following her gaze, Calan spotted Kyle in his NWU guard uniform standing beside a black van as the PKs emerged from the house. Two of them yanked Daniel between them, handcuffs around his wrists. Even caught, the godly man walked with confident and fearless authority. Though too far to tell, Calan thought he glanced at them and smiled before they shoved him into the van and slammed the door.

"I'm so sorry, Nyla."

"All this time, I thought it would be Marco who betrayed me," she mumbled.

"There they are!" one of the PKs shouted, pointing in their direction.

"Time to go."

Wiping her face, Nyla hopped on the back and wrapped her arms around him as Calan started the engine. Putting one boot on the ground, he spun the bike and peeled down the street as fast as his Harley would go.

St. Augustine, Florida, Two weeks later

There he was. After searching for an hour, Nyla finally spotted Calan on the beach by St. John's Pier. The past few weeks had been a flurry of frightening activity—packing what they could, gathering Tribby, Calypsey, and Spots without getting caught, selling Calan's Harley and buying a van, saying goodbye to dear friends, all while escaping the authorities at every turn.

The hardest part for Nyla was leaving Kyle. She wanted to at least say goodbye, to hear his explanation. But she couldn't risk it. It broke her heart to leave him. Still, she had no choice but to put him in God's capable hands.

The Two Witnesses continued their fiery preaching from Jerusalem, begging the world to repent and calling down plagues on mankind. Nyla would love nothing more than to visit Israel and see them—Moses and Elijah—*I mean, wow!* But that would be impossible. The sixth trumpet would soon blow, releasing a two hundred million strong army that would kill a third of mankind—the second woe. Whether that would happen before the midpoint of the Tribulation or after, no one knew, but they must prepare as best they could for whatever came.

After seeking God's will, they decided to travel up the coast, stopping along the way at each of the churches Daniel had planted, informing them of his arrest, and encouraging them to stay strong in the Lord. Turned out, Calan was quite the preacher. He had a natural gift for explaining Scripture and helping others see the Lord.

Nyla smiled as she headed toward him.

Their mission from the Lord? Go north, save the lost, heal the sick, deliver people from the bondage of the enemy, and start as many underground churches as they could. With Calan's gift of preaching and her gift of seeing, they made quite the pair. But of course, God already knew that and had chosen them for such a time as this.

Still, they missed those they left behind, but after much prayer and the laying on of hands, Javier and Elena assumed the mantle of responsibility for the Fort Lauderdale church. They sent Nyla and Calan off on their new assignment with many tears and embraces, but also with the knowledge that the church was in good hands.

During all of this, a deep sense of sorrow hung over Calan, and he often took off on long walks, needing to pray and be alone. Nyla understood.

She eased up beside him and slipped her hand in his. Without even looking her way, he smiled.

"You found me."

"I'll always find you."

"Promise?" Leaning toward her, he kissed her on the cheek.

They stood there for several minutes in silence, watching the waves roll ashore and spread their foaming filigree over the sand. Though the sky had cleared slightly, the afternoon sun struggled to punch its rays through the thick gray clouds. Much like the Son piercing the cloak of evil covering the earth with His light.

"Are you okay?" Nyla finally asked. "I know you miss Daniel."

"I do, but I know I'll see him again. It's not just that. To be honest, I've been struggling a bit. The last thing I wanted to do was lose him, fail him."

"I feel responsible for that."

"No." He took her hand and kissed it. "It was all part of God's plan. I see that now. God wanted me to trust Him with the decision. I had to choose. Your betrayal and then your willingness to stay made it more difficult. I mean, I would have hated to leave you."

Wind tossed her hair into her face, and she snapped it aside. "But your job was to protect Daniel. I get it. I can't imagine how hard that decision was."

"But it wasn't my decision. That's the point. It was God's. And that's where trust comes in. Despite my past mistakes, despite that it seemed I was making another, I had to trust that He knew best. I had to let go, you know?" He smiled at her.

"I do. More than you know. I think that's why it took me so long to commit to Him. I hate not being in control."

He chuckled. "I guess we are a lot alike that way." After several seconds, he added, "We've got quite the task ahead of us."

She nodded. "I know it won't be easy."

"And we'll probably not survive."

Nyla fingered the cross around her neck. "But as the Apostle Paul said, to die is gain."

"Ah, you've been reading your Bible." He arched a brow.

She looked up at him playfully. "Well, I have a boyfriend who happens to be a great preacher."

He laughed. "Boyfriend, eh? Maybe we need to find a minister who'll rectify that."

Nyla's heart leapt. "Are you proposing?"

Calan faced her and took both her hands in his. "Seems an odd thing to do in the Tribulation, but yes. There's no place I'd rather be during this time than by your side."

"Me too." Moisture filled her eyes as her thoughts drifted to a famous quote by Charles Dickens. "It was the best of times, it was the worst of times." She smiled. "How can I be so happy during such a miserable time in history?"

"God shines light even in the darkness." Calan drew her close and kissed the top of her head.

Ah, such warmth and strength, such joy to be in his arms. She could definitely get used to it. Nudging from him, she gazed into his eyes, so full of love and concern. "Yes. I will marry you, Calan Walker."

Lowering his lips to hers, he drew her close again, and for a brief moment the world with all its evil and deception melted around them. It was just them and their love. If only they could remain that way. But soon a wave swept over their feet and a siren blared in the distance.

Breathless, Calan took her hand and started walking down the shore. "First, after a kiss like that, we better make this legal." He chuckled, then grew serious. "Then we have work to do. There are still souls to save and saints to protect."

She nodded. "Until Jesus returns and makes all things new."

Nyla had finally found her purpose, her mission, and the man of her dreams. It was truly the best of times and the worst of times. Yet she already knew the end of the story—a glorious ending, an eternity of joy, peace, and love with the King of Kings!

"Thank You, Jesus," she whispered into the wind. "You saved me in every way possible."

"You must be most pleased, my friend," Anisian said to Ranoss as the two warriors stood guard behind their wards on the beach.

Ranoss had been unable to remove the grin on his face for weeks. "Most pleased. Out of all the daughters of Eve I have been assigned to guard, this one, this Nyla Cruz, gave me the most trouble." He shifted his stance and gripped the hilt of his sword. "I must admit there were times I doubted she'd ever enter the Kingdom."

Anisian nodded. "'Tis the way of the Commander. He never tells us the end, but merely asks us to trust."

"Praise His Name forever more!"

"Amen!"

"I feel for Zhaviel," Ranoss said. "His ward, Kyle, appears to be making no progress at all."

"Aye, 'tis true. Time will tell. The Father of Spirits will reassign him should all hope be lost."

Ranoss smiled as Nyla and Calan kissed. "Seems we shall be working together much in the future, Anisian."

Anisian chuckled. "Indeed. I am happy for them." He reached to grip Ranoss's arm. "And happy to be by your side as well. With the Commander's help, we will do our best to keep them safe."

"Indeed. I am up to the challenge, my friend."

Anisian stiffened and scanned the area.

"What is it?" Ranoss asked.

"The forces of darkness. They assemble against these two."

"To be expected." Ranoss grabbed the crossbow hanging down his back and swung it in front. "Soon, our enemy will fully inhabit the Antichrist and all hell will be unleashed."

Anisian drew his blade. "And we will defend these saints of the Most High with all our strength."

"For the Commander's glory!"

"To the fight, my friend!"

And they overcame him by the blood of the Lamb and by the word of their testimony, and they did not love their lives to the death. Revelation 12:11

Chapter 33

One month later, Washington, D.C.

Daniel stood, chained at his hands and feet, in a large, stone-walled room beneath the city that had once been the capital of the United States. Escorted there through dark twisting tunnels by two burly guards, he was actually happy to finally get out of the four-foot square isolation cell he'd been held in for the past month. He'd been questioned—more like tortured—during the first two weeks since his arrival by NWU officials who wished to know the locations of all the churches he'd planted, along with the names of each Deviant. When he wouldn't talk, they gave him drugs, which miraculously had no effect on him. When they finally realized they weren't going to get anything out of him, they'd stuffed him in a cell, which also served as his toilet, giving him nothing to eat or drink.

No doubt they assumed he'd crack and be willing to talk for food. But once again, the Lord Jesus provided, and Daniel woke up each morning to what he could only assume was Manna on the floor of his cell, along with water pooled in the cracks. Which only infuriated his captors more.

However, he assumed it was his nightly praise and worship, sung at the top of his voice, which prompted them to bring him to this place where he now stood.

Daniel had never seen a guillotine before, at least not in person, but the one that loomed before him looked quite new. All except the blood stains on the large blade perched at the top. He should be terrified, but all he felt was peace. Peace and an odd joy that his journey here had come to an end.

A door opened on the other side of the room and two men in NWU uniforms entered, scowls on their faces and hatred in their eyes. One took up a position by the guillotine while the other halted before Daniel, scanning a document in his hands.

"Daniel Cain?" he asked, finally lifting his gaze to Daniel.

"The one and only," Daniel answered.

The man's eyes narrowed. "You have been pronounced guilty of treason to the NWU, of spreading lies and causing insurrection, and of practicing an illegal religion. The sentence is death."

Daniel smiled. Finally. Finally, he'd be going home.

"Why are you smiling?" The man shook his head in disgust, then turned to the man behind him. "This one is nuts."

Facing Daniel again, he sighed as if he were bored. "You have one more chance, Deviant. Do you deny this Jesus? Do you deny He is God? And will you submit to the authority of the New World Union?"

Daniel studied the poor man, seeking wisdom on what to say, all the while silently praying for his salvation. "Jesus is God and the only way to eternal life. I urge you to repent of your evil ways, submit to Him, and be saved before it's too late."

Fury burned in the man's eyes, seething, loathing fury. He spat in Daniel's face.

The warm liquid slid down his cheek. Still Daniel smiled. "I take that as a no."

"You are going to die, Deviant. And when that blade cuts through your neck, finally that smile of yours will disappear."

"No, my friend, this smile is only the beginning."

Uttering a foul curse, he nodded for the guards to drag Daniel to the guillotine, force him to his knees, and place his head into the holder.

He stared at the splatters of blood on the basin before the other man laid a plastic sheet over it.

"Jesus, please receive me. I'm coming home."

He didn't even hear the blade drop, didn't feel an ounce of pain. Instead, he felt his body lift to a standing position.

An immense glowing being, wearing gold armor and a sword at his side, smiled down at him. He held out his hand. "Come, brave saint. The King awaits."

"Who are you?"

"I am Nazare, your guardian. I have waited long for this day."

Daniel gripped his hand and instantly they sped through the roof, into the sky, and into space, zipping past a multitude of stars so fast, they looked like streaks.

They broke through an invisible barrier with a loud bang and landed in an enormous meadow covered in velvet grass and brilliant flowers. Music floated across a golden sky.

It was like nothing Daniel had ever seen. "Where are we?"

Nazare pointed to a massive city with golden spires glistening with a light all its own.

But Daniel's eyes quickly moved to two figures walking toward him. His heart nearly stopped. Angelica? Isaac?

He took off in a mad dash to get to them. Angel! It was her! And his son, Isaac, beside her. Huge smiles lit their faces as he finally reached them and flew into their arms. He dove his head into Angel's hair and drew in the scent of her, then lifted Isaac off his feet and spun him around. "Son, my son!!"

"Dad!" Isaac shouted. "We've been waiting for you!"

"You have?" Daniel put Isaac down and stared at Angel, still finding it hard to believe. She was more beautiful than he remembered. Gone was the exhaustion lining her face, the sorrow in her eyes, the pain of life on earth. "Angel, I've missed you so much. Both of you."

"We've missed you too." She kissed him on the cheek and embraced him again.

"I'm sure you wondered if I'd ever make it."

Pulling back, she laughed. "At first, yes, but the Father told us you'd come eventually."

"Well, I'm finally here now. And we will never be parted again."

Isaac gripped Daniel around the waist. "I'm sorry I never knew you on earth."

"We have a lot of catching up to do, son." Daniel draped an arm around the boy, then glanced up at the magnificent city.

Angel followed his gaze. "You aren't going to believe how wonderful it is. Come. There are many anxious to see you, your mom included."

His mother? Of course. It was all too wonderful to imagine. "But there is One I wish to see first."

Angel nodded, her eyes sparkling. "Yes, indeed. The King of kings. He awaits you at the gate."

"He's waiting for me?"

"He greets everyone personally. He loves you very much, Daniel. He has told me so on many occasions."

Daniel swallowed a lump of emotion. "I can't wait. Shall we?" He glanced over his shoulder to ask Nazare to join them, but the warrior angel had already left.

Facing the heavenly city, Daniel looped one arm around Angel and another around Isaac and the three of them started on the golden path to the eternal city. There, awaiting them was a future filled with joy, peace, purpose, love, and endless wonders, basking in the glory of the one true and living God.

About the Author

AWARD WINNING AND BEST-SELLING AUTHOR, MARYLU TYNDALL dreamt of pirates and sea-faring adventures during her childhood days on Florida's Coast. With more than twenty-nine books published, she makes no excuses for the deep spiritual themes embedded within her romantic adventures. Her hope is that readers will not only be entertained but will be brought closer to the Creator who loves them beyond measure. In a culture that accepts the occult, wizards, zombies, and vampires without batting an eye, MaryLu hopes to show the awesome present and powerful acts of God in a dying world. A Christy and Maggie award nominee and two-time winner of the RWA Inspy Reader's Choice Award, MaryLu makes her home with her husband, six children, four grandchildren, and several stray cats on the California coast.

For a peek the characters and scenes from the book, visit my When Angels Battle Pinterest Page!

If you enjoyed this book, one of the nicest ways to say "thank you" to an author and help them be able to continue writing is to leave a favorable review on Amazon! Barnes and Noble, Goodreads, Bookbub (And elsewhere, too!) I would appreciate it if you would take a moment to do so. Thanks so much!

Comments? Questions? I love hearing from my readers, so feel free to contact me via my website:

https://crossandcutlass.blogspot.com

Or email me at: marylu_tyndall@yahoo.com

Follow me on:
BLOG: http://crossandcutlass.blogspot.com/
PINTEREST: http://www.pinterest.com/mltyndall/
BOOKBUB:https://www.bookbub.com/authors/marylu-tyndall
AMAZON: https://www.amazon.com/MaryLu-Tyndall/e/B002BOG7JG

To hear news about special prices and new releases sign up for my newsletter on my website Or follow me on Bookbub!
https://crossandcutlass.blogspot.com
https://www.bookbub.com/authors/marylu-tyndall

Other Books by MaryLu Tyndall

THE REDEMPTION

THE RELIANCE

THE RESTITUTION

THE RANSOM

THE RECKONING

THE RECKLESS

THE FALCON AND THE SPARROW

THE RED SIREN

THE BLUE ENCHANTRESS

THE RAVEN SAINT

CHARITY'S CROSS

SURRENDER THE HEART

SURRENDER THE NIGHT

SURRENDER THE DAWN

FORSAKEN DREAMS

ELUSIVE HOPE

ABANDONED MEMORIES

ESCAPE TO PARADISE TRILOGY

SHE WALKS IN POWER

SHE WALKS IN LOVE

SHE WALKS IN MAJESTY

VEIL OF PEARLS

WHEN ANGELS CRY

TEARS OF THE SEA

TIMELESS TREASURE

WRITING FROM THE TRENCHES

Made in United States
Orlando, FL
09 July 2022